# PORCELAIN
*keys*

## DATE DUE

# Praise for *Porcelain Keys*

"Emotionally gripping, this beautifully crafted young adult romance will pull at your heartstrings from tragic beginning to happy ending. A must-read for fans of contemporary romance, both young and seasoned." —Julie N. Ford, author of *Count Down to Love*

"*Porcelain Keys* is a fresh, heart-wrenching take on boy-meets-girl. Using fantastic and musical imagery to tell the poignant love story of Aria and Thomas, Beard leads the reader to a swelling crescendo as if we're part of the song—and what a beautiful song it is."—Cindy C Bennett, author of *Rapunzel Untangled* and *Geek Girl*

"With a fresh new voice and theme, Sarah Beard opens the musical world of her characters and tells a unique and profound story that will keep readers on the edge of their seats until the very end. I loved this story and highly recommend it!"—Lynn Gardner, author of the Gems and Espionage series

"*Porcelain Keys* is a well-crafted story that is guaranteed to make you cry, smile, cheer, and cry some more. The author uses not only words to tell her heart-warming story, but she also taps into the powerful language of music, making this a unique and fulfilling read. Aria is a heroine worth rooting for, and the plot is an emotional melody that weaves a spell so potent, it can only be broken by reaching the end. And even then, I couldn't stop thinking about Aria and her story."—Heather Frost, author of the Seers trilogy

"Emotionally rich, elegant description, beloved characters—*Porcelain Keys* is a masterpiece with more heart than most love stories. A boy and a girl rise above the storms of tragedy to find hope and forgiveness. Sarah Beard delivers a fresh, new novel that will go on my list of classics." —Stephanie Fowers, author of *Meet Your Match* and The Twisted Tales trilogy

"A lyrical love story that will leave your heart singing, *Porcelain Keys* is a masterpiece with emotional depth, young love, and family angst. Beard takes us on a journey of self-discovery, second chances, and ultimately, sweet resolution."—Heather Ostler, author of The Shapeshifter's Secret series

# SARAH BEARD

SWEETWATER
BOOKS

An Imprint of Cedar Fort, Inc.
Springville, Utah

ISBN 13: 978-1-4621-1396-5

Published by Sweetwater Books, an imprint of Cedar Fort, Inc.
2373 W. 700 S., Springville, UT 84663
Distributed by Cedar Fort, Inc., www.cedarfort.com

LIBRARY OF CONGRESS CATALOGING-IN-PUBLICATION DATA

Beard, Sarah, 1977- author.
  Porcelain keys / Sarah Beard.
     pages cm
  Summary: Seventeen-year-old Aria is a piano prodigy whose abusive father forbids her from going near a piano and whose only friend Thomas goes missing just as she braves everything to audition for Juilliard.
  ISBN 978-1-4621-1396-5 (perfect bound)
  [1. Pianists--Fiction. 2. Fathers and daughters--Fiction. 3. Child abuse--Fiction] I. Title.
  PZ7.B380234Po 2014
  [Fic]--dc23
                              2013034836

Cover design by Kristen Reeves
Cover design © 2014 by Lyle Mortimer
Edited and typeset by Melissa J. Caldwell

Printed in the United States of America

10  9  8  7  6  5  4  3  2  1

*For Keith,*
*who gave me wings and a reason to fly.*

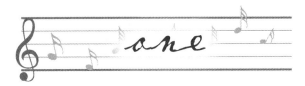

# one

I fled barefoot through the backyard, my spine tingling with the fear of pursuit. The grass was cold and wet, and the sound of my name echoed in the chilled mountain air.

"Aria!" Dad's abrasive shout fractured the night again and again, like the bark of an agitated dog. I pushed my legs harder, unable to differentiate between the thud of footsteps behind me and my own quick heartbeats. I could see the vague outline of the barn ahead like a beacon in the darkness, and I blazed toward it, blind to everything else. My only chance of losing Dad was to reach the trees behind it.

"Get back here!" His growl was right behind me. The anticipation of his hand hooking my arm threatened to paralyze me, but I pushed the expectation aside and forced my feet forward. I flew past the barn and into a dense cluster of pines, their branches whipping my face as I raced through them. It was darker in the trees, and I held my hands out like feelers to navigate the way. But it was my knee that found the fence at the edge of our yard, and I stifled a cry as it slammed into the rough wooden post.

I clambered over it into Mr. Euler's orchard. My legs trembled beneath me as I ducked under the apple-heavy branches. The orchard had been neglected for years, and the smell of rotten fruit squishing beneath my feet reminded me how Dad had smelled when he'd dragged me out from under the piano just minutes earlier. At the thought of him still out there in the yard searching for me, I lengthened my stride and tried to stay on the balls of my feet.

When I emerged from the orchard, I started running again, past the cluster of cottonwoods sprawled like cobwebs over Mr. Euler's vacant house, and across a stream that cut through his land. Frigid water splashed onto my skin and rocks jabbed into my already sore feet. A sharp one stabbed my heel, and I lunged for the dry bank and stumbled to my knees. I sprang up and kept going, bringing a thick layer of dirt on the soles of my feet.

In all the years I'd had to flee from Dad, he'd never found my hiding place. But if I slowed down, he might follow me and discover it, and I would have nowhere to go in the future when his volatility forced me out of the house. I started through a field of long yellow grass that stretched uphill toward the mountain. My lungs felt like they might burst, but I didn't slow down.

Dew from the long grass clung to the fray on my shorts, and chirping insects saturated the summer night with their music. I drew in my arms, hoping no spiders or crickets were hitchhiking on my back. I'd taken this path countless times in my seventeen years, but the Colorado

mountains were always more eerie at night. A chill ran down my spine as I saw a dark movement in the shadow of the trees, and I reminded myself that the only real monster was far behind me.

"Be brave," I whispered to myself through labored breaths.

It wasn't until I entered a grove of aspens skirting the base of the mountain that I felt safe enough to ease my pace. I weaved through a labyrinth of white trunks until I reached a clearing, then stopped and exhaled a sigh of relief.

A massive ash tree stood in the center of the clearing, ancient and otherworldly in the silvery moonlight. Five enormous limbs spread out from the squat trunk like an open hand, and nestled in the hollow of the palm was a tree house.

Using blocks of weathered wood nailed to the trunk, I climbed up to a narrow porch and stepped through an open doorway. Moonlight seeped through water-stained windows onto the wooden floor, making it a dusty gray. Cabinets and shelves lined one wall, and the open rafters provided a perfect place for spiders to spin their webs.

I shivered and rubbed my bare arms, wishing I'd worn something more substantial than a tank top and cut-off shorts. Not that I could have anticipated spending the night outdoors, or had time to change. One minute, I was asleep under Mom's piano, and the next, Dad was yanking my arm and demanding to know why I'd broken his rules *again*. I chided myself for being so careless and getting caught, for crawling under the piano to lie down instead of being satisfied with the four hours of Chopin and Beethoven I'd been able to sneak in while Dad was out falling off the wagon again.

I yanked a flashlight and sleeping bag from a shelf, then unrolled the sleeping bag and inspected it for spiders before sliding in and curling into a ball to warm up.

Trying to relax, I drew in a few deep breaths. My heart was still racing, my hands still shaky. I clutched a handful of down-filled nylon and shut my eyes. *I'm not going to cry,* I told myself. I felt the burn in my throat and the moisture gathering on my lashes, but I forced them back. Tears never did any good. They didn't provide comfort or explanations, and never helped me make sense of my situation.

Instead, I sat up and wiped the itchy wetness from my lashes. I opened a narrow cabinet and removed a thick wirebound notebook. Propping the flashlight against the wall, I slid a pencil from the coiled wire and opened the notebook. Musical staves lined each page, some filled with fragments of music Mom had written, others with my attempts at adding to hers. Other than the piano that remained locked in the parlor, Mom's notebook was my most cherished possession and one of the few things I'd been able to snag before Dad squirreled away all her things after her death.

I ran my hand down the page and picked out a short snippet of Mom's, then copied it onto a blank page. Humming the exquisite melody, I tapped my pencil to the rhythm. Then I pressed the lead tip to the page to add to it. I echoed her first passage, then carried her bass line for two measures and added a trill before a descending run. Measure after measure, passage after passage, I intertwined my music with hers until my pulse slowed and my nerves settled.

I awoke to a creaking sound, like wood bending under the weight of a heavy foot. But when I opened my eyes, there was no one there. Only a blue jay perched on the threshold of the doorway, his plumage vibrant in the early morning light. He tilted his crested head and stared at me curiously with one eye, then ruffled his feathers before going still again. He appeared to be listening, waiting expectantly for something.

Wanting to sleep longer, I shut my eyes. Every joint in my body ached as if I'd hiked a mountain the day before. The blue jay called again, a musical whistle that sounded like a rusty old swing. I picked out the notes and the melodic interval. *B-flat to G,* I thought, *a minor third.* He repeated the call again and again, but soon another creak silenced him.

I sat up in my sleeping bag, my ears suddenly attuned to the sounds outside the tree house. Weak wood whining against the strain of pressure. The tread of a shoe gripping the edge of a step. Labored breathing.

Someone was climbing to the tree house.

The blue jay's crest bristled outward in warning, and in one movement I shed the sleeping bag and shot to my feet. The bird beat its wings and let out a hawk-like scream before flying up into the rafters, trapping itself along with me.

My first thought was that Dad had finally found my hidden sanctuary. If he saw me here, I could never come back. As stealthily as I could manage, I scooped up my sleeping bag and receded into a shallow space behind a tall cabinet. My sleeping bag bulged around the corner, and I hooked my leg around it and drew it as close to my body as possible. The sounds of the blue jay's escape attempts only added to my anxiety. A thump against a window, a clatter against the roof, an ear-piercing warning call. Every now and then I saw a flash of blue feathers in the rafters. My heart beat as wildly in my chest as the trapped bird's wings.

A shadow stretched from the doorway across the floor, and I held my breath and stiffened my body, hoping Dad would take a quick glance, then go on his way. But instead I heard the creak of steps. They were slow and tentative, and were coming closer. My lungs burned for want of new air, and I eased the stale air out and silently drew in more.

Another step closer. Too close. I guessed he was right around the corner of the cabinet. If I moved a fraction of an inch, he would hear me. My muscles cramped up from being tense for so long, but I couldn't release them without being discovered. I heard one more step, then my stomach contracted as someone stepped into my line of vision.

It wasn't Dad.

It was a boy, tall with dark, tousled hair. His back was to me, but a moment later he turned to face me and his eyes locked with mine. The look of surprise I expected to see was strangely absent. Instead, his expression seemed to say, *Oh, there you are.*

I must have looked terrified because he raised his palms and said gently, "Don't be scared. I won't hurt you."

I knew I should say something, explain myself, but all I could do was stare up at the blue jay, still thrashing its wings against the rafters. The boy followed my gaze, then turned away and stepped out of view. I peered around the corner to see what he was doing.

He went to a wall and tugged at a latch that secured the

roof. It came loose; then he went to the opposite wall and unlatched another. Taking hold of a joist, he gave a few jerks until the roof opened like a sliding lid on a wooden box.

Mr. Euler had been an astronomer, and he'd used the tree house as his personal observatory. But it had been years since he'd slid open the roof to view the night sky, and the wheels made a crackling sound as they rolled over dirt and dried leaves along the track. The free corners of the roof moved over the deck on wheeled posts, and when it opened halfway, the blue jay dove toward the deck, then flew away. I turned back to the boy, wishing I could have flown away too.

The boy watched the bird disappear into the nearby aspens, then he turned to me. His lips parted as if to say something, but instead he pressed them back together and looked down, seeming as uncomfortable as I was. He scratched the sparse stubble on his jaw, then lifted his gaze to try again.

"I'm Thomas," he said. "Frank Euler's grandson." When I gave no response, he tilted his head and raised a dark eyebrow. "And you are?"

Blood rushed up my neck and into my cheeks, bringing my voice with it. "I . . . I'm sorry," I stammered. "I'm Aria. I live next door. I just come here sometimes to spend the night—for fun. Your grandpa knows, or knew, when he lived here." It all came out in a nervous rush, and I bit down on my tongue, trying to keep more words from spilling out.

The corner of his mouth twitched as he leaned his shoulder against the wall and shrugged. "It's okay. You're not in trouble. I just wanted to know who you were." He watched me, as though waiting for me to do or say something.

When I didn't move or speak, he rubbed the back of his neck and gave an encouraging smile. "You can come out of there . . . if you want."

I coerced my shoulders to loosen a notch, then stepped tentatively out of the shadow into the light, still clutching my sleeping bag to my chest.

He squinted against the sunlight falling through the open roof and took a step toward me, his face gradually brightening in recognition. "I think I've seen you before."

"When?" I asked, searching his face for familiarity but finding none.

"A couple years ago—when we helped my grandpa move to the nursing home. You came up the driveway and started talking to him." He paused and studied the floor a moment, musing privately on the memory. "You hugged him, then left."

As if sifting through a box of old photos, it took me a minute to retrieve the memory. But it was there. I'd been fifteen, crying, and all too aware of the cute dark-haired boy watching me from the window.

In the light of this memory, I appraised him again more attentively. He was still cute. In fact, he put cute to shame. His clothes were nothing spectacular—just a snug T-shirt and loose jeans—but the way the morning sun highlighted the lines of his face made him look like some Victorian masterpiece. I couldn't help but contrast his appearance with mine. With my dirty bare feet, scuffed knees, and snarled hair, I probably looked more like something hanging from the rafters of Dad's barn than in the borders of a gilded frame. "Yeah," I finally said, twisting my hair over one shoulder in an attempt to tame it. "That was me."

"My grandpa must have been a good friend to you." From his gentle tone, I guessed that he was still picturing my tearful fifteen-year-old face in his mind.

I nodded. "Is he back from the nursing home, then?"

He diverted his eyes to the window and twisted his mouth like he was tasting something bitter. "He . . . passed away a few weeks ago."

"I'm sorry," I said, feeling the all-too-familiar sting of loss in the pit of my stomach.

"Yeah. Me too." He hooked his thumbs in his pockets and sighed. "It was unexpected, so I didn't really get to say good-bye." A long silence stretched between us, until he turned to look at me and offered a little smile. "Anyway, we're just here until the spring to get his place ready to sell."

I'd been searching for a way to make a dignified exit, and his words opened a gate. "Well, I guess I'd better get out of your hair, then."

He started saying something about how I didn't need to go, but as I went to the doorway and tossed my sleeping bag to the ground, he trailed off. I glanced up at him, and his pointed gaze was fixed on my arm. When I glanced down, I gasped at what I saw.

Three bruises banded my upper arm like a cuff. They were barred, the size and shape of a man's fingers.

Instinctively, my hand came up to cover them. He turned away and absently opened a cabinet door, his face composing into a careful mask as he searched the empty shelves for absolutely nothing.

I tried to think of something to say, but no words came to mind. Only images from the night before.

Dad's callused fingers clamped down on my arm, his

thorny hangnail digging into my skin. His lips pulled tight over his teeth as he reprimanded me for doing the only thing that made me happy.

My vision wavered behind the pressure of unshed tears. But not wanting to cry in front of Thomas, I bit down hard on my lip, fortifying the dam keeping the tears at bay.

Thomas turned back to me and tried to smile. "I guess I'll see you at school, then. It starts Monday, right?"

Whether his evasion was for his sake or mine, I didn't know, but I was grateful I wouldn't have to come up with an impromptu explanation. "Right—Monday," I said vacantly.

Without another word, I descended from the tree house, snatched up my sleeping bag, and walked away, raw humiliation leaving me stunned. As soon as I was safely blanketed in aspens, I broke into a run. I didn't see their white branches whip past me, or the tunnel that closed over me as I passed down a row of apple trees, or the wooden fence as I clambered over. In their place, I saw Dad's eyes, bulging and wild. I saw the porch light cutting through the parlor window, making his red hair look like flames. I saw his hand on the piano key cover, slamming it shut. But worst of all, I saw Thomas's eyes, wide with alarm and fixed on the glaring evidence of Dad's abuse.

With each stride, the pressure behind my eyes built until the dam began to crumble. And when I reached Dad's barn, I pressed my back against the side and slid to the ground, where I buried my head in my arms and released the tears.

♪ ♪ ♪ ♪ ♪ ♪

The kitchen was dark when I stepped through the back door to get ready for work, and all my senses were on high

alert. The faucet dripped slowly in the kitchen sink, but the rest of the house was silent. An open bottle of brandy sat on the kitchen table, waiting to be finished. I tiptoed inside, the old floorboards creaking underfoot, and as I approached the living room, I saw Dad stretched out on the carpet at the base of the stairs.

He lay on his back, one arm resting across his muscular chest, the other propped up on the bottom step. His thick red hair shot out in every direction as if he'd been tugging at it all night, and he still wore the plaid flannel shirt I'd mended the day before. Oddly enough, it was still tucked neatly into his jeans. His abdomen slowly rose and fell, and his face was relaxed and peaceful. The way he used to look before Mom died, the way he'd begun to look again before his relapse the night before. It made my heart grieve over the loss of the good father he'd once been, and the three months of sobriety he'd thrown away.

A long rectangle of sunlight stretched across the carpet from the parlor door, and I was surprised to see it still open. The piano beckoned to me from inside the small room, but with Dad sprawled out on the floor just feet away, it wasn't exactly an ideal time to interpret *Fantasie Impromptu*. I went to close the door, but first stepped inside to pick up the sheet music that had fallen to the floor the night before. The morning sun spilled through the tall windows, washing the room with a heavenly golden hue.

Dad viewed the parlor as a sacred sepulcher, a forbidden place where memories of Mom dwelled, sleeping and inaccessible. But for me, it was where I came to be with her. I couldn't run my hands across the worn piano keys without seeing her own, couldn't sit on the bench without feeling her warmth beside me. Even the tendrils of dark hair that spilled over my shoulders when I played reminded me of her. Her hair had been the same shade as the dark mahogany piano, and when she wore it down, it shrouded her shoulders and back like a hooded cape, melding her and the piano into one inseparable instrument.

With a heartsick sigh, I turned around and left the parlor, locking and shutting the door behind me, just the way Dad wanted it. As I approached the stairs, I could feel Dad's hunting prizes watching me. I could almost hear them say, *If you go in there again, you'll be next.*

Dad didn't know, but I had names for all his furry trophies. Ann, the red fox on the side table, was polite, kept mostly to herself, and had impeccable posture. Harriet and Ned, two quails on the wall, constantly quarreled about whose fault it was that they'd ended up stuffed and mounted to a tree branch. Of all the stiff specimens in the room, I related to Harriet and Ned the most. Wings forever spread as if in flight, yet suspended, unable to go anywhere.

And then there was Knox, Dad's prized possession and my least favorite resident. The large gray wolf was preserved pushing off his hind foot, the rest of his body leaping into the air in attack position. Every time I walked past him, I felt him stalking me, waiting for an opportunity to tear into my calf with his razor teeth.

I heard the crackling sound of tires rolling over the gravel driveway outside—one of Dad's customers, I guessed. I always thought it ironic that when Dad wasn't running around in his fireman's uniform saving people, he ran a taxidermy business in our barn, preserving what others had killed.

I glanced through the lace curtains that were the last remains of Mom's decorating influence and saw a middle-aged man getting out of a silver car. A nervous tremble rippled down my abdomen as I recognized him from the night before. He'd shown up and argued with Dad in the driveway, and although I hadn't heard their conversation, it had set Dad off on his drinking rampage. And now, here he was again. I didn't know him, and from his appearance I guessed he wasn't one of Dad's customers. His sandy-blond hair looked like he'd spent half the day styling it, and he wore a starchy dress shirt and vogue square-rimmed glasses. Dad's customers were inclined toward dungarees, flannel shirts, and duck canvas vests.

I didn't have time to deal with him, so I stepped over Dad and went upstairs to get ready for work. Already late, I skipped the shower and went to my room to change. As I slipped the sheet music under my mattress with all my other music, there was a knock on the front door, loud and urgent. But I ignored it, taking off my dirty tank and shorts and throwing on an unflattering lime-green bussing shirt and black slacks.

The doorbell rang, and I poked my head into the hallway to see if Dad was waking up, but he hadn't stirred. I crossed the hall to the bathroom, where I did my best to make myself presentable by dabbing on some makeup and wrangling my hair into a bun. Luckily the sleeves of my bussing shirt were long enough to conceal the bruises on my arm. The doorbell didn't ring again, and soon I heard the man's car rolling back over the gravel and his engine fading away. I came back down the stairs and stepped over Dad, gave him one last pitiful look, and then left for work.

two

Despite the rock already filling my gut, I fetched my lunch sack from my locker Monday afternoon and went to the cafeteria. Students gathered in their new back-to-school clothes at long tables or lined up with trays, poking and flirting as they waited for pizza and fries. I leaned against the brick wall and browsed the tables for a place to sit. A couple of girls from English Literature waved at me from a table by a window, but I didn't have it in me to join them. With my nerves still frayed from what had happened over the weekend, I didn't feel like putting on a show and pretending that everything was okay. I didn't want people asking what was wrong or why I was wearing long sleeves and jeans in August or what I did this summer.

A tall, dark-haired boy with a black T-shirt and loose jeans strolled in. With his back to me, he paused and scanned the lunchroom. Even before seeing his striking profile, I knew it was Thomas.

I felt anew the humiliation of the other morning, and not wanting to risk running into him, I backed out of the cafeteria and fled down the hall. Turning a couple corners, I came to the heavy door that led to the auditorium stage. I glanced around to make sure no one was watching, then snuck inside.

I found the old upright piano tucked behind layers of black curtain and opened the key cover, then sat on the bench and locked down the soft pedal. With my sandwich in my left hand and my right hand on the keys, I practiced the melody of Debussy's *Reverie*. I switched sides and practiced the bass line. When my sandwich was gone and both hands were free, I sank into the lulling passages without reserve, expressing the things that were not safe to say.

My hands moved up and down the keyboard, summoning great waves of music, each one crested with sorrow, loneliness, and anger. Tides of emotion rose and fell, gradually finding their way down my arms and to the keys, becoming harmonies that filled and then dissipated into the air like mist.

When the lunch bell rang, I lingered for a few minutes so no one would see me come out, then gathered my things and went to class.

My World Civilizations class was bubbling with chatter when I walked in, the various tones and timbres of students' voices mixing like the cacophony of an orchestra warm-up. I skirted around the back of the room until I found an empty seat, but the moment I sat down, I regretted it. One row over and two seats up sat Thomas. He gazed down at his notebook with pencil in hand, making long, slow movements across the page.

"Choose your seat wisely," Mr. Becket said, twisting the corners of his overgrown mustache, "because I'm starting around the seating chart."

Feeling uneasy about sitting so close to Thomas, I scanned the room for another open seat. There were only two. One was right in front of Thomas, and the other was across the room, behind Dirk Page and Trisha Rosenblatt. I briefly wondered if they were back together, and which would be more tolerable—sitting so close to Thomas or watching Trisha give suggestive looks to Dirk all year.

Realizing I couldn't avoid Thomas forever, I decided to stay where I was. But I dreaded looking into his eyes again. I dreaded the sympathy I would see there, the questions he might ask, and the things he might say. I wondered if he'd keep what he'd seen to himself, or if, within days, the entire school would be casting pitiful looks at me. My pride and reputation were at his mercy. I felt like a small helpless bird enfolded in his hands—he could either crush me or set me free.

Mr. Becket was pacing with hands clasped behind his back in front of the room, giving a travelogue of all the countries he'd visited over the summer and claiming he'd learned to speak at least one phrase in every language. "Name a language," he challenged, "and I will say something in it." A couple kids called out German and Chinese, and he demonstrated each with nonchalance. "Come on," he urged, "give me a challenge."

Bulgarian and Yiddish were requested. He spewed out a phrase in each.

"Dutch," someone called out.

"*Nog een prettige dag toegewest*," said Mr. Becket.

"You mean *toegewenst*?" Thomas chimed in with a half-raised hand.

"Ah!" Mr. Becket's face brightened. "Do you know Dutch?"

Thomas lifted a shoulder in a casual shrug. "Enough to get by."

Mr. Becket stammered through another phrase, and Thomas replied with a long and fluent-sounding string of Dutch. The class reacted with yawns and eye rolls. But I was suddenly intrigued, wondering how on earth Thomas knew how to speak Dutch.

Trisha raised her hand, waving it in the air like a beauty queen.

"Miss Rosenblatt," Mr. Becket said, "do you have another language request?"

"Actually," Trisha replied, twirling a tendril of long golden hair around her finger, "I was wondering if I could change my seat."

"We already filled out the seating chart," Mr. Becket said.

"But I can't see very good back here, and it's giving me a headache." She pressed her fingers to her forehead, and Dirk turned around to shoot her a skeptical look.

Mr. Becket considered a moment, scanning the front of the class for an empty seat before gesturing to the desk in front of Thomas. "Come sit in front of Mr. Ashby."

*Ashby.* There was something lyrical about his name, like I could string the letters together on a staff to form a melodic phrase. *Thomas Ashby.*

Trisha happily popped out of her chair and perched herself in front of Thomas, flashing him a sultry smile before facing the front of the room. It was too easy to see how this would turn out. They would go to homecoming, hold hands in the hallway, and get married right out of high school. She angled her body sideways and crossed her bare legs, no doubt so Thomas could get a better view. But he didn't seem to notice. He kept his head down and his pencil moving across his notebook as Mr. Becket transitioned into a lecture on the Middle Ages.

As though fearing Thomas would forget she was there, Trisha made a point to move every minute or so. She gathered her hair to one shoulder, then the other. She uncrossed her legs and crossed them again. She trailed her pencil along her jaw, then tied her hair into a loose bun. A moment later as she pulled out the elastic band, she "accidentally" flung it into the aisle behind Thomas.

He reached back and picked it up, catching my eye as he did so. There it was—that look of commiseration that made me feel as small as the lead tip on my pencil. He paused and acknowledged me with a little smile before turning back and handing the elastic band to Trisha.

The fire spread from my cheeks to my ears, and I eyed the door, once again feeling like that little trapped bird. *Set me free*, I thought. *Don't look at me again. Don't talk to me. Just forget about me and what you saw.*

For the remainder of class, Thomas sat unnaturally still. He didn't take any more notes, and he didn't seem interested in Mr. Becket's lecture. He appeared distracted, and the unfocused glances he cast at the window made me wonder if he was watching me from the corner of his eye. I sensed he wanted to talk to me, but it was a conversation I didn't want to have.

With five minutes of class left, I gathered up my things. Thomas glanced back at me with an anxious expression, then gathered up his things as well. I watched the clock and eyed the door. He watched the clock too. I gauged the distance from each of our desks to the door. His was closer, so I would have to move fast. It would be a race for the door, and if I lost, I would have to face him to hear whatever he had to say.

The instant the bell rang, I dashed for the door. Glancing back, I saw Trisha stand and intercept Thomas. It was the first time in my life I felt gratitude toward Trisha.

When I got home, I found Dad clean shaven at the kitchen table, drinking coffee and eating dry toast. He was probably sobering up because he had to work the next day.

"Hey, Dad," I said as though he hadn't been missing for two days, as though he hadn't left a mark on me the last time I'd seen him.

He lifted his eyes from the *Field and Stream* magazine on the table. "Aria." He nodded, a look of contrition on his face.

I dropped my backpack on a chair and walked to the fridge, opening the door.

"How was school?" he asked.

I wanted to tell him it was awful, that I felt sick all day thinking about what happened over the weekend, and that I ate lunch alone because I didn't want people to see I was upset. But having an honest conversation with Dad was about as appetizing as the raw pheasant that had been sitting in the fridge for the last three days. "Fine," I said. "I like my teachers."

"Will you come sit down for a minute?"

*Here it comes,* I thought. I shut the fridge and joined him at the table in the chair farthest from him. One of the buttons on his flannel shirt cuff was undone, and he buttoned it. Then he unbuttoned it. Then buttoned it again.

"I'm sorry about the other night." He hung his head and ground his knuckles against his mouth. "I just . . ."

"It's okay," I said, knowing that guilt would only give him more momentum for the next ride.

When he lifted his face again, his eyes were misty and his mouth contorted in pain. "No—it's not okay." His eyes swept over me. "Did I hurt you?"

I shook my head. "I'm fine."

"Why are you wearing long sleeves? It's ninety degrees outside."

I glanced at my shirt and shrugged. "It was cool this morning."

"Did I leave a mark?"

"No." The sooner he moved past what had happened, the sooner he'd get back on the path to sobriety.

A strained silence filled the space between us, and I watched his face slowly turn from remorse to frustration. "I don't understand why you go in there," he said, referring to the parlor, "when you know what it does to me."

"It won't happen again." But what I meant was, *I won't get caught again.*

He studied me for a moment as though trying to measure my sincerity, then from his wallet pulled out five twenties and pushed them across the table. "I know it's not much, but you could probably use some new school clothes."

I stared at the money and nodded. "Thanks, Dad."

He stood and hooked his thumbs through his belt loops. "Well, I need to give one of my customers a call."

"Cody stopped by on Sunday for his marmot," I said, assuming that was the customer he needed to call. "I took him out to the barn and he found it. He said he'd already paid, so I let him take it."

PORCELAIN *keys*

He nodded, shame returning to his expression. "Thanks, Aria. I'll give him a call to make sure he's happy with it."

Dad went to the phone, and I folded the twenties and slid them in my back pocket, already knowing the money would go in my savings account and not toward my wardrobe. I didn't own a car, a cell phone, or new clothes. But I had freedom money waiting for me. I'd accumulated a meager savings bussing tables over the summer, and the moment I graduated high school—in less than nine months—Woodland Park, Colorado, would have one fewer resident. I didn't know where I would go yet, but it didn't really matter. Anywhere I could get a full-time job, a cheap apartment, and a thrift-store piano.

Dad started dialing a number, and I grabbed my backpack and went upstairs to my room, not wanting to hear him lie to his customer about where he'd been all weekend.

I sat on my bed and unzipped my backpack, then pulled out the Rachmaninoff book I'd picked up on my way home from school. I slid it inside my binder to use as a cover, then leaned against the wall and browsed the pieces. I found the most difficult one, with abundant sharps and flats, tightly stacked notes, and an array of dynamics. Determined to learn it, I took a pencil and began making fingering notations, all the while planning how I would avoid Thomas Ashby the next day.

# *three*

The air was muggy the next morning as I pedaled away from the house, and a wing of ashen clouds was sweeping in, turning the mountains a gloomy lavender. Foreseeing rain, I pulled up the hood of my sweatshirt and tucked my hair down my back. By the time I got to the highway, it was drizzling.

My bike tires cut through puddles on the roadside, forming little walls of water and splashing my sneakers. The smell of wet foliage and earth saturated the air, invigorating my senses.

A distant rumble echoed through the trees, but it wasn't thunder. It was an engine, loud enough to recognize from a mile away. Maybe Dad still felt bad about this weekend and was coming to offer me a ride to school. The roaring vehicle grew louder as it came up the highway behind me, and the engine's pitch lowered as it decelerated.

As I whipped around to see if it was Dad, my front wheel slipped off the wet pavement and into a rut. The next thing I knew, I was flying off my bike and crashing into the

muddy gravel, my palms scraping across the sharp rocks. I cried out in pain and glanced back to see an old red Bronco pulling over. It wasn't Dad. And it only took an instant to recognize the driver.

*Thomas Ashby.*

He jumped out and rushed over with an alarmed expression and an extended hand. "Are you okay?"

As if I needed another way to humiliate myself in front of him. I stood up without taking his hand and tried to swipe the muddy gravel from my jeans, but my palms were so raw I gave up. "I'm fine."

"I'm sorry. I didn't mean to startle you."

"You didn't," I said flatly. "I just slipped off the wet road." I picked up my bike and climbed back on.

"Hold on." His brows pulled together like he was calculating what to say next. "I . . . I need to talk to you."

*No—you don't.* I sheltered my face from the rain with my hand. "Can it wait until we're not being poured on?"

"It's dry in my truck. Can I give you a ride?"

"I like the rain," I lied. I put my foot on the pedal to leave, but his hand came over mine on the handlebar. It was warm, and his large fingers encased mine like an electric blanket.

"Wait—just let me—" He sighed, and a cloud of his breath hung in the crisp morning air. "You're cold. Your lips are trembling."

I bit down on my lip to make it stop.

He raised a hand to shield his face from the rain. "Let me give you a ride." His face was pleading, and for the first time, I noticed the striking color of his eyes. Brilliant azure, like the wings of the blue jay I'd seen the other morning. Something about them calmed me, and for a split second, every ounce of fear inside me was dispelled. I was cold, and the cab of his Bronco looked inviting. It had to be toasty to keep his hands so warm.

"What about my bike?"

He pointed his thumb at the back of his Bronco. "I'll put it on the rack."

I got off my bike and handed it over, then climbed into his Bronco and sat on the brittle, cracked leather seat. The heavy door squeaked loudly as I slammed it shut.

He climbed in and we got back on the road. The moisture in the cab clung to the windows, and he reached over and flipped on the defrost. When I clutched my wet backpack against my chest and shivered, he switched it to heat. Warm air blew loudly through the broken slats on the vents.

"So, about the other morning," he started.

I held my breath, bracing myself for the dreaded confrontation.

"I'm sorry if I made you feel uncomfortable," he said. "I should have just left you alone and gone back to the house."

"It's okay. You didn't know I was there."

"Actually . . ." He pressed his lips together. "I did."

"What?" At first I wasn't sure I'd heard him right. But then he gave me a guilty-looking sidelong glance.

"I came up there earlier and saw you sleeping. I was going to just leave you alone, and I started walking back to the house. But then I started wondering . . . what if I never saw you again?"

"Would that have been such a bad thing?" I didn't know whether to feel flattered or more embarrassed.

"Yeah—I mean, I'd be left wondering for the rest of my life who that mysterious girl in my grandpa's tree house was." He glanced at me, his full lips curving into a smile,

but his eyes were still troubled. "Anyway, it wasn't my intention to embarrass you or anything, so I'm sorry if I did. And I want you to know that even though we're living there now, you're welcome to use the tree house whenever you want."

So this was his indirect way of bringing it up, by letting me know that I still had a refuge. "It's okay," I said, shaking my head. "I'm getting too old to hang out in a tree house anyway." The windshield wipers were on high-speed, but they barely kept up with the raindrops pelting the glass. I gazed into the storm through the blurred window, hoping he would just drop the topic.

"Well, I'm just saying that—"

"Really," I cut him off and turned to him, letting out a little exasperated laugh. "It's okay." Desperate to change the subject, I asked, "So, how is it exactly that you know Dutch?"

It took him a minute to switch gears, but slowly his uneasy frown relaxed into a straight line. "I just returned from living in the Netherlands for a year."

"Is your dad in the military?"

"No. My mom's an astronomer like my grandpa, and she had a research project there."

"Are you going back there after you sell your grandpa's property?"

He shook his head. "She's finished with her research there, for now anyway. So we'll go back to Pasadena, where we're originally from. My parents still have a house there."

In order to keep him from going back to our first topic, I kept up a steady stream of questions. He seemed eager to tell me about life in the Netherlands, and as I watched him talk, I noticed a thin, inch-long scar above his right eyebrow. I wanted to ask him what it was from, but I didn't know if it was too personal a question to ask. I tried to imagine how he could have gotten it. Maybe a mountain-biking accident or an elbow to the face during a basketball game.

"Do you play basketball?" I interrupted.

He glanced at me with an amused smile. "Why is it that when someone is tall, people always assume they play basketball? Like being tall is the only requirement for the sport? It's like saying to a short person, 'You're short. You must be bound for the Kentucky Derby.'"

"Sorry—I didn't mean to—"

"It's okay." He laughed. "I played some lacrosse in junior high, but I'm not really into sports."

We rode in silence the rest of the way, him watching the road, me watching him from the corner of my eye. Apart from his stylish jacket, crisp jeans, and new hiking shoes, there was something strangely organic about him. Maybe it was the cracked skin over his knuckles, or the dirt embedded deep under his fingernails like he'd been working soil with his hands. Or maybe it was the stubble on his sharp-edged jaw and the tired lines under his eyes. I wondered if he'd slept roughly through last night's thunderstorm like I had.

He pulled into the school parking lot and we walked into school together. As we parted ways and I watched him disappear into the crowded hall, I realized that I liked Thomas. I wished that I could start over with him, like we'd only just met that morning. I decided that I would. I would forget about our first meeting in the tree house, and in time, maybe he would too.

When classes got out for lunch, I went to my locker, debating whether to go to the cafeteria to find Thomas or just retreat to the auditorium to get some piano time in. But as I shut my locker and saw Thomas a few feet away, his tall, lean figure leaning casually against the row of lockers, my decision was made.

"Hey," he said with a little smile that made a dimple appear at the side of his mouth. "Can I eat lunch with you today?"

I nodded with nonchalance, trying not to betray my acute interest in him.

In the lunchroom, I took a seat at an empty table while he went to join the lunch line. Before I could remove the sandwich from my lunch sack, Trisha and two of her friends swooped in with their lunch trays, tainting the air with coconut and nail polish.

Trisha's wide-necked shirt hung off one shoulder, revealing the sparkly purple strap of her dance uniform. Her long golden hair was secured on the opposite shoulder in a loose side ponytail, as if the display of her uniform was intentional. "Is Thomas eating lunch with you?" she asked, bewildered.

"So it would seem."

"Do you mind if we eat with you?"

I knew she'd stay regardless of my answer, so I asked, "Why aren't you eating with Dirk?"

As if on cue, cheering erupted from across the lunchroom, and we turned to see Dirk on a table, doing some shoulder-jerking dance move that resembled a cat coughing up a hair ball.

"Ugh. Are you kidding me?" Trisha rolled her eyes. "He's been doing the funky chicken on my nerves."

Dirk was a football star with broad shoulders, bleach-blond hair, and a toothy grin every girl in school found irresistible. But by the way Trisha was eyeing Thomas across the cafeteria, I knew she had found something more irresistible.

"You know," I said, feeling oddly protective of Thomas, "I don't think Thomas is your type."

"What does that mean?"

"I mean, I think he has a minimal supply of shoulder pads and tight pants."

"He could be in chess club for all I care," Trisha said, smiling at her friend Christy. "Can you just picture the way his bicep would flex as he moved his queen across the board? *Checkmate.*" She leaned on Christy and they giggled like twelve-year-olds.

Thomas came over with his tray, and since Christy and the other girl were sitting next to me, Thomas sat across from me next to Trisha. She dove into conversation with him, not wasting any time staking her claim. She asked question after question, and I noted that she didn't ask him anything unless it gave her an opportunity to say something about herself. Did he play golf? She did—her pro-golfer dad took her almost every weekend. Did he like sushi? She did—inari was her favorite, and she didn't mind the way wasabi made her sinuses tingle.

She said all these things with a glint in her eye and a smile that made her as sparkly as her dance uniform. It seemed her goal wasn't to get to know Thomas, but to put herself on display like a piece of merchandise on the home shopping network.

Thomas did a lot of smiling and nodding, but I couldn't

tell if it was because he was being polite or was genuinely interested.

I felt a tap on my shoulder, and I twisted around to see Dirk standing behind me in his letterman jacket with a tray of food. "Hey, Ariel. Mind if I sit with you?"

I gave him a withering look. "I've worked with you for three months, and you still can't remember my name?" Dirk's parents owned Pikes Pancake House, the place where I bussed tables. He held the position of underworked-over-paid host.

He stared at me blankly for a moment before smacking his forehead. "Aria . . . Ariel . . . You see why I get confused, right?" He wedged himself between Christy and me, and she scooted over to make room.

Trisha eyed Dirk warily, like he was intruding in her new social bubble. With an exaggerated eye roll, she turned back to Thomas and started talking about fortune cookies.

"So . . ." Dirk nudged me. "Do you like lemon Skittles?"

I arched an eyebrow. "Not really. Why?"

"I don't either." He pulled a deflated Skittles package from his jacket pocket. "I have a bunch in here I'm trying to get rid of. Trisha used to like them." His eyes flitted to Trisha and his shoulders slumped. "But not anymore." He glanced back at me, and his gaze latched onto my cheek. "What happened to your face?"

I reached up and ran my fingers over my cheek. It felt like sandpaper where the pine branches had whipped me the other night. "I . . . collided with a tree."

He let out a bark of amused laughter, loud enough that students at nearby tables turned their heads to stare. "Well, could've been worse. I collided with a goalpost last summer, and, *man* . . ." He shook his head vigorously as though trying to expel the memory.

While Dirk told me the story leading up to his run-in with the goalpost, I caught part of Thomas and Trisha's conversation. She'd asked him if he had a girlfriend. He said he didn't, then said something about how he didn't date.

"Why not?" she asked, biting her glossy lip while waiting for him to answer. I listened closely, curious to know the answer myself.

"I just don't," he said, a fleeting grimace rippling across his expression.

"Are you going to be a clergyman or something?" Trisha smirked.

He cleared his throat and smiled the way I did when people asked me how my mom died. "No," he said simply.

"Then why not date?" she pressed.

"It's not that I'm never going to date. Just not right now."

"Why not right now?"

The lunch bell rang, and Thomas stood with his tray. "See you guys in class." He gave that small, courteous smile again, then walked away.

"This makes no sense," Trisha whined as she gathered up her things. "What hot seventeen-year-old guy isn't interested in girls?"

"Maybe he's just playing hard to get," Christy suggested.

"He sounded like he meant it," I couldn't help saying as I stood.

"Well, if anyone can change his mind, it's me," Trisha insisted. "I've never been one to back down from a challenge."

"Or walk away once the challenge is over," Dirk accused with narrowed eyes.

Trisha aimed a death-ray glare at him and started spitting out her own accusations.

I didn't stay to witness the end of their fight, but from the way Dirk sulked through Mr. Becket's lecture, his pocket must have still been full of lemon Skittles.

Thomas gave me a ride home after school, and when he dropped me off, he got out to lift my bike off his rack. "I'll pick you up tomorrow morning for school, okay?" he said as he handed over my bike.

"It's supposed to be sunny the rest of the week. I should be fine riding my bike."

"You live next door. Why don't you just ride with me from now on?" The earnest way he cinched his brow and pursed his lips in anticipation of my answer was kind of cute. What would it hurt to just ride to school with him?

I sighed. "Okay."

He nodded and climbed back into his Bronco, but before shutting the door he said, "I'll see you tomorrow morning, then. Seven twenty."

♪ ♪ ♪ ♪ ♪ ♪ ♪

The house was quiet and dark as I came in on Friday afternoon after Thomas dropped me off. Dad wasn't scheduled to work at the fire station, but it was the busiest time of year for his taxidermy business, so he was probably hunkered down in his barn. I opened the kitchen blinds to let some light in, and that's when I noticed the garage was empty.

On the table lay a piece of yellow notebook paper with Dad's handwriting.

*Got called into work. Be back in the morning.*

A sense of respite came over me, a feeling that for a small space of time, I was free to be myself. My fingers tingled with anticipation, and I hurried back to the living room and pulled a pin from my hair. As I was about to pick open the parlor door, there was a tap at the front door. Feeling thwarted, I slid the pin back in my hair and opened the door. Vivian Dobbs, our thirty-something neighbor who had a relentless crush on Dad, stood on the porch holding a golden-tipped meringue pie. She'd moved here a couple years earlier from Mississippi, seeking a drier climate and, from what I'd gained from our brief conversations, a new start in life.

"Hey, darlin'," she said with a southern drawl and a brilliant smile that lit up her youthful eyes. "I bet your Daddy ain't never tried a caramel banana pie." She handed me the pie.

"Probably not. But it looks delicious."

She craned her neck and looked past me while twirling her long beaded necklace around her finger. "Your daddy home, or is he off savin' folks today?"

"He's working. He'll be back in the morning."

"Darn." Her disappointment was evident as she tapped her high-heel boot and blew a lock of blonde hair from her face. "Well, I guess I'll go deliver somethin' sweet to the new neighbors." Her face suddenly lit up. "You seen them yet? Now who would've thought old Frank had such a good-lookin' grandson?"

"Yeah, his name is Thomas. I actually—"

"I have an idea!" she squealed, grabbing my arm in a death grip. "Why don't you go get dolled up, and you and I can go over there for a little visit. That way you can have first dibs on him before all the other girls at school move in on him."

"It's too late." *Besides,* I thought, *first dibs don't matter when you've already ruined the first impression.* "The other girls are already moving in on him."

"It's never too late." Her eyes swept over my clothes, and her expression turned sour. "You know, I have some size-four clothes that I can't quite squeeze into anymore. I went a little shopping crazy after the divorce, trying to start new and all." She sighed. "But it was lonely too. And after months of keeping company with Sara Lee and Little Debbie, it'd be easier to squeeze myself through a biscuit cutter than into those new clothes." She eyed the pie in my hands. "Why don't you go put that in the kitchen, then come on over and try some on."

"I have homework."

"It's Friday."

"And chores."

"Chores, schmores." She took the pie from my hands and walked past me into the kitchen to set it on the counter. "So this is what your kitchen looks like." She shook her head. "Needs a woman's touch. But another time. Right now, you're comin' with me." She grabbed my wrist and led me out of the house.

Vivian lived down the road in a tiny two-bedroom bungalow. Her living room overflowed with the woman's touch, from her floral sofas to her brass and glass shelves filled with knickknacks.

She gave me a tour of the house, which lasted less than sixty seconds, and we ended up in a guest bedroom full of collectible dolls. She slid open the closet door. It was full of clothes, some still with tags on. "Try somethin' on," she instructed, "then come out and show me."

I pulled out an airy white blouse and miniskirt and

changed into them while trying not to be creeped out by the hundreds of doll eyes staring at me.

It turned into sort of a fashion show, though it probably looked more like I was walking the plank instead of strutting the catwalk. Most of the clothes actually fit me really well, and I was grateful that I could update my wardrobe without having to take money out of savings.

"Anyone ever tell you how pretty you are?" she asked as I came out in the last outfit, a sleek black sweater and skinny jeans.

I shrugged. "Not really."

Her penciled eyebrows raised a notch, and her lips curved into an almost mischievous smile. "Why don't you come in my room and let me do your hair and makeup."

What I really wanted to do was go home and spend the evening with Beethoven and Clementi, but the pleading look on Vivian's face told me she needed my company more. So I consented to stay and play as her dress-up doll. She sat me down at the vanity in her bedroom and ran her fingers through my unruly waves. "Most girls would kill for your looks," she said, studying me. "That long dark hair and milky complexion. You're like porcelain and earth."

She reached for a makeup brush and dabbed some rouge on it before brushing it over my cheeks. I looked up at her and thought how she was the pretty one, with her clear skin, green eyes, and full mouth, and I wondered why she didn't have a man in her life.

"Vivian, what happened with you and your husband? I mean, why did you get divorced?" As soon as the words were out, I realized what a rude, nosy question it was. But she didn't even flinch.

"Honey, I used to pick men the same way I picked accessories. As long as they looked good around my neck or slung over my shoulder, I didn't care about the price." She picked up an eyeliner pencil. "Shut your eyes." I did, and I felt her precise, confident strokes above my lashes. "My husband was the most gorgeous accessory you'd ever seen. Full head of golden hair, a smile like a crescent moon. But he turned out to be one bull shark of a purse. And I realized in the end, he wasn't worth the price I was paying."

I opened my eyes. "And so you left?"

She sighed and gave a sharp nod. "A woman shouldn't have to pay anything for a good man, because a good man gives himself to you for free. So I tossed him in the trash like the worthless piece of dollar-store jewelry he was."

I smiled. "Well, I hope you find a free designer man someday."

"I think I may have found one," she said with a loaded tilt of her brow, "but I'm not so sure he's free."

I knew she was referring to Dad, but not wanting to encourage her, I didn't say anything. She didn't know Dad very well, and if she did, she would realize that not only was he broken goods, he was far from free.

"Now," she said, brushing a last touch of lipstick on my lips. "Let's go over and visit the Ashbys."

"Uh, no," I objected, shaking my head. "I think I'll just head home."

"Look at you, Aria!" She turned me to face the mirror. "You look gorgeous. It would be a waste for you to sit here with me all night. You need an admirer!"

"No, I don't."

"You do! Come on," she pleaded. "We'll bring them a pie. I have an extra one in the kitchen."

"But why would I tag along with you to bring them a pie?"

"Who cares? It's Friday night. Thomas is probably out with friends anyway."

I sighed. "Fine. I'll go." I grabbed a tissue and dabbed off some lipstick. "Can we at least soften my eyes a little? If he is there and I show up like this, he'll think I'm only trying to get his attention."

"You *are* trying to get his attention."

"I'm not. He's my friend. He only sees me as a friend."

She pulled me to my feet. "Come on!"

She picked up the pie from the kitchen and I followed her out the front door. Vivian walked fast, like an ostrich on a mission, and I had to hop every few steps to keep pace.

"So what's our story again?" I asked as we walked down Thomas's sycamore-lined dirt driveway.

"We don't need a story, honey. We tell it like it is." She looked over at me. "Don't look so scared, darlin'. It's not like we're walking into the jaws of death."

On Thomas's doorstep, Vivian handed me the pie. She rang the doorbell, then leaned over and whispered, "By the way honey, *you* made the pie."

"What? No, I didn't!" I tried to give the pie back.

"You did." She waved a dismissive hand, rejecting the pie. "And don't be so modest about it!"

"No, Vivian. I—" The door opened before I could finish my objection.

*four*

W ell, hello!" A petite, brunette woman opened the door. She was covered in white dust, from her friendly face down to her canvas sneakers.

"Hi, Elsie," Vivian said, then gestured to me. "I don't think you've met your neighbor, Aria."

"So this is Aria! Thomas has told me all about you."

"He has?"

Vivian nudged me, but I felt a touch of panic as I wondered just how much Thomas had told her.

"I came by Aria's tonight," Vivian said, "and she said she was makin' this delicious pie to bring to ya'll." She gestured to the pie in my hands.

"Is this for Thomas's birthday?" Elsie asked.

"It's his birthday?" Vivian exclaimed. "What a coincidence!"

While Vivian went on, puffing me up and lying about my pie-making abilities, Thomas approached the doorway and stood behind his mom. Like her, his dark hair and shoulders were dusted white.

"Oh, hi Thomas!" Vivian said. "Happy birthday! Anyway, Aria let me come along to deliver the pie so I could say hi."

I wanted to tell them Vivian was lying and smash the pie in her face, but instead I handed it to Elsie and smiled.

"Well, how sweet of you," Elsie said. "What kind of pie is it?"

I glanced at the pie in her hands. "Apple?"

"Perfect—we have ice cream in the kitchen. Why don't you two come in and join the party?"

"I would stay," Vivian said, "but I've got some errands to run. But Aria told me she's free tonight."

I pictured the banana-caramel pie she'd made for Dad smeared all over her front door. Vivian pranced away and I turned back to Thomas, who was staring at me with a little lopsided smile.

"So," I said, "it's your birthday."

"Yeah—I'm finally old enough to vote. And get drafted. And be tried as an adult."

His mom slugged him in the arm. "I'm going to put this pie in the kitchen. Come on in, Aria. But watch where you step; it's like a war zone in here."

I hesitated, feeling awkward about crashing Thomas's birthday party. "Well . . . happy birthday. I should probably get my homework done since I have to work—"

He leaned down and grabbed my wrist, stopping me midsentence. "You have time for cake." He pulled me inside and closed the door behind me. Now I saw why everyone was covered in dust. The inside of Mr. Euler's house had been scraped to the bare bones, like an empty rib cage half-buried in sand. The wall separating the kitchen from the living room was stripped to the studs, and broken plaster littered the carpet-less floor.

He led me through piles of rubble to the kitchen where, other than Mr. Euler's old bulbous fridge, the walls were devoid of appliances and cabinets. "It's not much of a party," Thomas said, letting go of my wrist. "Most of my friends are on another continent."

A man pushed away from a folding table and stood, offering his hand. He was tall like Thomas, but with a thinner frame. A film of white dust coated his glasses, and his smile was broad and infectious. "You must be the famous Aria Kinsley." He took my hand and gave it a firm shake. "Hal Ashby."

"Famous?" I asked warily.

"Famous around here, anyway. Thomas talks about you all the—"

"Dad." Thomas shot him a warning look, then glanced at me. "I told them how you've been riding to school with me, and that's it."

Hal sat back down, a glint of playfulness in his eyes. He gestured to a folding chair, and I sat. On the folding table was a half-empty box of pizza and a Powerpuff Girls birthday cake.

Thomas must have seen me curiously eyeing the cake because he said, "My dad said it was the only one left, but I think it's just retaliation for winning our last Scrabble match."

"Don't believe a word he says," Hal said, "I've never seen a more enthusiastic Powerpuff Girls fan."

"And I've never seen someone try to spell 'pharaoh' with an 'f.' "

As they exchanged lighthearted jabs, I couldn't help contrasting their easy banter with my typically tense conversations with Dad. And the way Elsie smiled affectionately at the two of them tugged something loose inside me. I tried not to grieve over Mom, especially when others were around. I didn't want them to know how much losing her still hurt, because after five years, people expected me to be over it.

Elsie must have mistaken my discomfort for hunger because she put a slice of pizza on a paper plate. She had no sooner placed it in front of me than an enormous black cat bounded up on the table and nabbed a piece of my sausage.

"Tank!" Thomas slid his arm under the fat cat and dropped it to the floor.

"Sorry," Elsie said. "Pizza's his favorite."

Tank's paws lunged over the side of the table again, but this time the rest of his body didn't make it. His claws sunk into the tablecloth and took everything—Powerpuff Girls cake included—to the floor.

Tank shot out of the room like a black torpedo, and we all sat there a moment, still and silent as Dad's taxidermy projects. I glanced at Hal, expecting him to be livid, but his mouth turned up into an amused smile. "Sorry, Thomas. I know how much you liked that cake."

Thomas picked up a plate of cake from the windowsill and ate a forkful. "S'okay. I saved a piece."

"Well, it's a good thing Aria made us a pie," Elsie said, and my cheeks suddenly felt warm. She stood and licked her thumb, then wiped a dab of white frosting from Thomas's cheek.

"Come on, Mom!" He cringed. "I'm eighteen, remember? I can wipe my own face."

"You don't have to be so embarrassed just because there's a beautiful girl in the house." She grabbed a broom and

started sweeping the pizza from the floor. "He doesn't have any sisters," she whispered to me, "and he's not used to being around girls."

"And just because there's a beautiful girl in the house," he echoed, "doesn't mean you have to roast me." He set his plate down and scooped the bulk of the massacred cake into the pizza box.

"No daughters?" I asked Elsie.

"No, just two troublesome boys," Thomas answered for her. I glanced at him, expecting to see a playful smile, but his face was strangely somber.

"Maybe you'll have a granddaughter someday," I said.

Elsie nodded and smiled, but it was fleeting and didn't touch her eyes. A tangible tension settled over the room, and she swept in silence, like her thoughts were suddenly elsewhere.

Hal dropped his head and pursed his lips. Thomas turned away and quietly dumped the cake in the trash. The mood had shifted from jovial to serious in a matter of seconds, and I wondered if I'd said something wrong.

Hal rose and took the broom from Elsie. "I'll get this." She nodded, but she didn't make eye contact with anyone as she quietly excused herself from the room. Hal patted Thomas on the shoulder and gave him a consoling smile, then began sweeping. "Do you have brothers and sisters, Aria?"

I wasn't sure if he was really interested in knowing, or if he was just trying to distract me from the gloom hovering over the room.

"No," I said, watching Thomas slowly compose his face. I stood and picked the tablecloth off the floor. "It's just me."

"Here," Thomas said with an outstretched arm, "I'll put

that in the laundry." I handed it to him, and he disappeared down the hall where his mom had gone.

"So," Hal said with forced enthusiasm, "you ever heard of iridology?"

*Another distraction*, I thought. "No," I said, sitting down and playing along. "What's that?"

"I hadn't either, until I was commissioned to write an article about it. Would you believe that the iris of the eye can reveal a person's state of health?"

I gave him a skeptical look.

"Here, I'll show you what I mean." He put the broom aside and sat across from me, pointing to his left eye. "Now, see the little dark spot here under my pupil?"

I leaned forward and stared at his eye, but all I noticed was that they were the same bright blue as Thomas's.

"Come on, Dad," Thomas groaned as he walked back into the room. His cheerful countenance had returned, and he offered an apologetic smile. "Do I have to be embarrassed by both my parents tonight?"

"I'm just showing her something. Here, Thomas," he said, standing up. "Sit down across from Aria."

Thomas indulged his dad and sat down across from me.

"Now, lean in close." Thomas leaned toward me. "Both of you." I leaned forward until our faces were a foot apart.

As Hal explained the theory of iridology and how certain lines in Thomas's eyes could be linked to childhood illnesses, I was more intrigued by how gazing into Thomas's eyes made me feel. My heart seemed to beat a little faster, and a nervous flutter grazed my insides. The slight curve of his lips made me wonder if he felt it too. His eyes were expressive, filled with a thousand untold stories. There was something else in his eyes—something I recognized

because I saw it every time I looked in the mirror: pain. Not the acute, fleeting type, but the kind that nails down stakes and stays for a while. It was barely noticeable, but it was there.

"You going to read my palms next?" Thomas asked with a smirk.

"No—but you've given me an idea for my next project."

"My dad writes magazine articles," Thomas explained, leaning back into his folding chair.

"For what kind of magazine?"

"Any magazine, any topic imaginable. Gardening to robots." Hal folded his arms proudly across his chest. "Something sparks my interest, so I learn about it, then write about it so other people can learn about it too."

Elsie didn't come back into the room as we talked, and Thomas occasionally threw a concerned glance at the hallway.

"Thomas," Hal said, "maybe you could set up the telescopes this week for your mom. She could probably use some sky time after all the work we've been doing."

"Already done. The tree house needs some cleaning up though. And one of the windows is broken."

A little gasp escaped my lips as I remembered that Mom's music notebook was still sitting in the cabinet there.

Thomas glanced at me curiously, and I pushed out my chair. "I should go," I said, eager to get the notebook before he found it.

He followed me to the porch, and I expected him to stay there, but then he followed me down the steps. "I'll walk you home."

"It's okay," I said, turning and walking backward. "It's not far."

He looked up at the sky. "There's not much of a moon. What if you get lost in the dark?"

I stopped and heaved an internal sigh. "I'm actually not going home right away."

"No?" He took a step toward me. "Where are you going?"

"To the tree house," I admitted. "I left something there."

"Are you sure? I didn't see anything there when I was setting up the telescope."

"Yes—it's in one of the cabinets."

He considered this a moment, then held up a finger. "Wait here." He ducked inside and came out a few minutes later with a lit lantern. "Come on." He tipped his head toward the tree house. "I'll go with you."

"You don't need to."

"I want to." He smiled and started toward the tree house, and I followed him through the cavern of trees surrounding his house. The night was warm, filled with the sound of leaves rustling in the breeze and crickets chirping in the long grass.

"I have something to confess," I said as I caught up to him.

"Another confession?" He glanced at me and lifted an eyebrow.

"I didn't make the pie."

He grinned. "I know."

"You do? How?"

"From the bewildered look on your face when Vivian said you made it."

"Oh." I shook my head and laughed lightly, then recounted how I'd ended up on his doorstep with the pie in my hands.

"I'm glad you came," he said. "It was nice to celebrate my birthday with someone other than my parents."

The trees grew denser as we entered the aspen grove, and the lantern lit up the white trunks, encompassing us in a luminous orb. It felt intimate, sharing a little place of light with him in the dark world.

"Your mom was upset tonight," I said carefully. "Did I say something wrong?"

He inhaled deeply through his nose and released a long sigh. "You didn't say anything wrong."

"But she was upset?"

"She's ultrasensitive about certain things. Particularly about grandkids."

"Why?"

He met my eyes, and with soberness in his own said, "She did have a granddaughter."

"Did?" Suddenly Elsie's reaction to my "granddaughter" comment made sense. "What happened?"

In the light of the lantern, I saw something change in his face. His brows drew together tightly and his lips flattened into a taut line. He didn't answer right away, and his silence was somehow intensified by the sound of twigs snapping beneath our footsteps. Finally, he said softly, "She died."

"I'm sorry." The words sounded so inadequate. I had the urge to reach for his hand to offer comfort, but I resisted. "Was she your brother's baby?"

"Yes. Her name was Emily."

"That must have been really hard for him."

"It was hard on us all." He looked at me and tried to smile, but abandoned it half-formed. "So . . . what exactly did you leave in the tree house?"

I was thrown off for a second by the abrupt change of topic, but quickly took the hint that he didn't want to talk about it. "Just a notebook."

"It must be important if you're willing to walk through a dark forest to retrieve it."

I thought about telling him how it was filled with Mom's and my music, but feared it would somehow get back to Dad. "It's just some ideas I've jotted down."

"What kind of ideas?"

"Oh, you know, trivial things like how to cure tuberculosis, and how to save the Laysan Finch from extinction."

He watched me curiously, seeming to decide whether to push me for a real answer. But then he let me off the hook and began pointing out constellations instead.

When we reached the tree house, he set the lantern on the floor and I saw how different it looked from the last time I'd been there. Shelves were filled with long metal boxes, lenses, and instruments. A large star map covered in red handwritten marks hung on the wall. And in the center of the room, an enormous telescope rested on a heavy-duty tripod.

I went straight to the cabinet and pulled out my notebook. Thomas eyed it inquisitively, and I hugged it to my stomach to conceal it as much as possible. "So," I said, nodding at the telescope in an attempt to divert his attention, "do you know how to use that thing?"

"Are you kidding me?" He grinned. "With two generations of astronomers in the family, I would be a dope not to know how to use it."

"Will you show me something? Your grandpa let me look through his telescope a few times, but it's been years."

"You don't have to get home?"

Remembering Dad wouldn't be home until morning, I shook my head.

He undid the latches on the wall and slid the roof along the wheeled track to the deck, opening the tree house to the night sky.

Thomas turned off the lantern, and it took a moment for my eyes to adjust. The crescent moon outlined Thomas's face and hands while he fiddled with the telescope, and for a split second I thought how nothing he showed me tonight could be as beautiful. Something about being with him made the tree house feel more elevated, like I could reach up and graze the stars with my fingertips.

He punched some numbers into an illuminated keypad, and the telescope moved slowly by itself across the sky, stopping over the east horizon. He looked through an eyepiece and adjusted some dials. "Okay—come here." He reached out and placed his hand on the small of my back to guide me in front of the telescope.

I leaned down and peered through the lens to see a planet with vague orange stripes. "Jupiter," I said, "and four of its moons."

"You've seen it before, then."

I nodded. "It was the first thing your grandpa showed me."

Thomas reached for the keypad and entered more numbers, and the telescope panned to a new location. After he made more adjustments, he gestured for me to look. When I did, I saw a faint blue ring, glowing against black space.

"A nebula," I said.

"How can I impress you with my vast knowledge of the universe when you already know what everything is?"

I straightened and smiled. "Are you trying to impress me?"

He didn't reply, just typed more numbers into the

keypad. When the telescope came to a rest, he raised an eyebrow and nodded to the eyepiece, offering a challenge.

I looked through the eyepiece and saw two bright stars close together, one a yellow hue, the other blue.

"This I haven't seen before," I admitted. "It's beautiful. What is it?"

"Albireo," he said. "It's a binary—two stars orbiting around each other because they're gravitationally bound." He started going on about stellar mass and parameters, but all I could focus on was the warmth of his body beside me, his woodsy scent, and the calming timbre of his voice.

"They're so brilliant," I said. "They seem alive."

"They are, in a way. There's a lot going on up there— almost every element in the periodic table is being created. Carbon, oxygen, iron—all the elements in our bodies were made in a star or during a star's death."

"Now that's impressive. No one has ever told me that I was once a star." I looked up at him. All I could see was the outline of his hair and shoulders, glazed in silver light. "You know, I've never had such a nerdy friend before. I think you're the only person I've ever discussed the periodic table with in a social setting."

"Next time we can discuss galactic winds."

"Sounds fascinating." In truth, though, I really was starting to become fascinated. Not with how stars create elements or with galactic winds, but with Thomas Ashby.

When I woke up Saturday morning, the remnants of Vivian's makeup job and my tousled hair made me look like I'd just finished an *Elle Magazine* grunge photo shoot. I tied my hair back loosely before going to work, but I probably should have washed off the makeup too because Dirk stared at me all day.

"See you Monday, Aria," Dirk said with a big grin as I left work. I noted it was the first time he actually called me by the correct name.

Within days, our lunch table grew more crowded with Trisha's pack of primped friends, and every day was the same awkward lunch party—Dirk flirting with me while occasionally eyeing Trisha, Trisha monopolizing Thomas, and me debating whether to extract myself and just go spend lunch playing the stage piano so I wouldn't have to watch Trisha flirt with Thomas. But I continued to endure it day after day because I couldn't seem to pull myself away from him. I wondered if he liked her, but it was hard to tell. He was nice to her, but then, he was nice to everyone.

"I was wondering," he said as he dropped me off on a Thursday afternoon, "where are some good hiking trails around here?" He nodded in the direction of Pikes Peak. "I noticed the colors are starting to turn up there."

Dad's truck was gone, so I said, "I have some trail maps inside if you want to come look at them."

He followed me through the front door, and I watched uncertainly as his eyes moved from one preserved animal to the next. He bowed before the wolf to study his snarled muzzle at close range. "Well," he said with a little smirk on his lips, "I know one thing."

"What's that?"

"Your dad's not a vegetarian."

I smiled. "Have a seat next to the wolf. I'll go find those maps."

After a few minutes sifting through Dad's desk, I found some trail maps. I went back downstairs, and uneasiness pulled at my insides when I found Thomas peeking through the parlor window. He turned to face me.

"That's a nice piano. You should play something for me."

"What makes you think I play?" I handed him the maps.

He rubbed the back of his neck and his cheeks darkened a bit. "Because . . . I heard you play."

I blinked. "When?"

A piece of his dark hair had fallen over his eyes, and he pushed it out of the way before gazing at me thoughtfully. "The first day of school, at lunch. I was looking for a familiar face to sit by, and when I didn't find you in the lunch room, I walked the halls looking for you. I heard a piano playing behind the backstage door." He shrugged. "I went in to see who was playing, and I saw you behind the black curtains. I didn't say anything because I didn't want to embarrass you."

"I'm not embarrassed." In fact, I was thrilled that he'd heard me play. Thrilled that he'd been looking for me.

"Good, because you shouldn't be. It sounded beautiful." He gestured to the parlor. "You should play something again."

A wave of apprehension swept over me and my palms grew moist. Not that I was afraid to play for him, but I didn't know when Dad would be home. What would I do if Dad showed up while we were in the parlor?

"Just one song," he said, his eyes pleading.

I bit one side of my lower lip, debating. Maybe if I played something amazing, he would forget about that morning in the tree house. He would see me as a prestigious piano prodigy instead of a helpless damsel in distress. And maybe, just maybe, he would fall desperately in love with me. I decided it was worth the risk.

I pulled a hairpin from beneath my ponytail and straightened it, then picked the lock.

"Why is it locked?" he asked as I swung open the door.

"To keep the ghosts inside," I said half-jokingly. "Have a seat." I gestured to an overstuffed claw-footed chair by the door, where Mom used to sit when she taught me.

As I sat on the bench, I realized all my sheet music was under my mattress, so I'd have to play one by heart. I turned to see Thomas making himself comfortable on the chair. He gave me a little smile and his eyes lit up with anticipation.

Turning back to the piano, I suspended my fingers over the keyboard, unsure yet where I would begin. I drew in a deep breath and closed my eyes, searching for the right piece. Something haunting and lovely. Intricate, yet soft. Something that would tug at his soul and make him want more.

Like the first stroke of color on a blank canvas, a melody flowed into my mind. I listened carefully as it gained more depth and texture, then I grasped onto it until I could name it.

*Chopin's first etude, A-flat major, opus twenty-five.*

The melody found its way to my fingers, and in turn my fingers found their position on the keys. As I began to play for Thomas, the awareness of his presence warmed me like sunlight on my back. An intense magnetism flared inside me, and each note became a brushstroke painting the lines of his face, the sound of his voice, and the warmth of his touch.

When I finished the piece and turned around to face him, I was surprised to see him standing right behind me. He stared down at me, a stunned look on his face. "I had to come see how you were doing that," he said quietly.

"Doing what?"

He circled the piano bench to sit by me, and I scooted over to make room. "I had to see what your fingers were doing to make the piano sound like that." His gaze locked with mine, a sort of reverence in his expression. "But then I saw your face, and the way your arms were moving, the way you were moving, and I realized it wasn't just your fingers, it was . . . I don't know. It was *you*." He paused. "It was the most beautiful thing I've ever heard."

His face was just inches from mine, a blue flame sparkling in his eyes. We gazed at each other, electricity passing between us.

"Some people bring the piano to life," he said softly. "But you, Aria—you make it *weep*."

"Was it that bad?"

"No—it was that *good*. It made me want to cry, or run through a sunflower field . . ."

I laughed lightly.

"Or kiss someone," he said, and I stopped breathing. "Where did you learn to play like that?"

"My mom taught me."

"She must be an excellent teacher."

"Yeah, she . . . she was." I wanted to lie—to tell him that my parents had divorced and my mom lived in Tucson. It wasn't often that I had to tell people that Mom was gone, and even now, five years later, it was excruciating for my mouth to form the words.

"She . . ." I shifted in my seat, as if being more comfortable would make the words less bitter. "Five years ago, she . . ." I still couldn't say it. But I didn't need to.

Sensing my struggle, he whispered, "I'm sorry," and his hand fell on mine with ease. "How?"

Dad had explained it to me so many times after she died, like he never wanted me to forget the reason she was gone. "She'd had diabetes since she was a kid, so she had problems with her kidneys." I paused, knowing the most bitter part of the explanation was next. "She wasn't supposed to have kids. Her doctor told her not to."

"But she had you anyway?"

"Yeah. I think I was . . . unexpected."

Thomas kept his eyes on me, but I looked away. I didn't want to talk about it. Talking about it meant feeling it—the guilt of knowing that if I weren't here, she would be.

He lifted his hand from mine and placed it on the keys. He started playing a song I'd never heard before. It sounded like he played a couple wrong notes, but it was a nice melody.

"I didn't know you played," I said as I watched his big fingers clumsily navigate the keyboard.

"I don't." He smiled. "I only know one song. And as you can see, I don't make the piano weep. I make it retch."

I laughed, and he started to sing along. What he lacked in piano-playing abilities, he made up for with his voice. As his soulful tones filled the room, I practically felt the hearts forming in my pupils. As I listened to the words, a tingly, peaceful feeling washed over me like a cool stream, leaving water in my eyes.

"Where did you learn that song?" I asked as he continued playing.

"From my mom. It's one of her favorites. It seems to help her when she's feeling sad about things."

I put my right hand on the upper keys and started playing along with him. "Sing it again. I want to hear the words." And I wanted to hear his voice again.

"I will, if you play another song for me. And if I can sit next to you while you play."

Before I could reply, I heard Dad's truck rumbling down the driveway. I unconsciously shot a panicked glance at Thomas and jumped off the bench. I slammed the cover shut and grabbed his hand, yanking it toward the door.

"Come on—we need to get out of here," I said with urgency.

He followed me out of the room, confusion and alarm flashing across his face.

"What's going on?"

I locked and shut the parlor door. "My dad can't know we were in the parlor, okay?" I said, trying to suppress the desperation in my voice.

"What?" He peered out the living room window, but Dad had already driven around to the back of the house. "Why not?" He glanced back at me, puzzlement cinching his brow.

"He's coming in now." I grabbed the trail maps from the side table. "Please—just don't say anything about the piano." I scurried away from the parlor door and sat on the couch, patting the spot next to me firmly for him to sit down.

"But why?" He moseyed over to the couch and sat next to me.

"Please, Thomas."

"Will you explain later?"

"Yes."

"Okay. We weren't in the parlor. I didn't hear you play rapturous music." One corner of his mouth lifted into a smile.

"Thank you," I breathed. Opening a trail map, I launched into a description of one of the trails and tried to appear calm as I heard the back door swing open. Dad came directly to the living room, and when he saw us on the couch, his expression turned surprised.

"Hey, Dad," I said, standing and gesturing to Thomas. "This is Thomas, our new neighbor."

Thomas stood and offered his hand. "Hello, Mr. Kinsley."

Dad came over, took his hand, and then, smiling, said, "You Frank's grandson?"

"Yes, sir."

Dad released his hand and folded his arms across his chest. "I'm sorry to hear about your grandpa. He was a good man."

"Yes, he was. Thank you."

"I'm surprised to see you here," Dad said. "You're the first person Aria's brought home in years. And here I thought she'd get through high school without making any friends." He meant to tease, but his words hurt.

"Aria was just showing me some trail maps." Thomas gestured to the open map in my hands.

"You hunt?"

"I fish, but I've yet to move on to bigger game."

"You should try Rampart." Dad pointed to the three-foot rainbow trout mounted above the television. "It's where I caught that beauty right there." Dad plunged into the story of how he'd caught the fish, a story I'd heard him tell a dozen times. I watched the way his hands moved and his eyes lit up with the enthusiasm of a zealous fisherman telling his story. It made me happy to see him this way, cheerful and sober. "I'm going to Rampart tomorrow morning with a couple buddies," he said. "You're welcome to come with me if you want."

Thomas glanced at me as if looking for permission. I smiled and shrugged, and Thomas turned back to Dad. "Sure. School's out tomorrow, so that sounds great. Can Aria come too?"

Dad eyed me with raised eyebrows. "You want to come, Aria?"

It had been years since Dad had taken me fishing. It used to be one of my favorite things to do, but after he banned me from the piano, I stopped going with him so that I could spend the time in the parlor. "Sure," I said, willing to give up a few hours of piano time in exchange for spending time with Thomas.

"Well, I better get home," Thomas said. "I told my dad I'd clean up the orchard this weekend, and if we're going fishing, I'd better get a head start."

"I'll see you tomorrow," I said, handing him the trail map. "You can return this to me then."

He took it, a small, intimate smile crossing his lips and touching his eyes. I couldn't help but notice Dad studying us from the corner of my eye. "Tomorrow," Thomas said, then he turned to Dad. "I'll see you bright and early."

## six

E arly Friday morning, Dad woke me up with a hand on my shoulder. "Aria, wake up."

I stretched and yawned, opening my eyes halfway in the dark room. "Is it time to get up already?"

"Listen, I got called into work. I should be back in the afternoon, but we'll have to go fishing another time."

"Okay," I mumbled and closed my eyes, wanting to go back to sleep.

"I need to leave right now, so I need you to get dressed and go tell Thomas that we won't be going."

I sat up and rubbed my eyes. "Why can't you just call?"

"I don't have their number. Besides, it's too early to call. I don't want to wake up his parents. Just get dressed and run over there."

"Can't you just stop there on your way to work?"

"Just do it, Aria," he said firmly. "I need to leave now or I'll be late."

I staggered out of bed, and Dad walked out. A few seconds later I heard the back door shut and Dad's truck

roar to life. I flipped on the light and shuffled to the closet, debating how dressed up I should get to deliver my message. Unsure if he was already waiting for us and not wanting to make him wait longer than necessary, I threw a green hoodie over my T-shirt and pulled on some jeans and sneakers. I stopped in the bathroom to brush my teeth and tie my hair into a ponytail.

As I walked away from the house through the cool grass, I drew in a deep breath, filling my lungs with the crisp morning air. The sun hadn't yet emerged from behind the east mountains, and the horizon was a jagged silhouette against a pale violet sky. I hopped over the wooden fence and walked through the orchard until his house came into view.

I saw him sitting in a white wicker chair on his porch, hands in the pockets of his black hoodie, one ankle resting on his knee. His hair was disheveled like he had just rolled out of bed, and my heart trilled at the sight of him. "Hey," I called out.

He turned to me and stood, his expression surprised. "Hey. I thought your dad was picking me up here, or I would have just come to your house."

"He got called into work, so we'll have to go another time."

"Oh," he said, sounding disappointed. "Well, you and I could still go. I could drive."

He didn't need to persuade me, but I hesitated, not wanting to sound too eager. "Okay." I shrugged. "I just need to go back and get my fishing gear."

"On second thought," he said, taking a step toward me, "why don't we just hike to the lake up here?" He pointed to the narrow canyon on the east side of his land. "I haven't been up there since I was a kid."

"It's a lot smaller, and it's not stocked. If you want to catch something, we should probably just go to Rampart."

He shrugged. "I'm more in the mood for hiking than fishing."

"All right—let me just go get some water and something for breakfast."

He unzipped his backpack, pulled out a granola bar, and handed it to me. "I have plenty of other snacks and water in here."

"Okay, then." I smiled. "Let's go."

He shouldered his backpack and we walked around his house and toward the mountain. At the edge of the orchard, he plucked a couple ripe apples and dropped them into the pockets of his hoodie.

"How did you convince your dad to let you out of cleaning up the orchard today?" I asked, seeing all the apples on the ground.

"I did some bartering. He said I could go fishing if you help me shovel apples later today."

"What?"

He grinned. "Don't worry, Aria. My dad's a sensible guy. As long as I have the orchard cleaned up before it snows, he'll be fine."

"Let's go, then, and I'll help you later," I said with a smile.

The sun broke over the mountains as we walked through the open field of long, golden grass. The seeded amber tips glowed in the morning light, bowing and swaying gently, and I held out my arms to feel their feathery texture under my fingertips. We quietly made our way through the grove of aspens and followed the stream into the canyon. A soft breeze blew through the trees as we hiked alongside the babbling stream, filling the air with the scent of pine.

"So," he said as we hiked along the narrow trail, "can you explain now?"

"Explain what?"

"Why can't your dad know we were in the parlor?"

My heart plummeted. How could I have forgotten that I owed him an explanation? I didn't have a ready answer, because the answer was so complicated. I couldn't tell him the whole truth, because he might tell his parents, and it would only make things worse to have the Division of Child Welfare show up at my door. Besides, I wanted Thomas's respect, not his pity. "It's just a rule he has," I finally said. "He doesn't like music in the house."

"Why not?"

"Um," I hesitated, trying to figure out how to explain. "Because it hurts him." When I didn't say more, he eyed me with a trace of skepticism like he knew there was more to it than that.

"He used to love to hear my mom play," I offered. "He would sit in the parlor for hours while she practiced, his eyes closed, like a sailor bewitched by a siren. I think her music is what he loved most about her. But when she died, things changed. He doesn't like to be reminded of her. He keeps the parlor locked, and he put all her things in the attic where he can't see them." I couldn't believe I was telling him this. I'd never talked to anyone about it.

"All her things?" he asked.

"Yeah—pictures, clothing, music." I thought privately about the last time Dad had found me in the attic. He'd dragged me down and secured the hatch with an abundance of four-inch screws. What Dad hadn't known was that I'd already taken one of her dresses to my room. I couldn't put it back in the attic, so I'd tucked it in a box and kept it hidden all these years in the hollow space of my box spring.

"He couldn't even bear to look at the plants she'd grown in the yard." I described how charming the house had looked with roses and jasmine climbing up the porch railing and marigolds popping out of window buckets—before Dad tore them out.

He was quiet for a long time, pondering my words. Finally he asked, "Did he let you play the piano before your mom died?"

I nodded. "He actually loved to hear me play. He would go to all my recitals and competitions, and beam with pride just like the other parents." I sighed. "I tried to play for him after my mom died because I thought it would comfort him, but it seemed to have the opposite effect. And eventually he locked the parlor door and forbade me from playing anymore. So I don't . . . at least not when he's at home."

"That must be hard for you." He studied me a moment, then shook his head and looked away, frowning thoughtfully. "Not to mention tragic. Your mom taught you, and she's gone. By forbidding you to play, he's cutting off this incredible emotional link between you and her."

Relief washed over me when he said those words, to the point that tears brimmed in my eyes. To share the burden of grief, to have someone understand, were things I had never known until that moment. But with the tears came a feeling of self-consciousness, and I walked faster to hide my emotion, swallowing the lump in my throat. "Anyway," I said, "I probably shouldn't have told you all this. I hope you won't say anything to anyone."

Thomas caught up to me. "I won't." He was quiet for

another long stretch, then he said, "You're stronger than you look, you know?"

"Is that why I'm out of breath right now?"

"No—listen." He stopped me, and laying his hand on my arm, he looked directly into my eyes. "You have a gift, and I'm not talking about a 'play at the county fair' kind of gift. I'm talking about Juilliard. Carnegie Hall. You belong on a grand stage, not hidden behind dusty black curtains in a school auditorium."

"Juilliard? I think you overestimate my abilities."

"No." He shook his head. "You *underestimate* your abilities."

"You've only heard me play two pieces. Maybe they're the only ones I know."

"I'm willing to bet your repertoire is larger than you let on."

"Maybe, but you've still only heard me play two—not enough to gauge my abilities."

He pinned me with a scrutinizing gaze, and his mouth eased into a playful smile. "You may not know this, but Beethoven was my third great-grandfather's second cousin . . . once removed . . . or something like that. So I have an uncommon ability to spot Juilliard material when I see it."

I rolled my eyes and smiled before turning away and resuming hiking. "Okay, I'll admit that I'm pretty good at the piano. But I can't do anything about it until after high school."

"What are you going to do after high school?"

"Get my own place and my own piano, then I can play as much as I want."

"That's it?"

I stopped and turned to him. "What do you mean, 'That's it'?"

"Your plan is to sit in an apartment and play for yourself?"

"Well, I . . ." I'd been so focused on securing my freedom that I'd never really thought beyond that point. "I don't know. When I get to that point, I'll figure out the next step."

"You should start preparing for Juilliard now. If you audition this year, then you can enroll next fall."

I gave a humorless laugh. "Okay, let's ignore the fact that I haven't taken formal lessons for five years, or that I can't get enough practicing in when I'm living with my dad, or that a semester's tuition is probably more than I earn in a year. I don't know the first thing about getting into Juilliard, other than that my chances are slim."

"You could find a good teacher to help you prepare. There's still time."

"I can't. It would be too hard to keep it from my dad."

"Maybe he would let you take lessons if you practice somewhere else."

"He would never agree to it. Do you know how many people offered to teach me for free after my mom died? He turned them all down. He told them that both he and I needed some time away from music, and he would let them know when things changed. Things haven't changed yet, and to be honest, I don't think they ever will." I shook my head and began walking up the trail again, silently cursing the emotion burning in my throat. It seemed to ignite something deeper in my soul, a desire I'd kept suppressed far too long. I wanted to take lessons. I wanted to chase the dream of Juilliard. It was where Mom had gone to school, and as a child, I'd wanted nothing more than to follow in

her footsteps. But Dad had torn the dream from my hands, and until that moment, I hadn't realized just how raw the deprivation still was. "I can't even think about this until after I move out," I said, my voice thick.

He walked quietly beside me, his face troubled. Finally he said, "I'm sorry for pressing you. I'm just . . . in awe of you, Aria. You're like a beautiful caged bird, and I want to unlatch the door and set you free."

I didn't respond right away, and for the remainder of our hike I steered our conversation to more lightweight topics, like friends and movies and school. When we reached the lake, we wandered around a bit, circling the grassy shore to find a place to settle in and enjoy the scenery. A flock of geese waded along one edge of the football field–sized lake, and we skipped rocks across the clear water as we moseyed along. Aspens and pines skirted the lake, and beyond the trees, the mountains rose around us.

"Aria!" Thomas called out from ahead of me with a beckoning wave.

When I caught up, he was standing next to an old fishing boat that was half-covered in moss.

"That thing has been there since I was a kid," I said.

His mouth slowly curved into a smile. "Can you swim?"

"Why?" I asked nervously.

He tossed his backpack on the ground and tipped the fishing boat right-side up. The seat was caked with dirt, and he kicked it off with his shoe, then wiped it clean with his sleeve before pushing the boat to the water's edge.

"Hop in," he said.

I laughed and shook my head. "Why don't you take it for a test drive first? And when you get back soaking wet, let me know how cold the water is."

He picked the weathered oars off the ground and peered into the boat. "I don't see any holes."

I leaned over and examined the boat for myself. "That's because they're hidden under all that dirt."

He reached down and scooped up a handful of water, tossing it playfully at me. I straightened and gasped as the frigid water splashed my face and neck. "See," he said, his eyes gleaming, "it's not so cold, is it?"

I wiped my face with the sleeve of my hoodie and glared at him. "In relation to the Bering Sea, no." I had an impulse to shove him into the water, but after taking a moment to size him up, I thought twice. He was a head taller than me, and my willowy frame was no match for his broad shoulders and muscular arms. Retaliation would undoubtedly result in getting dunked, so I gave up the idea.

"Come on," he coaxed, "we'll stay close to shore."

"Promise?"

He offered me the oars. "You're the captain."

"If I'm the captain, shouldn't you be the one rowing?"

"Aye, aye," he said, tossing the oars in the boat. "Get in, and I'll do all the rowing."

"Okay, but if we sink . . ."

"If we sink, I'll buy you dinner."

"I thought you didn't date."

"I don't. But if the boat sinks, I'll make an exception."

It sounded like a good trade-off. Be submerged in cold water, get a dinner date with Thomas. I hesitated just long enough not to look overly eager, then climbed in the boat, hoping it would sink.

He gave the boat a shove, then jumped in. I picked up the oars and started rowing.

"I thought I was supposed to row," he said, holding out his hands.

"I've got it," I said, aiming for the middle of the lake. If the boat was going to sink, we'd have to be far from shore.

"I thought we were staying close to shore."

"There's a great view of Pikes Peak from the middle of the lake."

He smiled, that little dimple surfacing on the side of his mouth. "You've got to give a guy a chance to be chivalrous."

I sighed and handed the oars to him. "To the middle of the lake," I ordered in my most authoritative voice.

"Aye, aye, captain."

He made it to the middle of the lake eventually, in a roundabout sort of way. We settled in, quietly taking in the scenery around us. The morning sun had risen above the trees, and golden light bounced off the water, flickering across his face. I watched him as he gazed into the water, his face relaxed and carefree. Being with him made me feel the same. Like all my worries were left behind in some forgotten place. It was just me and him, sitting on a still lake in the quiet morning.

I eyed the bottom of the boat, which was still dry, and silently lamented that I most likely wouldn't be getting a dinner date. I wanted to ask him why he didn't date, but I wasn't sure how to casually broach the subject. "So," I started hesitantly, "I couldn't help but notice that you avoided answering Trisha's question the other day."

"Which question was that?"

"Why don't you date?" I felt my cheeks begin to flush. "I mean, is it your parents' rule or something?"

He looked down at the clear water, then dipped his hand in and slowly swayed it back and forth, making little ripples.

"No. And I didn't answer her question because it's hard to explain. Most people don't understand my reasoning."

I gazed at him, hoping he'd trust me enough to explain.

"I know this sounds weird, but . . ." He bit his lip and paused. "I don't date because it's my way of protecting my mom."

"How does you not dating protect her?"

A little crease appeared between his brows. "She's just been through a lot these past couple years." I waited for him to expound, but he went back to quietly swaying his hand in the water. Back and forth, back and forth. Just when I thought the conversation had hit a dead end, he said, "I told you about my brother's baby."

I nodded.

"Well, Richard, my brother, was my age when he got his girlfriend pregnant, and that in itself was hard for my mom because they were going to give the baby—her first grandchild—up for adoption. But then . . ." Thomas took a deep breath and his expression darkened. "When the baby died . . ." He seemed to be having some inward struggle, like he was deciding just how much to share with me. It was a good minute before he spoke again. "Richard has always struggled with drugs and alcohol, and when the baby died, he sort of went off the deep end. In fact, he's in jail right now."

I still wasn't sure that I understood. "Do you think you would make the same mistakes your brother made if you dated?"

He paused briefly as he opened his mouth to speak, then with a slight grimace said, "Believe me, I've already made my share of mistakes. But . . ." He shook his head as though veering from what he was going to say. "It's more complicated than I can really explain. But if I have a girl-friend or if I drink or mess up at school, it'll just add to the stress she's already feeling."

"That's kind of a lot to put on yourself."

He shrugged. "I guess. But if it lightens her burden, it's worth it to me. And it's not like I'll always be this stringent with myself. I'll date someday—maybe when she's had some time to heal and I go to college, but for now, it's just simpler this way."

"Well, it's a good thing this isn't a date, then," I said half-jokingly.

He straightened and looked at me. "I'm sorry, Aria. I don't mean to lead you along or anything. I just . . . like being with you." He smiled, a glint of cheerfulness return-ing to his eyes. He gazed at me, the light reflecting off the water making his eyes a calming blue. "You make me feel at ease. I'm glad you're my friend."

Funny how what he said put my own feelings into words. He reached into his hoodie pockets and pulled out the two apples he'd picked earlier. He handed one to me and took a bite out of the other. "Mmm," he murmured as he chewed. "I love September apples."

When I bit into mine, it was crisp and sweet. Every-thing that morning was sweet. The golden light, the still water, and—sweetest of all—Thomas Ashby sitting three feet away, glowing warmer than the morning sun.

♪ ♪ ♪ ♪ ♪ ♪ ♪

To my surprise, we made it back to shore dry. As I helped him pull the boat back onto shore, something in the black dirt caught my eye. A small and white rectan-gular shape. I squinted and looked closer, and what I saw stopped my breath. It was a miniature book of sheet music, white porcelain with hand-painted music staves. I recognized it instantly, and it evoked a memory from five years earlier.

Mom and I knelt in front of my bed, a few months before she died. She put her finger over her lips and said "Shhhh," then pulled a cardboard box from beneath my bed. She opened it and pulled out a piano-shaped music box. It was the size of a shallow shoebox, and the white porcelain was adorned with hand-painted birds. "This is for you," she whispered. "I'm going to fill it with things that will remind you of me, of how much I love you. It's our secret, okay?" I interpreted the meaning of her gesture and latched onto her thin waist, sobbing into her blouse and telling her I didn't want the music box, I wanted her. She gathered me in her arms and told me to be brave.

I hadn't wanted to think about the music box back then. To me it was nothing more than a sad representation of what would ultimately replace her. She and her warm embrace would leave me, and in return I would get a cold porcelain box of trinkets. In truth, I'd forgotten about it. But now, here was a piece of it, in the dirt, a mile from the house.

With a trembling hand, I bent down and picked it up, folding my fingers over it before Thomas saw it. I stood there, clutching it in my hand, trying to figure out what this meant. How had it gotten up here, and where was the rest of the music box? Had Dad dumped it in the lake? Had he buried it? Destroyed it? The thought of never knowing what Mom had placed in it brought tears to my eyes. I swallowed them back, not wanting Thomas to see how upset I was.

"Aria? You okay?" I felt Thomas's hand on my shoulder.

"Yeah," I said, turning to him with an automatic smile.

He raised an eyebrow.

"Come on. Let's head back." I started walking away, but he caught my arm and turned me back toward him.

"You can trust me, you know?" His hand was warm on my skin, and goose bumps rose on my arm. Somehow I sensed the honesty of his words.

A sigh filled my hesitation while I tried to figure out the best way to explain. I opened my hand and showed him the little piece of porcelain.

"What's that?"

I brushed my thumb over it. "It's a piece of a music box." I explained where it came from, and that I didn't know what had happened to the box after Mom died.

"So how do you think a piece of it got up here?"

"I don't know. My dad must have brought it up here for some reason."

"Why don't you just ask him about it?"

I didn't respond right away because my answer was pathetic. *Because I'm too afraid to ask.* For the past five years I'd lived in fear. Fear of doing or saying anything that would remind him of Mom, because of how he reacted every time he was. But Thomas's question forced me to see the truth of my situation. I was seventeen. A senior in high school. When would I have the courage to face my own father?

"I don't know," I finally said. "But I will."

seven

The closer I got to home, the more determined I became to ask Dad about the music box. I left Thomas in the orchard, then walked home, trying to summon enough courage to confront Dad.

I clutched the piece of porcelain in my hand as I entered the kitchen through the back door. Dad was leaning against the counter, the phone to his ear.

"So it's true, then?" Dad said into the phone, looking at me. He jerked his head toward the table as if to say, *Sit down. I need to talk to you.*

I sat at the table, suddenly not feeling so brave anymore. I shoved the piece of porcelain in my back pocket, deciding to postpone asking about it until I knew what Dad wanted to talk to me about.

"All right. Thanks for looking that up for me," Dad said into the phone, then he hung up and turned to me, folding his arms across his chest. "I think you're getting a little too friendly with that neighbor boy. I don't want you hanging around him anymore."

I blinked. "Why not?"

"I was talking to someone down at the station today about his family. They said the Ashby boys have a record."

I shook my head. "I think you mean Thomas's brother, Richard. Thomas told me his brother got into some trouble with drugs or something."

"No—I mean both the Ashby boys. I don't mean to judge, and I don't know all the details, but I know for a fact that they both have criminal records."

"That can't be right. I mean, he doesn't seem like the criminal type."

"It is right. I just checked with Gabe. And I want you to stay away from him. The last thing I need is you getting into trouble."

"I'm not going to get into any trouble. And believe me, Thomas is as straight-laced as they come. He isn't the type to—"

"Let me be a little more specific, Aria. I don't want you doing anything illegal, and I don't want you doing anything that will get you pregnant."

"What?" I glared at him, my face turning hot with humiliation. "Having a baby is the last thing on my mind."

"A baby doesn't have to be on your mind to have one. In fact, that's rarely how it works."

"I'm seventeen, Dad, and I know how it works. Believe me, I won't be doing that any time soon. Thomas is just my friend. He doesn't even date."

Dad snorted. "Guys don't go around being friends with pretty girls just for the conversation. I saw the way he was looking at you yesterday."

"He's not like that."

Dad pinned me with an icy glare, and I wondered why

he was so upset. His mouth was tight, his neck turning red. "Believe me, Aria," he shouted. "It will ruin your life!"

"I'm not going to get pregnant!" I shouted back, angry that he would think so low of me.

We glared at each other, and after a while his breathing slowed and the tight line of his mouth loosened. "I just don't want you to get hurt," he said, and I wondered if he recognized the hypocrisy of his own words. "When you're eighteen, you can move out and do whatever you want. But for now, no boyfriends. Especially not Thomas Ashby. Got it?"

I clenched my jaw, trying to contain the turbulent swell of anger that rose with each breath. I opened my mouth to object, but the fire in his eyes seared it shut. I dropped my eyes and nodded, but my anger turned inward, going deeper, flooding my marrow with a toxic torrent.

"I've got a wildcat to skin," he said. "Come get me when dinner's done." The back door clapped shut behind him, and I stood there fuming. I'd come home intending to get answers from him, and instead I had to be the one to answer to him. How could he have so much control over me? The answer chimed inside me like an alarm clock. *Because I let him.* No—I had to be stronger than that. I wasn't like the piece of porcelain in my back pocket that would shatter if I tried to stand up for myself.

I marched out to the barn, determined to ask him what he'd done with Mom's music box. But the closer I got to the barn, the more hesitant I became. When I peeked inside and saw a wildcat hanging upside-down, Dad scraping out its guts, I almost turned around and went back to the house.

"Be brave," I whispered to myself, then stepped inside. I

wrinkled my nose at the acrid smell of dead flesh that filled the barn. Two long florescent lights hung from the rafters, along with a few tagged and numbered antlers. Containers of chemicals crowded the shelves—tanning cream, degreasers, pickling agents. Glass eyes and tongues filled a chest of drawers, and a couple freezers clung to one wall, lids rusted from years of corrosive blood. Half-completed projects lined a workbench—a deer hide waiting to be attached to a mannequin, a fox with hollow eyes, a duck, a beaver, and other hides I didn't recognize. As I approached Dad, a battle between terror and determination raged inside me.

"Dad?" I said when I was about ten feet away from him.

He whipped his head around, startled by my presence, then turned back to the wildcat. "What do you need, Aria?"

I gulped. My mouth was suddenly dry, and my heart throbbed in my throat. It felt as if a vice gripped my chest, making it difficult to breathe. Forcing in a deep breath, I wrestled the words out. "Remember when I was a kid, we used to . . . go fishing at the lake up here?"

"Sure," he said as he tossed the cat's innards into the garbage.

"Well . . . I went up to the lake today, and I found something."

He froze for a few seconds, then slowly went back to work.

My heart wasn't just throbbing now, it was about to leap out of my throat. My face and ears felt hot, but my hands were ice cold. Dangerous words teetered on the tip of my tongue, and I opened my mouth, willing them to fall out.

"What did you do with Mom's music box?" I whispered.

He paused again, then set his tool down on his workbench. He turned to face me, but to my surprise, his face wasn't angry. It was vulnerable. Pleading. And it gave me more courage.

"I don't know what you're talking about." His voice was firm, but laced with sadness.

I opened my hand to show him the porcelain sheet music. "Yes, you do. Your expression tells me you know."

"Aria. You wouldn't understand if I tried to—"

"That's what you said when I was twelve, Dad. Every question I asked you about Mom, you told me I was too little to understand. Well, I'm almost an adult. And I think I'll understand any explanation you can give me."

He turned back to what he was doing.

"Did you throw it in the lake?"

He carried on, scraping, tugging, cleaning.

"Or did you bury it?" I stood there, arms folded tightly across my chest, hands squeezing my arms, nails digging into my skin. If I held on tight enough, I could keep my resolve. I would stand here until he answered me.

But he didn't answer. He scraped every bit of flesh from the wildcat. He applied a salt rub. He rubbed and pressed and kneaded. A good five minutes later, he tossed the wildcat hide into a tub of salt solution.

"Why did you take it from me? She wanted me to have it. She said she was going to put things in it, things she wanted me to have."

He turned to face me, half-sitting on the thick edge of the tub. His lips were pursed, his face pale and beaded with sweat.

"Listen to me." His voice was weak, like it was difficult for him to speak. "When you lose something, the only way to heal is to move on." His hand trembled as he wiped sweat from his brow. "If you keep digging up reminders, the wound that's almost healed will just keep getting split open. Do you understand that?"

I'd never seen Dad so vulnerable. Normally I would have just nodded and gone on my way, but within my reach was the door to his heart, cracked open ever so slightly. If I wanted answers, now was my chance to pry it open.

"Almost healed? No, Dad. I'd say both our wounds are still wide open." My voice broke and tears brimmed in my eyes. "And remembering Mom isn't what keeps my wound open. Not being *allowed* to remember is what keeps mine open." The words flew from my lips like liberated birds. "My memories are all I have left of her, and you've spent the last five years trying to erase them. So, no," I said, shaking my head, "I don't understand."

He stood up straight, and I instinctively took a step back. He hadn't been drinking, so I didn't think he would hurt me, but maybe I'd just driven a nail too close to the edge of his tolerance, making it split. As he took a step toward me, I gulped down the fear that had suddenly risen in my throat.

"It's been five years. It's time to move on."

I closed my fist around the piece of porcelain and stared eye-level at the black button on his flannel shirt. "I can't—and neither can you."

He strode over and glared down at me, and his hands came up and rested on my shoulders. A shiver of anxiety shot through me, and I felt I might collapse under the weight of his hands. I focused on his button, unsure what to say or do.

"Trust me," he said, "You need to let this go."

I bent my head and gazed through blurred vision at my hands, twisting and fumbling like they were trying to untie an invisible, intricate knot. "You don't know how much you're asking of me," I whispered.

"Please, Aria. For me. *Please*." His voice was thick with emotion, and when I looked up at him, there were actually tears in his eyes. But the compassion I expected to feel didn't come. All I felt was anger and resentment.

"For you, Dad? What have you ever done for me?"

"What have I done for you? I've loved you as only a father can love his daughter. I've fed and clothed you. I've raised you. Isn't that enough?"

When I didn't answer, he dropped his hands, lifting the heavy burden from my shoulders. He wiped his tears with the sleeve of his shirt, cleared his throat, and walked out of the barn.

I stood there for a long time trying to process our conversation, until my knees began shaking and I sank to the floor. My fingers clutched a nearby towel, as if holding it would help me grasp the reality that my father had kept from me the things that mattered most to me. The piano. The music box. Pictures and memories of Mom. And now he wanted to keep Thomas from me as well. A sick feeling washed over me as I realized just how much he disregarded my feelings. I wrapped my arms around my waist and curled over, breaking into quiet sobs. The ounce of hope I'd had that he would someday change was gone.

The tide of anger I'd felt earlier spilled over, mixing with loneliness and despair. The torrent surrounded me, pressed on me until I was suffocating and gasping for air beneath its current. Darkness enveloped me, and my heart felt like a void, with nothing and no one to fill it. Dad was a sick man. As long as I stayed in his house, he would hurt me, hold me back, keep me in the dark. I closed my eyes and searched the darkness, groping for something to hold on to. An anchor . . . a pillar . . . something unmovable and dependable. In the darkness, I saw a face with bright blue eyes and a smile that made my spirit sing. I heard his name, like a sound on the wind or a whisper piercing through a crowded room.

*Thomas Ashby.*

The sun hung over the horizon as I emerged from the barn, and I hoped Thomas was still working in the orchard. I swiped at my tears and walked to the orchard, taking deep breaths along the way to calm myself.

The autumn evening had grown warm, and as I entered the orchard, fruit flies zipped around, feasting on rotten apples and buzzing in my ears. I found Thomas down a row of trees, shoveling apples into a wheelbarrow. He turned to look at me as I approached, his face glowing like honey in the light of the setting sun.

"Do you have another shovel?" I asked.

Dumping a shovel full of rotten apples into the brimming wheelbarrow, he paused to give me a little smile. He brought his shovel upright and his eyes swept over my face. "You asked him about it, didn't you?"

"Yeah." I sighed.

"What did he say?"

"Not much. He didn't really want to talk about it. I'll have to ask him when he's in a better mood." In truth, I didn't think I'd ever find out what happened to the music box.

"Do you think it's up there somewhere? Do you want me to help you look for it?"

"It's okay," I said, not wanting to pull him further into it. "It could be anywhere. For all I know, it's at the bottom of the lake."

"It wouldn't hurt to go take a look around."

I shook my head, feeling embarrassed that I'd already dragged him this far into my melodramatic family life. "It's not a big deal."

He gave me a skeptical look, then nodded and went back to shoveling. He must have sensed I didn't want to discuss it further, because although he looked troubled, he didn't press me for more details or ask me any more questions.

Seeing an extra shovel leaning against a tree, I picked it up and started helping him. I settled in beside him, and we worked in silence. Thomas shoveled continuously, letting beads of sweat drip off the tip of his nose. He was quiet, absorbed in the work.

I thought about what Dad had said about Thomas having a criminal record and wondered if there could be any truth to it. I stopped shoveling after a while and watched him, sweat mingling with dirt on his forehead, and I knew Dad was wrong. Thomas was everything but a criminal. He was a hard worker, an intellectual. He was kind and giving. Dad's claim was absurd. Surely someone had confused or coupled him unfairly with his brother, Richard. No, Thomas's entire being emanated goodness, and I knew I could trust him. A peaceful feeling came over me, and I knew that as long as I had him for my friend, nothing else mattered. It didn't matter what Dad had said about Thomas. I could never bring myself to stay away from him.

After Thomas walked me home later that night, I watched him stroll away through the long grass and disappear into the trees, but my thoughts stayed with him. I couldn't help wondering why he'd been spending so much time with me when he didn't date. Maybe his feelings for me weren't as intense as my feelings for him. Or worse, maybe he just saw me as a friend, a buddy to hang out with in a boring small town. But I couldn't deny there was a spark of attraction in his eyes whenever he looked at me.

His words from earlier came back to me. *I'm just . . . in awe,* he'd said. What had he meant by that? My mind then latched onto something else he'd said. *You could find a good teacher to help you prepare.*

A vague scene floated up on the screen of my memory, like a wisp of smoke that would vanish if I tried to grasp it. So I waited. Waited for it to form into something more substantial.

*Good teacher,* I repeated in my mind.

It was something about Mom's funeral. Someone who spoke to me. A man with a kind face and sandy-blond hair. He'd approached me when I'd left Dad's side to go sit on a bench. I was tired, worn down with grief, tired of people casting pitiful looks at me and saying trite things like, *Poor little sweetheart,* and *Time heals all wounds.* I'd retreated to a bench in the dim hallway of the funeral parlor to find solace, but I didn't find it for long. This man approached me and sat beside me. I'd never seen him before, but he acted like he knew me. He said something I couldn't now recall, but I remembered it made me feel different than the things everyone else said. Like he knew how I felt, like his sorrow was as great as mine. He told me he was a friend of my mom's, that they'd gone to Juilliard together. Then he handed me a card and told me to call him if I ever wanted to take lessons.

That was all I remembered. What was his name? What had I done with that card?

I went to my desk. I opened the top drawer and sifted through some papers but didn't find it. I searched the side drawers, turning over every piece of paper to make sure it wasn't tucked in somewhere. I remembered playing with the card at the funeral, bending and folding the corners, but what had I done with it afterward? The only thing I remembered keeping from that day was Mom's funeral program.

I knelt in front of my dresser and reached underneath, groping deep against the wall for a shoe box. My fingers bumped against it, and I grasped the edge of the lid and pulled it out. I fanned through the papers inside until I found Mom's funeral program, then let it fall open in my hand.

There it was. The man's card, with creases in the corners where I'd folded them over and over. I picked it up and held it in front of me.

**Nathaniel Borough, NCTM**
*Master's Degree in Music Pedagogy & Performance*
*Juilliard Graduate*

I looked at his address. He lived only twenty miles away in Colorado Springs. And then my heart began to pound as my eyes fell on the picture in the upper left-hand corner. The man in the photo, seated at a piano and wearing a tuxedo, was the very same man I'd seen a couple weeks earlier arguing with Dad. Was it possible that he had come to offer me lessons, and Dad had intercepted him? Anger lapped at me, but it was quickly washed away as fear and excitement began rushing dually through my veins. Maybe I could take lessons from him. It would drain my savings account, and there was a chance Dad would find out. But it was the only way I'd get into Juilliard someday. And the only sure way to keep Thomas Ashby *in awe* of me.

# eight

When I got home from work Saturday afternoon, I changed and went over to Thomas's to ask if he could give me a ride to Colorado Springs the next week to see Nathaniel. The front door was cracked open when I got there, but I knocked anyway.

"Come in!" Elsie called from inside. I stepped in to see her poking her head out of one of the bedrooms in the hallway. "He's downstairs," she said. "Will you see if he's done with his homework? I need his help scraping wallpaper in the bedrooms."

"Sure," I said. "Can I help too?"

"That'd be wonderful." She smiled. "I've got an apron around here somewhere you can use."

Near the front door, a long stairway led to the basement. I went down it into a big family room that was void of furniture save for an old sofa and Mr. Euler's upright piano. Light spilled from an open door at the end of the hall, so I followed it and found Thomas sitting on a stool at a desk, his back to me. He hovered over something and had earbuds in his ears. On the edge of the desk was a small iron and some colored blocks of waxy-looking material.

I approached him slowly, peaking over his shoulder to see what he was working on. He had some kind of heat tool in his hand, like a thick metal pen with a long electrical cord. He was brushing it on a canvas in small strokes. When the canvas came fully into view, my breath caught in my throat.

It was an impressionistic landscape painting, but not any landscape. It was undoubtedly the lake we'd gone to the day before, with yellowing aspens skirting the shore and Pikes Peak towering in the background. A little fishing boat drifted in the middle of the lake. In the boat was a boy and a girl, both with dark hair.

I smiled, my heart soaring with hope. He didn't notice me behind him, even though I was close enough to smell his familiar scent. So I plucked an earbud from his ear and put it in my own.

"Whatcha listening to?"

He jumped in surprise, and I recognized the music immediately. A piano piece. The Chopin Etude I'd played for him a couple days earlier.

He smiled and reached up to retrieve the earbud, the backs of his fingers grazing my cheek. "I can't seem to get enough of it."

I felt my cheeks warm, so I nodded to his canvas. "I didn't know you were an artist."

He shrugged. "It gives me something to do when I'm feeling restless."

"It's beautiful. Almost more beautiful than the real thing." I nodded to the tools on his desk. "What's the iron for?"

"For melting wax. It's called encaustics—basically painting with wax." He picked up a block of white wax and smeared it on the iron, instantly melting it. He added some blue and a little pink, then took a blank sheet of paper and spread the melted wax on the paper.

"It looks like a sunset."

"Exactly. Instant sky."

Tank leapt up on the desk, and his fur grazed the iron. Thomas shoved him off, but Tank swiped at the fabric-covered power cord and took the iron down with him. Thomas snatched the cord just before the iron hit the carpet.

"Stupid cat," Thomas muttered. "He likes the warmth of the iron, but sometimes he gets too close. One of these days he's going to catch himself on fire."

He reached down to unplug the iron and stylus, and I took the chance to glance around his room. An oak dresser. A twin bed. A notebook and his physics textbook lying open on a plain navy comforter. Dozens of unframed paintings and drawings were tacked to the walls. If he painted when he was restless, he must have been restless often.

I wandered from painting to painting, taking in the beauty and brilliance of his talent. There were people and landscapes, abstracts and wildlife. There were galaxies and nebulae, and all kinds of beautiful things you'd see through a telescope. Each one was bursting with color, texture, emotion. I lifted my hand to feel the texture of the paint, but hesitated at the last second, unsure if he wanted me to touch them. I glanced at him, and he was smiling.

"It's okay. You can touch it."

I ran my fingers over the surface, smooth in some places, sharp and coarse in others. There was something thrilling

about touching something his hands had created, like wandering through the terrain of his subconscious and discovering the beauty of his soul.

When I came upon a small painting of a girl, with cropped blonde hair and big brown eyes, I paused. She looked to be in her teens, and her face was pretty, though sad. I wondered who she was, but not wanting to betray my interest in her, I moved on to other paintings. I didn't see the other subjects, though, because the girl's face was burned into my vision as though I'd stared at a lightbulb for too long. I squeezed my eyes shut and tried to flick the image and my curiosity away. She was probably just a friend, I told myself.

I came to a crowded bookshelf, and my eyes were drawn to a shelf packed with various wire-bound notebooks. I took hold of one and started to slide it out, but Thomas snagged my wrist to stop me. I looked at him. The corner of his mouth was turned up and he was shaking his head. "Uh-uh. Those are my journals."

"Oh." I slid the notebook back in and dropped my hand. "There are a lot of them. Did you start journaling in grade school or something?"

He shook his head. "Only a couple years ago. I . . . had a lot of things to sort out."

I eyed him with curiosity, hoping he'd expound, but he turned away and began organizing the tools on his desk. I glanced back at the journals, wondering what kind of feelings could have required twelve hundred pages to sort out. I would have given anything to read them, but I let it go, instead perusing the dozens of spines on the upper shelves.

*The Encaustic Studio* and *Artistic Techniques for Working with Wax. The Feynman Lectures on Physics.* Carl Sagan's *Cosmos. The Songs of Distant Earth* by Arthur C. Clarke.

"Are you going to be an astronomer like your mom and grandpa?" I asked.

He shrugged. "I'm torn. Art and astronomy both appeal to my creative side, just in different ways."

"Astronomy is creative?"

"Incredibly. It's not just about looking through a telescope; it's understanding physics and trying to imagine how something was created. Like reverse engineering." He turned to me and leaned against his desk. "But to be honest, sometimes a blank canvas feels more intriguing to me than the mysteries of the universe. Maybe it's the simplicity that appeals to me."

"Reverse engineering the universe does sound like a pretty overwhelming task."

He smiled. "Sometimes when I sit down to do physics homework, it makes me restless. On a lot of levels, it's absolute, no bending or changing the rules. And I know there's a purpose and application for it, but right now it feels so abstract and distant." He picked up a block of wax. "But you apply some wax to a blank canvas, and you get an instant result, and one that is different every time." He looked down at the block of wax thoughtfully, shaving a bit off with his thumbnail. "But . . . I don't know. I want to either go to Berkeley for astronomy, or Paris Sorbonne for art. I just haven't decided which."

*Berkeley or Paris,* I thought with disappointment. Either way, he would be thousands of miles from Juilliard. "So," I said, recalling why I'd come over in the first place, "I was wondering if you'd be able to give me a ride to Colorado Springs Monday after school?"

"Sure. Why?"

"There's someone I need to see. He's an old friend of my mom's from Juilliard, and . . . I'm hoping he can give me lessons."

He brightened. "Really? That's great!"

"I'm hoping it will be. But my dad can't know about it."

"Of course." He nodded solemnly.

"And . . . there's something else."

He raised an eyebrow.

I sighed. I didn't want to make him feel bad, but if I was going to be more discreet about hanging out with him, he needed to know. "My dad is being weird . . . about you."

"What do you mean?"

"Nothing. It's just . . . instead of picking me up for school from now on, I'll just meet you at your house."

He looked down, his brow wrinkled in puzzlement. His lips parted to say something, but he was interrupted by his mom calling him from upstairs.

"Oh, I forgot," I said. "Your mom needs your help scraping off wallpaper."

Thomas didn't move, and when he raised his eyes to meet mine, they looked hurt. "So your dad doesn't want you hanging out with me?"

I hesitated, then shook my head.

He frowned. "Did he say why?"

"No. He's just being unreasonable, as always."

He nodded, but there was a trace of sadness in his face, and it made me regret saying anything.

"Just forget I mentioned anything, okay?" I nudged him in the shoulder. "We're still friends, no matter what."

He tried to smile, and his mom called again. I tugged on his arm. "Come on," I said with an encouraging smile. "Let's go scrape wallpaper."

♪ ♪ ♪ ♪ ♪♪♪

Monday afternoon, Thomas and I pulled up to a boxy cobalt-blue house on the outskirts of Colorado Springs. Wood trellises covered in white honeysuckle hung over the porch, and neatly trimmed bushes lined the walkway leading to the front door.

I turned to Thomas. "Will you come with me?"

He'd been quieter than usual today, seeming contemplative. He'd excused himself halfway through lunch, about the time Dirk started playing twenty-one questions with me and snatching cherry tomatoes from my lunch tray. Trisha had followed Thomas out into the hall like a puppy, and from the nauseatingly seductive looks she'd given him in English, they must have had an interesting conversation. But not wanting to betray my jealousy, I hadn't asked him for details.

"Of course," he said as he cut the engine.

My chest felt tight as we approached the porch, and as we climbed the steps I took a deep breath, hoping Nathaniel would be willing to teach me and that I still had time to prepare for Juilliard auditions. I'd put on my best clothes this morning, a light blue eyelet dress and white slipper shoes I'd gotten from Vivian. I'd even applied my makeup like she'd shown me and blow-dried my hair until it was shiny and straight.

Piano music seeped through the window panes, and I glanced at Thomas nervously. He gave me an encouraging smile. I rang the doorbell, and the music stopped. A few seconds later, the front door opened, and there stood the same man I'd seen arguing with Dad a couple weeks earlier. His face went slack, like he was surprised to see me.

We all just sort of stared at each other for a moment without saying anything. He was built like a poplar, tall and thin, with short sandy-blond hair and a well-trimmed beard. He wore a black dress shirt and the beginnings of wrinkles beneath his square-rimmed glasses.

"Are you Nathaniel?" I finally asked, though I was sure it was him.

"I am," he said, pursing his lips and nodding slowly. "And you're Aria."

"I'm sorry I didn't call first," I said. "Is this a bad time?"

He shook his head. "No—I'm glad you came. Please, come in." He waved us in.

We stepped into the living room, which was consumed almost entirely by a black Steinway grand piano. The room was bright, with white carpet, pale paint, and a sleek white sofa running the length of the tall windows. Open books of sheet music covered a narrow coffee table wedged between the sofa and piano, and more sheet music crowded the built-in shelves on one wall.

I briefly introduced Thomas, then Nathaniel gestured to the sofa. "Have a seat." His voice was deep and confident, and I recognized the sound of it from when he'd talked with me at Mom's funeral.

Thomas and I settled into the sofa, and Nathaniel sat on a chair beside the piano. "You're all grown up," he said. Then with a thoughtful expression, he added, "You look just like Karina."

"So people say." I never knew how to take the comment. Mom was pretty, so I knew I should take it as a compliment, but it sometimes made me feel invisible, like the speaker wasn't seeing me, they were just seeing Mom.

"I'm willing to bet you play as well as her too."

"Well," I said, fidgeting with my skirt, "I guess that's why I'm here. I found your card—I'd forgotten all about it until the other day. And I'm wondering . . . if you're still willing to teach me, and if I still have a chance at getting into Juilliard next year."

"Next year? Whew." He shook his head. "Auditions are in March. Prescreening videos are due in December. That doesn't give us much time." He must have seen the disappointment in my face because he added, "It's not impossible, but it depends on where you're at now. Have you been practicing?"

"Yes, when I can. But not as much as I'd like."

"Well, there's only one way to determine how much work you'll need." He gestured to the piano. "Why don't you come to the piano?"

I hesitated, my heart suddenly knocking against my ribs, then I nodded and rose. I had never really had performance anxiety, but now my legs felt shaky as I moved across the room to the piano. It felt like my future hinged on this moment. Would he tell me that I wasn't good enough? That Juilliard wasn't even a possibility?

I sat at the piano and turned to him. "What would you like to hear?"

"What do you have memorized?"

"Chopin, Liszt, Schubert, Beethoven. Take your pick."

He smiled. "Why don't you play a few of your favorites, then?"

"A few?"

He nodded.

I twisted around and caught Thomas's gaze. "Do you have time?"

"As much as you need." He gave a little smile that filled me with a surge of confidence. Even if no one else in the

world wanted to hear me play, Thomas would. I shut out the fact that Nathaniel was sitting beside me, that he would be scrutinizing every sound my fingers produced. Instead, I laid my hands on the keys and played for Thomas.

I started with a spirited Chopin sonata, then somewhere in the middle of a lulling Schubert nocturne, I lost myself in the music. Through Mozart and Beethoven and Liszt, I thought about Thomas sitting behind me, and each note I played felt like a needle pulling string through my heart, binding it to his with an unbreakable stitch.

I wasn't sure how much time had passed, but finally Nathaniel put a hand on my shoulder and nodded for me to stop. I waited for him to say something, but he just sat there like a stone, a faraway look etched on his face. After a good minute, he stood and began pacing behind me. Anticipation pulled at my stomach, and I swiveled on the bench so I could see his face. He looked uncertain, and I was suddenly terrified he was going to tell me that my abilities were mediocre, that piano would be a good hobby for me but nothing more.

"Can you practice five hours a day?" he finally asked.

"I can on the days my dad is at work."

"Your dad doesn't know about this?" He paused and stared at me.

I shook my head. "He doesn't know I'm here. And if you decide to teach me, he can't know about that either."

"Well," he said, "I can't say that surprises me." He resumed pacing. "How often does he work?"

"Usually ten days a month. But I can practice more than five hours on those days."

He shook his head. "That won't do. Can you come here to practice on the evenings your dad is home?"

I considered this. I'd have to lie to Dad about where I was. I'd have to tell him I'd picked up more hours at work. I'd need to find a way to get here. And I'd have to find time to get my chores and homework done.

"She can practice at my house." Thomas stood and crossed the room. "I live next door to her."

"What kind of piano?" Nathaniel asked suspiciously.

"A Baldwin."

"What model?"

Thomas stared at him blankly.

"Oh, never mind," Nathaniel said, waving an impatient hand. "What kind of shape is it in?"

Thomas shrugged. "Good enough, I think."

I gave Thomas a smile of gratitude, but his face remained as intense as Nathaniel's. They both looked like they were debating how to perform life-saving surgery on a dying person.

"Has it been tuned recently?" Nathaniel asked.

"We'll have it tuned."

Nathaniel nodded, then resumed pacing behind me. "Juilliard is one of the toughest schools to get into," he said. "You need three things to make an impression on the judges. You need good technique, and good song choices to show off that technique." He stopped and folded his arms across his chest.

"What's the third thing?" I asked as my heart thrummed against my chest.

"The most important of all," he said. "Passion. If you play a dull song with mediocre technique, but play it with enough passion, they'll know you're teachable. You need to cut yourself open and hand over your heart. You're not just displaying talent, you're showcasing your soul."

I sat there, trying to figure out what he was saying. "Do I have what it takes?" I asked nervously.

"You have excellent technique. Your mother taught you well. I can help you with song choices. And let me tell you something, Aria." He sat and laid his hand on my shoulder. "You have artistic power in those fingers of yours, and passion I haven't heard since . . ." A small, thoughtful smile appeared on his lips. "Since your mother."

A medley of joy and relief swelled in my chest, pushing tears to my eyes. "Thank you," I whispered. "You don't know how much those words mean to me."

"I think I know," he said with a wink and a little smile. He patted my hand and rose. "Listen—if you can commit to practicing five hours a day, then your chances of impressing the judges are good."

He began gathering a stack of sheet music from the shelves on the wall, and I glanced up at Thomas. He was gazing at me thoughtfully, a sparkling reverence in his eyes. Nathaniel summoned me to the sofa, where we went over some pieces he wanted me to work on. When we finished, we discussed scholarship options, and then he walked us to the door.

"Oh," I said as I stepped onto the porch. "How much are lessons?"

He folded his arms and gazed down at the porch, his brow furrowed in contemplation. After a moment he looked up at me and said quietly, "You can pay me, Aria, by giving this your all, by making something of the gift your mom passed on to you."

I nodded, completely humbled by his generosity. "Thank you, Nathaniel. For being such a great friend to my mom, and a friend to me now."

He patted my shoulder and smiled. "I'll see you next week."

On the way back to Woodland Park, I chattered to Thomas about the meeting with Nathaniel and my hopes for the future. After ten minutes or so, I realized I was the only one talking, and the only one smiling. He drove quietly, his eyes fixed on the road and his brow lowered as though weighed down by some perplexing matter. I watched him from the corner of my eye, wondering if he regretted offering his help and now felt burdened by his obligation.

"You don't really have to let me practice at your house every day," I said. "And you don't have to drive me to my lessons or anything. There are a thousand other ways to get to Colorado Springs."

He glanced at me. "I don't mind at all. I'm glad I can help."

I watched him and waited for the shadow to lift from his expression, but it clung to him like pine sap. "Is everything okay?" I asked. "You seem upset about something."

"Can I ask you something?" he said, ignoring my question. "Has anyone asked you to homecoming?"

My heart tripped into a run. Was he asking me? "No, not yet," I said, trying to suppress the bubbling excitement in my chest.

His jaw tightened. "Well, I'm sure someone will," he said flatly, keeping his gaze on the road.

Confused, I asked, "Have you asked anyone yet?"

"No. Someone asked me though."

It took me a minute to find my voice again. "I thought you didn't date."

"I don't. It's just that, well . . ." He shrugged. "It's not technically a date. I mean, it's a school function."

"Oh." I didn't know what else to say. I was taken off guard, like being shoved unexpectedly off a cliff. I didn't want to ask who had asked him because I already knew, and because a lethal amount of jealousy would surface in my voice.

"Trisha cornered me," he volunteered, and I felt the sharp rocks at the bottom of the cliff pierce through my heart. "She said you were going with Dirk, and asked if I wanted to go with her and maybe double with you and him."

"What? Dirk? He hasn't asked me, and I'm sure he won't." I clenched my jaw, anger tensing every muscle in my body. Why would Trisha say that? Was she really low enough to lie just to get a date with Thomas?

"I'm sure he will." His hands tightened on the steering wheel, as though this bothered him.

"What makes you so sure?"

"Locker-room talk. That's all I'll say."

"Good. Don't say any more," I said with a cringe. I smiled, trying to appear unaffected by this awful turn of events. "So . . . you're going with Trisha," I said cheerfully, though the words tasted bitter on my lips. "You'll have the prettiest date at the dance." My stomach recoiled as I visualized them together on the dance floor.

"The second prettiest," he said, glancing at me. "Anyway, maybe we can double."

I almost scoffed at the suggestion. Nothing could be more torturous than spending an evening watching my nemesis devour Thomas with her manicured tentacles and come-hither eyes. "Sure," I said, "though I doubt Dirk will ask me." In fact, I was counting on it.

Thomas turned out to be right about Dirk. At the pep rally on Friday, Dirk asked me to homecoming in a way that was impossible to refuse. He called me down to the court, and in front of the entire student body, he handed me a rose and recited some cheesy thing about how I was as beautiful as a freshly bloomed rose. I'd never been so embarrassed in my life, nor felt so utterly trapped. I wanted to say no, but with everyone leaning forward on their seats with gleeful anticipation on their faces, "yes" came out of my mouth. The crowd erupted in cheers as though I'd just accepted a marriage proposal, and as I looked into the bleachers at Thomas, his expression was somewhere between annoyed and sympathetic. Trisha sat next to him looking smug. I knew in that moment that homecoming would go down as the worst night of my adolescent life.

*nine*

T hese three measures should be forte," Nathaniel said, pointing at the sheet music propped on his piano. "Now go back and play from measure twenty."

I played it again, doing as he asked. He sat beside the piano, swaying his hand to the rhythm. "Perfect. Now, sometimes the inner voices get buried in broken octaves, but the goal is to uncover them and let them be heard."

He played a passage to demonstrate, his long, lemur-like fingers striding across the keyboard effortlessly. I followed, trying to replicate the beautiful way he'd played. For an hour we went back and forth, him showing me different dynamics and phrasing, me trying to copy. It was a process I'd become accustomed to in the five weeks since our first meeting.

"You're coming along wonderfully," he said as I gathered my sheet music at the end of the lesson. "Next week we'll choose the final pieces for your audition."

"Do you think I have a shot?" I asked as he walked me to the door.

"Of course. But how close you get to the mark will depend on how much work you put in these next few months. If you're as hard a worker as your mom, you'll be spot on." He swung open the door, and I glanced at the empty driveway. We'd ended a bit early, and Thomas wasn't yet back from running errands for his dad.

I turned back to Nathaniel. "Can I ask you something?"

"Sure thing."

"You knew my mom pretty well, right?"

He nodded. "We actually met before Juilliard, at a federation competition."

"What was she like? I mean, I know what she was like as a mother, but sometimes I wonder what she was like outside of that role. My dad doesn't like to talk about her, so I was wondering if you could tell me what you remember about her."

His brow creased thoughtfully, and after a long moment, he said, "She had two left feet. She was always tripping over things. But somehow when she got on the stage, she pulled off poise and elegance." He smiled, as though reflecting on some specific memory. "She was stubborn, but deeply loyal—once she made up her heart about something, there was no distracting her from it. And intense—she always seemed to feel everything with about ten times the emotion as everyone else. Which could be good, such as when she was playing, and bad, because she often overreacted to things.

"She had incredible intuition. She seemed to always know what people were thinking and what they were going to do even before they did it. In fact, I think she knew your dad wouldn't support your music the way she wanted after she died."

"How do you know?"

He hesitated. "She came to see me, before she . . ." He trailed off, like the word was as hard for him to say as it was for me. But this time, I was the one to tackle it.

"Died," I said quietly.

He gave me a sad smile and shook his head. "It had been years since I'd seen her, and she looked so different." He released a disheartened sigh. "She was so thin and fragile-looking. It broke my heart to see her that way. She spent the entire time talking about you, about how much she loved you and how talented you were. She was worried that after she died, Jed wouldn't foster your talent the way she wanted. She asked me to teach you and to help you get into Juilliard. And . . ."

"And what?" I prodded.

"I thought this was a little odd, but she asked me to keep an eye on you, to look out for you and make sure you were okay. I never understood why, of all people, she would ask me. I mean, you didn't even know me. I suggested to her that she ask one of your grandparents or an aunt or something, but she insisted there was no one else. So I accepted the assignment."

"You must have been a good friend to her."

"Well, I wish I would have been a better friend." He let out a long sigh. "I'm sorry to say that I let her down. I tried to come see you a few times over the years, but I was still traveling a lot, and your dad was a hard man to get around. He wouldn't let me come near you or even talk to you on the phone."

"I saw you. A few weeks ago, arguing with my dad in our driveway."

He nodded. "I'd been feeling guilty about not fulfilling

the promise I made to your mom, and I came to try to convince your dad to let me teach you. Of course, you saw how that turned out. But all these years, I've been hoping you'd remember the business card I gave you and that you'd come see me." He smiled. "And here you are. I'm so glad you found me."

"I am too," I said.

♪ ♪ ♪ ♪ ♪

The day I'd been dreading for weeks finally arrived, and on a Friday afternoon in mid-October, I lay on my back and slid under my bed. The underside of the box spring was open, and I wiggled a cardboard box from a hollow space between the wood slats. Then I slid back out and sat up, folding my legs beneath me.

With great reverence, I opened the box and lifted out Mom's evening gown. I stood and held it up in front of a full-length mirror. It was pale periwinkle, with wide lace straps that hung just off the shoulders and a soft, rounded lacy neckline. A wide band of embroidered chiffon cinched the tiny waistline, and a fluttery, cascading swirl of chiffon and lace layered the floor-length skirt. It was ethereal, a timeless dress fit for a goddess. Mom had looked so beautiful in it with her long neck and slender frame as she performed Shostakovich with the Colorado Springs Philharmonic years ago. It had been her last concert and the only time I'd seen her perform onstage. My eight-year-old body had tingled with wonder and awe as I watched her, and as I looked around at the expressions in the audience, I knew they felt the same way. It was the first time in my life I really understood who my mother was. From that moment, I wanted

to be like her. I wanted to be able to put my fingers on an instrument and make people *feel* whatever I wanted them to feel. Anger, passion, hope, serenity, love. There was power in music, and I wanted to be able to channel and manipulate it the way she did.

The dress was the one thing I'd snagged from the attic before Dad screwed the hatch shut after finding me there one too many times. I hadn't intended on wearing it to homecoming, but after spending hours searching through a sea of sequined bodices and frilly skirts that belonged on Cinderella or Glinda the Good Witch, I realized all other dresses paled in comparison to this one. This was the only dress good enough for Thomas. I wasn't going to homecoming with him, but this dress would make it impossible for him not to notice me.

Dad had gone deer hunting for a week, so I'd have plenty of time to put the dress back in its hiding place before he got home. I hung the dress on the back of the bathroom door as I showered, letting the steam unwrinkle it.

Still dripping wet after my shower, I heard the doorbell ring. Dirk couldn't possibly already be here, so I threw on a bathrobe and went downstairs to look through the peephole. It was Vivian, holding a plate full of something. I cracked open the door.

"Hey, darlin'," she said, "I brought you some macaroons." She looked at the towel wrapped around my head. "You goin' somewhere tonight?"

"Homecoming," I said.

She gasped. "With Thomas?"

"No," I said, and I could hear the disappointment in my own voice. "He's going with someone else."

"What? Who?"

"Trisha. She's blonde and beautiful and has the body of a dancer."

"Oh, honey, we've got some work to do."

She handed me the macaroons and dashed away. "I'll be right back!"

She was back before I could put the macaroons on the counter, bursting through the front door with an oversized purse. "Upstairs, darlin'. Now."

After drying my hair and rolling it into huge rollers, she pulled out a massive case of makeup. "Lie on your bed," she said.

"What?"

"Just do it. It'll relax your face and get rid of that little crinkle between your brows."

"I have a crinkle between my brows?"

"Not for long. Lie down, sweetheart." I lay on the bed and she tucked a pillow under my neck to keep my head from crushing the rollers. She scooted my desk chair over and sat down. "Now, close your eyes, relax, and no talking." I closed my eyes, and for the next twenty minutes I felt all kinds of textures on my skin. Sponges, brushes, pencils, Vivian's fingertips. "Okay," she finally said, "now for the hair."

I sat on my desk chair, and Vivian took out the rollers. As she twisted my hair and pinned it loosely at the nape of my neck, I tried to do the same with my emotions. I mentally coiled and twined, pinned and tucked my feelings for Thomas. It was the only way I'd be able to keep myself from unraveling when I saw him with Trisha on the dance floor.

With my hair and makeup finished, Vivian went out and I slipped into the dress, zipped up the back, and

turned to look in the full-length mirror. I gasped at the sight of myself. Vivian had done an amazing job, but it wasn't just that.

I didn't have a lot of vivid memories of Mom, but seeing her in this dress was one of them. And looking at my reflection, with my perfect makeup and my hair all done up, was like looking at her.

My hand came to my mouth and I inhaled deeply through my nose to stifle the emotion rising in my chest. Now more than ever, I missed her. An acute, piercing pain stabbed at my heart, and I wrapped my arms around myself, wishing she were the one filling the dress, not me. Tears welled up in my eyes, and I blinked them back, not wanting to mess up my makeup. Suddenly I wasn't sure it was such a good idea to wear her dress. My feelings for Thomas had me feeling fragile enough. Did I really need to add another thing to be emotional about?

I backed up to the desk chair and sunk into it. "Mom," I whispered, still trying to hold back tears, "I wish you were here."

A car honking jarred me from my reverie, and when I looked out the window, I saw a shiny black Mustang parked in front of the house. I glanced at the clock—twenty to six. Was Dirk here already? Vivian burst into my room with offense written all over her face. "There had better be a rabid heifer in your driveway, because if it's your date—"

"Unless heifers drive Mustangs, it is my date," I said, slipping on my strappy ivory heels.

"Oh, no you don't," she said, waving her finger at me. "You're not going anywhere until he comes to the door and knocks like a gentleman." She sat me down on the bed and held my hand. "By the way," she said, eyeing my dress, "you're gonna knock every boy at that dance off their feet, including Thomas."

*Honk. Honk.*

"Somebody needs to go smack that boy upside the head."

"I should just go down. It's not like I'm ever going to go out with him again."

*Honnnnnnnnnnkkkkkk. Honk.*

"Thanks, Vivian," I said, giving her a hug, "for everything."

We walked out of the house together, and she watched me walk to Dirk's car. I pulled on the door handle, and it was locked.

I tapped on the window, and he reached over and unlocked the door. A draft of cologne assaulted me as I swung open the door, and I breathed in one last breath of fresh air before ducking into the car. I waved at Vivian, who was glowering at Dirk like he'd just insulted her banana-caramel pie.

"Sorry I didn't come to the door," he said. "We're running late for dinner."

"Where are we going?"

"Pikes, of course. But my dad wanted us to get there before the evening rush. It's Friday night, you know."

"We're eating at work?"

"I told my Dad to save us the back booth. Is that okay?"

I shrugged. "Nothing tastes better than a free dinner."

After he pulled onto the highway, he eyed me up and down and whistled. "By the way, you look smokin'."

"Um, thanks." I wrapped my arms around my waist and wished I'd brought a sweater. "So, weren't we supposed to double with Thomas and Trisha?"

"Huh? Said who?" He snorted. "Like I would double with my ex."

"Oh. I guess I misunderstood."

We stopped at Pikes Pancake House, and as Dirk promised, we ushered ourselves to the back booth. Dirk had the Mountain Man Skillet, and I picked at a chicken salad. I tried to be somewhat attentive, but all I could think about was Thomas. Where had he taken Trisha for dinner? Had he really nixed his no-dating policy for her? I attempted repeatedly to distract myself through conversation with Dirk, but it was difficult when his eyes never left my dress, and all his responses sounded something like, "Is that lace?" as if he'd never seen lace before.

We arrived at homecoming just as things were getting busy on the dance floor. As we stepped into the gymnasium, a pool of pulsating music and spinning color immersed us. A rainbow of lights twirled on a canopy of streamers draped from the ceiling like a circus tent, and the energy in the room thumped through my body with the beat of the music. Couples crowded the dance floor, an array of tulle and chiffon skirts swaying, curls piled on top of heads, skin shimmering with spray-on glitter—as though the sparkle from their rhinestone jewelry wasn't enough.

My eyes squinted into the dizzying display of lights and fog and swept the room for Thomas. I finally found him, sitting beside Trisha on a row of chairs lining the wall. They were engaged in conversation. He sat leaning over, elbows resting on knees, but his head was turned toward Trisha. All I noticed about Trisha was her legs. If she was wearing a skirt, I couldn't see it. Her legs were crossed, bare from her silver stilettos all the way to the sparkly fabric bunched in her lap. When she started tracing shapes on his back with her finger, I had to look away. That one fleeting glance at them was all it took to loosen the emotions I thought

I'd bound up so tightly. Trying to steady myself, I tucked them back into place as I followed Dirk to the dance floor.

"Sweet! I love this song!" Dirk yelled as he turned to face me. I stood there in frozen awkwardness as Dirk broke into a bouncing, jerking rhythm. I knew I should dance, but I couldn't seem to bring myself to do it. Dancing was for celebrating, and what did I have to celebrate? Thomas was being pawed by a half-naked girl, and I was on the dance floor with a wild hyena who was happily convulsing one second and heatedly staring at me with hungry eyes the next.

Soon a circle of clapping, bouncing kids had formed around Dirk, and I extricated myself to the outskirts of the crowd. Oblivious to my absence, Dirk just kept dancing, basking in the spotlight as he jerked and twisted, his face like an excited chimpanzee.

Watching him made me dizzy, so I went to the refreshment table to get some punch, wondering why I'd even bothered coming. As I sipped from my icy cup, someone stepped up beside me. I looked up to see Thomas, stunningly handsome in a tuxedo. My heart palpitated wildly at the sight of him, and I squared my shoulders, trying to appear unaffected. His dark hair framed his adorable face, and it was styled just right, like he'd taken the time to position each gelled lock in the perfect place.

"Aria," he said softly. "You look . . . amazing."

My cheeks warmed and I managed a little smile. "Same to you."

His lips parted as if he was going to say more, but then he turned away to grab a couple of empty cups.

I wanted to turn away, to feign interest in the dance floor, but I couldn't peel my eyes from him. I watched him

fill the cups, ignoring the fact that he was filling one for Trisha. When they were full, he came back to my side, and his sweet, earthy scent made my knees weak.

"Looks like there's only room on the dance floor for one," he said with an annoyed tone.

Dirk was surrounded by a crowd, still having a one-man dance-off. "I hope he doesn't mind dancing alone," I said, "because I don't think I can keep up." Feeling Thomas's eyes on me, I glanced up at him, quick enough to see his expression change from a troubled frown to thoughtful smile.

"Where's Trisha?" I asked.

He nodded to the gym doors. "In the bathroom. She won't admit it, but she's not feeling very well. I've been trying to convince her to let me take her home, but she insists on staying." Just then, Trisha appeared in the doorway. Her gaze homed in on us, and she loped toward us as quickly as her stilettos would allow.

It took all my effort to stay composed as she approached us. Her dress was look-at-me fuchsia, and the sequin-speckled skirt was so short I was almost embarrassed for her. As she came closer, I saw what Thomas meant about her not feeling well. Her eyes were bloodshot, her nose red and swollen, and even her thick makeup couldn't hide her skin's clammy sheen.

She sidled up to Thomas, wedging herself between us and looping her arm through his. He stiffened a little as he handed her a drink. Her glittered eyelids looked heavy as she took a sip and gazed up at him, and I wondered how much cold medicine she'd taken before the dance.

As the song ended and a slower one began, Dirk appeared at the punch bowl, all out of breath and face gleaming with sweat. He chugged two cups of punch, then hopped to my side. "That was awesome," he said with a huge grin. "Did you see me?"

"Yeah," I said. "I think everyone saw you."

Trisha blew her nose into a wadded-up tissue, then tugged on Thomas's arm until he followed her to the dance floor. Jealousy gnawed at me as she clasped her hands behind his neck, and once again I felt myself unraveling.

Dirk muttered something I didn't understand, and when I looked at him, he was staring at Trisha, raw envy in his eyes. "I'll make her sorry," he said, seeming to forget I was standing beside him. "Come on, let's dance." He grabbed my wrist and pulled me back to the dance floor, dramatically twirling me, then pulling me close. He'd taken off his tuxedo jacket, and his shirt was moist with sweat. I inched my body away from his until I was at a more comfortable distance. He looked past me as we swayed, and from the hard set of his jaw and the anger in his eyes, I knew he was watching Trisha.

"Doesn't Trisha look weird?" he asked.

"I think she has a cold."

"She looks kinda like a zombie or something." He let out a little laugh. "That would explain how she so heartlessly dumped me."

As we rotated, Thomas and Trisha came into view. She had her arms wrapped tightly around his neck, clutching her fat tissue wad in one hand. She rested her head on his chest, her halo of blonde curls drowning his chin. But with the greenish circles under her eyes and the monstrous cold sore above her lip, I had to admit she did look slightly zombie-like. Only, instead of a stiff body, hers seemed limp in his arms, like he was holding her up. And the back of her dress was cut so low, the only place for Thomas to put his hands was on her bare skin.

My stomach recoiled against the image of them together, and my breaths turned shallow. Dirk must have thought I was reacting to him, because he pulled me closer and slid his hand lower on my back.

Thomas caught and held my gaze. His expression was restless, and a worried crease pinched his brows. Trisha demanded his attention and he dipped his head to hear her better. She raised her lips to his ear and whispered something. I looked away.

Things sped back up on the dance floor, and Thomas and Trisha made their way to the exit. Just before disappearing through the streamer-covered doorway, he turned and waved at me, mouthing something I couldn't decipher.

I suddenly felt weak, and I found a chair and sunk into it. Dirk recommenced his gyrating dance-floor extravaganza, and I gripped the seat of the chair, trying to ground myself. The blaring dance music assaulted my frail emotions, pulsing under my skin and saturating my ears. Dirk found me and tried to pull me to my feet. I stayed planted on the chair, shaking my head in objection. "I don't feel well."

"Maybe you have what Trisha has," he shouted over the music.

I nodded, wishing I had what Trisha had.

We were one of the last couples to leave the dance, and Dirk chattered the entire way home about what a hit he was on the dance floor, speculating about which photos would end up in the yearbook. As we finally pulled into my driveway, I reached for the door handle, but he stopped me by seizing my knee.

"Wait," he said. "Are your parents home?"

His assumption that I still had two parents made me realize how much he didn't know about me. "Yeah," I lied. "I'd better go in."

"Hold on. I'll open your door."

I opened my own door and climbed out as he strutted around the car. He held out his arm for me, but the night chill bit my skin, so I rubbed my arms instead of taking his. He followed me to the porch, and as I turned around to say good-bye, his face was suddenly inches from mine.

"Don't I get a hug or something?" he asked, his arms outstretched.

Before I could say no, he stepped up and snared me in his arms. As I peeled away from him, his chin was lifted and his lips slightly puckered. I tried to break free from his embrace, but his arms didn't budge. With half-closed eyes, his face moved in, and I turned my head, leaning away as much as his grip would allow.

There was a creaking sound to my right, and with a start, we turned to see what had caused it.

Out of the shadow of the porch walked the sweetest sight I'd ever seen.

Thomas Ashby was on my porch, waiting for *me*.

# ten

A warm sensation rushed through me, and suddenly the night didn't seem so cold. My pulse did a double beat, and Dirk did a double take. "Dude. What are you doing here?"

Thomas cleared his throat as he stepped into the yellow glow of the porch light. "Aria's dad was tired, so he asked me to stay up and wait for her—since we're good friends." He caught my eye and winked.

Dirk shot me a questioning look. I just shrugged.

"Um, 'kay. Can you give us a sec?" Dirk asked incredulously.

"Sure, take your time." Thomas folded his arms across his chest.

Dirk stared at Thomas and lifted an eyebrow. "Dude. I mean, like, alone."

"I'm supposed to make sure she gets inside safe," Thomas said. "Now that she's home, I'd better keep my eye on her until she's inside."

Dirk snorted and looked at me. "Whatever, Aria. See

you at work tomorrow." He turned and stormed back to his car.

We watched him peel away, then I turned back to Thomas. His hair was kind of messy, and I hoped *his* fingers had been the only ones combing through it.

"Where's Trisha?" I asked.

"At home, probably in bed surrounded by tissues."

"How long have you been here?"

"I don't know. An hour? Maybe two? I came right after I dropped off Trisha. I thought you'd be home sooner." His voice was laced with uneasiness, like he'd been worried about me.

"So what are you doing here?"

He leaned back against the porch post. "Well, Dirk was bragging in the locker room earlier about his *list*."

"List?"

"Apparently he keeps a list of all the girls he's kissed—twenty-nine so far."

"You say that like it's news. I'm surprised it's not more."

"I just wanted to make sure *you* weren't number thirty."

"Thanks," I said, taking a step toward the door, "but I can defend myself. His lips weren't coming near mine."

"But they were. I was watching."

"Why?" I spun around to face him. "Why do you care if he kisses me?" My tone was harsher than I intended. I wasn't angry. I was thrilled that he was here, that he cared. But I had to know if he was just looking out for a friend, or if he was jealous because his feelings extended beyond friendship.

"Well, I . . ." He scratched the back of his head and sighed. He pursed his lips and looked down, nervously kicking the floor with the tip of his black dress shoe.

"Just tell me why you're really here."

His expression was troubled and he chewed on his lip like he was trying to figure out what to say. After a long moment, he took a couple steps toward me until he was standing just inches away. "I'm here because . . . I didn't get a chance to dance with the girl I *really* wanted to dance with." He gently laid his hand on my upper arm, and my pulse stuttered as his fingers trailed down my arm to my hand, where they fastened to the curve of my palm.

My lips parted and the shallow breaths passing through them quickened. An electric current ran down my arms, making the hairs stand on end. "Are you"—I swallowed, trying to restore some moisture to my mouth—"providing the music?"

He pressed my hand to his heart, making my own heart swell and rise from its natural place, and he rested his other hand on my hip and closed the small gap between us.

A soft, sweet melody hummed from his lips, and with each sway of our bodies, he drew me nearer to him. He lowered his head and pressed his jaw to my temple. My heart beat furiously inside my chest, and I nuzzled into him, breathing in his woodsy scent mixed with a hint of musky cologne. I closed my eyes and took in every sensation, in awe of what it was like to be held, touched, wanted.

This wasn't a crush or a fleeting infatuation. I could feel every flicker of his existence—the sound of his voice humming in my ear, his callused hand wrapped around mine, the curve of his shoulder as my hand clung to it—carve into my heart, marking it indelibly his. And I pleaded into the night, *Please let him love me too.*

He gazed down at me, his bright blue eyes sparkling with what seemed to reflect everything I was feeling. We stopped swaying, and he released my hand to tuck a stray tendril of hair behind my ear. The sensation of his fingers against my cheek caused a dizzying current to race through me, and I clutched the fabric of his tuxedo jacket to steady myself.

"Thomas," I said, "I have to be honest. I don't understand. You say you don't date, but you spend all this time with me, and then you go to the dance with Trisha. And now you're dancing with me?" I released his jacket and took a small step back. "Do you have any idea how confusing you are? You're like one of those imponderable questions, like 'which came first, the chicken or the egg?'"

"I don't mean to confuse you." He sighed and dropped his hand from my waist, and I suddenly felt cold and empty. "I guess that's why I'm here—I want you to know how I feel."

A suspenseful silence hung over us, but instead of quelling it, he leaned back against the porch post and hooked his thumbs into his pants pockets. My stomach tightened, and my fingers found a piece of lace on my hip and began twisting it. "And," I prompted, "how do you feel?"

His lips straightened into a thoughtful frown. "When I came to live here, I didn't want to get involved with anyone. I knew we wouldn't be here for long, and . . . there were some things in my past that kept me from wanting to get too close to anyone." He paused, pinning me with a gaze and a little smile. "But then I met you. And I found myself wanting to be around you. And the more time I spend with you, the harder it is for me to stay away from you."

"But if you like being around me, then why go to the dance with Trisha?"

"Because Trisha said you were going with Dirk."

"But—"

"Look, don't think I'm a stalker, okay? But Trisha made it sound like we were doubling with you, and I decided it was the only way I could keep an eye on you. I didn't want Dirk . . . I don't know . . . taking advantage of you." He looked down, like he was embarrassed for feeling this way. I suppressed a smile, trying to hide the sudden wave of hope that surged inside me.

He eyed my fingers, which were still twisting the piece of lace. With a smile, he came and gently pried the lace from my fingers, unraveling it and smoothing it out over my hip. "The truth is," he murmured, "I love being with you. You make me feel happy, at peace, like . . . like a part of me that's been missing has been found and locked into place. And when I'm away from you, that part goes missing again."

I couldn't speak. I was too busy trying to process his beautiful words.

"I care about you. And I don't want to cause you heart-ache or confusion. I don't want you to ever have to question my feelings for you, because that's not fair to you." He dropped his hand and sighed. "I thought I'd be okay just being your friend. But I can't just sit back and watch you get snatched up by someone else."

"I wouldn't have let Dirk snatch me up."

"I know. But what about the next guy? If I wait too long, someone else will come along, and I'll spend the rest of my life regretting not offering you my heart when I had the chance."

He took my hand and enfolded it in his. "What I'm trying to say is, even though I don't feel good enough for you, I want to be with you. And I'm hoping you'll tell me that you want to be with me too."

His words brought tears to my eyes, and I didn't bother trying to swallow them back. I was the one he wanted, and he'd wanted me all along. It seemed too good to be true, but I let his words linger in my heart, where I fastened them down safely to stay.

"Aria, say something," he pleaded.

"Thomas," I whispered as a tear trickled down my cheek, "how could I not want to be with you? You're the most wonderful person I've ever met."

He shook his head and his face turned somber, as though musing on some dark memory. "You don't know everything about me."

I wanted to ask what he meant, but it didn't seem like the right time. His past no longer mattered anyway. "I know enough. And I know who you are," I said, pressing my fingertip over his heart.

"Oh?" With his thumb, he brushed away my tears. "Who am I?"

I sighed and felt a warm blush burning in my cheeks. "You're just plain good. You're solid, like a steady, bright star fixed in the sky."

He gave a smile that reached into his eyes, making them shine. "Is that what you see?"

"Yes. But that's not all."

"No? What else then?"

I opened his hand in mine, tracing a circle in his palm as I tried to find the right words. "You're a melody . . . that plays over and over in my heart."

His smile widened, then slowly straightened. He lowered his forehead until it rested on mine. His face was so close to mine now, I could feel his warm breath on my lips. It took all my strength to resist the urge to rise on my toes and bring our mouths together. Instead, I listened to my pulse thrumming in my chest, counted the breaths passing through his slightly opened lips, and waited.

He slid his fingers under my chin and tipped my head, just enough that our lips met. His kiss was warm and tender, and his lips were sweet. Not sweet like sugar, but like Rachmaninoff's *Rhapsody on a Theme of Paganini*.

The sound of an engine roaring in the darkness burst our little electrified bubble, and I pulled away, uneasiness prickling under my skin. Headlights flashed behind the pines in our front yard, and I stepped away from Thomas.

"I thought he was hunting," Thomas said, unruffled.

"Maybe he already killed something." I tried to stay calm, but a nauseating dread rippled through me. "You'd better go."

Thomas didn't move. Dad's truck turned into the drive, and I caught the glint of animal eyes on the rear of his truck. Strapped atop camping gear and a blue tarp lay an enormous buck, neck bent over the side of the bed from the weight of its antlers. Dad's truck skidded to a halt on the gravel driveway, and his door creaked open. A loud groan filled the night as his boot crashed onto the gravel. My eyes flickered between Thomas and Dad, my pulse frantically pounding in my ears. Dad was drunk. He'd probably stopped at the bar after killing the deer for a celebratory drink. Thomas couldn't see Dad like this. It would ruin everything.

"Thomas," I said, trying to sound commanding, "you'd really better go. I'll call you tomorrow."

He glanced at me, concern and uncertainty cinching his brow. "Are you sure?" He looked back at Dad, who was leaning on the door of his truck, staring at me.

"Please go, Thomas," I said firmly.

"Karina?" Dad yelled out, stretching his arm toward me.

My heart sunk to the pit of my stomach and a paralyzing panic swept over me. I was in Mom's dress. He thought I was her.

He teetered across the driveway, and Thomas looked at me for an explanation, one that I couldn't possibly offer.

"Karina!" Dad cried again, his voice desperate and broken.

"Dad!" I called out, hearing the panic in my own voice, "It's me, Aria!"

Dad stopped and leaned on the handrail at the bottom of the steps. He squinted at me, his face gradually hardening as realization lit up his bloodshot eyes. He straightened and climbed the stairs with surprising steadiness, keeping a fiery glare on me the entire way. With exaggerated disgust, he stopped in front of me and eyed the dress from the straps on my shoulders to the lace shadowing my feet.

"Get inside," he breathed through clenched teeth, then turned to unlock the front door, completely disregarding Thomas.

Thomas shot me an anxious look, and I tried to smile. I had only two options. I could refuse to go inside with Dad and risk having him combust in front of Thomas, or I could go inside with Dad and deal with him in secret. "I'll call you tomorrow," I said to Thomas with forced cheerfulness, then followed Dad inside. I turned to wave at him, but he didn't wave back. He stood as still as stone, and as I closed the door, his expression was a mixture of apprehension and distress.

The house was dark, lit only by moonlight filtering through the window sheers. I reached over to flip on the

light, but my hand met Dad's chest instead. A jolt of terror shot through me. I didn't dare reach around him, so I turned into the darkness and headed for the light switch at the foot of the stairs. Better yet, maybe I'd just run upstairs and change out of Mom's dress before turning on the lights.

"Get over here," Dad growled.

"I'm just going to—"

"Get over here!" he shouted.

I skidded to a stop and slowly turned around to face him. Fear clamped on my heart like a bear trap as Dad's dark silhouette moved toward me.

He stopped and hovered over me, so close I could feel his rank breath on my shoulders. "Where did you get that dress?" he hissed.

I couldn't answer. My heart throbbed desperately in my ears, telling me to run. But I couldn't. I was too afraid to move. And even if I could, Thomas was outside somewhere. If I ran, he would know. It would ruin everything.

"Answer me." Dad's voice was eerily calm as he slowly enunciated each syllable. Maybe he was restraining himself because he knew Thomas might still be outside. "Where did you get that dress?" he repeated, his dark eyes demanding an answer.

"From the attic," I whispered.

The muscles in his jaw bulged as he contracted them. "So you've been hiding it from me all these years? And you think that when I'm gone you can just take it out and wear it to impress some shady, good-for-nothing thug?"

My throat ached with threatening tears, but I lifted my chin and fought them back, trying to be brave.

"You think you can do things behind my back without me finding out. But I know everything you do." His words raced out in a tight growl. His controlled countenance was steaming, gaining pressure and ready to burst at any moment. "I know you still go into the parlor. I know you've been going around with that boy, even though I told you not to. I knew you'd be with him tonight. I have lots of friends, Aria. And when they see you, they tell me about it." The dark shape of his hands clenched and unclenched at his sides. *Clench. Unclench. Clench.*

When he spoke again, his voice was shaky, like he was ready to crack. "One of my hunting buddies saw you in Colorado Springs at his neighbor's house. So I asked who his neighbor is. Do you know who his neighbor is?"

*Nathaniel,* I thought, panic choking my voice.

"What were you doing at Nathaniel's?" The words burst through his lips like a fiery explosion. The ghastly sound rang in my ears, stunning me. I wanted to sink to the floor and bury my head in the shelter of my arms. But terror kept me plastered against the wall.

Not wanting to look into Dad's crazed eyes, I redirected my gaze to the side table. The fox's glass eyes stared at me, appearing alive and full of warning. *Run,* she seemed to say, *before you share my fate!*

I gathered what remained of my courage and turned to flee. But the back of Dad's hand was faster.

# eleven

I held my stinging cheek as I flew through the back door and sprinted away, kicking off my heels as I went. Dad called after me, but I knew if I ran fast enough I could get out of his sight and he wouldn't be able to find me. Tears clouded my vision as I ran, but I kept running, faster with each step, farther and farther away from home.

I reached the wooden fence and clambered over. On the way down my skirt caught on something and I fell hard on my back. In the darkness, I couldn't see what it was caught on. I felt out blindly and discovered a protruding nail, but my hands were shaking so badly I couldn't seem to unhook it. I tugged, but I was caught like a trout on a hook.

In the distance, Dad's voice split through the night like a chain saw. His shouts grew closer, and I thought I saw a dark shadow moving through the pine trees. I yanked hard on the dress and it tore, but I was free. I scrambled to my feet and ran, too afraid to look back.

The grass was moist and cold, making my bare feet ache. I ducked into the cover of the orchard but didn't slow my pace. Midway through, I heard footfalls behind me, and my heart lurched with fear.

"Aria!" a voice called out. The moment I heard it, I knew it wasn't Dad. I stopped in my tracks and whipped around to see Thomas jogging toward me down a row of trees.

Not wanting him to see my face, I turned away and continued my path through the orchard. A clammy coat of tears covered my cheeks, and I reached up to wipe them away. I was suddenly more afraid of facing Thomas than of being hurt by Dad.

He caught up and hooked my arm in his hand. "What's going on?" he asked between heavy breaths.

My hair had come unpinned, and feeling my cheek begin to swell, I let my tangled locks fall over my shoulder to shield my face. "Nothing," I said. "It's no big deal. I just . . . just . . ." I couldn't finish my sentence. What believable excuse could I offer? I freed myself from his grasp and kept walking.

He followed me and grabbed my arm again, this time swiveling me to face him. I turned my head to the side.

"Aria," he said softly, "you're shaking. Tell me what happened."

I shook my head. If I spoke, the sobs I was holding back would slip through my lips.

"Did he hurt you?"

I yanked free and walked away again.

"Where are you going?" he called after me.

"Please just leave me alone, Thomas," I called over my shoulder.

"It's cold out here. Will you at least come in my house—then I'll leave you alone?"

PORCELAIN *Keys*

I ignored him and continued toward the tree house, and he followed silently a few yards behind. I reached the tree house and started climbing, hoping he wouldn't follow, but knowing he would. Once inside, I nestled into a corner and gathered my legs to my chest. I shivered, wondering how I was going to make it through the night without my sleeping bag.

Thomas appeared in the doorway a few moments later and knelt in front of me. I buried my head in my shaking arms.

"Please," I pleaded, "just leave me alone."

We both sat there, silent and motionless, for what seemed like an eternity. I finally had to glance up to see if he was still there. He was—still kneeling, watching me. The moon's silvery light slipped through the window behind him, outlining his hair and shoulders.

He finally moved, laying his hand on my goose bump–covered arm. "Aria," he said so quietly it was almost a whisper, "you don't have to tell me what happened, but I can easily guess. I have to confess—the first day I found you up here, I saw those bruises on your arm. And once I got to know more about you, it didn't take long to piece two and two together."

I grimaced at the memory of that humiliating morning and sank my head deeper into my arms.

"I'm telling you this," he continued, "because I don't want you to feel like you need to explain—or hide anything from me. Nothing you can say will change the way I feel about you. I still want to be with you, no matter what. I just want to help you. I wish you'd let me."

While I debated whether or not to open up to him, he took off his jacket and wrapped it around me. It was warm and comforting. And even in a time like this, I couldn't ignore how good it smelled.

As he turned on a lantern and a soft glow filled the tree house, I repeated his words in my mind. *Nothing you can say will change the way I feel about you.* I clung to those words, then took a leap of faith. I lifted my stinging face to look at him. "Please don't say anything to anyone," I whispered.

He swept a lock of hair away from my face and leaned in for closer examination. I winced as he grazed my cheek with his fingers, and he drew his hand back, inhaling sharply and exhaling through his nose. "I don't understand how he could—" The muscles in his jaw went taut and his eyes darkened with fury. "Someone needs to teach that scumbag a lesson. I'm going to go over there and—"

"No." I clutched his arm. "It'll just make things worse." I reached over and turned off the lantern. If Dad was still out looking for me, the light would lead him here.

"You need to tell someone," Thomas said.

I shook my head. "No."

"Why?" he asked angrily, folding his arms across his chest.

"Do you know what would happen? They would put me in foster care. Foster care!"

"That sounds better than the way you're living now."

"I'm seventeen. I'm moving out the second I graduate. I can deal with him for seven more months."

"What about family? Friends? Isn't there someone else you can move in with?"

"No. Besides, I don't want to. This is where I live. This is my life. I have a plan for my future, and stirring the pot now will only mess it up."

He brushed his thumb along my cheek. "What about

next time? If he hits you hard enough, you may not have a future."

"There won't be a next time."

"How do you know?"

"I'll just have to be more careful. I know what sets him off, and if I don't mess up, he won't get mad."

"What? Are you saying it's your fault he hurt you?"

"No. I know it's not my fault. But it is, in a way, when I don't obey his rules, when I do things I know will upset him." I drew in a deep breath, trying to calm myself. "He found out about Nathaniel. I should have waited to take lessons until I moved out. And he didn't want me hanging out with you; then he came home to see us standing on the porch. And to make things worse"—I gathered my lace skirt in my hands—"I'm wearing my mom's dress. When my dad saw me tonight, he thought I was her."

"So that's why he called you Karina?"

I nodded. "I shouldn't have worn it. It's my fault he got so upset." I tried to choke back the tears welling in my eyes, but they came too fast and trickled down my cheeks.

"No," he said, "it's *his* fault he got so upset. You shouldn't have to live your life fearing that you'll get hurt just because you take piano lessons or dance with a boy or wear a dress. You can't go back there, Aria. Promise me you won't go back there."

"Where else am I going to go?"

"I don't know. I'll figure something out."

"You don't have to figure something out. You don't have to save me. I'll be fine."

He wiped my tears away with his thumb. "You're shivering," he said. "Let's go to my house so you can get warm."

I shook my head. "Your parents—"

"They'll understand. They would probably even let you spend the night if we explained."

"They can't know about this. No one can."

He huffed out a frustrated breath. I wrapped his jacket tighter around me and shivered.

"Well, if you won't come in, at least let me get you some blankets. Can I do that?"

My feet were numb, and I knew it would be a miserable night if I didn't have something warmer than his tuxedo jacket. "Okay," I said, "but please don't say anything to your parents."

He nodded reluctantly, then stood and stepped out of the doorway. "Don't go anywhere. I'll be right back."

As if I had anywhere else to go.

Twenty minutes later, he came back with a backpack, and he'd changed into jeans and a sweatshirt. He unzipped the backpack and produced a pair of blue plaid flannel pajamas and some thick wool socks. He placed them in front of me.

"Put these on. I'll be back with a sleeping bag and pillow."

I waited until he had climbed back down, then I slipped out of Mom's dress and put on the much-too-large pajamas. I pulled the socks on my freezing feet, then peeked in the backpack to see bottled water and some granola bars. Despite the situation, I couldn't help but smile.

Thomas tossed in a sleeping bag and pillow, then disappeared for a couple minutes before returning with another sleeping bag and pillow.

"What are you doing?" I asked as he spread out two sleeping bags on the floor.

"I'm not letting you sleep up here alone."

"I've slept up here alone countless times before."

"But I didn't know it at the time. Now I know. So you're not sleeping up here alone."

"What about your parents? Do they know where you are?"

"It's taken care of."

"Did you tell them?"

"No."

"Then what did you say?"

"Doesn't matter. All that matters is that you're safe and warm. And not alone."

"What about your mom? Won't she be worried about—"

"Aria." He put his hand on my shoulder. "You need to stop worrying. She'll be fine. She knows I won't be coming home until morning. Okay?"

I stared at him, speechless. I'd never known someone so selfless, who seemed to care about me more than he cared about himself. I knew there was no point in trying to convince him to let me sleep here alone, so I slid into my sleeping bag and let my head sink into the soft pillow. I winced from the sting lingering on my cheek, and I applied my cold hand to soothe it.

He sat beside me, gently sweeping the hair from my cheek and neck. "I wish I could make it better," he murmured.

I drew in a deep breath, calmed by the comforting tone of his voice. "Remember that song you sang to me at the piano a few weeks ago?" I asked.

He was quiet for a moment, then said, "Yes, I remember."

"Will you sing it to me again?"

He slid into his sleeping bag and lay next to me, lacing his fingers through mine. Stroking my hand, he began quietly singing, his soothing tones joining the rhythmic sounds of the night. His song tugged at my heart and beckoned to me, and I drew nearer to him. He smiled and opened his arm, inviting me in. I lay my head on his chest, listening to the beating of his heart and the sound of his voice, and let all my troubles drift away on the wings of his song.

♪ ♪ ♪ ♪ ♪ ♪ ♪

The first thing I saw when I opened my eyes in the morning was Thomas sitting against the tree house wall, arms resting on his knees, the glow of early morning softening the edges of his figure. His eyes were troubled, and fastened on me. I met his look with a smile, my insides tingling at the memory of being in his arms the night before.

"Good morning," he said softly. A little smile passed across his lips before his expression became serious again. "I was thinking—I should come home with you this morning."

It was a terrible idea. I didn't know how Dad would react, and I didn't want to find out. I sat up and twisted my messy hair until it looked like a frayed rope. "You don't need to. I'm working today, so I'll go home just long enough to change. I'll be fine."

"Like you were fine last night?"

My hand instinctively came to the tender bulge on my cheek, and I winced in pain. "He's probably sleeping right now," I said. "I'm sure he was up all night."

"And if he's not?"

"Then he'll be too hungover to get out of bed." I slid out of the sleeping bag. Mom's dress lay nearby on the floor, and I folded it and placed it in a cabinet where it would be safe for now. When I glanced back at Thomas, his expression was full of doubt. "He's not going to hurt me again,"

I assured, "at least not today. He's going to feel bad about what happened. He'll say sorry and try to do something nice to make up for it."

A muscle in Thomas's jaw tightened, and he folded his arms across his chest. "How do you know?"

"Because I've been through this enough times to know how he works. I promise, I'll be okay. If you want to help me, you'll stay here. It'll just complicate things if you come home with me."

He hesitated, then said, "Can I at least give you a ride to work?"

I nodded. "I'll go home and change, then meet you at the end of your driveway."

As I walked to my house, the wind moved restlessly around me, stirring up the smell of dirt. Dark clouds billowed in the western sky, moving toward me, blanketing the blue sky like a shade sliding over a sunroof. I entered through the back door, hesitating on the threshold. The wind rattled the windows in the kitchen, and the last sunlight shining through them slowly darkened, smothered by storm clouds.

With a pounding heart, I crept into the kitchen, ears peeled for any sound. I'd told Thomas that Dad wouldn't hurt me. But now I realized how uncertain I was about that. I'd never seen Dad as upset as he was the night before, and maybe he was lurking around a corner with a knife, ready to plunge it into my heart.

The parlor door was wide open when I stepped into the living room, and just as raindrops started pelting the windows, I noticed a white, narrow rectangular block lying on the floor. "No," I mouthed. I moved slowly across the floor, strangely unable to feel my legs beneath me. The closer I got to the parlor and the more that came into view, the more my body began to tremble.

Piano keys on the floor, broken in pieces. The entire lid detached, leaning against the wall and a broken window. The shiny lacquer cracked and dented like it had been pummeled with a baseball bat.

My mind fought against the image, my hands clenched at my sides. I shut my eyes and tried to calm myself, tried to slow my breaths, but I couldn't take in air fast enough, couldn't think beyond the deluge of pain that washed over me. Trying to escape it, I turned away from the parlor and floated numbly up the stairs, knowing I needed something from my room, but not remembering what. As I passed Dad's room, I saw him strewn out on the carpet, face down. His back expanded and deflated slowly, rhythmically. A crow bar lay on the floor next to his legs.

I backed away slowly and turned into my room, only to find it in complete disarray. Every piece of furniture was turned over, the contents of my drawers scattered over the floor. Lightning flashed in the window, followed by deafening thunder cracking over the house.

At my feet lay Mom's music notebook, torn into a thousand pieces.

I didn't know why I was there. All I knew was that I no longer had the strength to stand. I sank to the floor, into a nest made of Mom's shredded music. I picked up a piece and stared at it in my open hand. In the notes and rests, the staff lines and tempo marks, I saw myself. And in the ragged edge that broke the music in half, I saw Dad.

Another bright flash filled the room, and raucous thunder rattled the window, shaking me to the core and striking down what was left of my strength.

Sorrow bore down on me, crushing me to the floor until I lay curled up, debilitated with despair. I shut my eyes, thinking that if I never opened them again, I wouldn't have to see again what Dad had done. I pressed my hands over my ears, trying to block out the sound of my own anguished cries.

♪ ♪ ♪ ♪ ♪♪♪

I felt someone kneel beside me, but I couldn't lift my head or open my eyes. I wanted to stay where it was dark and pretend I was somewhere else, someone else. There was a soft touch on my back and the sound of Thomas's voice speaking my name, but I couldn't move.

I heard the creak of steps, the sound of someone moving about the room. I heard my closet door slide open, and a zipping sound. I pried my eyes open a sliver, and through blurred vision I saw Thomas's feet walking back and forth, his arms carrying things, putting them in a bag on the bed. I shut my eyes again.

I felt Thomas's hand on my shoulder again. "I'm taking you away from here." His voice was gentle. "I have some of your clothes and your school stuff. Is there anything else you need?"

*Taking you away.* The words echoed in my mind, reverberating and gathering energy. *Away. Away.*

The power in his words washed through me, and I found the strength to sit up and look at him. He was crouched at my side, his face a duality of encouragement and worry. His lips straightened into a sad smile. "Let's go," he whispered, offering me his hand. His blue eyes offered conviction and strength, and I held his gaze, trying to glean the courage I needed to take an unknown path. I didn't know where I would go, but as I glanced around my overturned room again and thought about Mom's piano downstairs, I knew I couldn't stay.

A low moan came from the hall, and I turned to see Dad standing in the doorway, face twisted up like someone was holding a rotten fish under his nose.

"What are you doing?" He spoke slowly, still too hungover to function at normal speed. His hair was a firebomb, and his face a shade of red to match.

Thomas was suddenly standing in front of me. "She's leaving," he said with firmness.

Dad's eyes swept over my room and widened as he took in the extent of damage. His gaze finally landed on the bulging duffel bag near Thomas's feet, and understanding lit up his face. For a split second, sadness and regret curled around the edges of his mouth. "She's not going anywhere," Dad said, his expression hardening again. He pointed at Thomas. "But you are. Go home, Thomas."

"I'm not going anywhere without her." His voice was calm but unyielding.

"If you don't get out of here," Dad said, his voice growing louder, "I'm gonna—"

"You're going to what?" Thomas tossed back. "Hit me the way you hit your daughter?" He opened his arms. "Go ahead. Hit me. Then you'll be charged with child abuse *and* assault."

Dad stood there, huffing through his nostrils like a provoked bull, his bloodshot eyes staring Thomas down. I could see his mind turning like a tornado, trying to pluck useful words or actions from the storm inside him. But he must have ultimately seen that Thomas would stand his ground, because the storm weakened. The huffing slowed,

his shoulders slumped. "Go ahead," he said, his voice flat and defeated. "I should have let you go a long time ago."

"She's not coming back," Thomas said. "And if you try to contact her again, in any way, I'm reporting you to the authorities."

Dad just stared at the floor and said nothing.

"Aria," Thomas said, keeping his eyes on Dad and stretching a hand out to me, "you ready?"

I looked around my room. There were still clothes and books and knickknacks I'd collected over the years, but at the moment, they seemed worthless. The only thing I wanted was my freedom.

I put my hand in Thomas's and he pulled me to my feet. Grabbing the duffel bag, he took me by the hand and led me out of the room.

As we walked past Dad, a rage ignited inside of me. A rage that had been pent up and gradually swelling over the past five years. It suddenly broke free with explosive power. I ripped my hand from Thomas's and turned and charged Dad. I shoved him in the chest with all my strength and he stumbled back, his face stunned. "How could you!" I cried. "How could you do that to her piano? And her notebook! They were all I had left of her!" The dumbfounded look on his face only fueled the fire inside me, and I stepped into him, swinging my fists wildly, not even sure where my blows were landing. He lifted his arms in front of his face, completely on the defense for once. "I hate you!" I screamed and stepped back. There were so many things I wanted to say, so many emotions burning inside, so many whys I couldn't put words to.

I felt Thomas's hand on my arm, and I turned to see his pleading, anxious expression. He slid his arm around my waist and led me down the stairs and outside into the rain.

We walked down the lane through a canopy of blazing red maple trees, and rain dripped from the leaves onto our heads and shoulders. I shivered from the wet chill.

"I'll go get my car," he said as we neared his driveway. He handed me my duffle bag, then turned and jogged away.

I sidled up to the trunk of a maple tree to keep out of sight. My entire body trembled. I set down the duffle bag, and soon found myself sitting beside it. I clutched the handle like it was a lifeline. It and its meager contents were all I had left. The magnitude and uncertainty of my situation washed over me, and I felt like a lost child in a sea of people at a train station. I didn't know which train to get on, which one would take me home.

I squeezed my eyes shut, trying to push out the fear, and instead focused on the pattering of rain on the maple leaves. It sounded like applause, congratulating me for standing up to Dad, for setting myself free.

The rumble of Thomas's Bronco joined the sound of rain, and I opened my eyes to see him standing before me with an outstretched hand. He picked up my duffle bag and pulled me to my feet. Once in his Bronco, we rolled down the lane with the wipers on. He stopped at the highway and handed me his cell phone.

"What's this for?" I asked.

"You're calling in sick."

I debated a moment. I was still wearing Thomas's damp pajamas. My cheek was swollen and my eyes puffy from crying. My hair was snarled and my makeup non-existent. I'd have to explain myself to Dirk. Dirk, who'd tried to kiss me the night before. And I didn't have a home anymore, so

I probably needed to spend the day figuring out where I'd be living from now on.

I dialed Pikes Pancake House, and Dirk answered. I told him I had what Trisha had. It wasn't really a lie. I did have what Trisha had. I had caught Thomas, an incurable condition that made my heart, stomach, and lungs do all sorts of unnatural things.

Thomas had pulled onto the highway while I spoke with Dirk, and now we were driving southeast. "Where are we going?" I asked.

"For a drive," he said. "Until we can think of some place better."

Nothing came to mind, so I settled into the seat and gazed out the window, still too shaken to think productively. We drove along in silence, passing blurs of pine and rock and highway dividers. Every time I tried to think of where to go, I was overcome with a frightening sense of falling. So I focused instead on the feel of my feet on the floor and the warmth of Thomas's hand around mine.

As we neared Colorado Springs, Thomas squeezed my hand gently. "We should stop and get something to eat. Then we can figure out what to do."

I glanced down at my pajamas—Thomas's pajamas—and shook my head. "I need to change."

"I'll pull over at the next exit and get out so you can change."

As he pulled off the highway, I realized we were only a few streets away from Nathaniel's house. An idea came to me then. "Wait. Let's go to Nathaniel's."

He looked at me uncertainly. "Are you sure?"

I nodded. "He can help."

We arrived at Nathaniel's a few minutes later, and

Thomas walked with me to the door. I rang the doorbell, and after some shuffling inside, the door opened, and Nathaniel stood there with a piece of paper and pencil in his hand.

"Aria?" Nathaniel said with surprise as his eyes swept over me. "You look awful. I don't want to sound rude, but what happened to your face?"

I glanced into his house to see if he had a student, but it was clear. "Can we come in?"

"Of course. Come in." He put his paper and pencil on the piano and gestured to the sofa. We sat, and Nathaniel stood in front of us with arms folded across his chest. "What's going on?"

I bit my lip and looked at Thomas for strength, and he took my hand in his.

"Some things happened last night," I started.

"Obviously," Nathaniel said, his lips thinning in anger. "Did Jed do that to you?"

I nodded.

"I knew it. I knew that sad excuse of a man wasn't fit to be a father. I should go over there and—"

"Thomas already threatened him," I said, holding up a hand.

"And Aria pummeled him with her fists," Thomas added.

"Good, good! I'm sorry I wasn't there to see it!"

I lowered my eyes. "So, I was wondering if I could hang out here today. I just need somewhere safe where I can figure out what to do. I mean, I'll probably need to pick up more hours at work and find a cheap apartment and . . ." I paused, checking the emotion rising in my voice.

Nathaniel dropped his chin into his hand and started

slowly pacing the room. "If you pick up more hours, you'll have less time to practice. You're coming along so well, but getting your own place right now would just throw a wrench in your spokes."

"I know. But I don't know what else to do. I can't go back home."

"I didn't say you should go back home. In fact, that would be worse than getting your own place."

The doorbell rang, making my heart plummet to my feet as I pictured Dad on the other side of the door.

"I'm expecting a student," Nathaniel reassured. "Have you two had breakfast? There's oatmeal and cereal in the pantry. Why don't you go in the kitchen and make yourselves at home, and we'll talk some more after my student leaves."

Thomas and I went to the kitchen, and I sat by the window at a small mahogany table overlooking a garden bursting with fall perennials. Thomas opened the pantry door and perused its contents. I heard Nathaniel's student come in, a chatty girl who gave him a rundown of her week before they started their lesson. She began playing a Clementi piece that I'd learned as a child, and although she got the notes right, it sounded mechanical, like a music box.

"What do you feel like eating?" Thomas asked. "I can make you some oatmeal, or he's got a big selection of fiber-rich cereals." He turned to look at me, and I made a queasy face.

He came and sat across from me, and with a worried crease between his brows, he opened my hand and gently rubbed his thumb over my palm. "Do you have grandparents somewhere?"

I shook my head. "They're all gone."

"Aunts? Uncles? Cousins?"

"A few, but we're not close, and they live across the country."

Nathaniel's student finished playing the Clementi piece, and there was a long pause before I heard Nathaniel say, "Good. Um, yes. That was . . . that was fine. Let's move on to the Chopin piece."

"I didn't have a Chopin piece this week," the student said. "Do you mean Bach?"

"Oh. Right. That's what I meant. Let's hear the Bach." It was apparent that Nathaniel was distracted, and I felt bad that because of me, his student wouldn't get the instruction she needed.

"What about friends?" Thomas asked. "You're pretty close to Vivian, aren't you?"

I considered a moment. "She would probably let me stay with her, but . . . I don't know. It's too close to my dad, and it would be awkward living with someone who has the hots for him."

Thomas's eyebrows rose a second before they went back to being furrowed. He pulled his smart phone from his back pocket and began tapping at the screen.

"What are you doing?"

"Maybe we can find someone who's looking for a roommate, or renting a single room so the rent is inexpensive."

We spent the next thirty minutes searching in vain for an apartment or room that would fit in my meager budget, while Nathaniel's student serenaded us with parlor music.

Finally the music stopped, and I heard the student leave. Nathaniel returned to the kitchen, mumbling something like "painful." After acknowledging us with a brief smile, he began pacing the travertine floor.

"I've been thinking," he said after a long silence, steepling his hands to his chin. "You need somewhere safe to stay. And if you're going to get into Juilliard, you need somewhere you have access to a piano, where you can practice as much as you need. And somewhere free, so you don't have to pick up more hours at work."

"I'm open to suggestions," I said.

He came and joined us at the table, sitting kitty-corner to me. "Does your dad know you're here?" Nathaniel asked.

"No," I said. "But he found out I'm taking lessons from you."

His eyebrows slanted into a frown. "Well, hopefully he won't come around here looking for you. But just to be safe, it's probably best if no one, other than Thomas here, knows where you are." He drummed his fingers on the mahogany surface, then leveled an intense gaze at me. "I guess what I'm saying is, what if you moved here? I mean, I know you've only known me for a couple months, and I don't want to make you feel uncomfortable or anything, but it seems like the best solution."

I glanced at Thomas, and he gave me an encouraging nod.

"You can take some time to think about it, of course." Nathaniel said. "And you're welcome to stay here until you make a decision."

I thought for a moment and realized that I couldn't have imagined a better solution. I slowly nodded, and tears seemed to spring out of nowhere. I was so relieved, so grateful for his kindness, I didn't know what to say.

Nathaniel patted my hand and smiled. "All right, then." He leaned back in his chair and rubbed his jaw thoughtfully. "I don't have an extra bed, but we could go pick one up today. We can put it in my office, since I do most of my work at the piano anyway. But we'll need to move some furniture around. Thomas, do you think you can help with that?"

Thomas nodded, and from his relieved expression I could tell he was as grateful as I was for Nathaniel's generosity.

"Thank you, Nathaniel," I said as I swiped at my tears. "I don't know how I'll ever repay you."

"It's the least I can do for my best student." He smiled, and his face softened into a rueful expression. "And for her mother."

# twelve

We fell into a new routine over the next couple weeks. Thomas woke up extra early to pick me up for school each day. Some days he'd bring me back to Nathaniel's after school, and other days I came home with him. We'd do our homework and have dinner with his parents, then I'd practice on the upright in his basement while he painted. On clear nights, we'd bundle up and climb to the tree house and talk for hours under a blanket of stars.

Nathaniel convinced me to quit my job at Pikes, reasoning that I needed as much practice time as I could get if I was going to get into Juilliard. It was a change I gladly welcomed.

After an intense week going through a stack of sheet music that was almost taller than me, Nathaniel and I finally selected six pieces to perform at my Juilliard audition. Then the real work began. My music came with me wherever I went. On the stage during lunch hour, in Thomas's basement, in Nathaniel's living room, I practiced the pieces again and again. Days were filled with music, a string of notes tied together in one monumental loop. The notes became a part of me. My fingers moved in my sleep and trilled on my desk at school, and the melodies hummed in my soul. I dreamed of Bach's *The Well-Tempered Clavier*, sweet and flowing like a lullaby. I saw Beethoven's *Appassionata* as I scribbled out math equations, and I heard Schubert's *4 Impromptus* whenever Thomas laced his fingers through mine.

Nathaniel taught me how to add layers of nuance and to use my own intuition to phrase and shape the music. He drilled me on articulation, pace, and rhythm. He taught me how to move my hands effortlessly across the keys, regardless of tempo. "Your arms should be a pendulum," he said, demonstrating with his hands. "Swing fast, swing slow, but swing."

But it was time that swung like a pendulum, rhythmically, effortlessly, swinging from morning to night and back again. Constant movement, never time to stop and look at the calendar.

With fingers crossed, we sent my prescreening video to Juilliard. And when we celebrated my audition invitation with a piano-shaped cake, I realized my life had become something new. There were moments when I felt like a different person, like I was living someone else's life. But each morning, the mirror testified that *I* was the one with a safe home, a musical mentor, and a stunningly handsome boy by my side.

There were moments of great fear and anxiety as well. Whenever I exited the school, my eyes scanned the parking lot for Dad's truck. I sunk low into my seat every time we passed Dad's house to go to Thomas's. And with each knock at Thomas's or Nathaniel's door, my heart thudded with dread, wondering if it was Dad at the door. But as the weeks passed without any sign of him, the tension in my nerves eased, and I accepted that maybe I was finally free of him.

♪ ♪ ♪ ♪ ♪ ♪

On Christmas Eve, Nathaniel was out of town visiting his parents. He'd offered to take me with him, but I stayed behind to spend Christmas with Thomas. Around six o'clock, Thomas showed up at my door, his cheeks adorably flushed from the cold. "My heater's on strike," he said with his hands balled in the pockets of his peacoat. My pulse stuttered as I took in the sight of him, and I wondered if I'd ever get used to the effect he had on me.

After bundling up, I climbed into his Bronco and we got on the road. The skies were clear, and snow-covered pines sparkled under the moon as we drove from Colorado Springs to Woodland Park.

"Sorry I was late picking you up," he said. "I've been working on your present."

I smiled, wondering what it could be, and looked down at the wrapped gift in my own hands. I'd bought him an encaustics stylus with twelve different tips for making different textures. I was sure he'd love it. I'd also knitted him a herringbone scarf, dark gray with blue specks to match his eyes. I still needed to bind and weave in the ends, so I'd left it in my room, intending to finish it later that night.

When we arrived at his house, we got out of the Bronco to see Vivian stepping off the front porch. She waved excitedly and rushed over to greet us. "Aria!" She threw her arms around me. "Where have you been, darlin'?"

"I moved in with a friend," I explained, pulling back.

"Why?" She grabbed my arm. "What's going on?"

I gave a little shrug. "I'm just happier this way."

"Why, sweetheart? Your daddy not treatin' you nice?"

"Let's just say we're better off without each other."

She shook her head. "I'm so sorry. Why didn't you say somethin'? You know you're welcome at my place anytime."

"I know, Vivian. Thanks."

"You know, I brought some cherry mash bars over to your daddy last week, and he didn't say anything about it. I asked where you were, and he just said that you'd been real busy."

"Maybe he doesn't want anyone to know. Anyway, it doesn't matter. I'm sure he's glad I'm gone."

"I don't know about that, honey. He seems real down. I always see him moping around the yard and sitting on the front porch staring at nothin'. Maybe he misses you."

"I doubt it," I muttered.

"Well, maybe you should wish him a merry Christmas all the same."

"Vivian," Thomas said, "would you like to have dinner at our house tonight?"

She waved a hand, brushing away his suggestion like it was a pesky fly. "Your mom already asked me, but I'll be fine on my own. I'm so full of cookie dough right now, I probably couldn't fit dinner in me anyway. Besides, I still have a dozen plates of treats to deliver." She wished us merry Christmas and walked away humming.

The familiar scent of pine greeted us as we stepped into Thomas's house. In his newly renovated living room, glittering wreaths and garlands adorned the walls and fireplace. Gold ribbons, beads, and twinkling lights trimmed

the tree, which sat cozily in a nest of wrapped gifts. There were poinsettias and snow globes and all the warm glitz of Christmas.

As we sat around the dinner table spread with an abundance of food, my thoughts turned to Dad. I watched the loving way Hal talked to Thomas and felt a sense of loss as I recalled what a good father Dad had been before Mom died. I tried to imagine what he was doing tonight. Maybe he was at a bar, drowning his miserable holiday in brandy. Maybe he was gutting a reindeer in the barn. Or maybe he was sitting alone on the couch, staring at the wall where we used to put the Christmas tree, wishing he still had a family.

After dinner, we gathered around the crackling fireplace and I did my best to participate in their conversation about the possible effects of antimatter in black holes. Although I felt immensely happy spending Christmas Eve with Thomas's family, a sad feeling kept poking at me. No matter how much I tried, I couldn't ignore the empty place inside me where my own family had once resided.

I reflected on what Christmas was like in my younger years, when Dad twirled me in front of the Christmas tree and Mom filled the house with sparkling lights, beautiful music, and ribboned boxes under the tree. Those gifts meant nothing to me now. I would give them up in a heartbeat if I could exchange them for my family—the way it was before Mom died.

I glanced at Thomas, the lines of his face glowing in the light of the fire, the curve of his lashes creating soft shadows in his blue eyes. I focused on the sensation caused by his thumb stroking the top of my hand. Soothing, reassuring. This Christmas, he was my gift.

A knock at the door pulled me from my meditation, and as Elsie rose to answer it, I wondered if Vivian had changed her mind about spending Christmas Eve alone. But when the door swung open and Elsie released an uncharacteristic squeal of excitement, I knew it had to be someone else.

Into the living room stepped a young man, pulling a suitcase in one hand and catching his mother's embrace with the other. "Richard!" she said with laughter in her voice. "Why didn't you tell us you were coming?"

We all rose from the sofa to greet Thomas's older brother. He was shorter than Thomas, but his bright eyes and chiseled facial features affirmed they were brothers. He looked to be in his early twenties, and his jet-black hair was messily spiked all over his head. A small silver ring pierced his eyebrow, and the head of a snake tattoo slithered from the shadow of his coat collar.

Thomas's hand grasped mine, and I glanced up at him, just now noticing how tense he appeared. His hand was stiff, and as he locked eyes with Richard, his stance straightened defensively as though bracing for a fight.

With her arm still around Richard's waist, Elsie looked lovingly into his face and murmured, "It's so good to have you home." She turned and introduced me, and Richard nodded a greeting but didn't smile. His expression was menacing as he gave me the once-over. I felt self-conscious under his gaze, and I turned into Thomas, who put his arm around me protectively.

"I hope you're hungry," Elsie said, "because we have plenty of leftovers." She left the living room to go heat up a plate for Richard, and Hal went upstairs to prepare a bed for him. For a long moment after their parents had left the room, Thomas and Richard locked eyes as though some unseen challenge were occurring between them.

"So," Richard finally said, eyeing me again, "this must be the consolation prize."

The words surprised me, and not knowing how to take them, I looked up at Thomas for an explanation. But he didn't explain. And the tense look on his face told me that Richard's words weren't meant as light-hearted banter.

"Shut up, Richard," Thomas growled. "You don't know what you're talking about."

"Actually, I do." He winked at me.

"You must be home because your sentence was up," Thomas said. "Because they never would have let you out of the slammer for good behavior."

Richard smiled. "You never were very good at comebacks."

Hal came down the stairs and went to Richard's side, patting him on the back. "Hey, Rich, I've got a bed made up for you upstairs. Why don't we take your suitcase up there?"

Richard tore his eyes away from Thomas and followed his dad upstairs, dragging his suitcase behind him. Thomas looked after Richard with an indignant expression I hadn't seen since the night Dad had hurt me. After a long moment, his shoulders lowered and his expression relaxed. He turned to me. "Sorry," he said. "Richard and I don't exactly get along."

I was still stinging from Richard's "consolation prize" comment. "Why not?" I asked, hoping his answer would explain Richard's words.

He opened his mouth to say something, but then closed

it, as though something he saw in my face made him change his mind. "Just one too many rifts."

"Rifts about what?"

He sighed hard and pushed a hand through his hair, then tilted his head toward the sofa. "Let's sit down." We sat, my mouth turning dry from the fear of what he might tell me.

"Aria . . . I . . ." His eyes were pained, almost terrified, and he leaned in and rested his forehead against my temple. I could feel his warm breaths on my cheek, their shallowness betraying his anxiety.

"You can trust me, you know?" I whispered, echoing the words he'd once said to me.

He leaned back and smiled at me, but his expression was still wary. "I know." He took my hand in his and rubbed his thumb over my knuckle. "We were in a car accident a couple years ago, and even though he was driving, he blames me."

I reached out and touched the scar above his brow. "Is that how you got this?"

He nodded.

"What other rifts?" I asked, looking specifically for an explanation for Richard's comment. But when Thomas remained silent, I asked a more pointed question. "What did he mean when he said I was your consolation prize?"

"You're not a consolation prize for anything. Richard just likes to stir things up."

"But he was referring to something."

"It's nothing—it doesn't matter."

"If it doesn't matter, then you can tell me."

Thomas gazed at the Christmas tree, the sparkling lights reflecting in his troubled eyes. "He was referring to Sasha."

I felt a pang in my heart at the sound of another girl's name on his lips. She must have been the girl in the painting on his wall. I wanted to ask him who she was, but couldn't bring myself to say her name. So I waited, hoping he would explain.

"She was my friend," he continued. "We grew up across the street from each other. And when I was fifteen, my feelings for her started to change into more than friendship. And that's when Richard swooped in and swept her off her feet."

"Did he know you had . . . feelings for her?"

"Yeah, but he insisted it wasn't about competition. He told me he'd had feelings for her since junior high." He shrugged. "Maybe he did, but he never showed it before then."

"And then he got her pregnant?"

He nodded. "He treated her like a burden after that. She used to call me up and cry about it. I tried to get her to break up with him, but I think she really loved him."

He stroked the top of my hand while I sat there, suddenly feeling terrified. What if he had loved Sasha more than he admitted? What if he still loved her? Her painting was still on his wall. Was he still grieving over losing her to his brother? I felt my own breaths quicken, and I tried to subdue the emotion rising in my throat. He must have noticed because he pulled back and looked into my face.

"Aria," he said gently, lifting my chin so that I would meet his gaze, "you have nothing to worry about."

I must not have looked convinced, because he tucked a piece of hair behind my ear and said, "You have to understand, when she started dating him, I backpedaled and left my feelings at friendship." He gathered me in his arms and fastened his gaze on me. "So what he said has absolutely no merit. You're not a consolation prize. You're . . ." His face was close to mine, his voice soft. "You're a rare treasure, that I was lucky enough to find." He placed a gentle kiss on my forehead, then looked at me again. "Do you believe me?"

I shrugged. "I guess so."

He smiled sadly, then stood and reached for my hand. "Come downstairs with me. I need to show you something." We went downstairs to his room, where he turned on the light and led me to his desk. A painting lay on his desk, and I gasped when I saw the subject.

It was my house, how it looked in the spring before Mom died. White jasmine grew up the side of the porch, peace roses hugged the railing, and fuchsia blossoms bloomed from peach trees in the side yard. In the window of the parlor, a dark-haired girl sat playing at the piano. A boy with dark hair sat on the porch swing outside.

He sat on the stool and took my hand. "I've been working on it for weeks," he said quietly. "I hope you like it."

"Who's that?" I whispered, pointing to the boy.

He didn't answer, but from the way he was looking at me, I knew that the boy in the painting was him.

"I know I can't replace what you've lost," he said, "but maybe someday I can give you something similar."

*Or better,* I thought.

"Did I get it right?" he asked. "I mean, how it used to be?"

I swiped at a runaway tear and scanned the painting, amazed at how much he'd gotten right. But there was one thing missing. I pointed to the windows. "There were window boxes with orange marigolds." I couldn't seem to speak louder than a whisper.

He reached down to plug in his heat tools. He melted some brown and orange wax on his iron and stamped the edge of my painting just below the windows. Then he went back with a stylus and added more lines and texture. "Is that better?"

I couldn't speak. I couldn't figure out how I'd gotten so lucky to have Thomas. He knew my heart, my soul, what I needed to hear and see to feel healed, whole, at home. I nodded and gazed into his eyes. He put down his stylus and wrapped his arms around my waist, resting his head against mine.

"I've been thinking," he murmured. "There's a good astronomy program at Columbia University."

"But I thought you wanted to study art in Paris."

"Paris is more than three thousand miles away from Juilliard. And Columbia is only three."

I pulled back and stared at him, my pulse racing with the realization of what he was saying. He was making long-term plans. With me.

"I want to be where you are, Aria." He pulled me into his lap and brushed my hair over my shoulder. "I already sent in my application, and my mom is calling one of her colleagues there next week to try to pull some strings."

"But what if you decide you want to do art instead?"

"There are a lot of art schools in New York."

"What if I don't make it into Juilliard?"

"You will."

"What if—"

"'What if' doesn't matter," he said, cutting me off with his finger over my lips. "Let's replace 'what if' with 'even if.' "

"Even if?"

"We will be together, *even if* I don't get into Columbia. *Even if* I scrap my astronomy plans. *Even if* you don't get into Juilliard—which you will. *Even if* anything. I would follow you around the world if I had to." Then leaning his forehead against mine, he whispered, "Because I love you."

The words washed through me, cleansing any remaining fear or doubt. I pulled away and looked into his blue eyes. Just like the first time I gazed into them, they were full of untold stories. Only this time, I could easily read them. They were stories of us together, in the future. Bent over our newborn baby, stealing hushed smiles at each other. Watching our children open presents on Christmas morning. Sitting together in a sunny room, me at the piano, him in front of an easel, his hands wrinkled and discolored with age. All the while, his painting hanging above our fireplace mantel. Story after story, going on forever. It no longer mattered what I'd lost. In Thomas, I could have all I'd lost and more.

"Now do you believe me?" he asked.

I opened his hand and placed a kiss in the center of his palm, then whispered, "I love you too."

He closed his eyes as though taking a moment to absorb my words, then gently curled his hand around the nape of my neck. He leaned down and brushed his lips over mine, a soft and unhurried kiss I wished could last forever. When he pulled away, I wrapped my arms around his neck and drew him nearer, wanting to linger in the exquisite sensation his touch produced. He didn't object.

When the wax on his painting had cooled, he rolled up the canvas and gave it to me. The house was quiet and dark as we went upstairs, and figuring everyone had gone to bed, we spoke in hushed voices as we went outside to get in his

Bronco. Thomas started the engine and I set the canvas in the back seat, but I couldn't bring myself to climb in. I stared through the moonlit night in the direction of Dad's house, and I had an overwhelming desire to go check up on him.

"You want to go say hi?" Thomas asked as if reading my thoughts.

"It's Christmas Eve," I shrugged. "It wouldn't hurt to wish him a merry Christmas."

Thomas cut the engine and nodded. "I'll go with you."

We walked down the tree-lined street, ice crunching beneath our feet in the silent night. He took my hand and smiled at me, like he could sense how nervous I was. He lifted my hand and kissed it. "It'll be okay."

When we reached Dad's house, all the lights were off, but we stepped onto the porch and I knocked anyway.

"Do you think he's working tonight?" Thomas asked when there was no answer.

"Maybe." I stepped off the porch. "I'll see if his truck is here." I began circling the house, but I stopped in front of the parlor window and looked inside. The room was unchanged since the last time I'd seen it, the window still broken, the floor littered with pieces of Mom's piano.

Thomas must have seen the hurt look on my face because he came and folded his arms around me. "You know," he murmured into my hair, "it's possible that he'll change someday. Maybe someday your relationship with him will be mended."

"I doubt it," I said. "He's broken, and a broken man can't be fixed."

"Yes, he can. Someone will come along and give him what he needs, mend his wounds, and he'll be almost as good as new." He sighed. "That's what you've done for me, Aria. So I know it's possible for him as well."

I looked up at him, wanting him to elaborate, but something else caught my attention. The sky behind him was lit up with a strange orange glow. He must have seen the wonder in my face, because he turned around to see what I was looking at.

It only took two seconds for us to register what it meant.

"Fire!" Thomas yelled as he broke into a sprint toward his house.

# thirteen

I raced down the road behind Thomas, slipping and stumbling on ice as I went. Through the trees, I saw flames consuming the second floor of his house, black smoke billowing out through broken windows. He got there long before I did, and I found him on the porch, alternating between kicking and slamming his body into the front door. When he saw me, he stopped just long enough to fling his cell phone at me.

"Call 911!"

The phone slipped through my shaking fingers, and I fished it out of the snow, my hands taking much longer than they should to place the call. As I shouted instructions to the dispatcher, Thomas picked up a chair on the porch and launched it through a window. The glass shattered, and smoke came pouring out. A second later, the front door opened, and a figure came rushing out, coughing and choking.

It was Richard. He stumbled to his knees on the porch.

"Where are Mom and Dad?" Thomas shouted.

He couldn't seem to get any words out between coughing and gasping, so he pointed in the house. Thomas charged into the house, disappearing into the smoke.

"Thomas!" I screamed, tossing the phone at Richard and running in after him. Instantly, the smoke blinded me and choked my breath. I found Thomas with my outstretched hands and threw myself at him, pulling on his coat. My own strength surprised me. I didn't know what I was doing; I just knew I couldn't bear to lose him. He ripped my hands from his coat and pushed me back out of the house, throwing me down on the porch. "Stay here!" he yelled, then rushed back into the house.

Without thinking about consequences, I ran back into the house. "Thomas!" I managed to scream before the smoke hit my lungs. I dropped to the floor. I tried to call his name again, but my voice was squashed by a deafening crash. Black ash and flames flurried around me, blinding me. A sudden wave of heat washed over me, and it felt like my skin was on fire. I couldn't breathe, couldn't see, but I inched my way farther into the fire. I couldn't go back, not without Thomas.

The smoke closed in on me, filling my mouth, my nose, my lungs. I was drowning in a black, boiling sea, unable to surface for breath. I wanted to call out his name, but I didn't have any air to exhale. So I searched with my arm, waving and reaching, crawling and groping. It grew hotter and darker until I was on the threshold of consciousness. Sirens wailed in the distance, but I knew the firefighters were too late. His parents were gone. Thomas was probably gone. And I might be gone too. In a delirious dream-state, I thought I saw Thomas's face. But then the image turned into black vapor, and I knew it was only

a matter of time before the rest of him vanished into a puff of smoke.

For days after the fire, I stumbled through a haze, each moment spent trying to decipher what was real. My skin was stained with the smell of smoke, of death, constantly testifying that what had happened was real. Thomas's parents had died an unspeakable death. He had tried to save them and failed.

Thomas spent a few days in the hospital for smoke inhalation and a third-degree burn on his arm, and I didn't see him much in the two weeks after the fire. He stayed at a motel while he worked with the fire department and tried to plan his parents' funeral. I spent my days worrying about him, wondering how he was feeling, and spent each night reliving the fire in horrendous detail.

One night I dreamed that Thomas hadn't survived the fire. I saw the firefighters carry him out on a stretcher, his body burned and lifeless, and I woke up in a cold sweat, my cheeks wet with tears.

With a trembling hand, I reached through the darkness for the phone at my bedside. I had to hear his voice, had to know my dream wasn't real. I dialed his number and put the phone to my ear.

It rang. And rang. And rang.

"Hey."

I heaved a sigh of relief, then bit my lip to keep tears at bay. "Did I wake you?"

There was a long pause, followed by, "No."

"Can't sleep?"

"No."

"Can I come see you?"

"You don't have to. It's the middle of the night." His voice was flat, emotionless. It terrified me.

"I want to. I'll borrow Nathaniel's car."

He sighed, and in the long silence that followed, I mouthed the word *please* a dozen times. "I'll come see you tomorrow," he finally said.

After we hung up, I got up and paced my room, worrying about him. He wasn't sleeping. He was alone. I had an overwhelming feeling that he needed me, so I got up and threw some clothes on. I coiled the scarf I'd made for him around my neck and put on my coat, then left a note for Nathaniel and swiped the keys to his car. Twenty minutes later, I showed up at Thomas's motel. I parked next to his Bronco and knocked lightly on his door.

When the door opened and I saw Thomas, it was like coming up for air after being underwater for two weeks. He looked pale and his face seemed thinner, like he hadn't eaten for days. He tried to smile, but only managed to straighten his lips. I threw myself into his arms, assuring myself that he was still living and breathing.

After a long hug, he pulled me into his room and closed the door behind him.

"I'm sorry," I said. "I had to see you."

The bathroom light was on, casting a dim glow into the room.

"Where's Richard?" I asked.

"He went back to California." His voice was reserved, quiet. He stepped back and sat on the edge of the bed.

I took off my coat and the scarf, tossing them in a chair by the window, then sat beside him. He seemed tense, like if he relaxed, the weight on his shoulders would crush him.

I laced my fingers through his; they felt cold and lifeless. I wanted him to look at me and tell me everything he was feeling, but he kept his head down and his eyes on the floor.

"How are you?" I whispered, desperate to hear his voice.

It took him a long time to answer. "It was my fault," he finally whispered, so low I barely heard him.

"What do you mean?" I angled myself toward him and touched his forearm. He winced, and I realized there was a bandage on his arm where he'd been burned.

"The fire started downstairs. In my room."

"How do you know?"

"The fire chief told me. I left my heat tools on, and somehow . . ." He shook his head. "Somehow . . ." He leaned over and dropped his head into his hands. His back began shaking, and his sniffles filled the quiet room. "They're gone because of me."

"No," I said, shaking my head. "It was an accident."

He lay on the bed, and turning on his side, he burst into tears. I was curled behind him in an instant, sliding my arm under his neck and cradling his head against mine. I wrapped my other arm around his chest and felt his abdomen shake as he cried.

"Talk to me," I whispered.

"I . . . can't . . . ," he said between ragged breaths. I rubbed his chest and he drew in a stuttered lungful of air, trying to catch his breath. "I can't stop thinking," he cried. "I keep replaying that night over and over, calculating, reliving, trying to set things right. If I would have installed the smoke detectors like my dad asked. If the door wouldn't have been locked. If I could've found my stupid keys. If Richard would have woken up my parents before he saved himself. If you—"

My heart stopped as I registered what he was about to say. "If I hadn't pulled you back."

"I don't know. Maybe. Maybe I would've had time to get them before the second floor came down."

"Thomas, I'm so sorry. I . . . I didn't have time to think. I just didn't want to lose you."

"It doesn't matter. None of that would matter if I hadn't been so thoughtless and left on my heat tools." Another heartbreaking cry broke through his lips.

"Thomas . . ."

"Shhh. Don't, Aria. Don't." He put his hand on mine.

I stayed quiet, trying in vain to find words that might comfort him. Over the years, the pain from Mom's death had dulled somewhat, like an overused knife. But hearing Thomas crying and feeling him tremble in my arms sharpened my pain again. Not like the sting of a razor, but like a serrated blade, sawing back and forth, cutting deeper with each stroke. I saw myself in him, and I felt his pain because I knew it all too well. And I knew from experience that nothing I could say would make a dent in the agony he was feeling. So instead I kissed his head, stroked his hair, rubbed his chest.

I held him for the rest of the night, listening to him cry, feeling his body shake with each new wave of emotion. I cried my own silent tears, not wanting him to feel the need to comfort me. He finally drifted off to sleep in the early hours of morning, just as the sky started to light up. And when he fell asleep, I finally fell asleep too.

♪ ♪ ♪ ♪ ♪ ♪

It was late morning when I woke up, and Thomas was lying next to me on his side, still asleep. I propped myself

on my elbow and looked at him. I hadn't noticed the night before, but he was in his jeans and sweater, and his hiking boots were still on his feet. His hair was disheveled and his lips were dry and chapped, but his face was peaceful. I decided he needed to eat something, so I went to the motel office to get some continental breakfast. I loaded a tray with bagels, yogurt, and fruit, then added two tall glasses of orange juice.

He was sitting at the desk when I came into the room, spinning a pen on the surface. "I thought you could use some food," I said, setting the tray in front of him.

A fleeting smile passed across his lips when he saw the food, the first smile I'd seen from him since Christmas Eve. He picked up the orange juice and chugged the entire glass.

"You can have mine too," I said, placing it in front of him.

I sat on the bed with my legs folded beneath me and watched him pick at his food. He managed a few bites, then went back to spinning the pen, a troubled frown creasing his brow. I sensed the spinning pen mirrored what was going on in his own mind.

"The funeral is next Friday in Pasadena," he said, his voice quiet and somber.

"I'll come with you."

He turned to look at me. "You need to stay here and prepare for your audition. It's only weeks away."

"It doesn't matter. I'd rather be there for you."

He got up and sat next to me on the bed. "It does matter. You have to get into Juilliard. And you can't afford to miss a week of practice. It could make all the difference."

I raised a shoulder. "I'll be fine. And anyway, there's always next year."

He laid his hand on mine. "No. I want you to stay here."

He gave me a pleading look I couldn't argue with. A look that reached inside me and rattled something loose. His expression darkened, and he looked down at his hands. "Besides—I don't think I'll even go to the funeral."

"What?"

He stood and went to the window, where he stared through the pane and blew out a ragged breath. "What am I going to say to people when they ask what happened?"

I hesitated. "You're going to say it was an accident."

He shook his head, then mumbled something under his breath that sounded like, "They've already heard that one."

Wondering if I'd misheard, I rose and went to him. "What do you mean?"

He was quiet for a long time, then said, "Nothing." There was a despondency in his face I'd never seen before, and it sent an uneasy chill down my back. I searched for the words to reel him back in, to rescue him from the ravine he seemed lost in. But my seventeen-year-old mind had no wisdom to offer, no counsel to help him make sense of what he was feeling. All I could offer was myself. I wrapped my arms around his waist, and his hand fell on my back, but it felt stiff.

"Are you coming back here after the funeral?" I asked.

His silence answered the question.

I pulled away and stared at him. "You're not coming back?"

He released a sigh. "I'm going to stay in Pasadena until I graduate."

"But what about—"

"Our plans are still the same, Aria." He looked down at me. "I'll come get you in June, and we'll drive to New York together. We'll still be together, okay?"

"June is five months away. Why can't you just finish high school here?"

"Where am I going to live?"

"Where will you live if you go to Pasadena?"

"My parents still have a house there. Richard's moving in. That's one of the reasons I need to stay there for a while. My parents have a ton of stuff in their old house and in storage, and I need to go through it and decide what to do with everything. If I leave it up to Richard, he'll just pawn it all and spend it on drugs."

I felt my breath accelerate, my hands go cold. I thought about what he'd said the night before, how he might have had time to save his parents if I hadn't held him back. Maybe he was more angry with me than I realized. "Please . . ." The broken plea sounded desperate as it escaped my lips.

His eyes softened. "Aria," he groaned, "please don't make this harder than it already is."

"Please don't leave me," I whispered as my eyes filled with tears.

He put his palm on my cheek and wiped away the tears that were spilling over. "I can't stay," he said, tears brimming in his own eyes. "Right now I need to get as far away from here as I can."

I dropped my head.

"Listen to me," he whispered as he slid his hand behind my neck. "I love you. I could never live without you. I just . . . need to get away from here . . . to settle the storm that's whirling around in my head."

The only response I could muster was a sad, broken cry.

"Look," he said, "you're going to get accepted to Juilliard, and in the summer, I'll come pick you up."

I nodded as more tears rolled down my cheeks.

"Do you trust me?"

I nodded again.

"Then believe me when I say that I can't stay. Trust me that I will come back for you. Trust that we'll be together."

He leaned in and kissed me in a way that sealed his promise.

After packing his few things into a backpack, he slung it over his shoulder and opened the door, letting the morning sun and the cold winter air spill in. I put on my coat and picked up the scarf, then went and stood in front of him.

"I didn't get a chance to give this to you," I said, lifting it over his head and pulling it snug around his neck. I had been right: the blue in the scarf matched his eyes perfectly. "It was supposed to be for Christmas."

He looked down and picked up one end of the scarf, examining it. "Did you make it?"

I nodded.

His eyes glistened as they met mine. "Thank you," he whispered, pulling me into his arms.

We went out to where our cars were parked. He opened his car door and tossed his backpack on the passenger seat, then turned to look at me. "Aria, there's something else you need to know."

"What's that?"

He leaned against the driver seat and took one of my hands in his. "One of the firefighters told me . . . that your dad was the one who found you and carried you out. He saved your life."

I was speechless, stunned. I couldn't even begin to speculate what that meant. So I nodded and pushed it to the back of my mind, focusing instead on the fact that

Thomas was about to get in his Bronco and leave me for five months. He reached in the backseat, pulled out the painting he'd given me on Christmas Eve, and handed it to me. I took it, then leaned into him and wrapped my arms around him. He held me and planted a kiss in my hair. I clung to him, wishing I never had to let go, fearing that if I did, I'd never see him again.

"I love you," I whispered. "Promise me you'll come back."

"I'll see you in June," he finally said, pulling away from me.

"June." I tried to sound cheerful, but the word came out wrapped in despair. Then he got in his Bronco, pulled out of the parking lot, and disappeared.

# *fourteen*

After a couple weeks at school of people asking me where Thomas was, I went back to eating lunch by myself in the auditorium so I wouldn't have to explain what had happened or that I hadn't heard from him. I hadn't called him because I knew his plate was full, and I wanted to let him take care of things at home without worrying about me. He had Nathaniel's number. He would call when he was ready to talk.

To keep my mind off Thomas, I thought about Dad instead, contemplating and analyzing just what it meant that he'd saved my life. Did it mean he cared about me after all? Did he rush into the burning house to save me because he knew I was there, or simply because he was on duty? I wondered if he regretted the way he'd treated me and how he felt now that I was gone. Sometimes the little girl in me wanted to show up on his doorstep and say, "Remember me? Remember how you used to push me on the swing so high that it felt like my toes would brush the clouds? Remember how you used to smile and

pat my head as I awkwardly coiled a worm on my fishing hook?"

I wondered if we could ever return to the easy relationship we once had. Maybe he was sorry but was too ashamed to approach me. But even if he apologized, was it possible to repair a breach that had been so long in the making? Even after all this time, I didn't understand what had gone wrong. All I knew was that the demise of our relationship had begun shortly after Mom's death.

I thought about these things for weeks, and one February afternoon, I borrowed Nathaniel's car and drove to Dad's house to get answers.

Instead of pulling into Dad's driveway, I parked on the street behind the pines, giving myself a couple extra minutes to figure out what to say. It had stormed the night before, and a thick layer of snow blanketed everything in sight. I took a deep breath, trying to calm my nerves. "Be brave," I breathed. "It's not a big deal." I got out of the car and walked slowly up the drive, listening to the snow crunch beneath my feet.

I found him on the porch, tossing shovelfuls of snow over the railing. When he saw me approaching, he stopped and held the shovel upright. He looked surprised, and after I climbed the steps, we just stared at each other for a moment, each of us waiting for the other person to speak.

I wanted to at least thank him for saving my life, but when I finally broke the silence, the words didn't quite come out that way. "Why did you save me?" I asked. "If you don't love me or care about me, why did you bother?"

He bowed his head, his brow wrinkled with an odd mixture of confusion and shame. "Of course I didn't want you to die. I knew you were probably in there, so

I went in and found you." He looked up and released a long sigh. "It's cold out here. Would you like to go inside and talk?"

I shook my head. The last time I'd been in his house, he'd left me with a visible reminder of his volatility.

He backed up a few paces and brushed some snow from the porch swing before sitting down. After setting aside the shovel, he gestured to the space next to him. I stared at him, appraising his expression and posture. His shoulders were slumped contritely, his face sober and penitent. But I couldn't bring myself to join him on the swing.

"I haven't been a good father to you," he said after a long silence. "I've known that for a long time. But when you left, I realized just how awful I've been." He shook his head. "What a horrible person I must be to drive you away like that. I've made a lot of mistakes, but I do care about you, Aria. And I've done the best I could under the circumstances."

I wasn't sure which circumstances he was referring to, but I assumed he was referring to having to raise me as a widower. I thought briefly about all the other single fathers out there who had raised their children without hurting them, without keeping them from the things they cherished most. I didn't know whether or not to believe his penitent words. There was one way, I thought, to find out just how sincere he was.

"If you care about me," I said, "then tell me what you did with Mom's music box."

He stared at me for a long time without moving, until his mouth began twisting and pursing. But no words came out.

"Please, Dad. You don't know how much it means to me."

I could almost see the words in his mouth, fighting to get out. After another painfully long pause, he said matter-of-factly, "It's gone."

I felt an irritated muscle twitch near my shoulder blade, calling my attention to the tenseness gripping my entire body. I willed my muscles to relax, but they remained taut as though preparing for a fight. "What was in it?" My voice was calm, but I could feel flames beginning to crawl beneath my skin.

He took off his gloves, then put them back on, then off again. All the while, his face grew more and more pale.

"What was in it?" I repeated impatiently.

He finally met my eyes and allowed his lips to release one word. "Letters."

"Letters?" I repeated in a vacant whisper. "What letters?"

His face was blank now, like he'd retreated elsewhere and left only his lips to do the explaining. "There were six of them. One for each birthday up to your eighteenth."

Air rushed out of my lungs, like I'd been smacked in the ribs with a baton. I pictured her precious words, written on sheets of stationary, all lost to me now. "What did they say?" I asked weakly.

"How much she loved you, and . . . some advice—things she wanted you to know when you were older."

"What advice?"

His eyes grew cold and his expression became defensive. "It's been almost six years. I can't remember the details."

I narrowed my eyes. "Why did you keep them from me?"

"Because I loved you. I thought it was what was best for you."

I shook my head. "That doesn't make sense. How would keeping Mom's letters from me be best for me?"

"The things she had to say . . . would have put a wedge between us. And I didn't want that."

"Keeping her letters, and the piano, and her memory from me is what put a wedge between us. A music box and words of advice couldn't have changed the way I felt about you if you had treated me with kindness."

A wave of sorrow washed over his face. "I'm sorry, Aria. I did what I thought would be best. And as bad as things were between us, they would have been worse if you'd read those letters. But I regret other things. I regret treating you the way I did. I regret hurting you."

"Do you regret tearing Mom's notebook into pieces? Do you regret taking a crow bar to her piano? Because those things hurt me even more than the physical pain you inflicted."

He grimaced. "Yes, I regret those things too."

I spun around and marched down the porch steps and through the snow to the parlor window. I cupped my hands over my brow and peered in. Just as it had been on Christmas Eve, the broken piano pieces still rested on the floor, untouched, now collecting dust. Anger burned down my arms, scorching my fingertips.

I heard Dad's footsteps, and I spun around to see him standing behind me. "Aria, I—"

"You're not sorry," I said through tight lips. "If you were, you would try to fix the things you've broken. You would tell me what Mom's letters said. You would tape up the pieces of her notebook. You would fix her piano." My voice grew louder and sharper with each exclamation. "You would have called me sooner and begged for my forgiveness instead of waiting for me to come to you! You saved my life, but not because you love me. You did it because you were on the clock and it was your duty!"

He didn't say anything. He just stared down at the snow, his face falling into a guarded expression. The fire under my skin spread down my legs and to my feet, licking at my heels and urging me to escape from the man who had robbed me of love and security, of dreams and of the priceless words of a deceased mother.

Without saying another word, I turned and walked away.

I cried the entire way home, and soon my tears for Dad turned into tears for Thomas. I thought how if I could just talk to Thomas, it would make all the pain go away. It had been over a month since he left, and I was desperate to hear his voice tell me that everything was still the same between us.

Nathaniel was at the piano with a student when I came in, his back turned to me. I slipped past and into my room, where I quietly closed the door. Snatching up the phone from the bedside table, I dialed Thomas's cell.

My heart leapt at the sound of his "Hello," but then plummeted to my feet when it was followed by "please leave a message."

*Voice mail.*

I hung up, my hands suddenly clammy with anxiety. Why hadn't he answered? And why hadn't he called me yet? I picked up the phone again and called the number he'd left me for his parents' house in Pasadena, then paced the room, counting the rings.

Richard answered.

"Is Thomas there?" I wanted to sound calm, but my voice rose, betraying me.

Richard snorted. "No, and if I ever see him again I'm gonna beat his head in with a bat."

After recovering from his threatening words, I asked shakily, "Where is he?"

"Like I would know." Richard started calling Thomas all kinds of expletives, then said, "The last time I saw him was two days ago, when he gave me stitches. Right above the eye. He's lucky I'm not blind." He spouted off more insults, then added, "He tore the house to pieces too and left me to clean it up."

Richard kept talking, but all I could hear was my pulse pounding in my ears. The things he was saying about Thomas sounded all wrong. Thomas didn't give people stitches and tear houses apart. Thomas comforted, mended, healed. Richard must have provoked him.

"So if you see him," Richard finished, "tell him I'd better never see him again." He hung up.

I set down the phone, feeling like someone had just pummeled *me* with a bat and dropped me in the middle of a desert without a compass. I shut my eyes and took a deep breath, trying to calm myself so that I could think rationally. If he'd left his parents', then maybe he was on his way here. Maybe he would call soon, and I could talk to him and make sure he was okay, that *we* were okay.

I tried to take comfort in the prospect, but something Richard had said nagged at me. He said that Thomas had torn the house to pieces. But no matter how hard I tried, I couldn't imagine Thomas doing something like that. Maybe Richard had exaggerated to upset me. From the way he'd treated me on Christmas Eve, I wouldn't put it past him.

I went and stood in front of Thomas's painting tacked on my wall. I gazed at the boy with the dark hair sitting on the porch swing, and the sharp uneasiness dulled somewhat. I studied the intricate texture of the trees and flowers, details that his hands had spent hours creating just for me.

I was certain that within days, I would hear his voice, or better yet, see his face. He would explain what had happened with Richard, and I could tell him about Dad, and all my fears would be put to rest.

♪ ♪ ♪ ♪ ♪ ♪

I stood on the ninth floor of the Empire Hotel in New York City, staring out the window at the feathery snowflakes falling to the street below. In less than two hours, I would walk down the snow-covered sidewalk to The Juilliard School and spend fifteen minutes showcasing the pieces I'd spent hundreds of hours perfecting. The melodies that had been constantly playing through my head were now silent. Like a cast of performers who'd spent months rehearsing, they were now quietly tucked backstage in folds of black velour drapes, impatiently waiting for the curtain to rise.

Despite the imminence of my audition, my mind wasn't on Chopin and Beethoven, or on the four judges who were sitting in the fifth-floor studio of Juilliard right now. It was on Thomas. I still hadn't heard from him, and it had been three weeks since I'd spoken to Richard.

I heard the door open, and I turned to see Nathaniel with a small paper bag in his hand and two white Styrofoam cups in a cup holder. The thought of eating made me nauseous, and I felt my face recoil.

"Don't look at me like that," Nathaniel chided. "You need to eat something if you're going to be at your best. Here—come sit down." He set the food on a table by the window, and I sat. The room was bright, with clean modern lines and white and olive furnishings. Square white lamps and bulbous vases of daffodils were sprinkled about, and a swirly sculpture rose from the table like a silver flame.

He pulled out a softball-size blueberry muffin and set it in front of me. "Eat up."

I pinched off bite-size pieces from the muffin while Nathaniel sat across from me and gave me a last minute pep talk, reminding me of all the nuances we'd worked on over the last couple months—building up crescendos and punctuating staccatos and a million other things I didn't need him to remind me of. "I've got it," I mumbled.

He stopped talking and watched me pick at my muffin. "I know you do," he said over the rims of his square glasses. "But your thoughts are somewhere else."

I swallowed a bite, which took much more effort than it should have, then whispered, "Why hasn't he called?"

"Who?" Then understanding lit up his face. "Oh. Thomas."

The sound of his name made my insides twist up. "Something is wrong." I hadn't told Nathaniel about my conversation with Richard, so I told him now about Richard's harsh words, about Thomas leaving, and about the stitches.

"Thomas gave his brother stitches?"

I nodded. "It doesn't sound like something he'd do. But if it's true, it makes me wonder what state of mind he's in. If he's not at his parents' house, then why hasn't he come here? Where is he? You would think he would have called me, or that he would answer my calls. What if something happened to him?"

Nathaniel laid his hand on my shoulder and let out a heavy sigh. "No need to imagine the worst. He just lost his parents, and he's probably sorting through a mountain of emotions right now. Just give him some time. His head will eventually clear up, and when he's ready to call, he'll call."

I imagined Thomas somewhere, all alone and grieving.

It hurt me that he wouldn't let me be there for him. But maybe he wasn't alone at all. Maybe he'd found comfort in someone else. An image assaulted me, one of a blonde girl painted on a canvas on Thomas's wall. *Sasha.* I felt a stab of jealousy as I wondered if she'd attended the funeral, and I dropped the bit of muffin in my grasp.

Nathaniel leaned back in his chair and studied me for a moment. "I've seen the way he looks at you, like you're the most precious thing in the world to him." A reminiscent smile crept over his lips. "You should have seen his face that first day you came to see me, when you played for me. You had the kid spellbound. I've never seen someone so enamored."

I managed a smile, and my heart did a little flip at the memory of playing for Thomas. Nathaniel was right. Thomas didn't love Sasha; he loved me.

"He has some deep wounds right now, but that doesn't mean his heart has changed." Nathaniel took my hand and patted it gently, a line of concentration deepening between his brows. "You've always been good at infusing your emotions into your music. Today shouldn't be any different. Take everything you're feeling, and lay it out on those keys."

I nodded in understanding, then went to my room to get dressed for the audition. I put on an airy black dress that fell just above my knees, and pumps that were low enough that I wouldn't stumble on my way to the piano. I pinned my hair into a loose bun and put on some simple pearl earrings.

We bundled up and walked down the bustling sidewalk, past tourists pointing cameras, men in suits hailing cabs, and scraggy musicians playing behind open cello cases.

Nathaniel tossed a twenty into one of them and complimented the man's playing.

We came to a grandiose white marble building bearing the name of "The Juilliard School" and entered through two sets of heavy glass doors into the lobby. Our footsteps echoed as we crossed the cavernous room to the elevator, where Nathaniel pressed the button for the fifth floor. "You nervous?" he asked as the elevator began to rise.

"No," I said. "I feel strangely calm." It was true. I felt subdued, like every nerve in my body was peacefully sleeping, and I wondered if it was the effect of grief.

As we stepped out of the elevator, a large woman with unnaturally red hair walked by. She glanced at us, and when her eyes fell on Nathaniel, her face lit up.

"*Regarde qui viens là!* Mr. Borough!" She rushed to him and air-kissed him on the cheeks. Wrinkles framed her eyes behind her rhinestone-speckled glasses, and I was unsure if the red puff of hair on her head was real or a wig. "What gives us the pleasure?" Her French lilt made her voice musical, and the last word rose and fell like the sound of a door bell.

Nathaniel gestured to me. "This is my student, Aria Kinsley. She's auditioning for piano today."

The woman's hands flew to her face and she gasped. "Oh, this is wonderful!" She reached for my hand, clasping it in hers like we were old friends. "I'm sure he taught you well, did he not?"

"Yes," I said, glancing at Nathaniel. "I wouldn't be here without his help."

"Aria," Nathaniel said, "this is Margo D'Aramitz. She's been an instructor here for . . ."

"Twenty-eight years," Margo finished.

"Margo, Aria is Karina's daughter."

"Is your mother here?" She stared at me expectantly.

"Karina passed away," Nathaniel answered for me.

Margo gasped and placed a ring-covered hand to her heart. "Oh, *quelle tragedie.* I'm so sorry." She cupped my cheek in her palm. "Well, if you're half as good as your mother, you'll have no problem getting in." She patted my cheek lightly. "Good luck, *ma chérie.* We'll see you in the audition room."

"See," Nathaniel whispered as she walked away, "you already have an advantage. Knowing even one judge removes you from the crowd of nameless faces."

It was then that I noticed the hallways lined with other Juilliard candidates. They were poring over sheet music, fine-tuning violins, listening to iPods while playing along on air-instruments. Seeing all the competition should have made me nervous, but instead, I remained calm. I wasn't thinking about impressing the judges. I was thinking about Mom and Thomas and Elsie and Hal. I wasn't auditioning; I was playing a tribute to the people I'd loved and lost, and for the boy who held my heart thousands of miles away. Maybe if I played well enough, they'd somehow be able to hear me.

When it was my turn, I walked into the audition room. A Steinway grand piano sat on one end of the room, and four judges with pens in hand sat at a long table on the other. My shoes tapped across the wood floor as I approached the piano, and one of the judges coughed, nicking the silence.

"Start with your choice," Margo instructed as I sat on the padded piano bench.

I took a moment to clear my mind, then I placed my hands on the keys and began with Schubert's *4*

*Impromptus.* As the delicate strains enveloped the room, images of Thomas played through my mind like scenes from a movie.

His warm hand folding over mine in the cold rain, his blue eyes beckoning to me. The beautiful contours of his face, traced by the light of the stars. His fiery lips pressing softly against mine, making the cold autumn feel like summer. His hands slowly, meticulously moving colors around a canvas, creating beauty in the wake of his strokes.

My feelings for him could not be expressed in words, but the music gave voice to my heart. I imagined how it would feel to be in his arms again, to see him standing on my doorstep in June, to drive to New York with him and never have to be separated from him again.

I knew all too well the torment of separation, and as I played Bach and Chopin, drawing ripples and swells of song from the piano, I thought about Mom. She had auditioned like me in this very room, possibly at this very piano. Her hands had graced these keys and her music had pierced these walls. My heart ached for her, and my spirit wept at the sting of her absence.

With one more piece to go, I struck the dramatic opening fanfare of Beethoven's *Sonata No. 23 in F Minor.* As I did so, an unexpected fury flared up inside me and unwelcome memories sprayed into my mind like gasoline on a fire. The desperate look in Mom's eyes as she lay on a hospital bed. Her yellow-tinted skin and the coldness of her hand as I'd held it for the last time. The word *Mother* engraved on a new tombstone, and Dad's warm hand on my shoulder. A hand that had grown cold and hard in the weeks that followed.

PORCELAIN *keys*

Every tear I'd cried in the last six years seemed to burn again in my throat, and each slap I'd received at Dad's hand stung anew on my skin. I forged away at the keys as though striking the things I couldn't put names or faces to. For the chains Dad had bound me with, for death and its merciless sting, for life and its indiscriminate unfairness.

Nathaniel's words from months earlier came back to me. *You need to cut yourself open and hand over your heart.* I felt the blade puncture my skin, felt blood exiting my veins along with the notes I played. They sounded like indignant flames licking the walls, consuming, destroying, fueled by my despair and rage. But the music wasn't enough. Despite the fast tempo, it was like being forced to walk when my body wanted to run. My fingers were already sprinting across the keys in a blur, but there were not enough notes to contain my anger, and it consumed the room beyond the piano. As I played the final abrupt chord, the remnants of Dad's chains shattered from my wrists like porcelain, and I bit down on my lip to smother a sob.

The room remained silent until Margo began clapping and blubbering something in French. I swiped at my tears and stood to face the judges.

Three of them had their eyes down, their pencils scribbling furiously across their papers. Margo was standing, fanning her face with her fingers, still exclaiming words I didn't understand. "*Magnifique!*" she exclaimed. "*Comme ta mère!*" The other judges glanced at her with bored or annoyed expressions, and one of the judges looked at me and said flatly, "Thank you, Miss Kinsley. You'll receive a letter within four weeks. Please don't call. Just wait for your letter."

I nodded and walked out, and Nathaniel greeted me with open arms. He wrapped his arms around me and I shed a few more tears. Then he stepped back, put his hands on my shoulders, and looked in my eyes. "You did it, Aria. You did it."

# fifteen

I sat on a padded wicker chair on Nathaniel's back patio, soaking in the warm rays of early spring. It was the first week of April, and snow crocuses pushed through the scattered remnants of snow on the lawn. Purple, yellow, and white. Their bright petals hinted at the promise of warmer days and sunshine, holding so much hope in such tiny packages. Hope that no matter how hard I tried, I couldn't seem to feel.

Three months. Thirteen weeks. Ninety-one days without a phone call, a letter, or a knock on the door. I tried to imagine where Thomas was, tried to come up with excuses as to why he hadn't called, but they all left me feeling frustrated and delusional.

I heard the sliding glass door open behind me, and I twisted around to see Nathaniel step out onto the patio. He wore a jogging suit and sneakers, and his forehead glistened with sweat.

"Why are you crying?" he asked. "You haven't even opened it."

I wiped the back of my hand across my cheek and sat up straighter. "Opened what?"

It was then that I noticed a couple envelopes in his hand. One long and white, the other square and pink. He came and sat in the wicker chair beside me and handed me the white envelope. It was thick and heavy. "From Juilliard," Nathaniel said. "I guess you didn't see it."

My pulse picked up, and I looked at Nathaniel, suddenly unsure I wanted to see the contents.

"Looks promising," he said. "Open it."

I rubbed my thumbs over the envelope and stared at it, too terrified to break the seal. What if it said, "Thanks but no thanks," and it was only thick because it included a long list of alternate schools to audition for? I handed it back. "You open it."

I watched Nathaniel tear open the envelope and slide out the folded papers. I listened to him read it, the words "pleased" and "acceptance" and "scholarship" bursting in my ears like fireworks. I stood up and threw my arms around Nathaniel, like it was the most natural thing to do. "Really?" I said the word again and again, with Nathaniel patting my back and answering, "Yes, really."

I pulled away, and my first impulse was to run for the phone and call Thomas. But when I remembered that wasn't possible, I sank back into my chair, my tears of joy turning into tears of sorrow.

"What's wrong?" Nathaniel asked.

I hugged my knees to my chest and buried my head in my arms, shaking my head to indicate I didn't want to talk about it.

"You're still waiting for a call," Nathaniel said perceptively.

All I could manage to get through my lips was a broken

cry. The sun was still shining on my back, but the air suddenly felt more chilled and lifeless.

"Did he tell you he'd call when he left?" Nathaniel asked.

"No, just that he'd come get me in June."

"Well then, he'll come."

"But why wouldn't he want to talk to me in the meantime?"

Nathaniel was quiet for so long I finally turned my head to look at him. His face was sad and introspective. "Grief can do strange things to people," he mused. "I lost someone important to me once, and for three months I couldn't even function. I was like a sloth on Valium. I had to turn students away, tell them I'd gone on sabbatical, because I couldn't even pretend I was okay."

"Who did you lose?"

"A close friend." He shrugged. "But eventually I got back on my feet and rejoined society." He looked at me and offered a little smile. "I bet Thomas will call any time now, or show up at the door. Things will work out; you'll see. But for now, you need to focus on school and practicing. You only have a couple months of school left, but your acceptance to Juilliard is contingent upon your final grades." He handed me the pink envelope. "Here—I got you a little something."

I opened it expecting a congratulations card, but instead I found a belated birthday card and a gift card for a department store.

"I didn't really know what you needed, so . . ." He rubbed the back of his neck. "Anyway, I know it's late. I have a terrible memory when it comes to things like that."

He was late by a long shot. Eight months, in fact. I wondered when he thought my birthday was, but I didn't have the heart to say anything.

"Come on," he said. "I'll take you to a movie or something."

Over the next couple months, I clung to Nathaniel's words of hope and heeded his advice. I threw myself into practicing and studying and tried not to imagine where Thomas was or what he was doing. Maybe Nathaniel was right. Thomas hadn't promised to call; he'd only promised to come get me in June. I was sure he had a good reason for not contacting me. I trusted him. He would come and explain, and all would be right.

I watched blossoms grow on the crab apple trees in Nathaniel's yard, then watched them flutter away one by one. Tulips bloomed and wilted, and I graduated high school. The temperatures grew warm, and leaves unfolded on branches. When the big purple petals of the clematises bloomed, it was time for him to come. I spent the month of June with my fingers on the piano and my eyes on the window. I jumped at the sound of the phone, rushed to the door every time there was a knock—which was often since Nathaniel had a lot of students.

When sparklers and fountain fireworks lit up the street and firecrackers rattled the windows, I picked up the phone and called Vivian to see if she'd seen Thomas around, reasoning that maybe he'd returned to do something with his grandpa's property. But she hadn't seen him. So I rallied my courage and called Richard again to see if he'd heard from him. He laughed at me and told me to get a life.

I curled up on Nathaniel's white sofa and tried in vain to stop my whimpers from escalating into loud, heaving sobs. I listened to the popping fireworks and wondered

how anyone could celebrate when Thomas was lost to me forever. The world went on without him. But I was in my own little time capsule, where the hands of the clock stood still. I remained in the moment when Thomas held me for the last time, right before he climbed into his Bronco and disappeared from my life. I remained where I could feel his arms gathered around me, smell the woodsy scent of his skin, hear his breath in my ear, whispering in earnestness that he loved me, that he would come back for me. But there would be no phone call, no letter, no long-awaited knock on the door. And worst of all, there would be no explanation.

Nathaniel came in the front door with a paper bag in his arm and, without really looking at me, said, "I got some fireworks. Let me put this stuff away; then we can go outside." He set the grocery bag on the kitchen counter, and when I didn't answer, he turned to look at me.

"You all right?" he asked, coming to my side. "What's happened?"

I sniffled and shook my head. "He's not coming."

Nathaniel knelt in front of me. "It's only the first week of July. There's still time." His encouraging tone was forced, and I knew he didn't really believe Thomas would come.

I sat up straight and folded my legs beneath me. Nathaniel handed me a tissue, and my hand trembled as I lifted it to wipe my eyes. "Even if he didn't want to be with me," I cried, "wouldn't he at least have the decency to let me know?"

"Maybe he's still too distracted dealing with his parents' matters."

"Or maybe he's too busy hanging out with Sasha," I said bitterly through new tears.

"Sasha?"

I shook my head, not wanting to explain. "Or maybe he's just angry with me."

"Why would he be angry with you?"

"The night of the fire, he ran into the house to save his parents, and I pulled him back. Maybe he thinks he would have had time to save them if I hadn't, and he can't forgive me for it."

"You probably saved his life."

"That's what I thought too, but maybe he sees it differently."

"Well then, he's confused. And a thoughtless dope, I might add, to leave you hanging like this."

His words rang all too true. For the past six months, I'd felt like Thomas was dangling me over the edge of a cliff, and I was unsure if he'd pull me back to safety or let me plummet to the rocky shore below. If he was going to drop me, I wished he'd just drop me already.

Nathaniel put his hand on my shoulder and said something about the abundance of fish in the sea.

"You don't understand," I said. "He's one of a kind. Irreplaceable. No one else can make me feel the way he makes me feel. I don't even know who I am without him. I know that sounds pathetic, but it's true." I dropped my face into my hands and through broken sobs said, "I'm so scared."

He patted my back while I cried for another good five minutes. Then I looked up at him and whispered, "What am I going to do?" I could feel the lost, terrified expression on my face.

"I'll tell you what you're going to do," Nathaniel said confidently and without hesitation, like he'd been crafting a speech while listening to me cry. "You're going to pack

your bags. You're going to get on an airplane and not look back. You're going to walk through the doors of Juilliard and discover who Aria Kinsley is—without her mother, without her father, without some dopey, thoughtless boy. You're going to stand on your own two feet and find out just how strong and talented and beautiful you are."

I stared at him and sniffed, trying to catch my breath. "Okay," I finally said, mostly to appease him.

But soon I found myself in my room, sinking to my knees. I felt the floor crumble beneath me. I was falling, but there was nowhere to land.

As I wept silently through the night, slowly accepting Thomas's permanent absence from my life, I gathered up all my painful experiences—Mom's death, Dad's cruelty, Thomas's disappearance—and pushed them all deep inside, locking them in a hidden place where they could never afflict me again.

# sixteen

*Six months later*

I hovered over the desk in my bedroom on a January evening, painstakingly dotting manuscript paper with chords for a harmonization exercise. Occasionally my pencil would slip through the paper into a long scratch in the surface of the desk. No matter where I placed my paper, it always seemed to end up on the scratch. The sun was setting and the room was growing dim, so I turned on a lamp and stood to stretch and rub the kink out of my neck. I stepped over to the window to shut the blinds, pausing to take in the view. The setting sun cut through the cityscape, casting long shadows across the campus and making the snow-covered trees in front of the Lincoln Center sparkle like sapphires. It didn't take long for an unwelcome memory to spring up in my mind. Thomas, the morning he'd said good-bye, the winter sun sparkling in his sad blue eyes.

When memories of Thomas surfaced, which was often, I

had my own way of dealing with them. I closed the blinds, went back to my desk, and pulled out a piece of manuscript paper. Pressing my pencil to it, I started drawing notes on the staff lines, focusing on making each one the perfect shape. The wide hollow of a whole note, the two flags curving from the tip of sixteenth notes, the ascending beam connecting four eighth notes, the hook at the bottom of a quarter rest. I focused on my pencil leaving trails of lead on the white surface, and I wrote, unaware of what the music sounded like, until my mind had wandered elsewhere. Once I could focus on safer thoughts, I crumpled up the newly created music and tossed it into the wastebasket. I didn't want to hear the music my soul produced when thinking of Thomas.

I went back to my harmonization exercise, and the phone rang in the living room. I stayed put, knowing one of my roommates would get it. A few seconds later, the bedroom door cracked open and Nakira popped her head in.

"Devin's on the phone."

"I'm not here."

"Aria, he lives down the hall. He knows you're here."

"Then I'm sleeping."

"It's only five."

I glanced at her and did a double take. Her slick chin-length hair was a new color—black with pink ends. It had been streaked with blue the day before.

"I like the new color," I said.

She rolled her eyeliner-caked eyes. "So are you going to talk to Devin or not?"

I sighed. "I'm busy."

"Too busy for a one-minute conversation?"

"I have a test on Monday."

"Fine, I'll just tell him to come over then."

"Wait!" I jumped up and ran after her, but when I caught up to her in the kitchen, she was already inviting Devin over.

"I don't want him to come over!" I said as soon as she hung up.

"Chill out, Ari. Devin's nice. And cute. And it wouldn't kill you to have a social life."

"I have a social life."

"With who? Me? Brinna? Kadence? You rarely talk to us, and you live with us."

There was a playful tap on the door, and Nakira went to open it.

"Wait!" I said.

Nakira froze, her hand on the doorknob. She glared at me, daring me to convince her to keep Devin in the hallway.

"I really don't want to talk to him."

"Then *you* tell him you're busy." She swung the door open wide, and Devin Fineberg stood there, towering in the doorway with his usual easy smile. He wore designer jeans and a gray Beatles T-shirt with the black suit jacket he wore every day.

"Hey," he said, flicking a piece of shiny caramel hair from his forehead. He looked from me to Nakira and back again, and when I didn't say anything, Nakira invited him in. He planted himself on the wooden-armed sofa, resting his long legs on the coffee table.

"So, what are you girls up to tonight?" he asked.

I turned away to get a glass of water from the kitchen.

"I'm going out with Justin," Nakira replied, plucking

her purse from the counter. "I'll see you kids later. Have fun," she sang, smirking at me before disappearing out the door.

I felt Devin's eyes on me as I put my glass in the sink. Maybe he was wondering how long it had been since I washed my hair. I pondered that question myself for a moment, inconspicuously turning my head into the hair on my shoulder to take a whiff. Two days? That wasn't so bad.

"I think I'm going to catch a show tonight," he said. "You want to come with me?"

I walked over to the couch and stood in front of him. "I'm not exactly dressed to go out." I had on a faded black T-shirt and holey jeans, and it had been days since I'd made an honest effort at makeup. The only time I dressed up anymore was for performances and competitions.

"I'll wait for you to get ready. It's still early. You should wear that little red number you wore at the performance a couple weeks ago. You looked amazing in it."

I hated to admit it, but Devin was cute. His shaggy-cut hair fell in wisps around his copper eyes and defined jaw. His lips were full and perfectly shaped, and his infectious smile was famous.

"I don't know." I hesitated, though I knew full well I wouldn't be going anywhere with him. "I have a lot of studying to do."

"Come on. It's Saturday night. It wouldn't hurt to take a break."

"I'm sure you can find someone else to go with. Just pick someone off your *Date with Devin* waiting list." I'd watched him flirt with countless girls, only to leave each one heartbroken and bitter, and I was determined to be the only girl to resist his charms.

"Didn't I tell you? You're next on the list." He smiled, a glint of playfulness in his eyes.

"Brinna would never forgive me. She's still pining over you."

"Brinna?" He dropped his legs to the floor and leaned forward. "We weren't even that serious. She's nice, but too quiet."

"I'm quiet too."

"Yeah, but you're not afraid to speak your mind. I ask Brinna a simple question and her cheeks turn red."

"I heard you went out with Jen Sommers last weekend. Are you already tired of her?"

"Of course not. She's my friend."

"Is that what she thinks? Because she seemed overjoyed when you stopped seeing Brinna."

"You mean Amber? I stopped seeing Brinna two months ago." His mouth tipped in a lazy, flirtatious smile, and his eyes sparkled with razzing delight. He had a way of making the most chauvinistic things sound charming, and it infuriated me.

"Whatever. The point is, Jen sees you as more than a friend. I heard her say she'd been waiting for a shot with you since August."

He held open his hands and shrugged innocently. "Is it my fault she's misinterpreting my signals? I haven't done anything to encourage her."

"You don't think taking someone on a date is encouragement?"

"It wasn't a date. I was on my way to a movie and I saw her in the hall, so I asked if she wanted to come with."

The front door opened and Brinna walked in, juggling a violin case and a stack of sheet music. Brinna was my age, but with her petite frame, innocent face, and unruly curls,

she didn't look older than thirteen. She pushed the door shut with her shoulder, then turned to see Devin and me.

"Hey, Brinna," I said, conscious of how she must feel seeing Devin in our living room.

"Hi." She gave a fleeting smile, then dropped her head and went straight to our bedroom, closing the door behind her.

I turned back to Devin. "See? She's still upset about you," I whispered.

"There's nothing to be upset about," he whispered back. "We never even kissed. She's just quiet. That doesn't mean she's pining over me."

Just then, a melancholy strain of violin music played from the bedroom, like the theme of a tragic love story. I arched an eyebrow at Devin. "Either way, she's my roommate, and I don't want to risk hurting her feelings."

"Next week then, maybe?" He shrugged and stood to leave.

I huffed out an irritated breath and took a step closer to him. "I know this may surprise you, but you're not as irresistible as you think. Just because you've won a million competitions and have played concertos with major orchestras since you were fourteen doesn't mean you're God's gift to women. I've never wanted a shot with you, and I don't want one now."

"Come on, Aria." His hands fell open. "You know I'm just razzing you. I only do it because it gets such a rise out of you."

"What? You enjoy getting a rise out of me?"

"It's the only way you'll talk to me," he said, smoothing out his suit jacket over his muscular chest.

"Why do you wear that thing all the time, anyway?" I asked, annoyed.

"What, this?" He looked down and pinched the notched lapel of his jacket. "Because I'm a performer. And when I'm on stage performing, it doesn't feel restrictive or awkward because I'm already used to wearing it all the time." A wicked grin lit up his face. "See, you are interested in me. Otherwise you wouldn't have asked me about my jacket."

"Good night, Devin," I said, rolling my eyes as I opened the door.

"Until we meet again," he said melodramatically with his hand over his heart. He swaggered to the door and turned at the threshold, giving me one last, longing glance with his puppy-dog eyes.

I shoved him into the hall, which only made him laugh, and I shut the door firmly.

I turned and leaned against the door, listening to Brinna's mournful playing. The sound of it tugged at my heart, and I knew I wouldn't be able to stay here and listen to it if I wanted to keep my thoughts in check. Maybe I would go try to find an open practice room.

I gathered up some sheet music and took the elevator to the fourth floor. After a long search, I found an empty practice room. Velvet curtains dressed the walls of the small room, and the violet sky sulked through a sealed window. I set my music on the Steinway grand that filled most of the room and adjusted the bench before sitting down. With a pencil, I made some fingering notations, then sunk into the piece and began unraveling the complex passages. Measure by measure, phrase by phrase. Left hand alone, then right, then together. Slower, then faster, then up to tempo.

Work was the only thing I had control over. It kept me from thinking about the past, and kept me safe in my own little world. I had kept my distance from other people since I came to school, and soon everyone around me had become nothing more than background noise. Irritating at times, but easy to ignore. And harmless. Perfectly harmless.

♪ ♪ ♪ ♪ ♪♪

Nathaniel came to town a couple weeks later to see one of his old friends conduct a symphony at Carnegie Hall, and he invited me to the symphony and took me out to dinner beforehand. I took the opportunity to dress up and make use of my neglected makeup. I wore a dress I'd found on a discount rack, comfortable yet elegant, burgundy velvet with a knee-length skirt and capped sleeves. I curled my hair and left it down, then added a pearl necklace.

Nathaniel met me at my apartment, and we walked down Columbus Avenue to a cozy Italian restaurant with high-backed fabric chairs, linen tablecloths, and walls lined with wine bottles. Nathaniel pulled out my chair, then sat across from me after taking off his suit jacket and draping it over the chair back.

We exchanged pleasantries while perusing the menu, discussing everything from the pieces I was working on to my nonexistent social life. After we'd ordered and the menus were out of the way, Nathaniel leaned toward me, resting his elbows on the table.

"I met with Margo this morning," he said, a touch of concern in his voice. "She says you're struggling a little."

"No." I shook my head, confused by his statement. "I'm not. I've aced ear training, theory, chamber. Professor Nguyen told me that I'm the only one who's done every ear training exercise perfectly. And Margo is always complimenting me on my style and accuracy and fluency."

"No need to get defensive." He held up his hands. "I

think she was talking about the love of the art. Your passion for the music itself. She says you're struggling a little with taking a piece to heart and making it your own."

I fidgeted with my flatware. "I just find myself focusing a little too much on the technicalities sometimes instead of the emotion."

"Why do you think that is? I mean, you didn't used to be that way. Your emotional interpretations are what got you into Juilliard."

"I don't know. I guess sometimes it's just too emotionally taxing to throw my heart into a piece."

He gave me a long, searching look. "What's going on, Aria?"

I sighed. "I don't know. Maybe I'm just burned out."

"No, I don't think that's it. If you were burned out, you wouldn't be so strong with your accuracy and fluency. Margo said that you tackle technical demons like nothing. But that any time a piece requires more than a little emotion, you become distant and mechanical. It just surprises me."

I didn't respond, because he was right. And I didn't know what to do about it. He fixed an assessing gaze on me, and I averted my eyes to the group of customers entering the restaurant. Not that they were interesting, I just didn't want to meet Nathaniel's stare. A long silence passed between us, the clattering of utensils and glasses seeming to grow louder with each ticking second. He was waiting for me to explain, and I didn't want to explain. Instead, I stuffed corners of my napkin between the gaps in my fork.

"You know," he finally said, his voice gentle, "sometimes when we're trying to forget, or block something we don't want to feel, it can affect our playing." He paused. "I know what you're trying to forget. What you're trying not to feel. Aria, you need to allow yourself to grieve. It's the only way you'll be able to move ahead."

His acute perception and acknowledgment of my struggles brought an unwanted wave of emotion. I swallowed back the rising tears and spread my napkin over my lap, trying to get control of myself before I ruined my mascara. I took a few deep breaths, and when I felt in control, I looked up at Nathaniel. "I try not to think about him, about Thomas," I admitted, "but he always seems to creep in, especially when I'm playing. I have to shut him out. And I can't do that without shutting everything out. My playing suffers. Sometimes it sounds as flat and dead as I feel."

"So stop shutting him out."

I shook my head slowly. "Shutting him out is the only thing that keeps me sane. If you can consider me sane."

He reached forward and squeezed my hand with paternal affection. "You're stronger than you give yourself credit for. You can do this, Aria. You can take all that grief and sorrow inside you and do something useful with it. It won't kill you. It'll be hard at first, but it'll make you stronger." He let go of my hand and leaned back in his chair. "And it definitely wouldn't hurt to take a break from studying and make some friends. It's impossible to get through the pressures of Juilliard without a friend to talk to now and then."

We sat there quietly, him leaning back in his chair staring at me with concern, me watching customers come and go, until our food came. I prodded my lasagna with my fork, trying to think of a way to change the subject to more pleasant things.

Nathaniel leaned forward again after taking a few bites of his pasta. "Listen. There's nothing wrong with working hard. In fact, it's one of your greatest virtues. But don't let it become everything in your life. Ultimately, the only thing that brings true happiness is your relationships with other people. Yes, sometimes relationships fail. When they do, you shouldn't give up. Just try another."

He was talking like I could just put up a *For Sale* sign over my heart and find myself a new owner. "Have you ever been in love?" I asked a little too harshly, thinking he couldn't possibly know how I felt.

"Yes," he answered without hesitation. "But it didn't work out. And guess what? I became a better musician because of it. It was hard—sort of like having my heart scraped out bit by bit with a dull spoon. But I gathered up the pieces and moved on, and chose not to pathetically wallow in misery for the rest of my life."

His words sounded more severe than he probably intended, and his expression softened, as did his voice. "I just want you to be happy. This—Juilliard—it's what you wanted. It's what Karina always wanted for you. I'm sure she is happy for you, wherever she is. And so you should be happy too."

"I want to be happy, and I'm trying to be. I just don't know how to deal with all the grief I still feel."

"You can't deal with it unless you first acknowledge it. And once you acknowledge it, force yourself to move forward. Your grief will walk beside you for a while, but you will get stronger, and the grief will start to lag. But you have to keep moving, living, feeling. Take in what's around you, and you will find new things to love, to enjoy. The pain may not ever entirely go away"—he grimaced slightly

as he said this—"but it will be far enough away that it won't hurt so much."

"Nathaniel, who was the girl? I mean, the one who got away?"

He waved his hand as if to brush off the subject. "It was a long time ago."

I gazed at him curiously, hoping if I was quiet long enough, he would open up.

He finished chewing a bite of pasta, then set down his fork and sighed. "She was my wife."

My mouth dropped open. "Your wife? I didn't know—"

"I don't like to talk about it."

"What happened to her?"

He smiled humorlessly. "I said I don't like to talk about it."

I took a bite of lasagna and stared at him again, perfectly content to wait all night if needed.

Absentmindedly, he began running the prongs of his fork over the red sauce on his plate, making little parallel lines, then crossing them out with new ones. "We got married young, and we thought that love would somehow heal our differences." His fork switched directions, and now he made a row of loops. "She was a musician. But she wanted a life I couldn't give her."

"What kind of life?"

He set down his fork. "A small, quiet life where we didn't have to drag kids all over the world for our performances. She wanted to settle down somewhere and teach, and she wanted me to do the same. But I wanted to be on the stage, to see the world and meet new people. I wanted each day to be different than the last, to bathe in the sound of thunderous applause every night. In the end, we just couldn't reconcile our differences. So she moved on."

"Do you regret not giving her the life she wanted?"

He took a sip of water and paused, gazing past me into some long-forgotten place and time. "After spending years traveling and performing, I grew tired of the brutality of a concert career. I came to the sad realization that even though I woke up in a different place every morning, each day was the same as the last. Wake up in an empty hotel room, go to the airport to fly to a new city, practice all day by myself, perform for a thousand strangers, go back to an empty hotel room." He pushed a piece of bow tie pasta around on his almost-empty plate. "Yes—I regret not giving her the life she wanted. Every day of my life. I would give up every performance I ever gave to be able to go back and spend a lifetime with her."

"I'm so sorry, Nathaniel."

"It's okay," he said with a little smile, though the pain in his eyes suggested otherwise. "I made my choice, and now I have to live with the consequence."

The waiter showed up and asked if we wanted dessert.

"Which dessert has the highest calorie content?" Nathaniel asked the waiter.

"I'm not sure . . . probably the chocolate cheesecake."

"Great. She'll have a slice," he ordered, gesturing to me.

I arched an eyebrow.

"You've gotten too thin."

The waiter turned, but Nathaniel called him back. "Oh, and could you put a candle in it?"

"Why the candle?" I asked after the waiter nodded and walked away.

"For your birthday. It's this month, right?"

"Um, actually, my birthday is in August."

He was about to take a sip of his water, but he froze and

looked at me over his glass. "Your birthday is in August?" It was a question, but it sounded more like a statement. He stared at me with wide eyes, seeming stunned by this news. Then slowly, a strange, almost imperceptible pain eased into his eyes. "Why didn't you tell me last summer?"

"I don't know. I guess I didn't feel like celebrating. But why did you think my birthday was in February?"

"I could have sworn . . . ," he mumbled mostly to himself. "Huh. Never mind. Lousy memory." He pointed to his head. He suddenly seemed distracted, drumming his fingers on the table, his eyes darting about like he was solving some complex mathematical equation. His face went pale, and little beads of sweat formed on his brow.

"Nathaniel, are you all right?"

He stood abruptly. "Excuse me. I'm just going to run to the men's room."

I watched him dash off to the men's room, and soon I was surrounded by a handful of Italian waiters. One of them slid a slice of cheesecake with a burning candle in front of me and they all started singing, "*Tanti auguri a te.*" I smiled and blew out the candle, all the while wondering what was wrong with Nathaniel.

When he came back ten minutes later, he looked worse than when he left. The rims of his eyes were red, his face still pale and clammy. He didn't bother sitting down. "I'm sorry, Aria. I'm not feeling well. I think I'll go back to my hotel room." He pulled the tickets for the symphony out of his suit jacket and handed them to me. "You're welcome to go still. Maybe you can ask a roommate to go with you."

I nodded and took the tickets, though I couldn't think of anyone I wanted to go with.

We took a cab back to the school, and Nathaniel remained quiet and distracted. Before I got out of the cab, he told me he'd come see me the next day before he went back to Colorado.

I ended up handing my tickets to some people in front of the Lincoln Center. Then I spent the rest of the night holed up in a practice room working on a Liszt piece, trying to play with the emotion that Margo thought I lacked.

# seventeen

The next afternoon, I stepped into Margo's studio for my weekly private lesson. She sat at one of the Steinway grands, playing a romantic piece with flowing, unhurried tranquility. Her studio was homey, with rich red carpet, Victorian-style furniture, and the scent of flowery perfume. The walls were full of ornately framed photographs and old handwritten scores of famous composers. Some photographs showed her on stage in her younger years, a robust beauty with long, flowing red hair. Other photographs showed her posing with other world-famous conductors and musicians. Evidence of a life well lived, immersed in her passion for music.

She rose to greet me, her long flared skirt swaying as she approached me with open arms, graceful like a ballroom dancer. A jeweled lily brooch adorned her ruffled blouse, the buttons of which were almost popping over her buxom chest.

"*Bonjour!*" She laid hold of my arms and gave me air kisses, her puffy red hair tickling my nose. "I've been looking forward to our lesson, *ma chérie*. What did you bring today?" She eyed the sheet music in my hands.

"That Brahms Hungarian dance we were working on, and a Chopin waltz."

"Did you bring the Liszt piece I asked you to?"

"Yes, it's right here."

"Wonderful. Let's start with the Chopin."

Two grand pianos sat side by side on the carpet, and we each sat at one. I played through the Chopin waltz, whisking through splashes of rapid notes to produce a lilting rhythm. She nodded her head and breathed "Oomp-pah-pah, oomp-pah-pah" while waving her arms along to the pulse.

"Very good," she said when I finished, sliding on her glasses and turning to her keyboard. "But the repeat phrases need to be more distinct. Maybe try something more like this." She dove gracefully into the piece and easily tackled the passages with energy and fluent, nimble fingers.

I repeated the passages, trying to echo the way she played it.

"Yes, yes. That's it."

We went through the rest of the piece together, her listening, teaching, and demonstrating. I took in every word, every nuance her fingers produced, then tried to duplicate them.

Next she requested the Liszt, but since talking to Nathaniel the night before, I had been dreading playing this piece. It was a sorrowful, emotionally packed piece, and I was suddenly self-conscious playing it, knowing what Margo had said to Nathaniel.

I started playing, trying to make it sound as melancholy as I could.

"Stop, stop," she interrupted halfway through. "You're focusing too much on the technicalities," she said, pinching her index finger and thumb together. "You know the notes. Now try to interpret the song. Make it mean something to you."

"It does mean something to me."

"Tell me, Aria, what does it mean to you?"

"Music means everything to me."

"But what about this piece? What do you think it is about?"

"Sorrow. It sounds like sorrow."

"Then why do I not feel sorrow when you play it?"

I shrugged awkwardly, unsure how to answer.

"Let me tell you something about Franz Liszt. He led a tragic life, full of failed relationships, deaths of his children, alcoholism, and long periods of profound depression. He once said to a friend that he carried with him a deep sadness of the heart, which 'must now and then break out in sound.' You are right, Aria. This piece is about sorrow. Imagine what he must have been thinking about when he wrote it. And what are you thinking about when you play it? Are you thinking of sorrow?"

"I . . . I'm thinking about continuity, dynamics, tone."

"And that is why I don't feel sorrow when you play it. It sounds technical because you're thinking technical. Music is not meant to be a mathematical formula. It is meant to display and evoke the deepest hidden emotions of the human soul. If you don't put your heart and soul into this piece, no matter how well you play technically, it will sound flat."

Just then, the studio door opened, and I turned to see Nathaniel in the doorway. Margo leapt to her feet and greeted him with a hearty embrace and all kinds of French exclamations. "What brings you here, darling?" she gushed.

"I came to say good-bye to Aria." He glanced at me and smiled. He looked better today, not so pale, but still a little off.

I stood and went over to him. "Are you feeling better?"

"Yes. Sorry about last night. How was the symphony?"

"Oh." I looked down, feeling bad about wasting his tickets. "I didn't go. I gave the tickets away and spent the night practicing."

Nathaniel chuckled and Margo wrapped an arm around me. "Such a busy little bee." She laughed.

We spent a few minutes chatting, then we said our good-byes and Nathaniel left, promising to call me in a few weeks. Margo and I went back to the pianos. "Oh, my," she said with a sigh. "He is still so handsome, is he not? He and your mother made such a beautiful couple."

"My mom dated Nathaniel?"

"Oh, yes," she said, her expression igniting with her enthusiasm for torrid love stories. "For four years they were on and off, on and off. Tumultuous, I tell you. But I always knew how their relationship was going based on the way she played. She'd come in here one day and everything would sound sensuous and passionate. The next day she'd pound out her frustrations like thunder. It was all elation or misery, never in between, and never without passion. She was one of the most expressive pianists I've ever heard."

Margo took the conversation back to the Liszt piece, but my mind was going wild with this new revelation. It made me see Nathaniel in an entirely different way. He had loved my mother, more than just as a friend. For a split second I wondered if she had been the girl that he'd told me about

the night before. But I quickly decided it couldn't be. He would have told me if it had been my own mother. Besides, Mom had never said anything about being married before Dad. I shook the thoughts from my head, trying to focus on what Margo was saying.

"You are the instrument," she was saying. "The sounds that come from the piano do not originate from the strings, or the hammers, or even your fingers. They originate inside of you. It's not about the notes on the page; it's about making others feel what you feel, through the music. This piece is about the deepest yearnings of the soul. Now, I want you to close your eyes."

I gave a reluctant sigh, then closed my eyes.

"I want you to reach deep into your heart, and find something, someone that means something to you. Something you desperately want but can't have."

There was really only one thing that I desperately wanted, and his face had appeared in my mind the instant I'd closed my eyes. I made a mental effort to reconnect my mind to my heart, like torn fibers weaving back together. I focused on a single memory, the tender look on Thomas's face when I draped his scarf over his shoulders the morning we said good-bye. The love that emanated from his eyes, the tears that were proof that his heart was breaking just as much as mine. My heart ached with an unbearable pain at the memory.

"Now," Margo said, "are you ready to make this piece mean something to you?"

"Yes," I replied shakily, my heart suddenly pounding with terror of what I knew this allowance would cost me.

"Then open your eyes and play."

I played again, the entire piece, focusing on what each

note meant to me. My stubborn affection for Thomas
surged from my heart like a swell of water from an opened
floodgate. It spilled over as tears, rolling down my cheeks
and into my lap.

"There now," she said when I finished. "I saw your soul
in that one, and it was beautiful. You can't finagle or bluff
anymore, Aria, because I know what you're capable of."

Margo was pleased with my effort, but I paid for it later,
spending the rest of the day balled up in anguish beneath
the blankets on my bed. The tears wouldn't stop, no matter
how hard I tried to rein them in.

Nathaniel had told me that by coming to Juilliard alone,
I would discover what a strong, talented, beautiful person
I was. I didn't feel like any of those things. If anything,
I'd discovered how much I still had to learn, and just how
fragile I was.

♪ ♪ ♪ ♪ ♪ ♪ ♪

The next morning, I reorganized my forces. Dressing
in a white sweater and jeans, I pulled my hair away from
my face into a ponytail and looked in the mirror. My face
was still splotchy from crying so much the night before, so
I splashed some cold water on my skin and applied some
makeup. I went to the cafeteria for breakfast and sat on an
empty table by the east window, letting the sun warm my
back, then opened my *Counterpoint and Harmony* book on
the table in front of me. With a bagel in one hand and a
highlighter in the other, I worked on filling my head with
chromaticism and chord progressions, hoping to push out
the remnants of the memories I'd allowed myself the day
before.

"Good morning," a cheerful voice said, and I looked up to

see Devin smiling at me. I nodded at him, then went back to reading. To my chagrin, he sat across from me with his tray of scrambled eggs, toast, and bottle of cranberry juice.

"Reading ahead?"

"What?" I looked up at him, irritated at his interruption.

"You're in chapter twenty-four. Edelstein only assigned us through nineteen."

"I like to be prepared."

He flashed his famous grin, the corners of his eyes crinkling with humor like he was amused with my proactive study habits. Beneath his usual black suit jacket, he wore a white T-shirt with a monochrome print of a severe-looking Beethoven and the quote, "To play without passion is inexcusable!" Beethoven's eyes bore into me, as if seeing into my passionless soul. I dropped my eyes back to my book, if only to avoid Beethoven's all-seeing glare.

"Hey," Devin said after taking a few bites of his breakfast, "there's a concert later on at Avery Fisher. You want to go with me?"

"No," I said, taking a bite of my bagel and not lifting my eyes from my book.

"Don't I get a reason? I know you're done with your homework, seeing as how you're reading ahead. So what is it? Scrubbing your bathroom floor? Hot date with a tuba player? Your Chia pet need watering?" He paused. "Did you know that Chia seeds are packed with omega-3s?"

I almost smiled, but took another bite of my bagel instead and pretended to keep reading.

"Okay, I've got it," he continued. "You really, desperately want to go with me, but the word *yes* isn't part of your vocabulary. There are other words, you know. *Sure, okay, sounds good, love to, count me in.*"

"Why do you even want to go out with me?" I said, putting my bagel down and glaring at him. "There are a hundred girls here who would kill to go out with you, so why pursue the only one who's not interested?" A thought occurred to me. "Oh, I see. You just want what you can't have. Is that it?"

"Good guess, but you're way off."

"Then why? Why me?"

He dropped his eyes and pursed his lips. "I don't know." His brow wrinkled, and he looked up at me, his eyes full of curiosity. "I guess because you intrigue me."

"Why? Because I'm the only girl here who isn't falling all over you?"

"No," he said, his face more serious. "Because you sit alone in the lunchroom with a book open in front of you, reading five chapters ahead while everyone else is socializing. Because sometimes in class, you look like you're listening intently to the professor like the rest of us, but then you suddenly wince and get this look on your face like your family pet was just run over."

"You have to admit, some of the lectures are painful."

"And then," he continued, ignoring my attempt at humor, "you walk down the hall with your eyes on some point beyond the building, like you're seeing something the rest of us can't. I guess I just want to know *why*."

An idea came to me, a plan to get Devin to stop bothering me. If I dumped all my baggage out on the table, maybe it would satisfy his curiosity and he would move on to the next girl. He might tell other people, but did it really matter what other people thought of me? They probably already thought I was weird, so it didn't really matter. Spilling my guts was worth it if it meant repelling Devin.

I leaned forward and said, "Well, let me put an end to your intrigue." Then I proceeded to lay it all out, blood, guts, and all. "My mom died when I was twelve because of the strain I put on her body when she was pregnant with me. I was raised by a father who forbade me to play the piano, even though it was the only thing that made me happy, and when he caught me playing, he would leave bruises on me. Then last year, I met this amazing guy, who saved me and healed me."

I almost told him about the fire, but it felt like treading on sacred ground. "He left. He promised to come back for me, but instead he disappeared without a word. That's why I stare off into space, and that's why I sometimes look like I'm in pain. Because I am. Mystery solved. Now you can go on your way and find a cute, bubbly flute player to date."

I was hoping he'd get up and run away, but he stayed, his face thoughtful, like I'd just told him my favorite dessert was crème brûlée. "I'm sorry," he said, his voice sincere. "And so now you don't want to date because you're afraid of getting hurt again?"

"Not exactly." I tapped my fingers on the table, debating just how much deeper to plunge. I'd already dipped my feet in the water, and the temperature wasn't bad, so I jumped in. "I don't think it's possible for me to be hurt by someone else," I said, "because I'm still hurting from him. I don't want to date because I don't want to be reminded of him."

I kept waiting for him to get up and leave, but he just sat there, his copper eyes fixed on me, engrossed by every word that came out of my mouth.

"This guy—he must have been a huge jerk to make you feel that way."

"No. I feel that way because he was wonderful. I loved

him." It took almost every ounce of energy to say those last three words. "He had to leave for a few months, and he promised to come back for me, but he didn't come. No phone call, no letter. I've tried to reach him with no luck."

"How long has it been?"

I sighed. "Just over a year."

"And you're still waiting for him?"

"No . . . I don't know. See, there are only two possibilities."

"What possibilities?"

"Either he is dead . . . or he didn't love me."

He sat quietly, his brow creased in concentration as if deliberating what to say. After a couple minutes, he asked, "How old were you? Sixteen?"

"Seventeen."

"Was this guy the same age?"

"He was eighteen."

"Well . . . eighteen is so young. I don't think people really understand what love is when they're that young. And I doubt this guy was mature enough to understand what he was promising you. I hate to say it, but he probably found some other girl and forgot all about you. And you—you've been suffering all this time, and he probably hasn't even thought about you."

"Oh, and *you* understand what love is? You, who's broken every girl's heart in the whole school?"

His shoulders slumped and his face fell into a defeated expression, and I suddenly regretted my words. "No," he said. "I don't know much about love either. I guess that's why I haven't stayed with any girl for very long. I keep waiting to feel something—love, I guess—but I've never really been in love, so I don't know what it's supposed to feel like." He looked up at me with curiosity. "Maybe you can tell me. How does it feel?" The wistful tone in his voice caught me off guard, and his eyes were filled with such an earnest inquisitiveness that I couldn't help but give him an honest answer.

"It feels . . ." I paused, turning the highlighter in my hand. ". . . like an awakening of senses you never knew you had, and once they're awakened, you're never the same. The way you see the world is altered. Instead of riding down a road on your bike and thinking how the wind feels good on your face, you think, 'This is how it feels when he kisses my cheek.' You play a piece on the piano, and instead of imagining a crowd applauding, you only see him, sitting in the chair next to the piano, smiling at you. You catch the scent of sage in the air and think, 'This is how he smells.' But it's also kind of like being on a mousetrap ride. Exhilarating and terrifying all at the same time. You smile and laugh and feel a thrill inside of you, all the while wondering in the back of your mind if the car will come off the track at the next turn, or if your harness will come open and you will be tossed to the ground to your death."

"And you wonder why I can't stay away from you," he said with a smile that made my heart flutter unexpectedly. "Any other girl would have said something like, 'It feels . . .'"— he folded his hands under his chin and batted his eyelashes—"'like walking on clouds.'" His hands dropped to the table, and his brows pulled together in contemplation. After a long pause, he smiled softly. "Thank you for describing it for me. Now when I find it, I'll know." He leaned forward and added, "And I hope you find it again someday."

With that he got up and left, dumping his tray of half-eaten food in the garbage on his way out of the cafeteria. I sat there feeling completely flustered. I didn't like Devin.

But for the last few minutes, I'd seen a part of him that I'd never seen before. A side he kept hidden, a caring, vulnerable side. Maybe he wasn't a jerk. Maybe he was just searching for happiness like everyone else. And even though I was only trying to repel him by sharing everything, I had to admit it was nice to talk to someone. He would probably keep his distance from me now, but I felt my burden lighten slightly after sharing it with him.

During practice for the next week, I focused on trying to infuse more feeling into my playing. When I went to my next lesson with Margo, I felt I had progressed a lot and was eager to show her how I'd improved.

I brought back the Liszt piece and played it for her, feeling that she would be happy with my progress. But only a few measures in, she slapped my hands off the keys.

"Stop!" she exclaimed.

I pulled my hands to my chest and looked at her with wide eyes.

"Aria," she chided, "where are you?"

"I'm right here."

"No!" She tapped me in the chest. "Where are *you*?" She searched my face. "What is it that you're not allowing yourself to feel?"

"I'm trying—"

"No, you're not. You tried last week, but you're not trying now. You have a gift, and what you're doing with it is a pitiful waste. You're taking a nibble from it, then tossing the bulk of it in a pig's trough like a rotten corn cob."

"I practice eight hours a day! I would hardly call that nibbling."

"You can roll a grape around on your tongue all day without tasting it."

"I—"

"Bite down, Aria! Feel the texture! Taste the bitter and the sweet! I know you're capable of it. I've heard you do it before."

What she said made sense, but I didn't know how to fix it. I turned away from her and fought back tears.

"You have nothing to hide, *ma chérie*. Let the tears come. It will help."

I stayed turned away and even though I didn't want to let the tears come, they came.

"It's okay to have pain," she said, resting her hand on my back. "We all have it. You think your classmates are without pain? They are all struggling with problems of their own. Life is full of pain, but we can take it and put it to use. Name a composer, and I will tell you about tragedy. Franz Schubert. Robert Schumann. Peter Tchaikovsky. Any one of them. And I will tell you about loss, unrequited love, and unfulfilled dreams. And yet, they all channeled that disappointment and longing and despair to create music that lifts the souls of all who hear it."

I wiped my tears with my sleeve and turned to face her.

"Frédéric Chopin was desperately in love with a young woman named Maria. But in the end, their engagement was doomed. He placed Maria's letters in an envelope, and on it, he wrote the words *moja bieda.*" Margo placed her hand over her heart and sighed.

"What does that mean?"

"'My sorrow.'" Her hand fell to mine. "I see the sorrow in you, right under your skin. I see traces and footprints of whatever it is you've had to endure. But when you keep it inside, it becomes toxic. It will destroy your music and your happiness. So, Aria, the best thing to do with your pain is to take it from here"—she tapped my chest again with her free hand, softer this time—"and put it here." She put my hand on the keyboard. "Take something ugly, and turn it into something beautiful."

I stared at the keys, trying to figure out how to do what she was suggesting without falling to pieces.

"Don't play anymore today," she ordered. "Go home and think about what I said. You need to get those locked-up feelings on the very edge of yourself—to your very fingertips. Then go to the piano and liberate those feelings. Now go." She pointed to the door. I nodded, gathered up my sheet music, and walked out of the room.

# eighteen

It was four thirty and I didn't have any more classes for the rest of the day, so I wandered around for a while, thinking of everything Margo had said. She was right. My emotional disconnect was keeping me from becoming the great musician I wanted to be. After losing Mom, I'd used music as an outlet for my feelings. But after losing Thomas, and Elsie and Hal, it had all become too much to bear and I'd closed my heart to everything, somehow thinking it would protect me from feeling pain. As I wandered, I realized how totally, utterly wrong I was. Not only was I alienating everyone around me by my coldness, but I was also destroying myself, holding at a distance the healing balms of friendship, love, and music.

I ended up in the hallway where the practice rooms were, leaning against the brick wall and debating whether to disregard Margo's order to not play any more today.

Someone was playing piano in the practice room closest to me, and it caught my ear. A strain of delicate notes from a Chopin nocturne floated from the room, so haunting and exquisite it wrenched my soul. Whoever was playing was amazing. I stepped over to the small rectangular window on the door and peered in. It was easy to recognize Devin, with his broad shoulders beneath his black suit jacket and his shaggy caramel hair.

His entire body moved with the rhythm. His hands shaped the lyrical passages with controlled power in one moment, then with succulent tenderness in the next. Mesmerized, I watched him until he finished the piece, and when he started gathering up his things, I stepped away from the door and leaned back against the wall.

The door opened and he walked out with an armful of sheet music, doing a double take when he saw me. "Aria," he said, sounding pleasantly surprised. "You waiting for a room?"

"No." I looked away, a little embarrassed. "I was just listening to you play."

"Oh." He brightened. "Why were you listening to me?"

"Who wouldn't want to listen to you play?"

"Did you just give me a compliment?" He beamed.

"I gave your playing a compliment," I qualified.

"Well, I'll take any kind of compliment from you I can get."

I dropped my gaze to the floor and kicked my heel against the wall, feeling guilty for being so cold to him when all he'd ever been to me was nice. "Can I ask you something?"

"Please do."

I looked up at him. "What do you think about . . . when you play?"

He shrugged and casually leaned his shoulder against the wall. "Just depends on the piece. A lot of the time I don't really consciously think of anything. But then sometimes, when a piece needs that extra emotional element, I think about experiences I've had, or fictional characters, or friends. In fact . . ." He smiled in the way he always did right before he razzed me about something. "Just now, I was thinking about you. That nocturne is meant to be kind of dark and depressing, and you're the most depressed person I know."

I tapped him on the chest with the back of my hand. "You know, I'm working on this really pushy, agitating piece. Maybe I'll think of you the next time I play it." My sudden playfulness surprised me, and my cheeks grew warm.

"Whatever helps." He smiled, then his face turned more serious. "Hey, do you want to go get some coffee or something later? I mean . . . you know, just as friends."

"Um"—I eyed the room behind him—"I think I'm going to take advantage of that empty practice room after all."

"All night?"

"Margo's not happy with me right now. I have a lot of work to do." Margo had told me not to play any more today, but I didn't see the point in delaying my journey into uninhibited despair.

"You know, Aria," he said, "I think you misunderstand me."

I'd started walking into the practice room, but his statement made me turn around. "What do you mean?"

"I mean I'm not the bad guy you think I am."

"I know a dozen girls who would argue with that." I meant to tease, but his usually cheerful face fell into a solemn grimace.

"You're probably right." He sighed. "I'm sorry about that. It's just that, before I came here, I'd never really dated. My parents didn't allow it. They kept me busy with practicing, studying, performing, and meeting people who could boost my career. So when I came here and lived on my own for the first time, I was like a kid who'd never tasted candy set loose in a candy store."

"So, what? I'm just a flavor you haven't tasted before?"

"No," he said adamantly. "I'm tired of candy. It gives me a stomachache. I just want a nourishing, home-cooked meal. Something sustaining and real. And you seem . . . real. Even if you don't want to date me, I wish you'd let me be your friend."

I fidgeted with my sheet music and twitched my lips, but I couldn't find an appropriate response. I was still trying to understand what he meant by his reference to candy and a home-cooked meal, and I couldn't help picturing myself as a slice of roast beef.

"Have fun practicing," he said after a long pause. "And let me know if you ever need a friend." With that, he turned to walk away.

I watched him round the corner, then stood there feeling confused. Maybe he was right. Maybe I did misunderstand him. I sighed and leaned against the doorframe.

The barren-walled corridor stirred with students, coming in and out of practice rooms, standing in small groups conversing, or sitting on the floor making notes on sheet music. I watched them, studied their expressions, their demeanor and mannerisms. In some I saw peace and contentment, but in others I saw grimaces and sighs of discouragement. They were all struggling with their own problems. They were fighting their own demons and searching for their own happiness. In that, I was not alone. I listened to the sounds coming from the practice rooms. A cheerful dramatic flourish on a piano; a lonely, high-pitched cry of a

violin; a low despondent moan of a cello. I perceived that the difference between them and me was that their music was enhanced, not hindered, by their struggles.

Watching and listening to my fellow students was like watching a flock of starlings, free and unfettered, dancing in the open sky with the ebb and flow of life. While I, a caged bird, watched with painful yearning behind wire mesh and a latched door.

I looked down at my hands. I turned them over, bent and straightened my slender fingers. They were stronger and more competent than they had ever been in my life. They held the power and capacity to reach into people's hearts, draw out their innermost emotions, and give voice to the incommunicable. Yet I kept this power locked inside me, along with all the feelings I didn't want to give voice to.

A flame, ever so small, flared to life inside me. Small as it was, it was enough to illuminate the corners and shadows of my heart to see things hidden, to see the door keeping them inside. In order to liberate myself, to use the power I knew was in my hands, I needed to open the door and set these things free.

I went into the practice room and set my sheet music on the piano, suddenly determined to do whatever it took to break out of that cage. Nathaniel and Margo had said it would be hard, but that I would get stronger, and it would get easier. I needed to trust them. I settled myself at the piano, then closed my eyes and sent a silent, pleading prayer heavenward.

With my hands poised above the keyboard, I made a conscious effort to do as Margo asked, to get my feelings on the very edge of myself. I dove into the recesses of my heart and stood before the door where all my painful memories were hidden. My hand hesitated on the latch, terrified to open it, but I knew it was what I had to do.

"Be brave," I whispered to myself. I felt a warmth within me, a burning reassurance that I was strong enough to win this fight. With a gentle touch of the keys, I unlocked the door and set myself free.

I don't know how long I played, but when I stopped, the hall was quiet. All the students had gone, either back to their apartments or out for the night. My lap was wet with tears, but I felt stronger and suddenly liberated. Not like I'd joined the flock of starlings, but like I was a lone nightingale with an open sky all to myself.

Tears rolled down my cheeks, but this time they weren't tears of sorrow; they were tears of relief and gratitude. I thought of Mom, how proud she would be if she were here. I wiped my eyes with the back of my wrist, then lifted my hands and played the first part of a simple duet I used to play with her, a sweet and melancholy melody. To my surprise, I heard the second part of the duet.

At first I thought I was imagining it, but then I realized it was coming from the next practice room. I hesitantly played the next passage, and whoever was in the next room played along with me. I played the entire piece slowly, warily, the whole time being accompanied by the piano on the other side of the wall.

When I finished the song, the playing in the next room stopped as well. I sat there for a moment, waiting to hear more playing, or footsteps, or a door opening, but I heard nothing. Cautiously, I got up to see who was in the next room. I stepped into the hall and peered out, but it was

empty. The next door over was open, and I inched closer, craning my neck to see who was in the dark room. The piano came into view, but no one was seated there. I flipped on the light and walked into the room, but it was empty, save for a black suit jacket on the floor next to the piano bench. I looked out into the hall again, this time listening carefully for footsteps.

Empty. Silent. There was no one there.

I went over and picked up the jacket. It could have been anyone's, but I suspected one person.

I took the jacket back to my practice room and sat on the bench, holding it in my lap. A subtle scent lingered on the jacket. Devin's scent. I'd never really paid attention to it before, but it was distinct enough to recognize. Subtle, musky, and a little sweet, almost like vanilla. I wondered how long he'd been sitting in the room next to me, how much of my struggle he'd heard. I didn't know whether to feel annoyed or flattered. It was something I'd have to think about when I wasn't so physically and emotionally exhausted, and ravenously hungry.

I went back to my apartment and ate, then went to bed smiling for the first time since I'd come to Juilliard, deliriously satisfied with the progress I'd made.

♪ ♪ ♪ ♪ ♪ ♪

I carried the suit jacket with me to my classes the next day. Devin came into ear training class a little late, and I watched him as he sat down across the room. He was wearing a suit jacket, but it was dark gray, not the black one he usually wore. When class was dismissed, I approached him as he gathered up his things.

"Hey, Devin," I said, keeping his suit jacket behind me.

He looked up at me and smiled in surprise. "Hey, Aria."

"There's something I need to ask you," I said, getting right to the point.

He straightened and looked at me with a raised eyebrow.

"Were you in the practice room next to mine last night while I was practicing?"

He shook his head, but I could tell from the uncomfortable twitching of his mouth that he was lying.

"Is this yours?" I asked, taking his jacket from behind my back and showing it to him.

"Uh . . ." He stared at the jacket, squinting as if examining it. "No. I don't recognize it."

"It smells like you," I said.

"How do you know what I smell like?"

I grabbed the lapel of his gray jacket, pressed my nose against it, and inhaled. When I pulled back, his lips were curved into an amused smile. "Yep," I said. "It smells like you."

He sighed. "All right. You caught me." His brow wrinkled and his expression turned serious. "I went in there to practice, but then I heard you crying. I didn't know what to do. I didn't want to leave you alone, but I didn't want to bother you either. So I just stayed there and listened. And then when I heard you play that song, I don't know why, but I couldn't help but play along. Maybe it was my way of letting you know that you weren't alone. I left after because I didn't want you to think I was creepy or anything."

"It wasn't creepy," I said. "It was sweet of you."

"A compliment."

"Yes," I said. "And this time I'm complimenting you, not your playing." I smiled, and his face lit up. I realized it was the first time I'd ever really smiled at him.

"Is everything . . . okay?"

"Yeah. I mean, it will be."

"Well," he said, moving toward the door, "I need to get to my lesson."

"Wait," I said without thinking. He turned to look at me, but I didn't really know what to say. All I knew was I didn't want him to go. I wanted to talk to him more. I wanted a friend, and I wanted Devin to be that friend. "Are you doing anything tonight?" I finally asked.

"Yeah."

"Oh." I looked down, hoping the disappointment wasn't too evident on my face. "What are you doing?" I met his eyes again, and he was smiling.

"Whatever you want," he said.

♪ ♪ ♪ ♪ ♪

For the next week, I spent every spare moment working in a practice room, excavating all the emotions I'd spent years burying. I left the door to my heart wide open, and as each day passed, the pain and the sting of my memories lessened. The music helped me to see my past in a new perspective, as evidence of my strength, as a treasure of knowledge and experience, as sweet fruit within a bitter peel.

I went out with Devin a couple times that week, once to a little cafe on Broadway, and once to a student performance at Alice Tully Hall. I was surprised at how much I enjoyed his company once I gave him a chance. He was easy to talk to, always full of interesting things to say, and not expecting much from me in return.

The following week I walked into Margo's studio, prepared to show her the progress I'd made. She air kissed me, then put her hands on my arms. "So. How did it go?"

"I did what you asked."

"Wonderful." She put her hand on my back and gestured to the piano. "Show me."

I played the same Liszt piece I'd played the week before, and when I finished and turned to see mascara running down her cheeks, I knew I'd succeeded in fulfilling her expectations. She came to me, put her arms around me, and planted a kiss on my cheek. "You will be great, *ma chérie. Tu as un bon fond.*"

Later that night, Devin took me to dinner, and after that, we became inseparable. At first, dating someone besides Thomas was a little jarring, like stepping into a cold lake. It was shocking and uncomfortable, and I constantly debated whether to turn around and go back to shore. But Devin took me by the hand and, constantly reassuring me, lured me in with his sunny personality and unending patience. Once I was fully submerged, it became comfortable enough that I could breathe again.

I accepted that there would always be questions in my heart about Thomas, where he was and what had happened to him, but I wouldn't let those questions keep me from being happy or from loving someone else. My heart was forever changed because of him, but it was free and open.

Devin and I studied together, ate together, and played together. I kept waiting for him to get tired of me, to move on to the next girl, but every evening he would show up at my door, and we'd spend the night studying or going out to do something fun. I really saw New York for the first time since I moved there. We went to Broadway shows and walked through Central Park, kissed at the top of the Empire State Building and went skating at the Rockefeller

Center. We cheered each other on at competitions and enjoyed each other's performances at concerts.

In the summer, we toured Europe with the Juilliard Orchestra. Our days were spent sightseeing, our afternoons rehearsing, and our evenings performing. We took the stages of grand historical halls, basking in the exquisite acoustics and the applause of appreciative audiences. Every time the audience rose to their feet to fill the hall with thunderous acclamation, a thrill went through me, and I understood the lure of the concert career that Nathaniel had chosen.

With Devin by my side, I saw the ornate domes of the Berlin Cathedral and wandered through the dense forests of Grunewald. We saw Buckingham Palace and Tower Bridge, explored the shops at Covent Garden and toured the art of masters at the British Museum. We picnicked on rye sandwiches and fresh raspberries in Sibelius Park in Helsinki, Finland, and rode the Ferris wheel at the Linnanmäki Amusement Park.

With Devin's fingers laced through mine, we meandered down the cobbled streets of Lucerne's Old Quarter in Switzerland, and we watched through windows the breathtaking scenery as our train climbed to the summit of Mount Pilatus.

Day by day, touch by touch, and kiss by kiss, the memories of Thomas became quieter, like they were finally resigned to take their place on a shelf and only be called forth when I wanted them. And in little moments, in amused laughter over a plate of beetroot lasagna at a seaside cafe, or in an encouraging glance before I took the stage, my feelings for Devin grew stronger. One day, when I stood on the Chapel Bridge in Switzerland, Devin's arms around me and his lips in my hair, I realized that I loved him. It felt different than the love I had for Thomas in that it was a calmer, more subdued kind of love, but without a doubt, I loved him.

♪ ♪ ♪ ♪ ♪ ♪ ♪

"Thank goodness you're back," Nakira exclaimed from the couch as I walked into our apartment with suitcases in tow. She turned to face me, her expression annoyed. "This lady has been calling you nonstop for the last three weeks."

"What lady?"

"Some lady named Vivian. I kept telling her that you wouldn't be back until this week, but she kept calling anyway. I finally just stopped answering her calls."

I wondered what Vivian was so anxious to talk to me about, but only one possibility came to mind. Maybe she knew something about Thomas. I left my suitcases in the living room and picked up the phone in the kitchen, searching the call history for Vivian's number. I found it and hit *Send*.

"Aria?" she answered excitedly.

"Hey, Vivian."

"I'm so glad you're back! I've been trying to get ahold of you for weeks!"

"I know. I've been in Europe. So what's going on?"

"Oh, you'll never guess."

"What is it?" I asked anxiously.

She took a deep breath. "I got married," she squealed.

"You got married?" I hoped my voice didn't sound too disappointed. It was great news, just not the news I was hoping for. "That's wonderful! Who's the lucky guy?"

"Okay. Now this is where you need to brace yourself."

"Why do I need to brace myself?"

"Are you ready? Are you braced?"

"I'm braced."

"All right. I married . . . your daddy."

"What! You married my dad? When? How? Why?" I felt like I'd just come home to a scene from the *Twilight Zone*.

Vivian laughed. "Well, I invited him over for dinner one night and made this delicious Brunswick stew. He must have been real impressed, because the next week he invited me to a movie. All this time, I thought I'd win him over with sweets, and the real secret to his heart was stew. Why didn't you tell me sooner?"

"Uh . . . I didn't know. I've never made stew."

"Well, anyways, it doesn't matter because a couple months ago, we were sitting in his kitchen, and I was asking him all these questions about taxidermy, like how he keeps the skin on the mannequins, and how he makes 'em look so real, and he just looked at me and said, 'Vivian, would you ever consider getting married again?' and I said, 'Well, sure, if it was the right guy.' And he smiled and said, 'Do you think I'm the right guy?' And the next thing I knew, we were down at the courthouse, gettin' married. I'm selling my house, and we're moving all my things into his house as we speak."

I was stunned into silence, and I stood there trying to figure out how to respond. I was happy for Vivian because she seemed so happy. But I couldn't make sense of it. I couldn't imagine Dad sitting across the kitchen table from Vivian, smiling at her and asking her to marry him. I couldn't imagine Dad in a tux, Vivian's arm looped through his as they exchanged wedding vows. It seemed so unreal, like some impossible scenario I could have only conjured up in a dream.

"Aria? You there?" Vivian asked.

"Yes. I'm here. I'm . . . really happy for you. For both of you. Is he being good to you?"

"Oh, honey. He is wonderful. You know him—he's never been a talker, but he is so sweet and thoughtful. He's even been letting me decorate the house the way I want."

"Good," I said cautiously. "Vivian, I really am happy for you, but . . . I have to warn you. When he drinks . . ."

"Oh, I know all about that, sweetheart. I figured it out a couple weeks after we started dating. I found him in his barn one night, drunker than Cooter Brown. I sat him down the next day and I told him that I couldn't be with a drunk, that I've been in too many of those kinds of relationships. So he started cryin'. And I mean *cryin'*. I haven't seen waterworks like that since I accidentally axed my water line in oh-nine."

Before I could ask her what she meant by "axing her water line," she said, "Anyway, he opened up to me, sayin' how he didn't want to be that person anymore, that he wanted to be happy and free, so we went and found some of those AA meetings to go to. He's had a couple setbacks, but he's doing real good. Hasn't had a drink in six months."

"But why, Vivian? Why do you want to be with him?"

"Because he's a good man, and I love him. He's been through some tough things, like we all have, and he deserves a chance to be happy." She sighed. "Listen, I know you and your daddy aren't on the best of terms, but I know he really misses you. He always gets real sad when I talk about you. I think he wants to see you, to know how you

are, but he's too afraid to call you or come visit. He thinks you don't want anything to do with him."

"It's not that, Vivian. I wish things could be the way they were when I was younger. But so many painful things have happened between us that I don't even know where to begin to repair our relationship."

"Well, I think the first step would be coming to visit. How about you come home and visit us for the holidays?"

"I don't know . . ."

"Come on, darlin'. I'll even pay your fare. Listen, I wasn't supposed to say anything, but your daddy has a surprise for you. He'll be so disappointed if you don't come. And I'm redoin' your room and everything. Please say you'll come."

"I'll try," I said, but apparently my answer wasn't good enough because Vivian proceeded to beg and plead until I finally caved. "All right," I said. "I'll come home for Christmas."

# nineteen

At the last minute, Devin decided to come to Woodland Park to spend Christmas with me instead of his family, and on December twentieth we flew into Colorado Springs. After picking up a rental car, we stopped at Nathaniel's to have lunch. It was the first time he'd met Devin, and for some reason, Nathaniel seemed uneasy. As we went to leave, he stopped me in the doorway and put his hands on my shoulders, looking me in the eye.

"Brace yourself," he said.

"I'll be fine," I assured him.

"I know you will. But just . . ." His expression became guarded and his eyes flashed to Devin, like there was something he wanted to say but couldn't in Devin's presence. "Come see me again before you go back to New York," he settled for. "Call me if you need anything, or if you decide you want to come stay here instead."

"Okay, I will," I said suspiciously, making a mental note to call him later to find out what he'd really wanted to say.

As we drove along the highway toward Woodland Park,

I tried to prepare myself for a reunion with Dad. It had been a year and a half since I'd seen him, and until Vivian called a few months earlier, I'd avoided thinking of him. But since she called, he'd been in my thoughts almost constantly. Vivian had said that he'd changed, and maybe it was true. Maybe things could be different between us. I'd spent the last few weeks trying to wash away the painful memories of adolescence with the pleasant memories of childhood. The more I did so, the greater my desire became to repair my relationship with him.

"Are you nervous?" Devin asked.

I considered his question, and the thought of facing Dad again caused a tremor in my stomach that left me weak. I didn't want to discuss the past with him. I didn't want him to remind me of the times he'd hurt me and held me back. I didn't want him to say he was sorry, even if he was. That period of my life had already been laid to rest like dust after a windstorm. Why disturb it now? I just wanted to show up and have him take me in his arms, tell me he loved me and missed me, as though the last time I had seen him was when I was seven, not seventeen. So I wouldn't bring up the past. And I hoped he wouldn't either.

"It will be strange to see my dad married to someone else," I said, not feeling comfortable expressing all my thoughts to Devin. "I can't seem to picture it."

Devin squeezed my hand. "If it's too strange or uncomfortable, we can go stay somewhere else."

"We'll see," I said. "Vivian said he's changed for the better, and I'd like to give him a chance. He is my father, after all."

"Do you wish you could have gone to his wedding?"

"No." I shrugged. "We were in Europe anyway."

He was quiet for a moment, his expression contemplative. "You know, I've been thinking."

"About what?"

He glanced at me, cautious excitement in his eyes. "What if . . . ?"

"What if what?"

"What if you and I got married?"

"You . . . want to marry me?" He couldn't be serious. How could he be when we were so young?

"Yes." He smiled and squeezed my knee.

"Aren't you supposed to get down on one knee and offer me a ring or something?" I was trying to make a joke of it, but he didn't seem to see it that way.

"I can still do that if you want. Sorry, I wasn't planning on bringing it up. It just kind of came out."

My heart was suddenly pounding in my chest, but I couldn't tell if it was from excitement or anxiety. "Devin, I . . . I don't know. To be honest, the thought of marriage hasn't ever even crossed my mind. I mean, I haven't even had time to consider the idea."

"But what do you need to consider? You know me." He gazed at me with his puppy eyes. "We've dated for almost a year."

"Ten months," I corrected.

"That's what I said. Almost a year. And I don't think spending more time together will change the way we feel about each other." He sighed. "Remember the time we sat in the cafeteria, when you still hated me"—he smiled and gave me a sidelong glance—"and you described to me what love felt like?"

"I remember."

"Well, that's exactly how you make me feel. And I can't

imagine anyone else who would make me feel that way." He lifted my hand and pressed it to his lips. "You and I are perfect for each other. I can see us traveling the world together, just like we did last summer. We share the same passions. We understand one another. So what do you say? Let's get married." His eyes were alight with such fiery enthusiasm that I had to look away before I said yes without thinking.

He was right. We were perfect for each other. I wanted to say yes, but somehow, I couldn't make my mouth form the word. Maybe I just needed more time to get used to the idea.

"Do you love me?" he asked.

I stroked his cheek with my finger and gazed into his waiting copper eyes. "Yes."

He turned his face into my hand affectionately. "Why do you love me?"

"Because whenever I see you walk into a room, I can't help but smile. Because you make me feel safe, like you would never hurt me. Because every time I hear you play, I am completely mesmerized. And my life would be dull and drab without you."

"So then marry me."

"Devin, I just . . . don't feel ready. I'm only nineteen."

"My parents were eighteen when they got married, and they just celebrated their thirty-fifth anniversary."

I nodded slowly and turned to gaze out the window. Again, he was right. Did it really matter how old two people were as long as they were right for each other? And Devin and I were certainly right for each other. We got along, we enjoyed each other's company, we had everything in common. So what caused my hesitation? A face appeared in my mind, with dark hair and bright blue eyes, giving me the answer I already knew. I could never give my whole heart to Devin until I knew what had become of Thomas. But how would I find the answers I needed? Maybe when I got back to New York, I would renew my search efforts. I would call Richard again, and any other relatives I could find. In fact, maybe I would call them when we got to Dad's house and I had a moment by myself. If I still didn't find any answers, I would call hospitals and police departments and search online databases. Maybe I would even look into hiring a private detective. Though I had no way of paying for it.

I felt Devin's hand wrap gently around mine, pulling me back to our unfinished conversation. "Aria," he said, "you don't have to answer me now. I just want you to think about it."

I took his hand and pressed his open palm against my cheek. "I love you, Devin." I gave a rueful sigh and leaned against his shoulder, looping my arm through his. "I'm sorry I'm not ready to give you an answer. But I promise I will seriously think about it."

He kissed me on the head. "That's all I ask. And, remember, you already know how I feel about you. So when you feel ready, let me know and I'll drop down on one knee."

"You're too wonderful, Devin," I whispered.

"I know," he said. "That's why you should marry me."

A few minutes later, we pulled into Dad's driveway. His truck was gone, but a black sedan was parked on the gravel, and I figured it was Vivian's. We parked next to it and got out. The outside of the house looked much the same as the last time I'd seen it, including the white snow shrouding the roof and yard. While Devin pulled luggage from the trunk, I climbed the steps to the covered porch and

knocked on the door. There was no answer, so I turned the doorknob and found it unlocked. Slowly, I opened the door and stepped inside.

My first reaction at seeing Dad's transformed living room was a sense of disorientation, like I'd stepped into the wrong house. My second reaction was to smile. Vivian had certainly brought an element of warmth back to the house, but it looked like she'd had to work around the things Dad wouldn't give up. Harriet and Ned, the two quails, now shared their tree branch mount with bursting cherry blossoms, and a matching floral swag hung over their heads. Ann the fox was untouched on the side table, but she now sat on a white lace doily. Dad's old couch had been replaced by Vivian's floral sofas, and her glass knickknacks were lined up on the fireplace mantel. But the most notable difference was that Knox the wolf was missing. I wondered how Vivian had convinced him to give up his most prized possession.

"Hello?" I called out as I stepped further in.

There was no answer.

"Where should I put these?" Devin asked in the doorway, towing his suitcases behind him.

"Oh. Probably in the downstairs bedroom. It's the only spare room with a bed." I led him down the hall to the spare bedroom and flipped on the light. A large gray wolf with bared teeth welcomed us, and I jumped back into Devin and gasped. "So this is where she hid him."

Devin paused in the doorway and stared at Knox with wide eyes.

"I told you," I said, "my dad likes to hunt."

"Yeah, but I was thinking ducks or deer or squirrels. How am I going to sleep with that thing staring at me all night?"

"Sorry, I didn't know it was in here. It used to be in the living room."

Devin dropped his suitcase by the bed. "I'm a big boy. I'll be fine. Where's your room?"

"Upstairs."

"I'll go get your suitcase."

He left the room, and I wandered back into the living room. Through the window I saw Vivian pull into the driveway in a white pick-up truck. She got out and started talking to Devin. I was about to go out to greet her when my eyes were drawn to the parlor.

The parlor door was wide open, and the afternoon sun spilled out of the room. I slowly approached the parlor and stepped inside. Mom's piano stood, as always, in the center of the room. But the last time I'd seen it was after Dad had taken a crow bar to it. Now the lid was reattached and open with the lid prop. The broken keys had been replaced, and the shiny lacquer repaired. So this was the surprise— Mom's piano mended and made new. What did this mean? Did it mean that Dad was finally ready to have music in his home again? That his heart was finally healed enough to hear me play? Or did he just feel so guilty about everything that had happened that this was his way of making restitution? Regardless of the reason, I was overcome with emotion. With tears brimming on my lashes, I sat at the piano. I played a few keys and was pleased to hear it had been tuned.

Sinking gently into a Debussy piece, my ears and heart rejoiced at the rich, familiar tones of Mom's piano. It had been over two years since I played it, and it sounded just as sweet. Only my hands had grown more competent, making it easier and more natural to play. I breathed my soul into the neglected instrument, and it came to life and welcomed me back like an old friend.

Halfway through the piece, I sensed someone behind me. I glanced back to see who it was, and my hands froze on the keys. I stood with such swiftness that I knocked over the piano bench behind me.

It wasn't Dad. It wasn't Vivian or Devin.

Whether ghost, illusion, or flesh and blood, Thomas Ashby stood at the threshold of the parlor, his bright blue eyes fastened on me. His face, adorned in the ethereal afternoon light, was wistful and uncertain.

My mind couldn't seem to wrap itself around the scene before me. It could not accept the image my eyes were attempting to transmit. *You're lying,* my mind said to my eyes. But it didn't matter what my mind said. My heart received the message with foolhardy eagerness.

"Aria," he whispered, taking a step toward me.

At the sound of his voice, my heart lurched violently inside my chest and my knees started shaking. Maybe it was because I wasn't breathing, but I suddenly felt light-headed. I leaned back on the keyboard to steady myself, and the upper keys made a discordant crashing sound.

The front door opened, and Devin walked in carrying my suitcase. Vivian followed close behind, holding a paper bag full of groceries. "Goodness, Aria," Vivian said in a delighted voice. "Why didn't you tell me you were bringing a guest?"

I stared at Vivian with wide eyes, but I couldn't manage to get a single word through my lips. Luckily, she took control of the situation. She glanced at Devin.

"Devin," she said, gesturing to Thomas, "this is Thomas. He's an old family friend. He's going to be staying with us for a few days."

My mouth dropped open but still no words came.

Devin gave a small wave. "Hey. Nice to meet you." He nodded to my suitcase. "Where should I put this?"

"Oh," Vivian said. "Upstairs, second door on the left."

He carried my suitcase up the stairs, and Vivian turned to Thomas. "Thomas, honey, could you help me bring in the groceries?"

"Of course," he said, and after a quick glance at me, he turned and headed for the door.

I floated to the parlor window and watched him as he walked across the driveway to Vivian's truck. I couldn't pull my eyes away from him; it was like watching a ghost.

"Devin, honey," I heard Vivian say, "would you help Thomas bring in the rest of the groceries? There's something upstairs I need to show Aria."

Through the window, I watched Devin walk outside and meet Thomas at the truck, where they pulled bags of groceries from the bed. Devin was saying something to Thomas, but I couldn't hear what.

"Aria!" I swung around to see Vivian halfway up the stairs, waving for me to follow. I peeled myself from the window and followed her upstairs.

When I first stepped into my old room, I didn't recognize it. My antique white furniture was the same, but the walls were covered in gold and purple damask wallpaper, and the bed was buried beneath a skirt of flounced purple satin and a mountain of ruffled, embroidered pillows. Matching curtains hung over the window, and Vivian's doll collection was scattered about the room, on my desk, dresser, nightstand, and window seat. But my room didn't matter. There were more important issues at hand than my old room being transformed into a doll museum.

I sat beside Vivian on the bed and unleashed all my questions. "Why is he here? Where has he been? When did he get here?" My breaths were shallow, and I still felt light-headed.

"Calm down, sweetheart." She put her arm around me and pulled me close, speaking with quiet urgency. "All I know is this. He showed up here last night, and believe me, I was as surprised as you. He and your daddy went back into the guest bedroom and they talked for a long time. And they talked so quiet, I couldn't hear what they were saying, even with my ear pressed to the door. And when I asked your daddy about it later, he was not very specific about what they'd talked about. But what I did find out from Thomas is that he's been in the Netherlands these last couple years."

"What?" I asked incredulously.

"Yeah. I guess he was doing some kind of fishin' or somethin'."

"Fishing," I repeated in disbelief. "In the Netherlands." An unexpected surge of anger pulsed through my veins. I had spent the last two years in anguish over him, wondering where he was, worrying that he was dead, and he was *fishing?* "Well, why is he here then?" I hissed.

"He said something about needing to finish up some business."

The words only added fuel to my burning rage. So he was here on business, and he wanted to drop in and say hi. "But why is he *here*? In my dad's house?"

"Well, he was stayin' in a hotel, but your daddy insisted that he get his stuff and stay here."

"*Dad* insisted? Why?"

"I don't know why. But he's staying in the room right next to yours."

"But there's not a bed."

"There is now. We had so much extra furniture when we moved all my stuff in here." She let out an anxious sigh. "Oh, honey, I didn't know you'd be bringing Devin, and I thought you'd be happy to see Thomas. Do you want me to just tell him to go?"

"I . . . I don't know." I pictured Thomas leaving, and the thought made me panicky. "No. I need to talk to him. Did he say why he didn't call, or write, or let me know where he was?"

"No, I haven't had much chance to talk to him at all. He was gone this morning when I woke up, and then I went shopping, so this is the first time I've seen him today."

"Where did he go this morning?"

"I don't know, honey. But, listen, what do you want me to tell Devin? I mean, who should I say Thomas is?"

I shook my head. "I don't know. I mean, he is an old family friend, I guess."

"Done." She patted my knee and stood up to leave. "I better go get dinner started."

"Vivian," I said, standing and holding open my arms. "It's good to see you."

She took me in her arms and pecked me on the cheek. "It's good to see you too, darlin'. You look wonderful, by the way."

"Where's my dad?"

"At work until tomorrow morning."

I had to admit, I was more than relieved I wouldn't have to deal with two awkward reunions in the same day.

Vivian went downstairs, and I fell back on my bed and stared at the ceiling, marinating in my anger. Every tear I'd cried, every pain I'd suffered over Thomas had been made

in vain by four little words. *Fishing. In. The. Netherlands.*
A storm of emotion gathered inside me, building pressure
with each quickening breath.

I heard Devin's voice downstairs, and I wondered how
long it would be before he came upstairs for me. I didn't
want him to see me this way. A major meltdown was on
its way, and I needed some privacy. I jumped up and flung
open my suitcase, grabbed some clothes and toiletries, and
rushed across the hall to the bathroom, where I locked
the door behind me. There was only one place right now
where I wouldn't be disturbed. I turned on the shower and
stripped off my clothes, then stepped in and sat in the
cold porcelain tub. I pulled my knees to my chest and let
the water run over me. It grew warmer, and gave me the
cocoon I needed to grieve in secret. I lowered my head into
my arms and released quiet sobs, letting the water wash
away my tears.

How could I have mistaken his feelings for me? He must
not have cared about me as much as I thought he did if he
could so easily brush me off and leave the country without
a word. Two years without a word. Two years without a
thought of me. While I spent countless tears and sleepless nights on him. I felt betrayed and deceived, stupid and
gullible for believing that he loved me. I was relieved that
he was back, to know that he was okay. But I was furious
that he let me believe that he loved me and that he would
return to me. He had returned, but a year and a half late,
and only to take care of business. The sharpness of that
truth stung me to the core.

I cried until the water grew cold, then I forced myself
to stand and quickly wash my hair. I got out and wrapped
a towel around me, then looked in the mirror and took a

deep breath. I would be mature about this. I didn't know why he was here, but I didn't want him to know how much he had hurt me. I wanted him to see that I was happy with Devin, and that he would never have the ability to hurt me again.

Wanting to postpone the awkward dinner I knew was before me, I took my time getting ready. I put on a fitting red sweater with elbow-length ruched sleeves and dark jeans. I dried my long hair with a diffuser to bring out the natural waves, then made sure my bangs were swept perfectly across my forehead. Makeup was next, followed by simple silver earrings. I took one last look in the mirror, pleased with how pretty I looked.

When I opened the bathroom door, the dreamy passages of *The Venetian Gondola* drifted up the hallway from the parlor. Devin was performing in a Mendelssohn tribute in three weeks, so he would be practicing a lot while we were here. As I inched my way down the hall, the living room slowly came into view. Orange embers glowed in the stone fireplace. Devin sat in the parlor in his black suit jacket, swooning in the harmonies he drew from the piano. In front of the window, the Christmas tree sparkled with white lights and glittery ornaments. And Thomas sat on the sofa, ankle resting on his knee, head bent to the book in his lap. With a pencil in his hand, he made strokes in the book as though drawing something.

It was still shocking to see him sitting there, and I quietly observed him, taking in the visual details that had been lost to me for far too long. He wore a dark green zip-neck sweater, jeans, and hiking boots. His features seemed more rugged than before. The shadow of a beard framed the strong curve of his jaw, and his hair was longer, dark

shaggy waves falling across his brow and onto his collar. He appeared thicker, more mature and muscular. But what struck me the most was that he was even more arrestingly beautiful than I remembered.

His pencil paused, and he lifted his gaze to the parlor and watched Devin play for a moment. I couldn't see his expression, but his jaw tightened like he was annoyed. Or was he jealous? As though feeling my gaze on him, he turned his head and raised his eyes to meet mine. I caught a look of raw pain before he composed his expression into a small but warm smile.

I didn't know how to respond. I didn't know which mask to put on, or whether I should simply go without one. What was I going to say to him? I had so many questions to ask him, but I didn't know how to go about it. How could I talk to him with Devin here? And what if I had a chance to talk to him alone? Did I even want him to know that I wanted answers? Or should I just pretend I was not affected by him being here? While I was thinking all this, Thomas kept his gaze on me, his little smile slowly disappearing.

Vivian came out of the kitchen and announced that dinner was ready. My time for indecision was up. Thomas rose from the couch and followed Vivian into the kitchen. Devin came out of the parlor and stopped at the bottom of the stairs, holding his hand out to me.

"You look gorgeous," he said with a wide grin.

I met him at the bottom of the stairs and took his hand, and we walked into the kitchen together.

# twenty

W ow, Vivian," I said as I walked into the kitchen and saw that it had been transformed like the rest of the house. "You've been busy." The once-bland room was now a warm and colorful country kitchen, complete with red tile backsplash, rooster border, and plaid curtains.

"Like I said to you before," she said proudly, "it needed a woman's touch."

Devin pulled out my chair, then sat beside me. There was some shuffling on the other side of the table as Vivian awkwardly tried to figure out where to sit, whether to take the seat across from me or to leave it open for Thomas. Thomas sat across from Devin, putting an end to her dilemma.

After Vivian offered grace, an uncomfortable silence settled over the table as we dished up chicken cacciatore and roasted asparagus. Vivian kept glancing between Thomas and me, only adding to the discomfiture of his sudden reappearance.

"Where's your father?" Devin asked me, breaking the silence.

"At work," I said. "You'll get to meet him tomorrow."

"Jed is a firefighter." Vivian's green eyes beamed with pride.

"And a hunter, or so the wolf in my room tells me," Devin said. He smiled at me playfully. "Speaking of disturbing decor, you never told me you collected dolls."

I kicked him under the table. "I don't."

"Oh, those are mine," Vivian said apologetically, tucking a lock of blonde hair behind her ear. "Goodness, I hope they're not too disturbing. Most of them are family heirlooms. They seemed to go best in that room, seeing how it's the most feminine. I hope you don't mind, Aria."

"No, not at all," I said. "It's not my room anymore anyway." I glanced across the table at Thomas, who was looking down and tearing off a piece of chicken with his fork.

Devin must have followed my gaze, because he said, "So . . . Thomas, is it?"

Thomas looked up and nodded. His expression was flat, unreadable.

"How exactly do you know Aria's family?" Devin asked.

"Oh," Vivian broke in, "Thomas used to live right next door to Aria. And his Grandpa Frank lived there before that, isn't that right?"

Thomas nodded and gave Vivian a little smile.

I wished he would say something. I decided to ask him a question, if only to hear his voice. "So, Thomas," I stammered, and his eyes lit up like he was surprised to hear me addressing him. "The Netherlands?"

"Yeah," he said soberly. "Zierikzee, to be exact. It's about an hour from Rotterdam."

We'd performed in Amsterdam on our European tour, and it was unnerving to think that I'd unknowingly been only a couple hours away from him. "Vivian said you were fishing?" I tried to keep the incredulity out of my voice but didn't entirely succeed.

"Well, not recreational fishing. I've been working on a trawler."

"What do you fish?" Devin asked.

"Mostly plaice and sole."

"We tried some sole when we were in London, remember, Sweetie?" Devin asked me with a nudge. "It was good. Had a mild taste, like sturgeon."

"Yeah," I said weakly, "I think I remember."

"So," Thomas said, "you got into Juilliard. That's great."

"Yeah. It has been great."

Small talk. Stupid, fruitless small talk. We may as well be discussing fried eggs. I wanted to grab Thomas by the collar and demand an explanation, but I was forced to politely sit there and ignore the purple elephant sitting at the dining table.

"And what about you, Devin?" Vivian asked. "Tell us all about yourself."

Not that Devin ever needed much encouragement to talk about himself, but he seemed more eager than usual, maybe because he sensed competition in the room. While he gave a dazzling account of his life, including prestigious training and worldwide performances, I couldn't keep from stealing glances at Thomas. He sat there expressionless, mechanically eating and staring at a spot on the table like he was tuning out everything Devin was saying.

*Fishing,* I thought. *Fishing plaice and sole.* I imagined him on his vessel, breathing in salty sea air and feeling the sun on his shoulders, pulling in a net bursting with fish and smiling to himself, all while I lay curled in a ball on my bed, crying for him until I couldn't breathe. Maybe I didn't need answers. Maybe I should just tell him to go and never come back.

"Aria, are you okay?" I turned to see Devin looking at me anxiously, and I realized I was not eating.

"I'm fine," I said, spearing an asparagus and forcing myself to take a bite.

"Are you sure?" he pressed. "You look a little sick."

"You do look a tad pale, honey," Vivian added.

"I'm fine," I assured them again. "I think it's just jet lag."

"Why don't you go lie down?" Devin suggested. "I'll put your plate in the fridge for later."

"No, really. I'm fine."

Thomas pushed his chair out abruptly and stood. He lifted his plate and turned to Vivian. "Thanks for the delicious meal, Vivian. I have some errands to run, but I'll be back later."

"Oh. Okay," Vivian said, looking concerned.

Thomas walked to the sink and rinsed his dishes, then turned back to us. "Don't wait up or anything. I'll probably be back late." With that, he walked out of the kitchen, and I stared blankly after him.

I felt Devin's hand on my leg. "Go lie down," he encouraged gently.

I heard the front door open and close, and I fought an urge to jump up and run after him. "Okay," I conceded, feeling like I really did need to lie down.

I left the kitchen and went upstairs. As I passed the

room Thomas was staying in, I opened the door, wanting to make sure his things were still there. The plaid quilt on his bed was pulled back halfway and the sheet rumpled. His suitcase lay on the floor at the end of the bed. I went to my room, flopping onto the fluffy satin bedspread and trying to calm myself.

I heard Vivian and Devin cleaning up dinner downstairs, and I listened to the chatter between them. Devin was asking her about her doll collection, obviously to redeem himself for calling them "disturbing" earlier. I smiled, endeared by his attempt to reassure her.

Soon Devin came up and tapped on my door before coming in. He sat on the edge of the bed and stroked my hair.

"Are you okay?" he asked.

I looked into his concerned eyes, and I suddenly felt ashamed. Why did I care that Thomas was here when I had such a wonderful guy? I sat up, wrapped my arms around his waist, and leaned my head against his shoulder. "I'm feeling better," I murmured into his ear.

"Do you want to catch a movie or something?"

I shook my head. "Let's go down to the parlor and play some duets."

He smiled and patted my hand. "You're my kind of girl."

We spent a couple hours in the parlor, improvising playful duets from pieces that weren't meant to be duets. It was a pastime we'd grown into, and I recognized, not for the first time, what a good friend Devin was to me. I watched his hands move across the keyboard with absurd proficiency while he flashed his contagious smile, the way he always did when he wanted to pull a smile out of me.

Devin Fineberg was everything I'd ever wanted in a

man. And he had just asked me to marry him. Why wasn't I throwing myself into his arms and promising him my heart and soul? I wanted more than anything to be able to accept his marriage proposal. I'd told myself earlier in the car that I couldn't give him my whole heart until I knew what had become of Thomas. Well, Thomas was here, and now was my chance to get answers. For Devin.

I decided I would wait for Thomas to get back, then I would pull him aside and ask him the things I needed to know. Then I could move on with my life. I could get married and never look back.

♪ ♪ ♪ ♪ ♪ ♪

It was midnight, and Thomas still hadn't come back. Devin had gone to bed an hour earlier, and I'd spent the remaining time pacing in my room and glancing out my window every ten seconds. Where was he?

I shivered, and I wasn't sure if it was from the drafty window or from my nerves. I rubbed my arms, then grabbed an afghan from the window seat and wrapped it around my shoulders before resuming pacing.

Finally, around twelve thirty, headlights lit up the driveway. I looked out my window to see Thomas getting out of the rental car. My pulse was suddenly thrumming in my ears, and I sat on my bed and took a few deep breaths. Why was I so nervous? It was simple, right? I just needed to ask him some questions. I listened to him come up the stairs and softly shut the door to his room. I got up and paced a few more times, shaking my hands at my sides to release my nerves.

"Okay, Aria," I said to myself, "you can do this."

After a few more minutes of pacing and building up

courage, I opened my door and tiptoed into the hall, where I stopped in front of Thomas's door. I tapped lightly and waited a few seconds, but when I didn't hear anything, I cracked open the door. Soft light filled his room from the lamp on his side table, and he lay on the bed on his stomach, head turned away from me. My hand trembled on the doorknob as I slipped into his room and closed the door behind me. I waited for him to turn and look at me, but other than his back expanding with each breath, he didn't move.

"Thomas?" I whispered.

He remained still. Could he be asleep already? It hadn't been more than ten minutes since he got back. Then I noticed he was still in his clothes, boots on and everything. Different boots than the ones he'd been wearing earlier. They were heavy snow boots that came to his mid-calf, and they were caked with mud. Where had he been? What errand would have caused him to come back with muddy feet?

I circled the bed and saw that his eyes were closed. Whatever he'd been doing, it must have exhausted him. A strange heat flooded my veins at the sight of his face, leaving me weak. I sunk to my knees, letting the afghan fall off my shoulders to the floor. I leaned on the edge of the bed and stared at him, letting my eyes wander over the familiar lines of his face. Without thinking, I reached up and brushed his tousled hair away from his eyes. Between his brows was a faint line, as though he dreamed of something that troubled him. His lips, full and perfect, were chapped from being exposed to the elements.

I listened to his deep, rhythmic breathing and felt my own breath falling in time with his. It was like I'd been

unknowingly holding my breath since the day he left, and having him here allowed me to breathe again. The burning uneasiness that I hadn't even realized was there was gone, a calm replacing it. The relief was so overwhelming, I bent my head and released a wave of silent tears.

When I looked back up at him, I questioned my plan. Did I really want to hear him say the words that would pulverize my heart once and for all? Did I want to see him laugh and shake his head, and look at me condescendingly like I was delusional, like I was the one who was in the wrong? *What do you mean you waited for me all that time,* I imagined him saying, *I thought I made it clear when I left that I wanted nothing more to do with you.* Maybe his words wouldn't be quite so harsh, but it didn't matter. I would be torn apart by any way he phrased his rejection.

Maybe if I waited until tomorrow, I would feel stronger, more prepared to hear the words that would cut me off from him permanently. I stood and went back to my room, deciding I could wait one more day to get my answers.

I slept restlessly all night. Every time I closed my eyes and started to drift off, a jolt of fear would wake me up. Fear that when I awoke in the morning, Thomas would be gone. I knew the thought was irrational, so I forced myself to stay in bed. When I finally fell asleep for long enough to dream, I dreamed I was walking along a deserted seaside street in the Netherlands, searching for Thomas. I called out his name, and my voice echoed like I was inside a hollow cavern. The harbor was filled with boats, and the water beyond was unnaturally still, like a sheet of glass that would shatter if disturbed. He was not there. I ran down the streets and called out his name until my voice was hoarse, then I sank to my knees in the middle of a cobblestone street and wept bitterly into my hands.

♪ ♪ ♪ ♪ ♪ ♪

I woke up in the late morning to the sounds of Devin's arpeggio scales. I threw my blankets off and jumped out of bed, the terror of my dream forefront in my sluggish mind. I went straight to Thomas's room and flung open his door.

He was not there. But his suitcase still sat on the floor, with two pairs of boots next to it. A black peacoat and a heavier brown coat lay draped over the footboard. I breathed a sigh of relief.

With my head a little clearer, I came out of his room and approached the top of the stairs, staying in the shadows of the hallway. From a bird's-eye view, I saw Dad sitting on the sofa next to Thomas. They sat closely, angled toward each other and engaged in a hushed conversation.

I recalled the last time I'd seen Dad. We'd had a tense conversation on the porch before I left for Juilliard, and I'd left angry and hurt. I watched him now, waiting to feel something. But strangely, seeing Dad produced no effect on me. The tension caused by Thomas's presence supplanted everything else. I tried to set it aside but could only manage to peek around it, just enough to see Dad and the unavoidable task ahead of me. The task of greeting him, of surveying him, of determining where we stood.

Devin still played in the parlor, but Dad didn't seem bothered by it, or to even notice it. Thomas held an open book in his hands, and he was pointing to something in it and asking Dad a question. I watched their lips and strained to hear their words, but their voices were drowned out by Devin's scales.

I must have finally caught Thomas's eye, because he looked up at me. He closed the book and stopped talking, then nodded his head slightly in my direction, alerting Dad to my presence. Dad turned and glanced at me, then stood. A feeling finally came to me then, and it was easy to pinpoint.

*Dread.*

I thought about going back to my room. I was still in my pajamas, after all, and my long hair was tousled and tumbling over my shoulders. But they'd already seen me, so what did it matter? The sooner I got this over with, the better.

I stepped forward and slowly descended to meet him, a nauseating grip tightening my stomach with each step. What was I going to say to him? How would he react to me being here and to hearing Mom's piano being played? He'd been doing so well without me here. Would my presence dredge up feelings too difficult for him to handle? Would his words bring memories too heavy for me to bear?

Dad waited for me to get to the bottom of the stairs before he took a cautious step toward me. "Aria," he said with a nod.

"Hi, Dad." I glanced at the parlor, and Dad must have seen the anxiety in my face because he followed my eyes, then turned back to me with a reassuring smile.

"It's okay," he said. "A lot has changed around here." With his red hair trimmed short and his usual plaid shirt tucked into his jeans, he looked much the same as he did the last time I saw him. And yet he looked different. His blue eyes were clear and untroubled, his countenance relaxed and friendly.

"I can see that," I said, feeling myself relax a little too. "Thank you for fixing the piano. It means a lot to me."

He nodded once, seeming uncomfortable with the subject.

"Did you get a chance to meet Devin?" I gestured to the parlor, intending to officially introduce them.

"Yes," Dad said. "We met earlier, when you were sleeping. He seems like a really nice fellow." His face turned thoughtful, and a look of penitence wrinkled his brow. "It's good to have you home, Aria."

"Thank you," I said, unable to say honestly that it was good to be home. I asked him how his taxidermy business was going and how the guys at the fire station were doing. And to my surprise, he asked me about Juilliard. With vagueness and caution, I told him about my classes and my trip to Europe.

Thomas stayed seated while Dad and I talked, but my eyes kept flitting to him. Over a plaid cotton shirt, he wore a half-buttoned azure blue sweater that made his eyes stunningly bright. He was watching me, studying me.

Vivian came bouncing out of the kitchen, her youthful ponytail swaying back and forth. She teased me about sleeping in, then asked if I wanted some french toast.

"Sounds wonderful," I said, starving from not eating much dinner the night before. I felt Thomas's eyes on me as I followed Vivian into the kitchen, but I couldn't meet his gaze.

Vivian dished up a plate of french toast and set it in front of me along with a tall glass of orange juice. She started doing dishes while I ate, chattering away about something, but I wasn't hearing anything she said. All I could think about was Thomas, how I was going to pull him aside and

talk to him, and how I was going to preface and phrase all my questions.

"What's he doing all the way out there?" she asked.

I looked up from my plate, thinking I'd missed a question, but she was squinting out the window.

"Who?"

"Thomas. He's plowin' through the snow toward the mountain."

I jumped up and rushed to the window. There was Thomas, walking into some pines on the east side of Dad's barn. "Maybe he's going to check on his telescope." I turned to Vivian and grabbed her arm. "Vivian, I need your help."

"What with, sweetheart?" Her face was suddenly concerned.

I heard the playing in the parlor stop, so I whispered, "I need to talk to Thomas today. Alone."

"Say no more," she whispered back.

Devin came into the kitchen and I turned to greet him. He looked extra handsome in a snug V-neck sweater, the red color complementing the richness of his eyes. He put his arms around my waist and bent to kiss me. "Good morning, gorgeous."

"Good morning," I replied with a smile.

"Devin," Vivian said as she turned off the faucet and dried her hands on a towel, "I'm going to do some last-minute Christmas shopping today. I was wondering if you would be so kind as to come with me. I need someone to carry all my bags for me."

"Uh . . ." He hesitated, looking at me with uncertainty. I nodded and smiled to encourage him. "Sure," he finally said. "Can Aria come too?"

"Oh, no," Vivian said, putting her hand on her hip and

shaking her head. "I want you to help me pick out a gift for her, and I don't want her to see what it is."

Devin eyed me warily. "Will you be okay here alone?"

"I'll be fine. I need to catch up on my practicing anyway." It was true. I did need to practice. But it would have to wait until after I talked to Thomas.

I went upstairs and showered and dressed as quickly as possible, putting on a heather-blue sweater and jeans. I half-dried my hair and dabbed on some makeup, then came back downstairs. I looked out the front window to see Vivian's truck gone, and a black wing of clouds rising ominously on the north horizon. I slid into my coat and snow boots, then hurried out the back door.

A whirl of snow powder rolled across the drifts in the backyard, and a frigid gust of wind whipped my hair as I walked away from the house. I shoved my hands in my pockets and shivered. I thought about going back to get my gloves and hat, but I didn't want to waste any more time. Besides, I would be at the tree house soon, and it would provide enough shelter.

I followed the path Thomas had blazed in the calf-deep snow, past the barn and over the wooden fence, through the orchard and across the field of grass. The sky grew darker, and flurries of icy dust rolled across the landscape with each blast of winter's breath.

When I entered the aspen grove, Thomas's prints started to turn in an unexpected direction. Instead of leading to the tree house, they went east toward the mountain. I followed them to the mouth of the canyon, where I paused and stared at his boot prints leading up the snow-covered trail.

What was he doing hiking up a mountain in the snow? I

shivered and considered going back to the house to wait for him. But how long would it be before he came back? Now was my chance to talk to him. I had to take it. He couldn't be that far up the trail anyway.

I dropped my boot into his track and started up the mountain to find him.

# twenty-one

Tall pines and barren aspens shuddered and bowed in the restless atmosphere, and snow began tumbling down in thick waves. Between the veil of falling snow and the tangled, frosted undergrowth, the trail was almost impossible to make out. My only guide was Thomas's footprints, which were getting more indecipherable the farther I went.

I stopped, debating whether to just go back to the house and wait for him to return. I studied his tracks again. They looked fresh, so he had to be nearby. "Thomas!" I called out, my voice echoing in the canyon. I decided to go a little farther. I called out his name as I hiked along, getting colder and colder until my teeth were chattering. Reason told me to go back, but determination pushed me forward. He was up here somewhere. I had to find him.

I came upon an enormous log that was too high to step over. Its dead branches hung over the stream bank, and on the other end, the roots were twisted up in thorny shrubs. I peered over it, and there were Thomas's footprints,

continuing up the mountain. Not seeing a way around, I climbed over the log and slid down to the other side. But instead of my feet hitting solid ground, the snow collapsed beneath me.

I tumbled down an icy embankment to the frozen stream below, hitting the ice with such force it made a cracking sound and knocked the air out of me. I lay there a moment, groaning in pain, then carefully stood and stepped toward the bank. But on the second step, my right foot plummeted through the ice and frigid water flooded my boot.

I pulled my boot out and lunged for a twisted root protruding from the embankment. As I clung to it, the precariousness of my situation hit me like an icy snowball to the face, and with the sharp sting came a handful of terrifying words.

*Frostbite.*

*Hypothermia.*

*Death.*

In an instant, I saw a headline in the newspaper. *Juilliard Student Dies in Snowstorm.* I heard Margo saying to the other instructors, *"Quel dommage.* She had so much potential."

I pushed the thoughts away and forced myself to think rationally. There was a way out of this. One step at a time, I would make it back to the warmth of Dad's hearth. The first step was getting back up the icy bank to level ground. I began climbing back up, my bare hands stinging as they clutched tangles of frosted roots. Halfway up, I lost my footing and slid back down to the water's edge.

I raised my face to the sky and screamed Thomas's name one last time. It wasn't a beckoning call or a cry for help. It was an angry curse that slashed through the canyon walls.

The icy water in my boot was excruciating. I knew I needed to take it off and warm up my foot, but I had to get up the embankment first. I looked downstream, searching for a spot that might be easier to climb up.

Maybe it was my imagination, but I thought I heard footsteps. The space between the sounds grew shorter and shorter, like someone was running.

"Aria?"

I looked up to see Thomas sliding down the embankment toward me, his face etched with concern. Grabbing an exposed root, he skidded to a stop at the water's edge and held his free hand out to me. "Are you okay? Are you hurt?"

"I'm fine," I said angrily, even though I wasn't fine. "But my boot is filled with ice water."

He turned and climbed back up the embankment, then after tossing his gloves aside, he stretched a hand out to me. "Grab my hand." I put my hand in his, and he pulled me back up to level ground.

He picked up his gloves and led me to the shelter of a nearby pine tree. After kicking some snow off a log, he put a hand on my shoulder. "Here—sit down. We need to take your boot off." He knelt down in front of me, the knees of his black snow pants compressing the snow beneath him.

I had my arms wrapped around myself, and they refused to move from the warmth of my body, so he pulled my boot off for me. He peeled off my sock, then wrapped his warm hands around my foot. "Your foot is like ice." I shivered, and he looked up at me. "And where are your gloves? And hat?"

"At the house. I didn't think I'd need them."

"Put my coat on." He let go of my foot and stood, shrugging out of his coat.

"I'm not taking your coat," I objected. "You'll be cold."

Ignoring me, he draped his heavy coat over my shoulders. I shuddered from the warmth of it. "I don't get cold," he insisted, and when I shot him a skeptical look, he added, "I grew some thick skin these last couple years." He slid his gloves onto my hands, then pulled off his beanie, making his thick hair stand up in all sorts of directions. After brushing some snow out of my hair, he put his beanie onto my head.

"We need to warm up your foot," he said, taking my foot in his hands again. He straddled the log next to me and faced me.

"I'll take off my coat and wrap my foot in it," I said as I began unzipping my coat.

He shook his head and swatted my hands away before zipping my coat back up. "That won't warm it up fast enough. And you're cold enough as it is."

"Then what do you suggest?"

He looked down and pursed his lips, the way he used to when he was solving a tough mathematical equation. Snowflakes were sprinkling down from the pine branches above us and into his dark hair like confetti. And whether from the cold or from hiking I wasn't sure, but his cheeks were flushed in a strikingly flattering hue. Why did he have to look so adorable? He looked up at me with his bright blue eyes, and one side of his mouth pulled up into a little smile. "Well, the best way would be to put it against warm skin." He scratched the dark stubble on his jaw, then raised an eyebrow. "It's warm under my shirt."

My mouth dropped open. "I'm not putting my foot in your shirt!"

"Have you ever had frostbite?"

"Isn't there another way?"

"It depends on how flexible you are."

I pulled my foot toward my chest, trying to shove it under my coat. It wasn't happening. Why hadn't I been doing yoga? I rested my foot on my knee and let out an exasperated sigh.

"So what's it gonna be?" he asked, fighting a smile. "Awkward five minutes, or amputated toe?"

"Depends. Which is more uncomfortable? Frostbite? Or putting my foot up my ex-boyfriend's shirt?"

"Maybe you should ask yourself how uncomfortable it will be to press down the piano pedal when you don't have any toes."

I considered this. Maybe he was right.

"Aria. Just give me your foot." He grabbed my foot and swiveled me toward him on the log. In the same movement, he slipped it under his sweater and pressed it against his skin.

I stifled a gasp. As soon as I got over the shock of having my foot against his abs, I remembered why I was there in the first place. "What are you doing up here, anyway?"

He hesitated, opening his mouth as if to answer, then closing it.

"Are you avoiding me?"

"Would I be staying at your dad's house if I were avoiding you? And anyway, what are *you* doing up here?"

"Looking for you," I said angrily. "I need to talk to you."

"Why didn't you just wait for me to come back?"

"What reason do I have to believe you'd ever come back?"

He grimaced.

"I need some answers," I said.

He brushed some newly collected snow off his knee

with his bare hand, then looked up at me, his gaze wandering over my face. "You're right. Which answer would you like first?"

There were so many questions to ask. Where did I begin? "You said you were coming to get me to go to New York. Why didn't you come?"

His brows drew together. He stayed quiet for a long moment, like he was carefully framing an explanation in his mind.

"Were you angry with me?" I suggested, losing patience.

"What?" He looked at me in astonishment. "Where did you get that crazy idea?"

"From you. Before you left. You said something about how you might have had time to save your parents if I hadn't pulled you back."

He let out a frustrated breath. "I can't believe it. All this time, you've been under the impression that I was angry with you? Aria . . ." He pinned me with a hurt look. "You saved my life that night. If I would have gone up those stairs, I would have been crushed or burned to death when the ceiling collapsed."

"Then why? Why didn't you come back?"

He set his mouth in a grave line. "It's complicated."

"It's not complicated. Just tell me what happened after you left. Did you get in a fight with Richard? He told me you gave him stitches. Is that true? And where did you go after that? Did you go straight to the Netherlands? And why there? Why didn't you just come back to Colorado?" The questions poured out, my voice growing angrier and louder as I went on. "And if you didn't want to be with me, why didn't you at least let me know? I waited for you until August! Didn't I at least deserve a phone call?"

He sighed, a dark cloud of remorse settling over his face. "You deserved a lot more than that."

"Then why—"

"Look, can we slow down the interrogation a little? You're not even giving me time to answer."

"Fine. Answer." I folded my arms across my chest and clenched my jaw, trying to keep more questions from spilling out.

Another strained silence filled the space between us, but this time I waited for him to break it. Finally, with a weary voice, he said, "After I left, I just wasn't in a place I could call."

"What does that mean? Were you on a deserted island? The middle of the Sahara? Or do you mean somewhere figuratively? Can you not be so ambiguous?"

He rubbed my foot, as if I needed a reminder of the awkward situation I was in, and he stared at me, his expression turning amused. "You've changed. You didn't used to be so . . . demanding."

"Would you just answer my question?"

"Which one?"

"Ugh!" I breathed. "What did you mean you weren't in a place to call?"

He searched my eyes, seemingly weighing something. When he finally spoke, it was not the answer I was hoping for. "Devin seems like a nice guy. Does he make you happy?"

I was so thrown off by his reply that I couldn't immediately respond.

"I hope so," he said earnestly. "You of all people deserve to be happy."

"Devin is amazing," I admitted. "He's been so . . . patient with me."

"Why would he need to be patient with you?" The line between his brows deepened. "You never struck me as the type of person who evoked a need for patience."

"I wasn't ready to date for a long time after . . . after everything." *Or make friends. Or shower.* "He waited for me to be ready. And he loved me when I was at my worst."

He looked away with an oddly ruffled expression, and when his gaze returned to mine he studied my face as though trying to read my thoughts. "It must be nice to have someone with the same interests as you."

"How did we get on this topic?" I asked, annoyed at the detour our conversation had taken.

"I just want to know if you're happy." His voice was soft, his eyes clinging to mine. "Does he make you happy?"

I had a feeling his explanation would be altered depending on what my answer was, and I didn't want that to be the case. I didn't want to involve Devin in this. I just wanted the truth.

"No," I said, shaking my head.

Surprise flitted across his face. "He doesn't make you happy?"

"No, I mean, I'm not answering your question. You hijacked my interrogation. You're the one who owes me answers, remember?"

"You answer first."

I gave a sigh of frustration. "Yes, okay? I'm happy. Devin makes me feel . . . safe. I know that no matter what, he'll never leave me or hurt me. In fact, he just asked me to marry him."

His face slackened in astonishment. "Did you say yes?"

I stared at him, suddenly wishing I hadn't brought up Devin's proposal. "It's your turn to answer."

"The thing is, I don't want to ruin your happiness. If I tell you everything, you'll wish I hadn't. You'll be better off without me rehashing every awful thing both of us have been through the last two years."

"No," I responded automatically, "I'll be better off having answers to the questions that have kept me up every night for the last two years."

"Every night?" He seemed bewildered by this revelation. "Is that why you were in my room last night?"

"What makes you think I was in your room?" My heart dropped at the thought that he'd known I was there last night, watching him.

"Because you left your blanket on my floor."

I cursed myself privately as I felt my cheeks flush. "Yes, all right? I waited for you to come home last night because I needed answers. But then you were asleep, and I didn't want to wake you. So, please," I pleaded, "don't make me wait for those answers any longer than I already have."

"All right," he said after a long pause and a sigh of resignation. "Look, all you really need to know is that after my parents died, I became someone different. Someone you wouldn't have even recognized. I didn't want you to see me the way I was." His face darkened as if tormented by some painful memory. "And I felt like, in the long run, you would be better off without me. And look at you—you're better off for it. You have someone who is perfect for you, who makes you happy, and you're living your dreams." He smiled, but it didn't touch his eyes. "I'm really happy for you, Aria."

"If you think I'm so much better off without you in my life, then why did you come back? Why now?"

He combed his fingers through his hair, making flakes

of snow fall out. "I came back to do a favor for an old friend. And . . . I didn't want you wondering for the rest of your life what happened to me." His face was guarded, like he was hiding something.

"How kind of you," I said with heavy sarcasm, "to only leave me hanging for two years." I felt my temper rise, and I withdrew my foot, but not before giving him a healthy jab in the stomach. He didn't even wince, which angered me more. It seemed he wasn't affected by anything. I enclosed my bare foot in my gloved hands and leveled a fiery glare at him. "Why didn't you call me sooner to tell me you weren't coming back? You have no idea what it's like to have the person you care about most just drop off the face of the earth."

He opened his mouth to say something, but in my anger, I cut him off.

"For six months after you left, I couldn't breathe. For six months, I paced in front of the window, jumped every time the phone rang, rushed to the mailbox when I saw the mail truck. On the rare nights that I slept, I had nightmares of your Bronco mangled up on the side of some deserted road, and of you walking away from me even though I screamed your name until my throat burned!" It all came out with unrestrained severity, and I went on and on. My cutting words, my breaking voice, and my desperate expression unfurled with precision every pain, fear, and anxiety I'd had since the morning he'd driven away.

The longer I went on, the more he appeared to withdraw inside himself and shut down. When he could no longer bear to look in my eyes, he dropped his gaze to the snow-covered ground and listened to me with quiet forbearance.

After a few minutes and a lot of tears, I ran out of steam

and the space between us was still again. He looked up at me with an expression that betrayed just how much my words had wounded him. His eyes were shining, tears clinging to his eyelashes. The color had drained from his face, and his chin quivered for a split second before he set his jaw to make it stop.

I waited for him to say something, but I waited in vain. He wouldn't be saying anything else to me. I'd ruined whatever opportunity I might have had to get an honest explanation from him. I knew I should apologize, knew I should speak forgiving and encouraging words to get him to open back up, but I couldn't rein in my anger. It galloped full speed ahead, breaking through every feeble restraint, plowing over every attempt at reason and civility. Blinders of pain kept me from seeing anything but my need for justice and restitution.

A gust of icy wind pushed a flurry of snow through the trees, coating us in frozen white dust. "My foot is warm." My voice was flat, emotionless. "Let's get back." I looked down at my bare foot, then at my frozen boot. Before I could figure out how I was going to walk back down the mountain, Thomas pulled off his blue sweater, leaving only his plaid button-down shirt between him and the elements.

"Let me wrap up your foot so it doesn't get cold again." His voice sounded empty. He was on autopilot, like he was somewhere else, hidden away in a dark corner licking the wounds I'd just given him.

I watched as the cold air drew goose bumps from his forearms. "You can't wear just that in this weather," I protested.

He brushed off my concern and wrapped my foot in his sweater, tying the sleeves together to secure it. "I'll be fine."

I shrugged his coat off my shoulders. "Here. Put your coat back on. Mine is warm enough."

"No. You keep it on."

"I'm not putting it back on," I insisted, dropping it in his lap. When he hesitated, I picked it back up and pushed it toward him. "Just take it!"

With an irrational amount of reluctance, he finally took it. "All right. But keep my hat and gloves on."

"I'll be fine," I said, tossing his gloves and hat on the log between us. "You're not the only one who's grown thick skin."

He slid back into his coat and zipped it up, then picked up his hat. But instead of putting it on, he reached over and put it back on my head. "I have a hood," he said, his face inches from mine. "And unless you want to stop again to warm up your hands, put my gloves on." He straightened and handed me his gloves. I put them on.

He knelt down with his back to me. "Come on, I'll carry you down."

I cringed. "No, you're not carrying me."

"Aria," he said angrily and turned to look at me. "You can't hike in snow with a sweater for a shoe."

I ignored him and got up to start walking. On my first step, the sweater-shoe sunk knee-deep into the snow. It was clear I wouldn't get ten feet before his sweater was caked with snow and my foot was freezing again. I glared up at the snow falling from the sky. I couldn't meet his eyes, couldn't admit he was right.

"Here," he said, handing my frozen boot to me. "Hold this." I took it in my gloved hand, and he knelt in front of me again. "Hop on."

I hesitated, then submitted. I climbed on his back, and

he hooked his arms around my legs and started trekking back down the mountain. Flecks of snow continued to fall steadily from the sky, but he blazed a path close to the stream so we wouldn't lose our way.

Neither of us talked, and the only sound was the stomping of snow beneath his boots and his heavy breaths as he trudged along. He didn't pull up his hood, and my face was so close to his that he could probably feel my breath on his neck. Clinging to his solid shoulders, I could feel the strength of his body as he plowed through the snow. His familiarity saturated my senses—his rousing woodsy fragrance, his dark hair brushing against my cheek, even the sound of him breathing. It all made me breathless and weak, and I realized just how powerful my feelings for him still were. But the realization only angered me further. I didn't want to feel anything for him.

We eventually made it back to the house, and we entered the back door to find Dad sitting at the kitchen table. Thomas set me down.

"You okay?" Dad asked, his face concerned.

I pulled out a chair and sat. "I'm fine. My boot just got wet and I had to take it off, so Thomas carried me back." I took off Thomas's gloves and hat and laid them on the table. I untied his sweater from my foot, and as I handed it to him, our eyes locked. His expression was apologetic and hurt.

"Thomas," Dad said, "I was wondering if you could help me with a project today." He and Thomas exchanged an odd look, like they were communicating without words.

"Sure," Thomas said.

Dad took his mug to the sink, then turned to me. "Aria, I'm not sure if we'll be back in time for dinner, so if we're not, would you tell Vivian to put ours in the fridge?"

"Where are you going?" I asked.

"A few places." He turned to gather his keys and wallet from the counter. "There's a project I've been meaning to finish up for a long time, but it's not something I can do alone." He turned around and looked at Thomas. "You ready?"

Thomas nodded and collected his hat and gloves, then I watched wordlessly as they both walked out the back door.

I sat on the couch later that night next to Devin, who had nine pages of sheet music spread out on the coffee table. He tapped the tip of his pencil to the beat and hummed through the different passages, pausing now and then to make a notation. I glanced up from the book in my hands at the clock. It was eight thirty and Thomas and Dad still hadn't come back. I'd borrowed a novel from Vivian to keep my mind from speculating where they were and when they'd be back, but the melodramatic romance she'd given me only served to further agitate my uneasiness.

The anger I'd been unable to rein in earlier had begun to lose momentum. It trotted along now, slow enough that I saw things I hadn't noticed before. Like the fact that Thomas had probably saved my life earlier, or at the very least, the toes on my right foot. He'd pulled me out of the stream, given me his coat, gloves, and hat, and allowed me to put my ice-cold foot against his skin. Remorse poked at me, urging me to apologize for my anger and to thank him for helping me as soon as I got the chance.

"Would you stop bouncing your knee?" Devin said. "You're messing up my rhythm."

I hadn't realized I was bouncing my knee. "Sorry," I said, making a conscious effort to stop.

He turned to look at me. "Why do you seem so anxious? Is everything okay?"

The sound of the back door opening delayed my answer. They were back, and I felt a strange sense of relief come over me. I realized Devin was still waiting for me to answer, so I nodded to my book. "I'm in a tense scene."

Vivian came down the stairs and went into the kitchen to greet them. I listened as they chatted and dished up leftovers. They were talking fishing. My eyes stayed on the page, following the same line of text over and over, but I didn't comprehend a single word. All I could focus on was Thomas's voice, going on about nets and bait and trawlers. Dad laughed and shared his own fishing anecdotes like he'd found a new best friend in Thomas.

I'd gotten through two pages of my book, still not knowing what I'd read, when Thomas came out of the kitchen. He paused at the bottom of the stairs and turned to glance at me. His expression held an odd mix of remorse and impatience, like there was still more he wanted to say to me. I considered getting up and initiating a conversation with him, but Devin put his hand on my knee, and suddenly I was too concerned about what Devin would think. I turned back to my book, and Thomas went upstairs, closing the door to his room.

I glanced at Devin. His eyes were still on his sheet music, but his jaw was rigid. He turned and fixed an assessing gaze on me. In a hushed voice, he said, "It was him. Wasn't it?"

I raised an eyebrow. "What do you mean?"

"The guy you were so hung up about last year. It was him. Am I right?"

I dropped my gaze, then nodded reluctantly. "I'm sorry," I said quietly. "I didn't know he was going to be here."

"So . . . what is he doing here?"

"I don't know. I asked him earlier, but he gave me a vague answer."

"Huh." He was quiet for a moment, lost in thought. "So all that time you were pining over him at school, moping around like the living dead, he was just . . . hanging out in the Netherlands?"

I nodded slightly, but said nothing. I didn't want to have this conversation.

"Do you remember that night we went out after the concert at the Concertgebouw? There were some pretty seedy places in Amsterdam. Discothèques, drugs, legal prostitution. I think the legal drinking age is fourteen or something." His brow wrinkled in contemplation. "I wonder what he was doing there all this time."

"He was fishing."

"Yeah, but what does a fisherman do at night?"

I closed my eyes and grimaced, trying to shut out the images Devin had planted there. Thomas's words replayed in my mind. *I became someone you wouldn't recognize.* A sick feeling wrenched my insides, and I stood. "I'm tired," I said, and I was. Tired from the previous sleepless night. Tired from hiking all over a frozen mountain. Tired from the confusing thoughts and feelings that had continually bombarded me since Thomas's reappearance. "I'm going to bed."

He stood and hooked my arm, turning me around gently. "I'm sorry," he said. "I didn't mean to upset you."

I let out a long sigh. "You have nothing to apologize for."

"Listen," he whispered and threw an anxious glance up

the stairs. "I can see you need to get some answers from him. And I want you to know that you're free to do that. You don't have to tiptoe around me. I don't see him as a threat. I know you love me." His words were confident, but behind his eyes was a fear and insecurity I'd never seen before.

I put a hand to his cheek and looked in his eyes. "I do love you."

He bent and kissed me. "I trust you, Aria."

"Thank you," I said. "I'll see you in the morning."

I climbed the stairs, and as I passed Thomas's door, I paused. I listened, expecting to hear his movements. But all I heard was my pulse throbbing in my ears. I raised a fist to knock, but lost my nerve and lowered it. I rested my palm against the door with fingers splayed, the wood's proximity exaggerating my shallow breaths.

"I'm sorry," I whispered, knowing he wouldn't hear me. What else could I possibly say to him that I hadn't already said? What could I ask that I hadn't already asked? There was no reason that he would open up now when he had refused to earlier. So I stepped away and went to my room. I lay down and stared at the wall separating him from me, thinking how he may as well be thousands of miles away, back in the Netherlands. Soon, my weary eyes closed and I succumbed to much-needed sleep.

# twenty-two

The next morning I awoke just before seven, as the sky was starting to lighten in predawn pale blue. I got dressed and went downstairs to the kitchen to make breakfast. I halted in the doorway when I saw Dad sitting alone at the kitchen table.

"There's oatmeal on the stove if you want some," he said, glancing up at me and waving his spoon toward the stove.

Apprehensively, I went to the cupboard for a bowl and dished up some oatmeal. "Is Vivian still sleeping?"

"Yeah," he said. "She was up late wrapping presents."

I joined him at the table and smiled to cloak my uneasiness. "It seems Vivian has been good for you."

He nodded. "It's been nice to have someone to come home to, to talk to. I didn't realize how lonely I was until she forced herself into my life." He smiled to himself as though reflecting on her endearing persistence. After a long moment, his eyes returned to mine, and his expression turned apologetic. "Aria, there's something I need to say to you."

My grip tightened on my spoon, and I suddenly felt like I was ten again, standing in line next to Dad for the Zipper ride at the carnival. *It'll be fun,* he had said, and the next thing I knew, I was being hurled in a rickety deathtrap toward the pavement.

"You don't need to," I said with firmness.

He stared at me. "But I do. I—"

"Please." I held up a hand and let out a sigh. "I came here because I want things to be different between us. Better. But I don't want to revisit the past." My voice was pleading. "Let's just . . . start from here. Like a clean slate."

A disappointed crease appeared between his brows, and he said, "The problem is, it's still the same slate, and it needs to be wiped clean before we can start over."

I shook my head. "No, it doesn't. I know you're sorry. You don't need to say it. You don't need to explain. It will only cause me more pain."

His face fell, but he nodded slowly.

I paused, searching for a way to change the subject. "Are you working today?" He stared at me for a long moment as though still clinging to the prospect of his thwarted speech, then said, "Yeah. I volunteered so the younger guys could be at home for Christmas Eve."

*Christmas Eve.* My heart sunk with the realization that this would be a hard day for Thomas.

"That Thomas," Dad said as if reading my thoughts, "he's a good kid."

"You didn't used to think that."

"I know. I was wrong. He was a good friend to you, wasn't he?"

*He was much more than that,* I thought. "Yeah, he was."

"I saw him this morning—walking down the driveway toward the road."

"He's already up?"

"I think he went over to the fire site." He paused. "Today is the day they died, you know."

"I know," I whispered.

He rose and took his dishes to the sink. "I could be wrong," he said as he rinsed out his bowl, "but he's probably the one who needs a friend right now." He dried his hands and shrugged into his coat, then turned to me and smiled. "I'll see you tomorrow, for Christmas."

I nodded and returned his smile, then watched him walk out the door.

Imagining Thomas alone at the fire site made me uneasy. I leaned over my bowl of half-eaten oatmeal, recalling how a couple years earlier, he had been there for me when I needed him most. The least I could do now was be a friend to him.

I pushed away from the table and dropped my oatmeal in the sink, threw on my coat, hat, and boots, and hurried out the front door.

As I walked along the icy road, the sun peeked over the mountain, casting long shadows across the sparkling snow. The air was perfectly still and clear from the storm the day before.

Turning down his driveway, the cavernous tomb where his house once stood came into view. The blackened ruins stood out in the snow like ink splattered on white paper. All that remained was a scarred foundation littered with ash and rubble. Above it, singed and leafless branches arched like arms attempting to conceal the tragedy of what had occurred there.

In the shadow of the foundation, my eyes were drawn to a flicker of movement. There, camouflaged against a charred wall, Thomas leaned with head bent and hands stuffed in the pockets of his black peacoat.

I paused to watch him, puffs of my breath obscuring his figure with each exhale. His disheartened posture caused compassion to flood through me, making my heart ache with a desire to comfort him. Setting aside my own feelings and needs, I slowly approached him. When a twig snapped under my foot, he glanced up at me. His face was wet with tears, and his hand came up to wipe them away.

I lowered myself into the foundation and stepped carefully over the rubble to stand before him. His face was composed in a fragile mask, but beneath it his shining eyes were pain stricken.

"I'm sorry about yesterday," I said softly. "I shouldn't have gone off on you like that. It was selfish of me."

He nodded, a feeble smile touching his lips. "All things considered, I thought you went pretty easy on me." The smile gradually collapsed into a frown. "Aria—I'm so sorry. I never imagined my actions would hurt you so deeply. If I had known—"

I put a hand on his arm and shook my head. "It's okay. I mean, I'm okay now." I gazed into his face, searching his eyes for something, but not entirely knowing what. "What about you?" I asked gently. "How are you these days?"

His eyes strayed from mine, instead wandering over our dismal surroundings. Scraping his boot through the ash and decomposing leaves, he released a sigh. "It's hard to be here, to see . . ." His voice broke and he turned away. "I miss them."

Instinctively, I went to him and pulled him into an

embrace. He stiffened at first, then his body relaxed and molded into mine. "I know," I murmured, hoping he'd understand that in some way I knew how he felt and shared his burden.

"You do know, don't you?" His voice was faint, his lips buried in my hair. I could feel his chest trembling, like it took all his effort to restrain whatever storm was raging inside.

The woods around us were quiet, but somewhere off in the distance I could hear a blue jay's call. A warbling A-flat to C, like an old iron gate, swinging open and closed. Open and closed. Open and closed.

Thomas pulled away first, and it was then that I noticed a scarf coiled around his neck and tucked beneath his coat. Blue and gray herringbone. The same one I'd knit and given him for Christmas two years earlier. I reached up and touched it. The fibers were beginning to fray with wear. "You kept it," I said with wonder.

His eyes softened and a faint smile appeared on his lips. "I kept everything you gave me." His husky tone was rich with unspoken meaning. I gazed at him, waiting for him to expound, but he didn't.

"Please, Thomas. Talk to me. Tell me what happened to you."

He backed away, then slid down the blackened wall and rested his arms on his knees. "Does it really matter anymore?"

There had to be a way to make him see that he could trust me, that I was safe to confide in. I went and knelt in front of him, and in a gesture that took a great deal of courage, I slipped my hand into his. For a brief second, his face slackened in surprise, then his callused fingers softened and formed carefully around mine. I looked into his eyes. "It matters to me. I'm still your friend, and no matter what, I always will be."

He stared at our hands, and when he looked back at me, his fragile mask had all but disappeared. His face was hauntingly expressive, a medley of eagerness and terror.

"You left me that morning in the motel parking lot," I prompted when I could no longer bear his silence, "and then you went to Pasadena, and then what?"

I saw a change come over his face—like he'd been arguing with himself about something and had now made a decision. "I went to the funeral," he said, shaking his head. "It was awful. Having to face my parents' friends and our family, and explain to them what happened. Some were kind about it, but others . . ." His hand stiffened in mine, like he was reliving some hurtful memory. "I never realized it was possible for someone to offer condolence and condemnation all in the same look, with the same words. Richard made sure that everyone knew I was to blame. 'Thomas, the grim reaper.'"

I squinted. "Why would he say that?"

Something like guilt washed over his face. "Aria . . . there's something I should've told you a long time ago."

The air around us suddenly grew quiet. Not even the blue jay was singing anymore. All I could hear were his words, hanging, echoing between the beats of my heart. "What?" I asked, my voice barely audible.

"Do you remember when I told you I'd been in a car accident?"

I glanced at the thin scar above his right eyebrow and felt my pulse quicken with foreboding. "Yes, I remember."

"Well . . . I didn't exactly tell you the whole story."

The terror his words stirred in me robbed me of my voice. All I could do was stare at him and wait.

"A few years ago I was at a party with some friends. Richard came with Sasha. She was pregnant, about six months along, and she was upset that Richard had brought her there because she didn't feel well. She kept asking him to take her home, but he was too busy playing rounders and beer pong. So finally she tried to take his keys to drive herself home, and they got in a huge fight—he had this old Audi he'd put a lot of work into and was really protective of it. Eventually he gave in and agreed to drive her home. It was late, so I came along."

He pulled his hand from mine and began tugging on the fray of his scarf, twisting it between his fingers. "Richard was angry that she'd made him leave. So he kept driving up on the curb to scare her. We were both yelling at him to stop, to pull over and let Sasha drive, but he insisted he was in control and that he was just playing around."

He gritted his teeth and tore a piece of fray from his scarf. "He was laughing, while Sasha sat there crying, and it infuriated me. So when he started veering toward the curb again, I reached up from the backseat and yanked the steering wheel in the other direction." He dropped his hand from the scarf, gazing past me with empty eyes and a placid expression, like he was no longer with me. He was sitting in that car, reliving that fateful sliver of time.

He didn't need to tell me what happened next, because through the window of his eyes, I saw the scene myself. I saw the crumpled metal and shattered glass on blood-stained asphalt. I kept my expression steady, which strangely took little effort. I felt as numb as he looked.

"I woke up days later in the hospital," he finally said,

"with broken ribs and a torn spleen and stitches all over. I thought I had it bad, but then I found out that compared to Richard and Sasha, I'd come out unscathed. Richard was in the hospital for weeks with head and lung injuries. And Sasha . . ." Torment etched itself across his face, sweeping away the blanket of numbness.

"She didn't make it," I finished in a whisper.

He shook his head, tears welling up in his eyes.

"And the baby?"

"Emily lived long enough for everyone to fall in love with her," he said hoarsely. "But she was too early."

A tightness developed in my chest, and I realized I hadn't drawn air for quite some time. I willed myself to breathe, and with each breath came a stab of pain.

"If I hadn't yanked on the steering wheel," Thomas added, "or if I wouldn't have let Richard get behind the wheel in the first place . . ." He grimaced and shook his head. "I was fifteen. If I hadn't been drinking too, I could have swiped his keys and driven her home myself. Anyway, it doesn't matter now. Sasha and Emily are gone."

What little control I had over my emotions crumbled away, and I stood and turned from him so he couldn't see my face.

The few months I'd spent with him were laid out before me like an open field. This new revelation drove over it like a plough, scraping up the grass to reveal the hidden soil beneath. I saw my memories with him against this new backdrop. His bookshelf full of journals to sort out his grief. His walls covered in paintings to curb his restlessness. The hostility between him and his brother. That dark, tormented look that sometimes seeped into his expression. All those untold stories in his eyes, all those moments when it seemed he was holding something back. The words, *I don't feel good enough for you,* on the porch after the dance.

The plough and harrow then came over me, scraping my soul until it was raw with guilt. I must have been so selfish not to see his suffering. I thought about all the time he'd spent comforting me, helping me, and all the while he was suffering, silently carrying his own burden.

I didn't want to cry when I was the one who should be comforting him, but even pressing a hand over my mouth couldn't stop the first sob from erupting. Helpless to restrain the flood of tears that followed, I turned back and knelt in front of him, then putting my hands on his face, I forced him to look at me. "Why didn't you tell me?" I said fiercely through my tears. "Why didn't you tell me before?"

"I wanted to tell you so many times," he said, a tear trickling down his cheek. "But every time I was about to tell you, I would look at you, at your trusting face, and I'd think of everything you'd already been through, all the things you'd already had to carry. I just couldn't share it with you. Not because I was afraid that you'd think differently of me—though I was afraid—but because I couldn't put that on you."

"I wish you had put it on me," I scolded. "I could have helped you. You were there for me when I needed you. But you didn't let me help you. Do you have any idea how awful that makes me feel?"

His hands curled around mine and an intense flame ignited his blue eyes. "You did help me." He pulled my hands from his face and lowered them to his lap, where he clung to them. "When we first met, that first morning I saw you in the tree house, I was in a very dark place, trying to forgive myself for what happened. Every day was a struggle with loneliness, emptiness. But you . . . you were like this little spark of light in the blackness. You gave me something to live for—to live up to. You made me feel loved, needed, worth something, and you made me look outside myself and my own despair. It was the first time in my life that I cared about someone more than I cared about myself. All I wanted was to make you happy, to make you feel loved and protected."

"Then . . ." I shook my head in bafflement. "Why didn't you come back to me?"

His thumb traveled slowly over the ridges of my knuckles before he spoke again. "I wanted to. I was planning on it. But after the funeral . . ." He shook his head. "All my reason was smothered by guilt. Guilt for Sasha and my niece, compounded by my parents' deaths. Guilt like that has a way of blinding you to everything else. You can try to escape, but it traps you, consumes every thought, every breath. Whether you're awake or asleep, it replays your mistakes on a loop until you think you'll go mad.

"On top of that, I had to go through all my parents' things with Richard pacing behind me like a jackal, making biting remarks about how I'd robbed him of everything that was important to him. We got into an argument about who had hurt my parents and Sasha the most, and I just . . . snapped. I started throwing things, breaking things. Not just anything, but important things. Family pictures and awards and heirlooms. I clocked Richard in the jaw and sent him flying into a wall. Then we ended up pounding on each other until we were both bleeding. I left feeling like a despicable barbarian."

He looked at me, his face restless. "I was coming to Colorado Springs to be with you. I was going to find an

apartment and get a job and finish high school here. But as I approached the exit, I couldn't do it. I was a complete mess. I was so angry. At everything and everyone. I didn't want you to see me that way. I didn't even want you to hear me that way, so I didn't call. I was afraid it would scare you, or that it would hurt you. So I kept driving."

If only I'd known. I would have been out standing on the highway, waving him down with florescent flags.

"I spent that night in some place I don't even remember. And when I woke up the next day, I still felt like I needed to sort things out and get myself together before I came back to you. So I kept driving. I drove for days, expecting my head to clear or the intensity of the pain to lessen, but it was relentless. I thought that if I could just get far enough away, I could somehow escape it. So I got on a plane for the Netherlands.

"I stayed with my friend, Stefan, and I only planned on staying a couple weeks. But he was a little too generous with me. He gave me an empty room and a bed, and I stayed holed up in that little space for weeks, sleeping or shuffling around like the living dead. To be honest, I spent a lot of time wishing you had just let me go up those stairs."

He must have seen the distress in my face, because his eyes turned apologetic. "Not because I thought I could have saved my parents, but because dying would have been easier than dealing with the aftermath." He ran his fingertip through the wet ash on the ground, clearing a small spot of foundation. "Some days it felt like I would never be okay. And an irrational part of me felt like if I allowed myself to be with you, my bad luck would eventually come around to hurt you. The more I thought about it, the more I convinced myself that you deserved better than that."

He shut his eyes tight and a silent cloak of darkness settled over him. Whether because he didn't want to hurt me anymore, or because words were insufficient to express it, I knew he would never say just how bleak his life had become.

"I could give you a million reasons for my actions, Aria." He opened his eyes. "But I won't. All that really matters is that I was wrong to stay away. I was wrong to leave you hanging. But by the time I'd healed enough to figure that out, it was too late. I'd already hurt you, and I didn't think you could ever forgive me."

I opened my mouth to say something, but there were so many competing words that none of them could get out.

"So I settled for a different life," he went on. "I got the fishing job with Stefan's uncle, and to distract myself, I kept busy, working long hours at sea and doing anything and everything with Stefan on land."

I thought about what Devin had said the day before about Amsterdam's colorful nightlife. "What do you mean 'anything and everything'?" I could feel the sick look on my face. "Did you spend a lot of time in Amsterdam?"

He knotted his brow as though puzzled by my question. "No—not much." Then understanding swept over his face. "You know I've never been big on partying. And you have to know . . . I was never with another girl. Stefan brought girls home sometimes, but the thought of even touching another girl when I still had feelings for you . . ." He shook his head and his meaning was clear.

An involuntary sigh of relief escaped my lips. Not that it mattered, I reminded myself. Thomas wasn't mine anymore anyway. I was with Devin now. At the thought of

Devin, it registered just how long I'd been holding Thomas's hands. Not wanting him to misread my intentions, I withdrew my hands and slipped them into my coat pockets.

"I thought about you all the time," Thomas said. "I can't tell you how many times I started dialing your number, or how many times I wrote a letter only to crumple it up and throw it in the trash. But I could never find the right words to say, how to explain myself or how to encourage you to move on without hurting you more. I just hoped that you would go to Juilliard and move on with your life." A look of regret flitted across his face. "And you did move on. You have a new life now. A better life."

"And you have a new life too," I said slowly. "Don't you?"

"I guess so. But . . ." He hesitated, then pinned me with a meaningful look and said, "But I've spent every day for the past year wishing that I could go back to the life I left behind."

His words jostled something inside me, something I thought I'd laid to rest. Hope. Part of me wanted to forgive him and throw myself into his arms. But another part of me—a much greater part—was still hurt and confused. I couldn't afford to have hope. Not with him, not yet. So I stomped it back down.

"But I know that's not possible," he said sadly. "Funny how time is a healer . . . and a thief."

When I didn't say anything in return, he bent his head and studied his hands, open and empty in his lap. For the first time since his return, I noticed a pink mark on the inside of his wrist, stealing from the cuff of his coat sleeve. A burn scar. Without thinking, I reached out and touched it, as though needing to be convinced that he was healed. His small, answering smile told me that he was.

Dawn had broken over the edge of the foundation, had swept out the shadows and filled them with light. Thomas shaded his eyes against the brilliance of the rising sun, and we sat there gazing at each other, wordlessly acknowledging that the hardest part of our conversation was over.

"Thomas," I finally said, releasing his wrist, "how did you know I would be here and not in New York?"

He hesitated. "I called Nathaniel about a week ago to find out where you were."

"I can't believe he didn't tell me," I muttered to myself. And then another question sparked in my mind. "What finally made you decide to come see me?"

Thomas tugged his coat sleeve down over his scar, and when he looked up again, instead of meeting my eyes, he focused on some point in the distance. "I think someone is looking for you."

I whipped my head around to see Devin's figure wandering through the frosted orchard. He paused and glanced in our direction, then resumed meandering like he knew I was here but didn't want to interrupt.

"I better go back." I stood and looked down at Thomas. "How long are you staying?"

"I'm flying back to Zierikzee tomorrow."

"You're going back to the Netherlands?"

He nodded. "For one more season."

"One more season? What will you do after that?"

He shrugged. "My plans are kind of up in the air. I'm going to study art somewhere, I just haven't decided where yet."

At the thought of him being out of my life again, I felt panicked. But what could I do? I glanced at Devin again, who was waiting patiently for me in the orchard. In

a few days I would go back to New York with him, back to the life I knew and had grown to love. I turned back to Thomas. "Don't leave without saying good-bye," I said, the words catching in my throat.

He stared at me for a long moment before nodding slightly, and I turned to walk away.

"Aria."

I glanced back at him, and he was standing up with an anxious look on his face.

"Can you . . . can you come to the tree house tonight?"

The thought crossed my mind that I should say no, that I should go back to Devin and put Thomas out of my mind, but instead I said, "I don't know. Maybe."

"Meet me there at midnight, if you can. Wear something warm." He smiled, making that little dimple appear on the side of his mouth.

I ignored the flutter in my stomach and nodded, then turned to go meet Devin.

# twenty-three

"Hey," I said contritely as I approached Devin in the orchard.

"You could have left me a note." He smiled, but his expression was stiff, like he was trying to subdue his emotions. "I was worried."

"I'm sorry. I left the house this morning in kind of a rush." I considered telling him about the significance of this day for Thomas, but it seemed inappropriate. "I just wasn't thinking."

"It's all right. It wasn't too hard to find you." He took my hand in his and we began walking back to the house. "So . . . did you get the answers you need?"

I thought back on everything Thomas had told me, but there was so much I hadn't even swallowed, let alone digested. "I think so." It was the most accurate response I could give.

"When is he leaving?"

"Tomorrow."

"I was thinking. Maybe we should just go get a hotel

room or something. Or we could go spend the rest of our trip at your old teacher's place."

A small part of me wanted to consent, to pack up my things and be done with this place. But my heart revolted at the thought. There was still unfinished business here. Not only with Thomas, but with Dad. "We're leaving the day after tomorrow," I said. "I'd like to spend a little more time with my dad."

"So spend some time with him today, and we'll go check in somewhere tonight."

"He's at work until tomorrow morning. Besides, Vivian would be offended."

His hand tensed around mine. "Are you sure you don't just want to spend more time with *him?*"

"Devin—"

He stopped and turned to me. "Be honest, Aria. I'm not blind. I can see how much you're affected by him being here."

"Of course I'm affected. How would you feel if the person who was most important in your life vanished off the face of the earth, then reappeared out of nowhere years later?"

"But . . . who is the most important person in your life now?"

"You." The immediate response made my answer sound trite. I closed my eyes and pressed my fingers between my brows to ease the tension there. "I just need time to think. I've been bombarded with unexpected feelings and information—I need a chance to sort through it all."

I felt his hands on my shoulders, and I opened my eyes to see his perplexed face just inches from mine. "What do you have to sort through? He hurt you. Almost beyond repair. I remember how unreachable you were. I remember the sound of your sobs that night in the practice room. All because of him. I would never do that to you. I would never hurt you."

I brushed a piece of hair from my face and looked into his eyes. "I know."

"Please . . . just tell me nothing is going to change between us."

"Nothing is going to change between us." But as he wrapped his arms around me and held me uncomfortably tight, I could feel the uncertainty of my words. I buried my face in his chest. I felt unsteady, oddly pliable, like a piece of clay that could be molded and shaped by whomever's hands I was in. At the moment, even though Devin pressed me closely to him, I was in Thomas's hands. They possessed the power to alter the life I'd become accustomed to. And I floundered in my effort to find the strength or desire to resist him.

♪ ♪♪ ♪ ♪♪♪

*You're in trouble,* I texted Nathaniel once we were back at the house. *Why didn't you tell me?* I hit send and dropped the phone in my back pocket, then went to the parlor.

I spent all afternoon at the piano, with Devin working nearby on his sheet music. I played absentmindedly, my mind still back at the fire site with Thomas. Like watching a movie, I paused at certain frames, rewound phrases, and skipped over parts that were too hard to stomach.

I thought about the way his lips curved around the words, *I thought about you all the time,* and the piercing blue flame in his eyes when he said, *I kept everything you gave me.* What exactly had he meant by that?

*Meet me there at midnight*, he had said. Something stirred inside me again, like wings beating furiously to escape a captor's hand. I considered that maybe my heart was not as unfettered as I'd supposed.

Just before midnight, I slipped out the back door to go meet Thomas. I'd spent most of the evening debating whether to go, and finally acknowledged that I needed to make a choice between continuing in my relationship with Devin or taking a chance with Thomas. I told myself it was for this purpose—to gather the information necessary to make that choice—that I went to meet him.

The closer I came to the tree house, the stronger some unseen force tugged me toward it and the more my anticipation bubbled over. But when I got there, he was not there.

I expected to feel anxious, but instead a calm washed over me. He would be there soon; I was sure of it. I leaned against a wall and stared at the spot where I used to sleep on the nights Dad's behavior forced me out of the house. I recalled the morning Thomas had discovered me here, and the thought made me smile. I ran my fingers over the telescope in the corner, remembering all the nights we'd spent up here together, looking at objects in the sky. And then I waited. Waited for him to come. I paced slowly, peering out the windows on either side for a sign of him.

I heard a thud, then something like metal scraping against metal. I glanced out the east window and saw the yellow glow of a lantern coming nearer through the trees. I smiled and stepped away from the window, twisting my hands, my heart thumping against my chest.

When his face appeared in the doorway, illuminated by the lantern, I thought my heart would burst. He climbed into the tree house. His chest was heaving, like he'd been running. He slid off his backpack and set it down. "Sorry I'm so late," he said. "It took me longer than I thought it would to get here." He smiled and walked past me, assailing me with his alluring scent. As he set the lantern down, I noticed his hands were shaking.

"You're cold," I said. "We can go back to the house."

"I'm not cold." He took his gloves off. "I'm actually a little too warm."

"Then why are you shaking?"

"I'm tired."

I took his hand in mine to test the temperature. It was warm. It was also very rough. I turned his palm up, and saw that it was blistered and crusted with dried blood. "Thomas—your hands," I said with alarm. "What have you been doing?"

He pulled his hand away. "Working on something."

"On what?"

"A project."

"What project?"

"You'll see in a few hours."

"No—tell me now," I demanded.

He shook his head. "A few more hours. Right now, there's something else I want to show you." He unlatched the roof, then with a bit of a struggle, slid it along its tracks. Turning off the lantern, he lay down and gazed up at the open sky.

I stared at him, unsure what to do. He patted the space next to him. "Come here."

After a moment's hesitation, I joined him on the floor

and looked up at the star-filled sky. Every sense seemed heightened—the air I breathed, the tingle of the night on my skin, the silence of the winter air—it was all flavored by him, lying two inches from me.

"Are you cold?" he asked.

"No." It was true. I didn't know if it was an unusually mild night or if it was just the heat emanating from him, but I felt strangely warm. I waited for him to say something, to tell me what he wanted to show me, but he was quiet. I turned to look at him, and his eyes were closed. "So, what are we looking at?" I said in a hushed voice.

"Just wait. You'll see it in a few minutes." He glanced at me, a little smile on his lips, then turned his face back to the sky and closed his eyes again.

"It's strange being up here again," I pondered aloud.

"What do you mean?"

"I don't know . . . it's a bittersweet place for me. It was my refuge, but it reminds me of the reasons I needed a refuge. And it reminds me of you."

He opened his eyes, but kept his gaze on the sky. "Is that part of the bitter or the sweet?"

"Both." I whispered, but he didn't respond. Wanting to hear his voice again, I said, "Tell me about the place you live. What's it like?"

He started talking about Zierikzee, about the friendly people, the historic architecture, and the boundless sea. He told me how he'd been spending all his spare time in his apartment: writing, painting, listening to music that calmed him. I wondered what he'd been listening to, and I imagined a room somewhere in the Netherlands, filled with paintings that his hands had created.

Recalling something he'd said earlier, I said, "You said

you didn't visit Amsterdam—much. Does that mean you went there sometimes?"

A half-moon had risen over the wall, flooding the tree house with silvery light. He turned to look at me with a guilty expression that made my stomach drop. "I visited Amsterdam once, last summer."

"What for?"

His eyes turned rueful, and he propped himself up on an elbow. "My favorite piano concerto was being performed at the Concertgebouw, so I took a trip to see it."

It took me a few seconds to decipher his meaning. "You mean . . ." I sat up with mouth agape, feeling like the wind had been knocked out of me. "You saw me perform?"

He sat up. "I was at the train station with Stefan, about to board a train to Brussels, when I saw the poster. It was like fate sending a lightning bolt straight through my heart. I didn't know if you'd be performing, but I took a chance and got on the train for Amsterdam anyway. I didn't have any nice clothes, so I showed up at the Concertgebouw in shorts and a T-shirt." He paused long enough for my heart to knock against my ribs at least a dozen times. Then he turned to me and said wistfully, "You were amazing."

An unexpected surge of anger ripped through me. "Why didn't you come talk to me?" I slugged him in the chest, and there was nothing playful or gentle about it. My fist ached from the blow, and my eyes burned with tears.

He caught my wrist before I could pull away, and he looked me straight in the eyes. "You were with Devin. I saw you in the crowd after—with him. And you looked happy. Happier than I'd ever seen you. Like you'd healed from every heartache and injustice you'd ever suffered. I just couldn't bring myself to ruin it for you."

Slowly, the anger drained from my body, and all that remained was an agonizing sorrow that left me speechless. Thomas let go of my wrist, and I swiped the tears from my cheeks. Feeling a little faint, I lay back down. I recalled the performance in Amsterdam, remembering it had been one of my best that summer. There had been something in the air that night—something aromatic and euphonic and electric. It had elevated me to the peak of musical passion. The thought of him being in the audience as I performed unaware made my heart ache with regret.

"I went back home," he said sadly, "hoping I'd be able to let you go after seeing you so happy with someone else. But it had the opposite effect. My feelings for you only intensified. I couldn't eat or sleep, and I would lie awake at night, searching for the right words to come and ask for your forgiveness."

Thomas lay back down, folding his hands over his chest and gazing up at the moon. "Then one night, when the moon was shining through my bedroom window, something occurred to me."

"What?"

He drew in a deep breath and exhaled, making a puff of vapor in the crisp winter night. "You ever notice how, even though the moon is sometimes hidden in shadow, it never turns its face from the earth?"

"Ah—an astronomy analogy, of course," I teased in an unsteady voice. I looked up at the moon, at the crater that was a constant landmark on its surface. "I've never really thought about it, but yeah—you're right."

"Well, I guess I'm sort of like the moon. Only instead of being gravitationally drawn to the earth, I'm drawn to you. There will always be some unseen force that attracts me to you, something at the center of my soul that tugs and aches to be near you. And even in my darkest moments, when I've been lost in shadows, I've never turned away from you."

Even if I had known what to say, the sudden lump in my throat would have prevented me from saying it. My vision turned cloudy again, and soon tears were trickling from the corners of my eyes into my ears. If Cupid's arrow was a literal thing, this must be what it felt like to have my heart pierced by it. Painful and divine all at once.

He propped himself up on one elbow and gathered me into his arms, hovering over me so his face was just a couple inches from mine. His dark hair and the planes of his face glowed softly in the light of the moon.

"I love you, Aria," he whispered. "I've loved you since that first morning I found you in this tree house. Please . . . tell me I'm not too late." He brushed the back of his fingers over my cheek and lowered his head until his forehead touched mine. His lips lingered over mine, tempting me. "Please . . . just say the words." Feeling his warm breath on my lips sent my pulse racing.

He stayed there, as though waiting for me to tilt my face and make our lips meet, making the choice mine. Every nerve in my body tingled with anticipation, and soon enough, I gave in. Sliding my hand to the nape of his neck, I tugged his head down a fraction of an inch, just enough that our lips met.

His kiss was warm and tender, his breath sweet in my mouth. But the effect it had on me was anything but tender. It was as though my heart had lain lifeless in my chest for the past two years, and kissing him sent a jolt straight to it, stunning it back to life. An electric current surged through the rest of my body, leaving a trail of sparks under my skin and fire on my lips.

In that moment, I was helpless to deny what I'd already known for the last two days. I still loved him. I loved him so much it terrified me.

I was on the edge of a precipice, higher than I'd ever felt in my nineteen years of life. But as I looked down, my stomach lurched at the realization of just how far I could fall. My mind rewound to my first year at Juilliard, and I felt a sharp jab of pain as I remembered how deep my wounds had been. I thought about Devin, how much he'd helped me and how patient he'd been with me. And now he was asleep at Dad's house, completely unaware that in this moment, I betrayed him.

My desire for Thomas was overtaken by fear, and I gently pushed him away and sat up. "I can't be with you," I breathed.

He sat up and swept my hair behind my shoulder. "Why not?"

"Because of Devin. I can't hurt him, not after everything he's done for me." I shook my head. "I shouldn't have even come here tonight."

"Is that the reason? Because if it is, then I'll leave. Just tell me that you love him more than you love me, and I'll go back to the house and pack my bags. I'll be out of your life for good."

I opened my mouth, but I couldn't say the words.

"But I don't think that's the reason," he said. "Maybe it's wishful thinking, but . . ." He put a finger to my chin and turned my face toward him. "I think you love me."

When I didn't respond, he traced the ball of his thumb

across my cheek. "I felt it in your kiss. I can see it in your eyes. I can hear it in your breath."

I turned my face away and with futility tried to slow my breathing.

"You're afraid," he said, all too perceptively. "You're afraid I'll hurt you again."

"Can you blame me?"

"No. But if fear is the only thing keeping us apart, we can overcome it."

"It's not that simple." I gave a weary sigh. "I don't want to be your anchor."

"What do you mean?"

"Your mom was your anchor." I turned to fully face him. "Everything you did was for her, and she kept you grounded. But when she died, you . . . you drifted away from the people who cared about you. I can't be your anchor, Thomas. What about the next tragedy that comes along? Life is full of them. What if I die? Or what if we lose a child? Are you going to run away to punish yourself and your loved ones every time something bad happens?"

Frustration pinched his brow. "I've learned a hard lesson these last couple years. But it's not one I'll have to repeat. You're not an anchor. You're the girl I love and want to be with. It's taken me time—too much time, I know—to learn how to overcome grief and self-hatred. And I didn't do it for you, or for my mom, but for me. I wanted to be able to look in the mirror and not despise the person I saw. And I knew until I became that person, I didn't deserve you." He paused, then in a quiet voice said, "I found a new anchor—one that will never go away."

He was talking about God. How could I argue with that?

He reached for my hand and pressed it to his heart. "I love you, Aria. And I'll never hurt you again. But whatever happens between us now, you have to know that I have my own anchor." He said this with such earnest conviction, I knew he believed his own words. But I wasn't sure.

"I forgive you, Thomas, for every pain you ever caused me. But I don't trust you. Trust has to be earned."

"Can I ask one favor? Will you just . . . just give me a chance to earn your trust?"

"It would take a lifetime."

"That's all I ask."

I stared at him, wanting more than anything to say yes. But fear took over. Fear of hurting Devin, fear of getting hurt again, fear of making the wrong choice. And if Thomas ever hurt me again, I didn't think I would survive. I looked into his moonlit eyes brimming with tears, and I couldn't speak. I dropped my head and cried, slowly shaking my head. "I can't," I whispered. "I just want to feel safe."

"And you feel safe with Devin." It wasn't a question.

I didn't know how to respond. So I didn't. I just sat there, paralyzed with uncertainty and fear.

After a long silence, he leaned toward me and, cradling my face in his hands, brushed a featherlight kiss on my forehead. He stood and offered me his hand. "Come on," he said gently. "I'll walk you back to the house."

I didn't take his hand. I couldn't. How could I accept such a kindness when I'd just rejected him? I got up on my own and followed him back to the ground.

He walked a few steps ahead of me, but turned to glance at me every so often to make sure I was still behind him. Anxious with uncertainty, I almost called him back to tell him that I loved him, that I chose him. But, unable to overcome the hurdle of fear between us, all I could do was mouth his name with a soundless cry.

The distance between us grew as we got closer to the house, and the sound of snow crushing beneath his heavy step could have been the sound of my own heart breaking.

♪ ♪ ♪ ♪ ♪ ♪ ♪

Something hard jabbed into my spine as I rolled over in bed the next morning. I sat up and rubbed my tear-swollen eyes, then looked blearily down at the offending object.

A shoe box–sized gift, wrapped in red paper and a silver bow, lay on my bed. I picked it up and examined it. There was no tag to indicate the giver, but I assumed whomever it was from intended for me to open it in private.

I slid my finger under a fold of paper and peeled it away. My heart skidded to a stop and I cupped my hand over my mouth when the contents were revealed. A card with my name, written in Thomas's handwriting, and beneath the card, Mom's porcelain music box.

I threw my blankets aside and went straight to Thomas's room. His door was open, and his room was empty. His suitcase and shoes were gone, and his bedding lay in a heap on the floor. I remembered the card and rushed back to my room. I plucked the card from the bed and flipped it open.

*If you ever need me, this is where I'll be.*

Below that was a phone number and address in Zierikzee, the Netherlands. I dropped to the edge of the bed and stared at the porcelain music box, and all the puzzle pieces fell neatly into place.

The project he'd been working on. Him hiking up the mountain in the snow. His fatigue. The muddy shoes. All the time he'd spent away from the house. His callused and

bloody hands. My chest grew tight and my breaths staggered as I realized what this gift had cost him.

I opened the lid of the music box. It was silent, its gears stiff with corrosion, but as I pictured Thomas up on the mountain, picking away for hours at the frozen earth to find something that meant so much to me, my room was filled with music that seemed to burst forth from my soul.

An envelope with the words, *Aria: 18th Birthday,* lay in the box's velvet-lined alcove. *Mom's letters,* I thought as my pulse quickened.

I picked the envelope up, but it was light in my hands. Empty. I set it aside and glanced back at the alcove, instantly puzzled to see torn pieces of stationary. Beneath the torn stationary were more envelopes, all with my name and a birthday number. And below that, a ring, some pressed flowers, and other trinkets. I gathered the torn pieces of stationary and took them to my desk. At closer look, I saw they were covered in Mom's handwriting.

I dug through a drawer until I found some tape, then began piecing the letter back together. Soon, phrases and sentences started to form.

# twenty-four

I t was with a certain expectation that I pieced Mom's letter together—that whatever was written was of grave importance. A tense knot formed in my stomach as I wondered what it could be. What words were so important that instead of simply saying them before her death, she felt the need to write them down, to preserve and immortalize them? I thought about the other letters in the music box that hadn't been torn up, and I briefly considered reading them first. But I quickly discarded the thought. This was the most important letter. This one contained a revelation so impactful it had provoked Dad to tear it up and bury it.

*. . . that whether this knowledge brings you . . .*

*. . . loved him deeply, and . . .*

The more fragments I pieced together, the more my hands began to shake. It was becoming more difficult to hold the pieces in my hands. So I kept them on the desk and pushed them around with my fingertips, trying to line up words torn in two. My pulse surged as each new phrase was revealed.

*. . . but my divorce with . . .*

And then I pieced together a phrase that made me feel like I'd been cut open and turned inside out. I felt the blood drain from my face and my hands went ice cold.

*. . . pregnant with you, Nathaniel's child . . .*

I sat there in shock for a few seconds, then numbly went back to piecing the letter together, desperate to read all the words, to know the whole story. When I finished, I went and sat on the bed, where I held the patched letter in front of me and started at the beginning.

> *Dear Aria,*
>
> *It is with great regret that I write this letter, because it means I won't be here to give you this information myself, and because I know the topic will be painful for you. I've considered not telling you at all, but after months of wearisome deliberation, I've come to the conclusion that whether this knowledge brings you joy or suffering, it is your right to have.*
>
> *Years ago when I was a student at Juilliard, I dated a musician named Nathaniel Borough. I loved him deeply, and after graduating, we were married. But from the very beginning, things were stormy. We had so many differences that we didn't know how to reconcile. He wanted to travel the world to perform, and I wanted to settle down and teach so that we could have a family. Neither of us were willing to compromise, so after only a year of marriage, we separated.*
>
> *I met Jed Kinsley a couple of years later, and I was attracted to the simple life he had to offer. He was kind and giving, and I grew to love him. He asked me to marry him, but my divorce with Nathaniel*

*was not yet official, so I didn't feel I could give him an answer. So I went to see Nathaniel in New York to discuss the finalization of our divorce and have him sign the necessary papers. However, upon seeing Nathaniel and spending hours talking with him, I realized how much I still loved him. He felt the same, and we decided to try to work things out. I stayed the week with him, but before the week was over, we got into a huge argument, rehashing every disagreement we'd ever had, and both of us remained as unyielding in our views as ever. It became clear that even though I loved Nathaniel, Jed was the only one offering the life I wanted.*

*The divorce was soon finalized, and I returned to Woodland Park and married Jed a few weeks later. Within days of the wedding, I found out I was pregnant with you, Nathaniel's child.*

I paused and stared at the words *Nathaniel's child.* My lungs burned for want of air, but I couldn't bring myself to draw breath. I recalled that night at the Italian restaurant, a six-month-late birthday candle burning in front of me and Nathaniel sick in the bathroom. He didn't know. At least he hadn't until that moment.

I unlocked my eyes from the phrase. There were more words on the page. Maybe they would answer some of the questions that swept through me like a flame in a parched field of grass. I drew in a lungful of air and continued reading.

*I wanted to tell Jed the truth, but I was so afraid of hurting him. And at the time, I truly believed he would be a better father to you than Nathaniel.*

*The closer I got to my due date, the more difficult it became to tell him the truth. And when you were born, I watched Jed cradle you in his arms and smile at you like you were the greatest gift he'd ever received, and I couldn't tell him. As you grew and I saw how much you loved him, I couldn't separate the two of you. He always loved you as his own daughter, because he believed you were.*

*It was always my plan to tell Jed and Nathaniel the truth, but it never seemed like the right time. Or maybe I just wasn't courageous enough to do what was right. I won't try to justify my actions. I was wrong, and I regret my dishonesty. But as I write this, you are only eleven years old, and soon you will not have a mother. I feel it would be too hard on you to bring this to light at this time. Hence, the 18th birthday letter. If you have had a few years to grieve the loss of your mother, perhaps you will have the strength to bear this life-shattering revelation as well.*

*This horrible secret has been a source of great sorrow for me, but I have never regretted giving you life. My greatest joy and privilege has been watching you grow and seeing the gift of music bloom in your heart, even if my privilege was cut short.*

*If Nathaniel contacts you, it is because I have asked him to look out for you and to foster your musical gifts. It is up to you whether or not to share this information with him or Jed. But I fear they would both be devastated if they found out.*

*I can't tell you how sorry I am to have to put all this on you, but I couldn't go down to my grave without letting you know the truth. Forgive me for the pain*

*I know this letter will bring. But it would be more unforgiveable for me to withhold the truth from you.*
    *Wishing I was there to dry your tears,*

*Mom*

I sat there squinting at the letter as if further examination would make the content easier to digest. I read it again, then again. But I still couldn't accept it. It was like reading a fictional story, then having someone say, "By the way, that story is about you." It wasn't about me. It couldn't be. And yet it was. It felt like every single page had been torn from the book of my life, and I was left to rewrite every memory with this new perspective. It was too overwhelming, too big a task to accomplish all at once.

A movement in the doorway caught my eye, and I turned to see Dad standing there, staring at me. I didn't know how long he'd been there, but I instinctively hid the letter behind my back. It was too late, though. His slight grimace told me he'd already seen it and the music box on my bed.

I watched his face, waited for his jaw to tighten and his neck to redden, but instead, only relief swept over his face. "Looks like Thomas found it."

It took me a minute to register his words, and I narrowed my eyes. "You knew he was looking for it?"

"How do you think he found it?"

My mouth dropped open. "You told him where it was?"

He stepped into the room and shut the door quietly behind him. "As well as I could remember. I went up to the lake with him the day before yesterday to help him, but we didn't find it. I thought he'd give up—it's like picking through ice up there."

I stared at him, at the man who had raised me, who had fed and clothed me, and the truth slowly sunk in. This man was not my father. In the space of a few minutes, he had become foreign, almost unrecognizable. I didn't know how to feel or what to say. He *knew* he was not my father. He had known since Mom died. And he had kept the truth from me.

I dropped the letter on the bed and rose to my feet. "You knew, all this time." My chin began to quiver and angry tears pricked my eyes. I forced them back. "How could you keep this from me?"

With a pained expression, he motioned to the bed. "Sit down," he instructed.

I stayed where I was, not taking my eyes off him.

He sighed and sunk into the desk chair, leaning forward with his forearms on his legs. "Like I told you a couple years ago, I kept it from you to protect you."

I shook my head. "I don't understand. Make me understand."

He lowered his head and clenched his hair in his hands. After a lengthy pause, he said, "When she died and I found that letter, I was crushed."

"But why keep it from me? Why keep *everything* from me that mattered to me?"

He straightened. His face became distant, the way it used to when I knew he was thinking about Mom. But this time, instead of quietly withdrawing within himself, he opened up and let his secrets fall out. "As if losing my wife wasn't enough to suffer, I learned that she'd lied to me all these years, and that the daughter who I'd loved and raised as my own for twelve years wasn't even mine." A ripple traveled across his chin and he rubbed it with the back of his hand to still it. "I took that music box and its contents up to the lake and sat there all day trying to figure out what to do. I was so angry and hurt. But I realized that if she hadn't loved me, she would have left me when she first found out she was pregnant. I tried to see it from her point of view, and I knew she'd just made a terrible mistake. Even though it had been wrong of her to keep it secret, she was only trying to do what she thought was best for our marriage, and for you.

"And then I thought about you . . ." He fixed a heart-broken gaze on me. "About how much I loved you and how hard it would be to give you up. I tried to think about what was best for you. You'd already lost your mom. How could I take away the person you'd known as your father as well?" He shook his head. "I just didn't think you could bear losing your mom and me all in the same swipe."

The crushing weight of truth bore down on me, and I feared my knees would buckle if I heard anymore. But I needed to hear more. I needed to know everything. I backed up and sat on the bed to avoid collapsing.

"I finally decided that biology didn't matter," he continued. "You were still my daughter. My name was on your birth certificate. No one would ever know. So I buried the music box and the letters, intending to keep the truth from you forever. But . . ." He gave a sigh, and his face crumpled into a tormented expression. "What I didn't anticipate was how much resentment and pain I would feel. I couldn't bear to hear you play the piano—not because Karina played, but because I knew your father was a musician too. All I could think of when I heard you play was that you were not mine, you were Nathaniel's. I wanted to be a good father to you, Aria. I wanted to continue to love you

and give you everything you deserved. But I failed you. I harmed you. And I'll never forgive myself for treating you the way I did." His hand came to his face and he bent over in quiet anguish.

I sat watching him, unsure how to react, how to feel. Here was this man who should've been my father, who should have loved me and supported me, but instead had hurt me, neglected me, and twisted knives into my already gaping wounds. Now he was sorry. Now he finally saw the pain he had caused me. Deep down, I wanted to forgive him, to forget every horrible thing that had occurred between us, but I didn't know how. "Why now?" I asked. "Why tell me now? Why this way?"

After regaining some control, he straightened and said, "I wasn't going to tell you. I fixed your mom's piano, and I was going to just try and fix things between us without telling you the truth. But then Thomas showed up last week and asked me about the music box. He said he owed you something, and he begged me to tell him where it was so he could retrieve it for you.

"And I started thinking. I remembered how upset you were when you left for New York, when I wouldn't tell you about your mom's letters. And I realized that if I wanted a chance at obtaining your forgiveness, you would have to know the whole truth. I didn't know how to tell you myself though, so I decided to let your mother tell you in the way she originally intended. I drew Thomas a map of where I thought the music box was, but after a couple of days with no success, I went up there with him. I pinpointed the area where I'd buried it and we dug all day but didn't find it. He must have found it yesterday."

I waited for a response to form in my mind or for feelings

to flood me, but nothing came. I felt detached, like I was watching a scene from afar.

"I'm so sorry," he said, "for not loving you the way you deserved. For taking something painful and making it worse. I wish I could go back . . ."

The door swung open and Devin popped his head in, all bleary-eyed and tousled. "Hey. Merry Christmas."

Dad slowly stood. He hooked his thumbs through the belt loops of his jeans and looked down at me. "One more thing, Aria. The piano downstairs—it's yours. Whenever you're ready to take it, it will be here for you."

He walked out of the room, nodding at Devin as he passed him. Completely oblivious to the heavy mood in the room, Devin joined me on the bed, putting an arm around me and kissing my head. "Fabulous," he said with a huge grin. "I was thinking what a waste it was to have that amazing instrument sit here collecting dust. I hope you'll let me play it on occasion." He glanced at the torn wrapping paper and the music box on my bed. "What's this?"

I couldn't answer. My pulse was throbbing so loudly that Devin's voice sounded muffled in my ears. All I could think about was Nathaniel. *He's my father,* I thought. *My name should have been Aria Borough.*

I needed to see him, to tell him the truth, and I needed to tell him now. I looked into Devin's eyes. "Devin, there's something I need to do this morning. It's really important, and it can't wait."

"Okay," he said warily. "What's that?"

"I need to go see Nathaniel. Alone."

His eyes narrowed. "Does this have something to do with Thomas?"

"No. Thomas is gone."

A look of relief washed over his face. "Then what is it? Why do you need to go alone?"

"I just do."

"Well, can't it at least wait until after we have breakfast and open some presents?"

I considered briefly, but the need to see Nathaniel was so overwhelming that it would be excruciating to delay. "No. I'm sorry." I stood and opened my suitcase to find something to wear. "But I'll be back for lunch."

"Then at least tell me why you have to go."

"I can't." I shook my head. "It'll take too long. I'll explain when I get back."

"Aria—" he groaned. "Don't make me sit here all morning speculating. You've already given me enough anxiety these last couple days to triple my Ativan dosage. Just give me an abbreviated explanation and I promise I won't ask any more questions."

I stared at his worried face. "I'm sorry, Devin." I released a heavy sigh. "All right—I'm going to Nathaniel's because I just found out he's my real father."

After a stunned moment of silence, he said, "Oh."

"And I don't think I want to stay here another night. Would you mind if we stayed at Nathaniel's tonight?"

He slowly nodded, his face sober. "Of course not."

I kissed him on the cheek, then took my clothes to the bathroom to get ready.

♪ ♪♪ ♪ ♪ ♪♪

I knocked on Nathaniel's door and bounced on my toes, needing to channel my anxiousness somewhere. Nathaniel opened the door, his face surprised.

"Merry Christmas," I said.

"Aria! I wasn't expecting you so early."

"I had a change of plans."

"Well, come in."

I stepped in slowly, my legs feeling shaky beneath me.

"Where's Devin?"

"I wanted to come alone."

"Listen," he said, "I'm sorry I didn't tell you about Thomas. I was going to, but then—" He put a hand on my shoulder and his face turned concerned. "Are you all right? You don't look well. Here, come sit down." He guided me to the couch and I gratefully sat.

He sat next to me, and I stared at him. He suddenly looked so different. I studied his face with renewed interest, wonder even. It was so strange to think I was looking at my father, when that image had always been filled by someone else.

"Aria, what's going on?"

I dropped my eyes and took a deep breath. "Before my mom died, she wrote me some letters. My dad—Jed—kept them from me."

Nathaniel's expression went slack, and I watched as the color drained from his face.

"Yesterday," I continued, "Thomas found the letters for me."

Nathaniel cleared his throat and swallowed. "Where were they?"

"Buried in a music box by a lake near my old house."

His brows pursed. "That's odd."

I found myself staring at him again, looking for traces of myself in his face. His eyes, I noted, were the same shade of blue as mine. "One of the letters was torn up. I had to tape it together to read it." I took the letter out of my purse.

It was folded in half. The letter shook in my hand, so I dropped it in my lap.

"What does it say?" he asked anxiously.

I picked it up and handed it to him. "You read it," I said, my voice weak with emotion.

He took the letter and unfolded it. He read a few lines, then stood and walked to the other side of the room, leaning on the piano for support. His face was turned away so I couldn't see his expression. He read for another minute, then dropped the letter to his side. He bent his head and grasped the corner of the piano. I couldn't tell if he was angry or just shocked. Then he turned to face me. There were tears in his eyes, and he looked worried. He took a step toward me. "Aria, how do you feel about this?" His voice was thick.

"It's like the missing puzzle piece of my life. Only now other ones have gone missing. I'm still trying to make sense of it all."

He came and sat beside me. "But how do you *feel*? About . . . me being your father?"

I hadn't yet overcome the hurdle of shock to consider my feelings. I looked at Nathaniel, at his anxious face, and considered them now. "I'm . . . relieved. Happy, even."

His shoulders dropped a notch and his face relaxed in relief.

"And I already love you like a father," I confessed, giving him a little smile I hoped would ease his concerns.

New tears welled up in his eyes and he put an arm around me, pulling me to his side. I rested my head on his shoulder, and we stayed like that for a long time—me soaking in the truth, him occasionally lifting a hand to wipe tears from his face. His embrace felt so natural and comforting, like it was where I belonged, where I should have been for the last nineteen years of my life.

Eventually, he pulled away to look at me. "I have to admit—I had my suspicions."

"Since you came to see me in New York?"

He nodded. "When you told me your birthday was in August."

"Why didn't you say something?"

"Because I didn't know for sure. Your mom got remarried right after our divorce, so it was possible that Jed really was your father. I thought maybe she lied to me about your birthday just to avoid speculation on my part." He sighed. "But just the possibility of you being my daughter . . . it unhinged me. I couldn't stop thinking about everything I'd missed out on, how I'd been cheated out of raising my own daughter. I cried for weeks after." He patted my arm and smiled at me. "But all is as it should be now, isn't it? To know the truth and to be able to move forward is all I need. I must say this is the best Christmas gift I have ever received." A perplexed look crossed his face. "Though things could have been so different if she had told me. If only I'd—" He released a sad sigh. "If only I hadn't been so selfish back then."

"Nathaniel, why didn't you tell me you'd been married to my mom?"

"Because when she came to see me before she died, she asked me not to tell you. I didn't understand why, but I couldn't deny a dying woman's wish. And now that I think back on it, maybe she was trying to prevent the truth from coming out when you were too young to handle it." Slowly, his expression turned concerned. "Does your dad—I mean, does Jed know?"

"He's known since my mom died."

"Well, that explains a lot." He grimaced. "No wonder he wouldn't let me see you. That must have been hard for him to take."

"It was. It still is, I think."

"Well, I'm sorry for him. Kind of. I'd be a lot more sorry for him if he hadn't mistreated you the way he did. Let me give you my first official piece of fatherly advice: Men are scum. Stay far away from them."

"I've heard that before," I said with a smile. "But I don't think it's true. Most of the men I know are good." My thoughts immediately turned to Thomas. "Nathaniel— why didn't you tell me that Thomas would be in town?"

"Yeah, I'm sorry about that." He cringed. "I got a call from him a couple weeks ago. He wanted to know where he could find you. He said he needed to see you as soon as possible and he didn't want to waste time going to New York if you weren't there. I was pretty hard on him—I knew how much you'd progressed and that you were finally moving on with your life. I didn't think you needed him showing up and messing things up all over again, and I told him so. He started going on about how much he loved you and how sorry he was, and I didn't want to hear his sorry excuses so I ended the call. But then something started to eat at me."

"What do you mean?"

"There was something in his voice—this heartbreaking sound that reminded me of the way I felt when Karina left me the last time. I took pity on him and called him back to tell him you'd be in Woodland Park for Christmas."

"But why didn't you tell me?"

"Because I wasn't sure if he'd actually show up. And I didn't want you to expect him and then be let down again."

I nodded in understanding.

"How did it go, by the way?" he asked.

I sighed and dropped my chin into my hand. "Terrible. But . . . wonderful. I've never been so confused in my life." I told Nathaniel everything that had happened with Thomas over the past few days, from his shocking reappearance to the priceless gift he'd unearthed.

Nathaniel put his hand on my shoulder and looked me in the eye. "I see so much of Karina in you. She chose Jed because she perceived him to be the safer choice. Things weren't perfect between us, but we loved each other. I never would have done anything to hurt her. We could have worked out our differences, but she was too afraid to try."

He looked into my eyes with earnestness. "It's good to be careful, but just make sure the choices you make to keep you safe don't also keep you from what makes you happy. I saw how miserable you were when Thomas left. It was like a piece of you was missing. You still love him—I can see it in your face. Why not give it a chance?"

I thought about what he said, but I was still so scared.

"Just think about it," he said.

I nodded. "I will."

# twenty-five

As I drove back to Jed Kinsley's house, I began to emerge from the frozen shell of shock that had surrounded me the past few hours. As my emotions began to thaw, tears trickled down my cheeks like water dripping from melting ice. But each tear only served to thaw my emotions further, and before I could stop it, a deluge burst forth, leaving me no choice but to pull over and surrender to waves of uncontrollable sobs.

I felt dizzy, like I was a piece of clay on a potter's wheel. It had been spinning for the past nineteen years, shaping and carving the vessel of my life. All that had happened in the past few days, with Thomas returning and Mom's secrets being unearthed, had shattered that vessel into a million pieces. Up until this moment, I had only stood there in shock, staring at the pieces and trying to decide if it was salvageable. But now I realized that it wasn't. I could sweep up the pieces and try to put them back together, but they would never fit together the same way again.

I thought about Mom, about the burden of guilt she

must have carried alone all those years. If only she'd just told the truth from the beginning. But I couldn't bring myself to harbor a grudge against her for her mistake. From the words in her letter she was clearly remorseful, and I freely forgave her.

I reflected on my childhood and how Jed had loved me as his own daughter. But then he'd discovered the truth, and it had chipped away at his love until it was shaped into resentment. He had tried to love me. He had wanted to be a good father. But, as he had said himself, he had failed. And he was sincerely sorry for it. He had done terrible things to me, but those things were behind us. He had done right by helping Thomas find Mom's music box and allowing me to learn the truth. He had done right by restoring Mom's piano and giving it to me. And he had done right by marrying Vivian and trying to start his life over.

I visualized the broken vessel of my life again, and realized that it would do no good to try and carry around the broken pieces of my past. I could not repair it and make it what it once was. I needed to let go of what once was, give up what could have been, and accept what really was. I needed to take fragments of truth and use them to build a new vessel of life.

And to leave the old vessel behind, I knew with a deep conviction that I needed to forgive Jed Kinsley. I made a conscious decision to do so. I said the words out loud.

"I forgive you, Jed Kinsley." The words hung in the air like mist, to be blown away by a breeze. I realized that they wouldn't mean anything until they were sounded in Jed Kinsley's ears.

I pulled the car back onto the road and drove to his

house with that purpose in mind, clinging to the words of forgiveness and the promise of healing they offered.

As I came into the house, Vivian greeted me in the doorway and pulled me into a hug. Devin played Mendelssohn's *May Breeze* in the parlor, and I could tell by the hurried tempo that he was restless. Vivian held me for a long time, then said, "Jed told me." She pulled away and looked me in the eyes. "Don't tell me this will be the end of our friendship."

"It won't be," I said with a smile, though I wasn't sure how close that friendship would be.

"Devin said you two were leavin' early." Her voice wavered, and I could see she was fighting back tears.

"I'm sorry, Vivian. I—"

She shook her head. "It's all right, sweetheart. I understand. Anyway I put your gifts in your car. You can open them later."

"Thank you." I bent my head, feeling ashamed for jumping ship on Christmas.

She hugged me again. "Come visit us the next time you're in town, when everyone's emotions have settled into place, you hear me?"

I nodded and pulled away. "Where's Jed?"

"Upstairs, in his room. He's upset, but I think he'll be all right."

I went upstairs and found Jed sitting on the edge of his bed, facing the window. I stood in the doorway, and he turned to look at me. His eyes were red from crying, but he put on a brave face. I crossed the room and sat next to him on the edge of the bed. He seemed surprised, unsure. We sat there for a long time, both of us looking out the window at nothing.

"I'm sorry you lost my mother," I finally said. "You really loved her, didn't you?"

From the corner of my eye, I saw him nod slowly.

I folded my hands in my lap. "And I'm sorry you had to suffer even more from the mess she left behind."

"You're not the one who should be apologizing."

"I know. All I'm trying to say is that I can see now . . . I'm not the only one who suffered."

Other than his eyes welling up with tears, he didn't respond.

"I want to thank you," I continued, "for trying to set things right. And I want you to know . . . that I forgive you." My breaths seemed to come easier after I'd said the last three words, like they'd loosened a vice that had been cinched around my chest for the past several years.

His hands came to his face, and his shoulders began to shake. Great heaves rolled over his back like swelling waves of the sea. I'd never seen him break down this way, and the sight of it brought tears to my own eyes. I considered how heavy his burden of guilt must have been, and how great a relief my words must have provided.

I didn't know what else to say, but I felt that the words I had said were enough for now. I walked out of his room, unsure when I would see him again. It was something I couldn't predict and only time would tell.

I gathered up my things from the bathroom, and as I crossed the hall to my room, something in the room Thomas had stayed in caught my eye. A dark object poking out from a blanket on the bed. I strode over and slid it out from beneath the heap of blankets.

It was the book I'd seen Thomas holding more than once these last couple days. I picked it up and let it fall open in my hand. But instead of print on the pages, there was handwriting. Thomas's handwriting.

I sank to the edge of the bed, his lingering scent enveloping me, and hurriedly flipped through the pages. It was not only filled with his words but also with his sketches.

The piano had stopped playing, and I knew Devin would soon come upstairs to see if I was ready to go. I didn't want him to see me sitting in the bed Thomas had slept in, holding Thomas's book. So I shut the book and took it to my room, packing it in my suitcase with my other things. I tried to pack my thoughts of Thomas along with it. I knew I needed to address my feelings, but I wanted to wait until we got back to New York and I could be alone.

Devin came up and helped me carry my things to the car, and as we drove away from Jed Kinsley's house, I thought about how someday I would be back, if not to see Jed, then to see Vivian and to claim Mom's piano.

For the entire drive back to Nathaniel's, I thought about that book tucked inside my suitcase in the trunk. It was like it had grown arms and was pounding its fist against my backseat and chanting, *Read me, read me.* Devin asked me questions the entire way about what had happened that morning, but my explanations came out abbreviated. Every word I spoke seemed to take a great amount of effort, because even though my body sat in the passenger seat, I was elsewhere. I was in the trunk, turning the pages of Thomas's journal. I was in the tree house, hearing again the words Thomas had spoken. And I was standing before Thomas in an airport, saying, "Wait—before you go, I have to tell you everything that happened, because you're the only one who will understand."

But it was probably too late for that. He was probably

already on his plane back to the Netherlands. *I could call him,* I thought, eyeing the bag that contained the card he'd left.

Devin pulled my attention back to him by slipping his hand into mine, and I brushed my impulsive thought aside. *Not now. I don't even know yet what I want.*

♪ ♪ ♪ ♪ ♪ ♪ ♪

Later that night after Devin had gone to bed, I found myself on the floor of my room, digging through my suitcase. I found Thomas's journal and leaned against the side of my bed, and by the dim light of a lamp, I opened the book and perused its content. There were sketches throughout the book—some on clean pages, others at the end of an entry, and others in the midst of words. I studied some of the drawings and read their captions.

An hourglass with a boy inside, looking like he was drowning in sand. The caption read, *Time has been slipping away from me, like I have no past, no future. I live moment to moment, just struggling to survive, struggling to force each breath in and out.*

My heart ached to know how much he had suffered, to know that I had not been there for him. And then another thought occurred to me. Was his reaction to grief any different than mine had been? Hadn't I closed off my heart at Juilliard to protect it from further pain? He had done the same to protect himself, and for the first time since his return, I understood why he'd stayed away.

I flipped a few pages to another drawing. It was me and him, separated by a large body of water.

*Everywhere I look, I see her. Even the ocean separating us sparkles and shines like the blue in her eyes. In my heart is*

a cruel dichotomy between love and hate. *Love for her and hatred for myself, and I don't see how the two can coexist. And as long as I have reason to hate myself, I have reason to be separated from her, to protect her from more pain.*

I turned to another page. A boy, holding out his empty pockets, and a flame burning in his chest. *My hands are empty, my pockets are empty, my soul is empty. But my heart is full of her.* And on the opposite page, a barren landscape. *I've seen more places than I can remember, but I haven't really seen any of it. It's all the same. Foreign, empty spaces and masses of superficiality. It's all where she is not.*

Toward the end of the book, there was a sketch of a twisted, overgrown path leading to a glorious sunrise and the words, *When disappointment, grief, and fear are gone, sorrow forgot, love's purest joys restored.* They were the same words he'd sung to me the first time he sat beside me at Mom's piano, and in the tree house after the homecoming dance.

I went to the last page. On one side was what appeared to be a map of a lake, and I realized he must have used it to find Mom's music box. On the other side was a drawing of me. *Of all the things I've lost, Aria is the greatest loss of all.*

I closed the journal and held it to my chest, feeling my heart hammer against it. Here in my hands was the proof that he'd spent each day, each moment for the past two years fighting his way back to me. Everything he'd said to me was true. He loved me. He had always loved me.

Tears welled up in my eyes, but I tried to blink them back. I couldn't do this now—I had to pack up my things in the morning and fly back to New York with Devin. My decision would need to wait until then. I told my tears they would have to wait. But the more I insisted, the more they flooded my eyes until they were spilling down my cheeks. Once again, I had the urge to call Thomas. I caught the sound of his voice in my memory, and felt that familiar pull in my chest. The pull that I had never once felt for Devin.

I thought about the day I'd described to Devin what love felt like to me, and it occurred to me that those feelings had never applied to Devin. My feelings for Devin had always been calm and unworried, and I thought it was because I trusted him not to hurt me. But now I recognized that he had no power to hurt me, because the love I had for Devin was something different than the love I had for Thomas. Devin was my friend, but he was not irreplaceable.

With Thomas back in my life, Devin was like candlelight in a sunlit room. I could snuff him out and not even notice a difference. I felt callous thinking it, but it would be more callous to stay with him when I felt this way. He deserved someone who loved him, who saw him as her own sunlight.

But if being with Thomas meant that I would spend my life on an unpredictable ride, fearing at every turn that I might lose him again, I wasn't sure I wanted that kind of love either.

"Be brave," I whispered to myself. It all came down to courage. Did I have the courage to listen to my heart, to embrace Thomas and allow myself to love him, even if it meant I could be hurt again? Even if I would fear that he would leave again? Even if I didn't know what trials the future would bring us?

*Even if . . . Even if . . .*

His words from two years earlier came back to me. *I love you. We will be together, even if anything.*

I noticed a melody, sweet and peaceful, playing in my heart. I closed my eyes and listened to it carefully, blocking out all other sounds and thoughts. The melody wrapped around a pair of callused hands and over weather-chapped lips, wound through strands of dark hair, and melded into the irises of bright blue eyes. It grew more and more distinct, swelling and filling the space of my heart.

And suddenly, it all became clear. I knew what I wanted.

Soon I was on my feet, pacing the room and hugging Thomas's journal against my chest. The prospect of telling Devin the truth in the morning made my heart take a nosedive to my feet. I paced and paced, searching for the right words to deliver the blow. There were no right words. No matter how I phrased my rejection, it was still rejection. My only comfort was that Devin was resilient. Nothing ever seemed to keep him down for long, and I was sure that girls would be lining up at his door the moment news of his availability broke.

I don't know how long I paced, but I didn't stop until there was a quiet tap on my door. The door cracked open, and Devin popped his head in and looked at me curiously. "Are you all right? It sounds like you're doing late-night aerobics in here."

"Sorry. Did I wake you?"

"No. I wasn't asleep. What's going on?"

Feeling unprepared for this conversation, I sat on the edge of the bed and tried to gather my thoughts. He came and sat next to me.

"Have you been crying? What's wrong?" As he circled his arms around me, I searched for an explanation to offer. But what could I possibly say? How could I tell him the truth without breaking his heart?

He nodded at the book in my hands. "What's that?"

After a long hesitation, I said, "Thomas's journal."

Understanding swept slowly across his face, leaving sadness in its wake. He released me and gave a disheartened sigh. "This is one competition I can't win. Isn't it?"

I felt the sting of tears again behind my eyes, but I didn't want to cry in front of him. I didn't want him to feel the need to comfort me when I was the one about to sink a dagger into his heart. I felt like such a horrible person, wishing I didn't have to hurt a man who'd been so kind to me. But I couldn't make two people happy. I couldn't be with Thomas and Devin. And the truth was, there had never been a competition. It had always been Thomas.

"You deserve someone better for you," I finally said. "Someone who can give her whole heart to you."

"Does anyone really have their whole heart to give? I don't expect you to give me your whole heart, Aria. All I need is the greater portion."

I dropped my eyes and slowly shook my head, unable to tell him that not only did Thomas possess the greater portion, he possessed the entirety. But I didn't need to say the words. Devin received the message loud and clear.

"I see." A long silence passed between us before he said sadly, "I guess I'm not surprised. I sort of knew we were doomed the moment I saw you talking with him yesterday morning. There was something in your face when you saw me—like you wished I wasn't there."

"I'm so sorry. I never wanted to hurt you."

He shrugged. "As much as I love you, I want to be loved too." His face was carefully composed, but there was no hiding the hurt in his eyes. "Only one thing would hurt more than losing you. And that is being with you, knowing

that you love someone else." He stared at me for a long moment, then touched my heart with his fingers before pressing them to his own heart. "*Moja bieda,*" he whispered. It had been months since Margo told me Chopin's tragic love story, but I hadn't forgotten the meaning of the words. *My sorrow.*

This brought on a whole new round of tears, but neither of us made any further attempt to comfort each other. After a long stretch of silence between us, he said, "I guess I'll see you in class. You can go back to ignoring me, and I can go back to harassing you on occasion." The jab was meant to lighten the situation, but I couldn't bring myself to smile. His own smile was vacant, betraying the hurt behind it.

He left my room and I closed the door so that he could pack up his things with a measure of dignity. I sat there and listened to the zipping of his bags, the occasional creak of the floor beneath his footstep, and finally the whine and click of his exit through the front door. My heart felt heavy with guilt for causing him sorrow, but the more I thought about Thomas, the more certain I was that I was making the right choice.

I knelt down in front of the dresser and opened the bottom drawer, pushing my hand through stacks of sweaters until I found a cardboard tube. I pulled it out and turned it on end. A rolled-up painting slid out, and I unrolled it and held it in front of me. As I stared at the boy on the porch swing, I was filled with a sense of relief.

I was free to love Thomas. I was free to be with him. But he would probably be heading out to sea in the next few days, and I needed to be back at Juilliard before the new semester began. I pulled Thomas's note from my bag and stared at the phone number written on it. I wanted to talk to him, to tell him I loved him and wanted to be with him. I snatched my cell phone from the dresser and dialed his number. But instead of hitting the call button, I hit cancel.

I had a much better idea.

# twenty-six

*Zierikzee, the Netherlands*

Outside the cab window, ambiguous struc-
tures flew by in the darkness of predawn. Occasionally I could make out a windmill or a lighthouse, but most
of the passing farmhouses and barns remained hidden in
the shadows of trees. I glanced at the clock on the driver's
dashboard. It was just past seven thirty, and from the faint
glow on the east horizon, the sun probably wouldn't rise for
at least another hour.

The moon hung over the west horizon, racing along the
landscape as it kept pace with the car, occasionally reflecting off bodies of water as we crossed a bridge or dam. The
sight of it reminded me of Thomas's words a few nights
earlier, and with a smile I visualized his face in place of the
moon. Soon enough I would be standing on his doorstep,
knocking on his door.

I brushed my thumb over the card that Thomas had
given me, and anticipation swelled in my chest, leaving

little room for air. Within minutes, I would see him. The skin on my arms tingled with the expectation of feeling the warmth of his touch. In my mind, I ran through the words I would say to him, and I imagined how it would feel to have him pull me into his embrace. I laid my hand on my bag, feeling the shape of his journal beneath the fabric. I had read through the entire thing on the flight to Rotterdam, and each word had only cemented my choice.

"How much farther?" I asked the cab driver.

"Only a mile or two," he answered in a heavy Dutch accent. Thus far, the English-Dutch book I'd picked up in the airport was proving to be a useless purchase. Everyone here seemed to know some English.

Any direction I looked, there was some form of water. We crossed yet another bridge, and a handful of boats moved like shadows across the harbor, yellow lights glowing atop their masts. I wondered if Thomas was out there now, or if I'd find him at his apartment. I realized I didn't know how commercial fishing worked—if they'd be back at the end of the day, or if they'd be out at sea for a week.

"How long do the fishing boats stay out at sea?" I asked.

"Depends on the vessel. Some are out for a day, others for weeks or months."

I hoped I would find him at his apartment, or that if he was gone, he would return at the end of the day. I hadn't thought about what I would do if he was out to sea for weeks. I would have to go back to Juilliard without seeing him and find some other way of getting in touch with him.

As we got closer to Zierikzee, the roads narrowed and the buildings multiplied. The town was brimming with historic character, with flourished, centuries-old facades and decorative ironwork. Pathways of herringbone brick

lined the sides of roads and alleyways. The driver maneuvered tightly between walls of shops and apartments, and it was impossible to distinguish one building from the next because of their proximity.

The driver turned a corner, then slowed to a stop. He glanced up at a narrow brick apartment. "This is it," he said.

I paid and thanked him, then shouldered my bag and got out of the cab. As the cab disappeared down the channel of a street, I climbed the steps to Thomas's door, my heart pounding in my chest. I drew in a deep breath, and unable to suppress a smile, I knocked on his door.

As I waited for an answer, I slipped my hands in the pockets of my coat. It wasn't as cold as Woodland Park, but still chilly enough to freeze my anxious breaths.

There was no answer, so I knocked again, a little harder this time. I listened and waited, but there was nothing but silence on the other side of the door. I leaned over the iron railing and cupped my hands over my brow to peer inside. The apartment was dark, but not empty. Before I had a chance to take in more detail, I heard a man's voice addressing me.

"*Mag ik je helpen, kleine meid?*"

I whipped around to see an old man sitting on the steps of the apartment next door. He wore pajama bottoms and a wool coat, and, despite the cold, slippers. He took a long drag of his cigarette and stared at me, waiting for me to answer.

"I'm looking for Thomas," I said. "Do you know Thomas?"

He gave a lazy nod, then summoned me with a wave of his hand. I descended the steps and went to stand in front of him.

"*Hebt je papier?*"

I shook my head to tell him I didn't understand, then reached in my bag for my English-Dutch book. He waved his hand to stop me. Then he made a gesture with his hands, like he was writing something.

"*Papier*," he repeated.

"Oh," I said. "Paper." I searched my bag until I found a small notebook and pen, then handed them to the man.

He took a couple minutes to draw something on the paper, then handed it back to me. It was a map, with street names and arrows leading to a picture of a boat with the word "Lysander" written on it. On the boat was a stick figure with the name "Thomas."

"How long ago did he leave?" I asked, tapping my wrist.

He glanced at his watch, then with a shrug said, "*Een uur geleden.*"

I squinted at him as though it would help me interpret his words. He held up one finger. "*Een uur.*"

"One hour ago?" I asked.

He nodded and said with a thick Dutch accent, "One hour."

I thanked the man and hurried away, hoping I could catch Thomas before his boat headed out to sea. I pulled out my cell phone and debated whether to call him to let him know I was here. I didn't want him to know I was here until I was standing right in front of him. But I also didn't want him to be out at sea for weeks without knowing that I'd come for him. I decided to send him a brief text. I typed in two words.

*I'm here.*

Everything else could wait until I could talk to him in person. I pocketed my phone and made my way down a narrow street toward the waterfront. According to Thomas's

neighbor, I was an hour behind him. But surely it would take longer than that for his crew to prepare their vessel and push out to sea. Even so, I quickened my steps to a jog.

I followed the arrows on the map and was at the waterfront before I was out of breath. The walkway was flanked by shops on one side and a wide canal on the other, and it was so long I couldn't see the end of it. I pulled out the map the old man had drawn and stared at it. There was only one boat on the map. He'd made it look so simple. But as I lifted my eyes to the row of countless pleasure boats and fishing trawlers parked along the canal, I realized that finding Thomas's boat would be far from simple.

Not wanting to waste a second more, I began my search. I scuttled along, reading the names painted on the boats as I passed them. Some didn't have names, only numbers, and none of them appeared to bear the name "Lysander." My face must have reflected the anxiety I felt, because people glanced at me curiously as I passed them by. I began searching their faces, looking for Thomas while still searching for his boat. The more I searched, the more distinct his face became in my mind. There was no one like him. No one in this world would be able to take his place.

I passed rows of bicycles and people preparing for the day's work. I passed boat after boat, but I searched in vain. When I reached the end of the canal and the row of boats, I paused.

I turned in a circle, scanning the pathway I'd just come from. The sun was edging over the skyline, and its golden light lit up the air, softening the outlines of people and buildings, like everything was draped in gossamer.

I sat on a bench in front of a bakery to collect my thoughts. I squinted into the liquid horizon, hoping he would get my message, hoping that by the end of the day I would find myself in his arms. But if he didn't return today, I would have to go back to my hotel in Rotterdam and wait for his call. I decided I would go back to his apartment to ask his neighbor when Thomas might be back.

Just as I was about to stand and go back the way I came, I felt a buzz in my pocket. With a leap in my chest, I pulled out my phone to read the message. It was from Thomas.

*Where?*

I grinned widely, thrilled he'd gotten my message.

*Here in Zierikzee,* I started to write, then paused. There were so many words I wanted to say, but my fingers seemed completely inadequate to convey them. It would have been easier to channel the entire North Sea through my cell phone than to text what I was feeling.

*I need to see you,* I typed. But the words seemed so insufficient. I raised my eyes and swept the landscape as though it would help me devise the next sentence. There was a vague bustling of fishermen preparing their ships, mending nets, and loading and unloading supplies. But one figure stood out, because he wasn't moving at all. About fifty yards off, a young man with a heavy coat and dark hair stood at the edge of the water, looking down at something in his hands. The sight of him made my breath catch in my throat.

I squinted through the morning mist to make sure I wasn't mistaken, and as he turned his head slightly in my direction, I knew I wasn't.

It was Thomas Ashby.

I didn't remember rising to my feet, but I found myself standing and moving slowly toward him. My heart pushed against my chest, urging me forward, but my feet insisted on a snail's pace. He didn't see me. His attention was still

on the object in his hands. He lifted it to his ear, and my phone rang.

I paused and looked down to see Thomas's number gracing the screen of my phone. I turned it off and dropped it in my pocket. Like I was approaching a bird, I inched my way forward, fearing that if I made the wrong move, he would take to the sky. I heard his voice saying my name into his phone, a sound more beautiful than the swelling violins in *The Moldau*.

I drew nearer and nearer until I was standing beside him. He glanced down at me with a double take, then without taking his eyes off me, he lowered his phone and slipped it in his pocket.

"You didn't go," I said.

He stared at me in disbelief for a moment, then said softly, "You came." His eyes were brighter than I'd ever seen them, seeming to be illuminated from within.

"I thought you'd gone out to sea."

"I was . . . until I got your message."

"Don't they need you?"

"They'll survive." His expression turned curious. "How long have you been here?"

"I flew red-eye to Rotterdam last night, from Colorado Springs." I paused, letting my eyes soak in the sight of him. His hair was still damp and slightly ruffled from the morning breeze. His hands were tucked in the pockets of his coat. His cheeks were rosy from the cold, and the beginnings of a smile tipped one corner of his mouth. I realized he was waiting for an explanation. I reached into my bag and pulled out his journal. "I found this."

He took it, his brows knitting slightly. "You came five thousand miles to return it?"

"No. I came five thousand miles to tell you what I want."

His lips parted as if to say something, but nothing came out. Instead he kept his gaze on me and waited, his expression brimming with anticipation.

I pulled out his painting and handed it to him. He tucked his journal under his arm and slowly unrolled the painting. When he saw what it was, he bowed his head and a quiver rippled across his chin.

I pointed to the dark haired boy on the porch swing. "That boy there," I said. "He's all I've ever really wanted."

His eyes filled with tears, and I dropped my bag and closed the small distance between us. I unzipped his coat and slid my arms around his waist to draw him near. His arms enfolded me, fastening me to him. His body was warm and inviting, like cozying up to a blazing hearth after being out in the cold. I tipped my head up to gaze into his glistening eyes. "I love you, Thomas Ashby."

He lowered his forehead to mine, and a single tear trickled down his cheek.

"Don't cry," I murmured.

"I thought I'd lost you forever."

"You never lost me," I said. "I have always been yours, and nothing will ever change that."

"Even if I—"

I pressed a soft kiss to his lips. "Even if anything."

A smile slowly spread across his mouth and brightened his eyes. "Even if anything," he echoed solemnly before bringing his lips to meet mine again. Everything I thought I'd lost was in that kiss, reassuring me that the past didn't matter, because my future was full of him.

# Acknowledgments

I want to take a moment to express my sincere gratitude to all those who contributed to the completion and publication of this book. In the early stages of this project, I was fortunate enough to join a wonderful critique group, The Point Writers. Shauna Dansie, Sabine Berlin, Kylee Wilkins, Ami Chopine, Terri Barton, Chris Weston (C.K. Edwards), Darren Eggett, Alyson King, and Garrett Winn, you reined in [some of] my cheesiness, pointed out the things I did well, and weren't afraid to tell me when I could do better. I have gained vast quantities of knowledge from you and I can say with certainty that this book never would have seen the light of day without your guidance and enthusiasm.

Thanks to the wonderful staff at Cedar Fort who saw potential in my manuscript and helped make it the best it could be. Angie Workman, Melissa Caldwell, Alissa Voss, Kelly Martinez, you made the publication process smooth and painless. Kristen Reeves, for designing a gorgeous cover and enduring my fickleness.

A huge shout-out of thanks goes to my brilliant astrophysicist cousin, Amanda Ford, who patiently answered all my questions about astronomy and gave me feedback on an early version of *Porcelain Keys*. To Garrett Winn for proofing my Dutch, and Mike and Cindy Kemp for proofing my French.

To the girls of Real Writers Write, who saw me through

the publication process, provided encouragement, friendship, and grammar help. Heather Clark, Janelle Youngstrom, Sabine Berlin (again), Juliana Montgomery, Rebecca Scott, Caryn Caldwell, Nikki Trionfo, and Shari Cylinder, you guys took me in like family and made me feel right at home.

To my dad, who taught me about redemption and who shares my love of writing. To my mom, who taught me unconditional love and who shares my love of books. And to my sister and brother, who encouraged and supported me along the way, who never seemed to grow tired of my book-talk. You guys are the best family a girl could ask for.

Many thanks also go to other friends and family for their kindness and support during the writing of this book.

Over the years that I worked on *Porcelain Keys*, I grew to know and love the characters of Aria and Thomas. As I wrote down their story, I cried their tears and celebrated their triumphs. So even though it feels like acknowledging imaginary friends, I want to thank Aria and Thomas for telling me their story and for pressing me to finish it.

And last but not least, I want to thank my first critique partner and biggest fan, Keith. It has been a long journey, and you have cheered me on from the very beginning. You changed diapers and folded laundry while I slaved over my laptop, and each time I emerged from my office after a writing marathon looking like a writer (synonym: vagrant), you smiled and told me I was lovely. You gave me honest feedback that helped me improve the story and my writing. You have been the one unmovable, dependable thing in all this crazy business of getting published. You picked me up off the floor and said the words I needed to hear when I thought I couldn't take one more rejection. You came up with a beautiful title for my book, and believed in me when I didn't believe in myself. You were the first to read my finished book, and it says a lot about you that you read it in one sitting, with a flashlight, because the power was out. My heart is yours to keep; you have earned it a thousand times over.

# About the Author

SARAH BEARD graduated from the University of Utah with a degree in communications, and she splits her time between writing and freelance editing. She enjoys reading, composing music, and traveling with her family. She lives with her husband and three children in Salt Lake City, Utah. Her website is www.sarahbeard.com.